Winter Warriors

David A. Gemmell

CORGI BOOKS

WINTER WARRIORS
A CORGI BOOK : 0 552 14254 9

Originally published in Great Britain by Bantam Press,
a division of Transworld Publishers Ltd

PRINTING HISTORY
Bantam Press edition published 1997
Corgi edition published 1997
Corgi edition reprinted 1997

Set in 10pt Sabon by Falcon Oast Graphic Art

Corgi Books are published by Transworld Publishers Ltd,
61–63 Uxbridge Road, London W5 5SA,
in Australia by Transworld Publishers (Australia) Pty Ltd,
15–25 Helles Avenue, Moorebank, NSW 2170,
and in New Zealand by Transworld Publishers (NZ) Ltd,
3 William Pickering Drive, Albany, Auckland.

Printed and bound in Great Britain by
Cox & Wyman Ltd, Reading, Berkshire.

Thirty years ago I saw a young woman climbing a rock face in the pouring rain. She was too short to reach the higher holds, and there was no way she would make it to the top, but she clung to that rock face, refusing to be lowered, until exhaustion made her lose her grip. Twenty years later the same woman wanted to run the London Marathon in under four hours. She broke her foot at 15 miles – and ran on to finish in three hours fifty-nine minutes. *Winter Warriors* is dedicated with love to Valerie Gemmell.

Chapter One

The night sky over the mountains was clear and bright, the stars like diamonds on sable. It was a late winter night of cold and terrible beauty, the snow hanging heavy on the branches of pine and cedar. There was no colour here, no sense of life. The land lay silent, save for the occasional crack of an overladen branch, or the soft, whispering sound of fallen snow being drifted by the harsh north wind.

A hooded rider on a dark horse emerged from the tree line, his mount plodding slowly through the thick snow. Bent low over the saddle he rode on, his head bowed against the wind, his gloved hands holding his snow-crowned grey cloak tightly at the neck. As he came into the open he seemed to become a focus for the angry wind, which howled around him. Undaunted he urged the horse on. A white owl launched itself from a high treetop and glided down past the horse and rider. A thin rat scurried across the moonlit snow, swerving as the owl's talons touched its back. The swerve almost carried it clear.

Almost.

In this frozen place *almost* was a death sentence. Everything here was black and white, sharp and clearly defined, with no delicate shades of grey. Stark contrasts. Success or failure, life or death. No second chances, no excuses.

As the owl flew away with its prey the rider glanced up. In a world without colour his bright blue eyes shone silver-grey in a face dark as ebony. The black man touched heels to his tired mount, steering the animal towards the woods. 'We are both tired,' whispered the rider, patting the gelding's long neck. 'But we'll stop soon.'

Nogusta looked at the sky. It was still clear. No fresh snow tonight, he thought, which meant that the tracks they were following would still be visible come dawn. Moonlight filtered through the tall trees and Nogusta began to seek a resting place. Despite the heavy, hooded grey cloak and the black woollen shirt and leggings he was cold all the way to the bone. But it was his ears that were suffering the most. Under normal circumstances he would have wrapped his scarf around his face. Not a wise move, however, when tracking three desperate men. He needed to be alert for every sound and movement. These men had already killed, and would not hesitate to do so again.

Looping the reins over his pommel he lifted his hands to his ears, rubbing at the skin. The pain was intense. Do not fear the cold, he warned himself. The cold is life. Fear should come only when his body stopped fighting the cold. When it began to feel warm and drowsy. For death's icy dagger lay waiting within that illusory warmth. The horse plodded on, following the tracks like a hound. Nogusta hauled him to a stop. Somewhere up ahead the killers would be camped for the night. He sniffed the air, but could not pick up the scent of woodsmoke. They would have to light a fire. Otherwise they would be dead.

Nogusta was in no condition to tackle them now. Swinging away from the trail he rode deeper into the woods, seeking a sheltered hollow, or a cliff wall, where he could build his own fire and rest.

The horse stumbled in deep snow, but steadied itself. Nogusta almost fell from the saddle. As he righted himself he caught a glimpse of a cabin wall through a gap in the trees. Almost entirely snow covered it was near invisible, and had the horse not balked he would have ridden past it. Dismounting Nogusta led the exhausted gelding to the deserted building. The door was hanging on one leather hinge, the other having rotted away. The cabin was long and narrow beneath a sod roof, and there was a lean-to at the side, out of the wind. Here Nogusta unsaddled the horse and rubbed him down. Filling a feedbag with grain he looped it over the beast's ears, then covered his broad back with a blanket.

Leaving the horse to feed Nogusta moved round to the front of the building and eased his way over the snow that had piled up in the doorway. The interior was dark, but he could just make out the grey stone of the hearth. As was customary in the wild a fire had been laid, but snow had drifted down the chimney and half covered the wood. Carefully Nogusta cleaned it out, then re-laid the fire. Taking his tinder box from his pouch he opened it and hesitated. The tinder would burn for only a few seconds. If the thin kindling wood did not catch fire immediately it might take him hours to start a blaze with knife and flint. And he needed a fire desperately. The cold was making him tremble now. He struck the flint. The tinder burst into flame. Holding it to the thin kindling wood he whispered a prayer to his star. Flames licked up, then surged through the dry wood. Nogusta settled back and breathed a sigh of relief, and, as the fire flared, he looked around him, studying the room. The cabin had been neatly built by a man who cared.

The joints were well crafted, as was the furniture, a bench table, four chairs and a narrow bed. Shelves had been set on the north wall. They were bare now. There was only one window, the shutters closed tight. One side of the hearth was filled with logs. An old spider's web stretched across them.

The empty shelves and lack of personal belongings showed that the man who had built the cabin had chosen to move on. Nogusta wondered why. The construction of the cabin showed a neat man, a patient man. Not one to be easily deterred. Nogusta scanned the walls. There was no sign of a woman's presence here. The builder had been a man alone. Probably a trapper. And when he had finally left – perhaps the mountains were trapped out – he had carefully laid a fire for the next person to find his home. A considerate man. Nogusta felt welcome in the cabin, as if greeted by the owner. It was a good feeling.

Nogusta rose and walked out to where his horse was patiently waiting. Removing the empty feedbag he stroked his neck. There was no need to hobble him. The gelding would not leave this place of shelter. The stone chimney jutted from the wooden wall of the cabin here, and soon the fire would heat the stones. 'You will be safe here for the night, my friend,' Nogusta told the gelding.

Gathering his saddlebags he returned to the cabin and heaved the door back into place, wedging it against the twisted frame. Then he pulled a chair up to the fire. The cold stones of the hearth were sucking almost all the heat from the fire. 'Be patient,' he told himself. Minutes passed. He saw a woodlouse run along a log as the flames licked up. Nogusta drew his sword and held the blade against the wood, offering the insect a way of escape. The woodlouse approached the blade, then turned away from it, toppling into the fire. 'Fool,' said Nogusta. 'The blade was life.'

The fire was blazing now and the black man rose and removed his cloak and shirt. His upper body was strongly muscled and heavily scarred. Sitting down once more he leaned forward, extending his hands to the blaze. Idly he twirled the small, ornate charm he wore around his neck. It was an ancient piece, a white-silver crescent moon, held in a slender golden hand. The gold was heavy and dark, and the silver never tarnished. It remained, like the moon, pure and glittering. He heard his father's voice echo down the vaults of memory: 'A man greater than kings wore this magic charm, Nogusta. A great man. He was our ancestor and while you wear it make sure that your deeds are always noble. If they remain so you will have the gift of the Third Eye.'

'Is that how you knew the robbers were in the north pasture?'

'Yes.'

'But don't you want to keep it?'

'It chose you, Nogusta. You saw the magic. Always the talisman chooses. It has done so for hundreds of years. And – if the Source wills – it will choose one of your own sons.'

If the Source wills . . .

But the Source had not willed.

Nogusta curled his hand around the talisman, and stared into the fire, hoping for a vision. None came.

From his saddlebag he took a small package and opened it. It contained several strips of dried, salted beef. Slowly he ate them.

Adding two logs to the fire he moved to the bed. The blankets were thin and dusty and he shook them out. Away from the blaze he shivered, then laughed at himself. 'You are getting old,' he said. 'Once upon a time the cold would not have affected you this way.'

Back at the fire once more he put on his shirt. A face came into his mind, sharp featured and with an easy, friendly smile. Orendo the Scout. They had ridden together for almost twenty years, serving first the old king and then his warrior son. Nogusta had always liked Orendo. The man was a veteran, and when you gave him an order you knew it would be carried out to the letter. And he had a heart. Once, several years back, Orendo had found a child lost in the snow, unconscious and half dead from the cold. He had carried him back to camp, then sat with him all night, warming blankets, rubbing the boy's frozen skin. The child had survived.

Nogusta sighed. Now Orendo was on the run with two other soldiers, having murdered a merchant and raped his daughter. She too had been left for dead, but the knife had missed her heart, and she had lived to name her attackers.

'Don't bring them back,' the White Wolf had told him. 'I want them dead. No public trials. Bad for morale.' Nogusta had looked into the old man's pale, cold eyes.

'Yes, my general.'

'You want to take Bison and Kebra with you?' asked the general.

'No. Orendo was Bison's friend. I'll do it alone.'

'Was Orendo not your friend also?' said Banelion, watching him closely.

'You want their heads as proof that I killed them?'

'No. Your word is good enough for me,' said Banelion. That was a source of pride to Nogusta. He had served Banelion now for almost thirty-five years – almost all his adult life. The general was not a man given to praise, but his men served him with an iron loyalty.

Nogusta stared into the fire. It had been more than a surprise when Orendo had betrayed him. But then Orendo was being sent home. Like Bison and Kebra. And even the White Wolf himself.

The king wanted the old men culled. The same old men who had fought for his father, saving the Drenai when all seemed lost. The same old men who had invaded Ventria, smashing the emperor's armies. Paid off and retired. That was the rumour. Orendo had believed it, and had robbed the merchant. Yet it was hard to believe he had also taken part in the rape and attempted murder of the girl. But the evidence was overwhelming. She said he had not only been the instigator of the rape, it had been he who had plunged the knife into her breast.

Nogusta stared moodily into the fire. Had the crime shocked him? A good judge of men he would not have thought Orendo capable of such a vile act. But then all those years ago he had learned what *good* men were capable of. He had learned it in fire and blood and death. He had learned it in the ruin of dreams and the shattering of hopes. Banking up the fire he moved the bed closer to the hearth. Pulling off his boots he lay down, covering himself with the thin blankets.

Outside the wind was howling.

He awoke at dawn. The cabin was still warm. Rising from the bed he pulled on his boots. The fire had died down to glowing embers. He took a long drink from his canteen, then put on his cloak, hefted his saddlebags, and went out to the gelding. The back stones of the hearth were hot, the temperature in the lean-to well above freezing. 'How are you feeling, boy?' he said, stroking the beast's neck. The gelding nuzzled his chest. 'We'll catch them today, and then I'll take you back to that warm stable.' Back in the cabin he put out the remains of the fire, then laid a fresh one in its place, ready for any other weary traveller who came upon it. Saddling the gelding he rode out into the winter woods.

Orendo stared gloomily at the jewels, purple amethysts, bright diamonds, red rubies, sparkling in his gloved hand. With a sigh he opened the pouch and watched them tumble back into its dark interior.

'I'm going to buy a farm,' said the youngster, Cassin. 'On the Sentran Plain. Dairy farm. I've always loved the taste of fresh milk.' Orendo's weary eyes glanced up at the slim young man and he said nothing.

'What's the point?' countered Eris, a thickset bearded warrior with small dark eyes. 'Life's too short to *buy* hard work. Give me the whorehouses of Drenan and a fine little house high on the Sixth Hill. A different girl every day of the week, small, pretty and slim hipped.'

A silence grew among them, as each remembered the small, pretty girl they had murdered back in the city of Usa. 'Looks like we're clear of snow today,' said Cassin, at last.

'Snow is good for us,' said Orendo. 'It covers tracks.'

'Why would anyone track us yet?' asked Eris. 'No-one saw us at the merchant's house, and there's no roll-call until tomorrow.'

'They'll send Nogusta,' said Orendo, leaning forward to add a chunk of wood to the fire. It had been a cold night in the hollow and he had slept badly, dreaming awful dreams of pain and death. What had seemed a simple robbery had become a night of murder and shame he would never forget. He rubbed his tired eyes.

'So what?' sneered Eris. 'There's three of us, and we're not exactly easy meat. If they send that black bastard I'll cut his heart out.' Orendo bit back an angry retort.

Instead he rose and stepped towards the taller, heavier man.

'You have never seen Nogusta in action, boy. Pray you never do.' Stepping past the two younger men Orendo walked to a nearby tree and urinated. 'The man is uncanny,' he said, over his shoulder. 'I was with him once when we tracked four killers into Sathuli lands. He can read sign over rock, and he can smell a trail a hound would miss. But that's not what makes him dangerous.' Orendo continued to urinate, the water coming in slow, rhythmic spurts, sending up steam from the snow. He had endured trouble with his bladder for over a year now, needing to piss several times a night. 'You know what makes him dangerous?' he asked them. 'There is no bravado in him. He moves, he kills. It is that quick. When we found the killers he just walked into their camp and they were dead. I tell you it was awesome.'

'I know,' came the tomb-deep voice of Nogusta. 'I was there.'

Orendo stood very still, a feeling of nausea flaring in his belly. His water dried up instantly and he retied his leggings and turned very slowly. Eris was lying flat on his back, a knife through his right eye. Cassin was beside him, a blade in his heart. 'I knew they'd send you,' said Orendo. 'How did you find us so fast?'

'The girl lived,' said Nogusta.

'I thank the Source for that,' said Orendo, with a sigh. 'Are you alone?'

'Yes.' The black man's sword was sheathed, and there was no throwing knife in his hands. It does not matter, thought Orendo. I don't have the skill to best him.

'I'm glad. I wouldn't want Bison to see me now. Are you taking me back?'

'No. You will remain here, with your friends.'

Orendo nodded. 'Seems a shame to end a friendship this way, Nogusta. Will you take back our heads?'

'The White Wolf told me my word was good enough.'

Orendo felt a trickle of hope. 'Look, man, I was only the look out. I didn't know there was going to be murder. But it happened. There are enough jewels in that pouch to give us a life . . . a real life. We could buy a palace with them, you and me.' Nogusta shook his head. 'You could just tell them you killed me. And keep half the jewels.'

'That is what I will tell them. For you will be dead. You were not the look out,' said Nogusta, sadly. 'You raped the girl, and you stabbed her. You did this. You must pay for it.'

Orendo moved to the fire, stepping over the bodies of his companions. 'They were sending me home,' he said, kneeling down and pulling off his gloves. The fire was warm and he held his hands out to it. 'How would you feel? How does Bison feel?' He glanced up at the tall warrior. 'Ah, it is different for you, isn't it? The champion. The blade master. You're not quite as old as us. No-one's told you you're useless yet. But they will, Nogusta. The day will come.' He sat down and stared into the flames. 'You know, we had no intention of killing the merchant. But he struggled and Eris stabbed him. Then the girl ran in. She had been sleeping, and she was wearing a transparent shift. I still can hardly believe it happened. The room went very cold. I remember that, and I felt something touch me. Then I was filled with rage and lust. It was the same for the others. We spoke about it last night.' He looked up at Nogusta. 'I swear to you, Nogusta, that I believe we were possessed. Maybe the merchant was a sorcerer. But there was something evil there. It affected us all. You know me well. In all the years we have fought together I have never raped a woman. Never.'

'But you did three nights ago,' said Nogusta, moving forward, and drawing his sword.

Orendo lifted a hand. 'If you will permit me I will do the deed myself?'

Nogusta nodded and squatted down on the other side of the fire. Orendo slowly drew his dagger. For a moment he considered hurling it at the black man. Then the image of the girl came to his mind, and he heard her voice begging for life. Swiftly he drew the sharp blade across his left wrist. Blood flowed instantly. 'There is a bottle of brandy in my saddlebag. Would you get it?'

Nogusta did so and Orendo drank deeply. 'I am truly sorry about the girl,' said the dying man. 'Will she recover?'

'I don't know.'

Orendo drank again, then tossed the bottle to Nogusta. The black man took a deep swallow. 'It all went wrong,' said Orendo. 'Never put your trust in kings. That's what they say. It was all so glorious in those early days. We knew where we were. The Ventrians invaded us and we fought back. We knew what we were fighting for.' Blood was pooling on the snow now. 'Then the boy-king convinced us we should invade Ventria, to force the emperor to end the war. No territorial ambitions, he said. Justice and peace were all he wanted. We believed him, didn't we? Now look at him! Emperor Skanda, would-be conqueror of the world. Now he's going to invade Cadia. But he has no territorial ambitions. Oh no . . . the bastard!' Orendo lay back and Nogusta moved around the fire to sit alongside him. 'You remember that boy I saved?' asked Orendo.

'Yes. It was a fine deed.'

'You think it will count for me? You know . . . if there is a paradise?'

'I hope so.'

Orendo sighed. 'I can't feel the cold now. That's a good thing. I've always hated the cold. Tell Bison not to judge me too hard, eh?'

'I am sure that he won't.'

Orendo's voice was slurring, then his eyes flared open. 'There *are* demons,' he said, suddenly. 'I can see them. There are demons!'

He died then, and Nogusta rose, collected the pouch of jewels and walked to his horse.

He glanced up at the sky, which was blue, clear and bright. Not a trace of cloud.

Stepping into the saddle he gathered the other three mounts and headed back for the city.

There were demons in the air over the city of Usa, shroud-pale and skinny, their talons long, their teeth sharp. Ordinary eyes could not see them, and they seemed to pose no threat to ordinary folk.

Why then are they here, thought Ulmenetha? Why do they hover close to the palace? The large priestess pushed her thick fingers through her short cropped blond hair. Rising from her bed she poured water into a bowl and washed her face. Refreshed she silently opened the connecting door and stepped through into the queen's bedroom. Axiana was asleep, lying on her back, one white slender arm curled around a satin pillow. Ulmenetha smiled. Only a few years before that arm had, in the same manner, cuddled a stuffed toy – a woollen lioness with only one glass eye.

Now Axiana was a child no longer.

Ulmenetha sighed. Despite her bulk the priestess moved silently across the royal bedroom, casting an affectionate look at the pregnant Axiana. The queen's face shone in the moonlight, and, in sleep, Ulmenetha could just discern the child she had grown to love. 'May your dreams be rich and joyful,' she whispered.

Axiana did not stir. The fat priestess reached the window balcony and stepped out into the moonlight. Her white-streaked blond hair shone like silver beneath the stars, and her voluminous nightdress of white cotton shimmered, as if turned to silk. There was a marble-topped table set on the balcony, and four chairs. Easing herself down she untied her rune pouch and placed it on the table. Ulmenetha gazed up at the night sky. All she could see with the eyes of her body were the stars, shining bright. To her left a crescent moon seemed to be balancing precariously on the uppermost tower of the Veshin temple. Closing the eyes of her body, she opened the eyes of her spirit. The stars remained, brighter and clearer now, robbed of the twinkling illusion caused by human astigmatism and the earth's atmosphere. Tall mountains could clearly be seen on the far-away face of the crescent moon. But it was not the night sky Ulmenetha wished to see.

Above the palace three scaled forms were hovering.

For weeks now their malevolent presence had kept her chained to her flesh, and she longed to fly free. But the last time she had tried they had come for her, screeching across the sky. Ulmenetha had barely made it back to her body.

Who had summoned them, and why?

Closing her eyes she loosened the draw-string of her rune pouch and reached inside, her fingers stroking the stones within. They were smooth and round and flat, and for a while she continued to stir them. At last one stone seemed to call for her, and she drew it from the pouch. Painted upon it was a cracked goblet. Ulmenetha sat back.

The Broken Flagon was a stone signalling mistrust. At best it warned of caution in dealings with strangers. At worst it signalled treachery among friends.

From the pocket of her white dress she produced two leaves. Rolling them into a ball she placed them in her mouth and began to chew. The juices were acrid and bitter. Pain lanced into her head and she stifled a groan. Bright colours danced now on the edge of her vision, and she pictured the Broken Flagon, holding to the image and freeing her mind of conscious thought.

A silver serpent slithered up and around the flagon, slowly crushing it. The flagon suddenly shattered, the pieces exploding outward, ripping through the curtain of time. Ulmenetha saw a tree-shrouded hollow and four men. Axiana was there. Ulmenetha saw herself kneeling beside the queen, a protective arm around her shoulder. The four men were warriors, and they had formed a circle around Axiana, facing outward ready to fight off some unseen threat. A white crow was hovering over them all, his wings beating silently.

Ulmenetha sensed a colossal evil, about to sweep over the hollow. The vision began to fade. She struggled to hold the image, but it collapsed in upon itself and a fresh scene unfolded. A camp-fire beside a dark frozen lake stretching between high mountains. A man – a tall man – sitting with his back to the lake. Behind him a dark, taloned hand reached up through the ice, then a demonic form pulled itself clear. It was colossal and winged and stood blinking in the moonlight. The great wings spread wide and the demon floated closer to the man at the

22

camp-fire. It extended an arm. Ulmenetha wanted to cry out, to warn him, but she couldn't. The talons rammed into the back of the seated man. He reared up and screamed once, then slumped forward.

As Ulmenetha watched the demon began to shimmer, his body became black smoke, which swirled into the bloody wound in the dead man's back. Then the demon was gone, and the body of the man rose. Ulmenetha could not see his face, for he was hooded. He turned towards the lake and raised his arms. Through the surface of the ice a thousand taloned hands rose up to salute him.

Once more the vision faded and she saw an altar. Upon it, held with chains of iron, was a naked man with a golden beard. It was Axiana's father, the murdered emperor. A voice spoke, a soft voice, which she felt she should recognize, but it was blurred somehow, as if she were listening to a distant echo. 'Now,' said the voice, 'the day of Resurrection is at hand. You are the first of the Three.' The chained emperor was about to speak when a curved dagger sliced into his chest. His body arched.

Ulmenetha cried out – and the vision disappeared. She found her gaze focused now only on the bare, moonlit wall of the royal bedchamber.

The visions made no sense. The emperor was not sacrificed. Having lost the last battle he had fled with his aides. He had been slain, so it was said, by officers of his own guard, men disgusted by his cowardice. Why then should she see him sacrificed in this way? Was the vision symbolic?

The incident at the lake of ice was equally nonsensical. Demons did not live below ice.

And the queen would never be in a wood with a mere

23

four warriors. Where was the king and his army? Where were the royal guards?

'Dismiss the visions from your mind,' she told herself. 'They are flawed in some way. Perhaps your preparation was at fault.'

Axiana moaned in her sleep and the priestess rose and moved to the bedside. 'Be still, my pet,' she whispered, soothingly. 'All is well.'

But all was not well, Ulmenetha knew. Her *lorassium* visions were certainly mysterious, and might indeed be symbolic. They were, however, never false.

And who were the four men? She summoned their faces to her mind. One was a black man, with bright blue eyes, the second a huge bald man, with a white, drooping moustache. The third was young and handsome. The fourth held a bow. She remembered the white crow and a shudder went through her.

This was one sign she could read without interpretation.

The white crow was Death.

Kebra the Bowman dropped a small golden coin into the palm of the outraged innkeeper. The fat man's anger faded instantly. There was no feeling in the world quite so warming as that of gold against the skin. The seething anger at the thought of broken furniture and lost business receded into minor irritation. The innkeeper glanced up at the bowman, who was now surveying the wreckage. Ilbren had long been a student of human nature, able to read a man swiftly and accurately. Yet the friendship of Kebra and Bison remained a mystery. The bowman was a fastidious man. His clothes were always clean, as were his hands and skin. He was cultured and softly spoken, and he had a rare talent for creating space around himself, as if he disliked crowds and the closeness of bodies. Bison, on the other hand, was an uncultured oaf and Ilbren despised him. The sort of man who would always drink two more flagons of ale than he could handle, and then became aggressive. Innkeepers loathed such customers. Bison's saving grace, however, was that to reach the last two flagons he could drink an inn dry, and would make every effort to do so. This naturally created large profits. Ilbren wondered how Kebra could tolerate such a friend.

'He did all this?' asked Kebra, shaking his head. Two long bench tables had been smashed, and several chairs were lying in pieces on the sawdust-covered floor. The far window had been smashed outward, and shards of broken glass still clung to the lead frame. An unconscious Ventrian officer was being tended by the window, and two other victims, common soldiers, were sitting near the doorway, one still bleeding from a gashed cheek, the other holding his bandaged head in his hands.

'All this and more. We have already swept away the broken crockery and two bent pots, which cannot be used again.'

'Well, at least no-one is dead,' said Kebra, his voice deep and sombre, 'so we must be grateful.'

The innkeeper smiled and lifted a flagon of wine, gesturing the grey clad bowman to join him at a nearby table. As they sat down he looked closely at Kebra's face. Deeply lined, as if carved from stone, Kebra looked every inch his fifty-six years. The bowman rubbed his tired eyes. 'Bison's like a child,' he said. 'When things go against him he loses control.'

'I do not know how it started,' said Ilbren. 'The first I knew of trouble was when I saw that officer flying through the air. He hit that table there, and cracked it clean through.'

Two Ventrian soldiers came in carrying a stretcher. Tenderly they lifted the unconscious man onto it, and carried him out. A Drenai officer approached Kebra. He was a veteran, and well known to the bowman as a fair man. 'You'd better find him fast!' he warned Kebra. 'The wounded man is an officer on Malikada's staff. You know what the penalty will be if he dies.'

'I know, sir.'

'Gods, man! As if we haven't enough trouble with the cursed Ventrians as it is, without one of our men cracking the skull of one of their officers.' The Drenai swung to the innkeeper. 'No offence meant, Ilbren,' he said.

'Oh, none taken I am sure,' replied the Ventrian, with just a trace of sarcasm. The officer wandered away.

'I am sorry for the trouble, Ilbren,' said Kebra. 'Do you know where Bison went?'

'I do not know. He is old enough to know better than to wreak such . . . such devastation.' The innkeeper filled two goblets, passing one to Kebra.

'This has not been a good day for him,' said Kebra, softly. 'Not a good day for any of us.' He sipped the wine, then laid the goblet down.

Ilbren sighed. 'I heard of the king's decision. We all have. For what it is worth I shall miss you.' He smiled. 'I will even miss Bison.' He stared at the white-haired archer. 'Still, war is for young men, eh? It is way past the time when you should have settled down with a wife and raised sons.'

Kebra ignored the comment. 'Which way did Bison go?'

'I did not see.'

Kebra moved away, stepping past the injured men in

the doorway. 'It was just a bad joke,' said the soldier with the bandaged head. 'Then he went berserk.'

'Let me guess,' said Kebra. 'Something about his age, was it?'

The young soldier looked suddenly sheepish. 'It was just a joke,' he repeated.

'Well, I'm sure Bison didn't take it too seriously.'

'How can you say that?' stormed the second soldier. 'Look what he did to my face.' Blood was still seeping from his swollen cheekbone, and his right eye was closed tight, purple swelling distending the eyelid.

'I can say it because you are still alive, boy,' said Kebra, coldly. 'Did anyone see where he went?'

Both men shook their heads and Kebra stepped out into the fading winter sunlight. Across the square market traders were packing up their wares, and children were playing by the frozen fountain, scooping snow and fashioning balls which they hurled at one another. A tall black man in a long dark cloak moved through the crowd. The children stopped to watch him. Then one child moved silently behind him, a snowball in his raised hand.

'Not a wise move, child,' said the black man, without looking back. 'For if you throw it I shall be obliged to –' suddenly he swung around '– cut off your head!' Terrified the boy dropped the snowball and sprinted back to his friends. The black man chuckled and strode on to where Kebra waited.

'I take it he was not at the barracks,' said Kebra. Nogusta shook his head.

'They have not seen him.'

The two men made an incongruous pair as they walked off together, Nogusta black and powerful, Kebra wand slim, white-haired and pale. Cutting through the narrow streets they reached a small eating house overlooking the river. They took a table by the fire and ordered a meal. Nogusta removed his cloak and the sheepskin jerkin he wore below it and sat down, holding his hands out to the blaze. 'I, for one, will be pleased to say farewell to this frozen country. Why is Bison so depressed? Does he not have three wives waiting for him back home?'

'That's enough to depress anyone,' replied Kebra, with a smile.

They ate in companionable silence and Nogusta added another log to the fire. 'Why is he depressed?' he asked again, as they finished their meal. 'There must come a time when a man is too old for soldiering, and we are all way past that. And the king has offered every soldier a pouch of gold, and a scrip to give them land when they return to Drenan. The scrip alone is worth a hundred in gold.'

Kebra thought about the question. 'There was a time,' he said, 'when I could outshoot any archer alive. Then, as the years went by, I noticed I could no longer see quite as clearly. When I turned fifty I could no longer read small script. That was when I began to think of going home. Nothing lasts for ever. But Bison is not a thinker. As far as he is concerned the king has just told him he is no longer a man. And he is hurting.'

'There is some pain for all of us,' said Nogusta. 'The White Wolf will be leading almost two thousand men home. Every one of them will feel some sense of rejection. But we are alive, Kebra. I fought for the king's father – as you did – and I have carried my sword through thirty-five years of warfare. Now I am tired. The long marches are hard on old bones. Even Bison must admit to that.'

Kebra shook his head. 'Bison admits to nothing. You

should have seen his face when they called the roll. He could not believe he had been chosen. I was standing beside him. You know what he said? "How can they send me back with all the old men?" I just laughed. For a moment I thought he was joking. But he wasn't. He still thinks he's twenty-five.' He let out a soft curse. 'Why did he have to hit a Ventrian? And what if the man dies?'

'If he dies they will hang Bison,' said Nogusta. 'Not a pleasant thought. Why did he hit the man?'

'He made a joke about Bison's age.'

'And the others?'

'I have no idea. We'll ask him when we find him. The officer was one of Malikada's men.'

'That makes it worse,' said Nogusta. 'He might demand a hanging, regardless. He's a hard man.'

'The White Wolf would never allow it.'

'Times are changing, Kebra. The White Wolf is being sent home with the rest of us. I doubt he has the power to oppose Malikada.'

'A pox on Bison,' snapped Kebra. 'He's always been trouble. You remember when he and Orendo stole that pig . . . ?' The bowman's voice faded away. 'I'm sorry, my friend, that was crass.'

Nogusta shrugged. 'Orendo took part in a rape and a murder. It saddens me that he is dead, but he was the victim of his own actions.'

'Strange, though,' said Kebra. 'I am a fair judge of men and I would never have believed Orendo capable of such an act.'

'Nor I. Where shall we look for Bison?' asked Nogusta, changing the subject.

Kebra shrugged. 'He was drunk when he thrashed those men. You know Bison. After a fight he'll look for a woman. There must be two hundred whorehouses within walking distance. I do not intend to spend the night scouring them.'

Nogusta nodded, then he gave a wide grin. 'We could try just one, though,' he said.

'For what purpose? The odds against finding him are enormous.'

Nogusta leaned forward and placed his hand on his friend's shoulder. 'I was not thinking of *finding* Bison,' he said. 'I was thinking of soft skin and a warm bed.'

Kebra shook his head. 'I think I'll return to the barracks. I have a warm bed there.'

Nogusta sighed. 'Bison refuses to get old, and you refuse to stay young. Truly, you white men are a mystery to me.'

'Life would be dull without mysteries,' said Kebra.

After Nogusta had gone he ordered another flagon of wine, then made the long walk back to the barracks. The room he shared with Nogusta and Bison was cold and empty. Bison's bed was unmade, the blankets in a heap on the floor beside it. The Senior Cul no longer made inspections, and without the threat of punishment Bison had reverted to slovenly behaviour.

Nogusta's bed was tidily made, but he had left a tunic upon it.

Kebra's pallet was immaculate, the blankets folded into a square, topped by the pillow, the undersheet pulled tight, the corners overlapped with a perfect horizontal fold. Kebra moved to the hearth and lit the fire. He had cleaned out the ash and re-laid it that morning, the kindling placed with perfect symmetry.

Just about now Nogusta would be lying beside a fat, sweating whore. He would be, perhaps, the twentieth man she had opened her legs for that day. Kebra shuddered. It was a nauseating thought.

Silently he padded out to the bath house. The boilers had not been lit and the water was cold. Even so Kebra undressed and immersed himself, scrubbing at his body with soap. There were no clean towels on the rack. Angry now he searched through the large laundry basket and dabbed at his cold body with the cleanest of the used towels.

The collapse of discipline unnerved the bowman. Carrying his clothes he returned to the room and sat, shivering, in front of the fire. Then he took a nightshirt from his chest and slipped it on. It was crisp and clean and he could smell the freshness of the cotton. It eased his mind.

Ilbren's words haunted him. 'It is way past the time when you should have settled down with a wife and raised sons.'

Kebra felt the weight of the words, like a stone on his heart.

Most of Palima's customers thought of her as a whore with a golden heart. This was a view she cultivated, especially as she grew older, with age and the laws of gravity conspiring to ravage her features. The truth was more stark: Palima's heart *was* like gold, cold, hard and well hidden.

She lay now on her bed, staring at the hulking figure by the window. Bison was well known to her, a generous giant, unhindered by imagination or intellect. His needs were simple, his demands limited, his energy prodigious. For a year now – ever since the Drenai had taken the city – he had come to her at least once a week. He paid well, never troubled her with small talk or promises, and rarely outstayed his welcome.

This night was different. He had come to her bed and

had cuddled her close. Then he had fallen asleep. Bison usually paid with a single silver coin upon leaving. Yet tonight he had given her a gold half *raq* just after he arrived. Palima had tried to rouse him – not usually a difficult feat. But Bison was in no mood for sex. This did not concern Palima. If a man wanted to pay for a hug with gold she was more than happy to oblige. He had slept fitfully for two hours, holding her close. Then he had dressed and moved to the window. Bison had been standing there in the lantern light for some time now, a huge man, with great sloping shoulders and long, powerful arms. Idly he tugged at his bristling white, walrus moustache and stared out at the night dark square below.

'Come back to bed, lover,' she said. 'Let Palima work her magic.'

'Not tonight,' he told her.

'What is wrong?' she asked. 'You can tell Palima.'

He turned towards her. 'How old do you think I am?' he asked, suddenly.

Sixty-five, if you're a day, she thought, staring at his bald head and white moustache. Men were such children. 'Maybe forty,' she told him.

He seemed satisfied with the answer, and she saw him relax. 'I'm older than that, but I don't feel it. They're sending me home,' he said. 'All the older men are going home.'

'Don't you want to go home?'

'I was one of the first to join the White Wolf,' he said. 'Back when Drenan was beset on all sides and the king's army had been all but destroyed. We beat them all, you know. One after another. When I was a child my country was ruled from afar. We were just peasants. But we changed the world. The king's empire stretches for –' he seemed to struggle for a moment with the mathematics. '– thousands of miles,' he concluded lamely.

'He is the greatest king who ever lived,' she said, softly, hoping that was what he wanted to hear.

'His father was greater,' said Bison. 'He built from nothing. I served him for twenty-three years. Then the boy-king for another twenty. Twenty-six major battles I've fought in. There. Twenty-six. What do you think of that?'

'It's a lot of battles,' she admitted, not knowing where the conversation was leading. 'Come back to bed.'

'It's a lot of battles, all right. I've been wounded eleven times. Now they don't want me any more. Eighteen hundred of us. Thank you and goodbye. Here's a bag of gold. Go home. Where's home, eh?' With a sigh he moved to the bed, which creaked as his huge frame settled upon it. 'I don't know what to do, Palima.'

'You are a strong man. You can do anything you want. Go anywhere you want.'

'But I want to stay with the army. I'm a front ranker! That's what I am. That's what I want.'

Sitting up she cupped his face in her hands. 'Sometimes – most times – we don't get what we want. Rarely do we even get what we deserve. We get what we get. That's it. Yesterday is gone, Bison. It will never come again. Tomorrow hasn't happened yet. What we have is now. And do you know what is real?' She took his hand in hers and lifted it to her naked breast, pressing his fingers to her flesh. '*This* is real, Bison. *We* are real. And at this moment *we* are all there is.'

His hand fell away, then he leaned down and kissed her cheek. He had never done that before. In fact she couldn't remember the last time a man had kissed her cheek. Then he rose. 'I'd better be getting back,' he said.

'Why not stay? I know you, Bison. You'd feel better afterwards. You always do.'

'Aye, that's true. You are the best, you know. And I speak from a lifetime of having to pay for it. But I have to go. I'll be on charges. The Watch is probably looking for me.'

'What have you done?'

'Lost my temper. Tapped a few soldiers.'

'Tapped?'

'Well, maybe more than tapped. One of them laughed at me. Ventrian scum! Said the army would be better off without the greybeards. I picked him up and threw him like a spear. It was really funny. But he landed on a table and broke it with his head. That upset the Drenai soldiers who were eating there. So I tapped them all.'

'How many were there?'

'Only five or so. I didn't really hurt no-one. Well, not badly.' He grinned. 'Well, not *very* badly. But I'll be on charges.'

'What kind of punishment will you get?'

'I don't know . . . ten lashes.' He shrugged. 'Twenty. No problem.'

Palima climbed from the bed and stood naked before him. 'How did it feel when you were *tapping* them?' she asked.

'It was . . . good,' he admitted.

'You felt like a man?'

'Yes. I felt young again.'

Her hand slid down over his leggings. 'Like a man,' she whispered, huskily. She felt him swell at her touch.

'And how do you feel now?' she asked him.

He let out a long sigh. 'Like a man,' he said. 'But they don't want me to be one any more. Goodbye, Palima.'

Without another word he walked out into the night.

Palima watched him from the window. 'A pox on you and all your kind, Drenai,' she whispered. 'Go away and die!'

Banelion, the legendary White Wolf, gathered his maps and carefully placed them inside a brass bound chest. Tall and lean, his long white hair tied at the nape of the neck, the general's movements were swift and precise, as he packed the chest with the expertise of a lifetime soldier. Everything neatly in its place. The maps were stacked in the order they would be needed during the 1400 mile journey to the western port. Alongside them were notes listing the names of tribes and their chieftains, way stations, fortresses and cities along the route. As with everything else he undertook the journey home would be planned meticulously.

Across from the broad desk a young officer in full armour of gold and bronze stood watching the general. The old man glanced up and gave a swift grin. 'Why so sad, Dagorian?'

The young man took a deep, slow breath. 'This is wrong, sir.'

'Nonsense. Look at me. What do you see?'

Dagorian stared at the white-haired general. Leathered by desert sun and winter winds, the White Wolf's face was seamed and wrinkled. Beneath bristling white brows his eyes were pale and bright – eyes that had seen the fall of empires, and the scattering of armies. 'I see the greatest general who ever lived,' said the younger man.

Banelion smiled. He was genuinely touched by the officer's affection, and thought momentarily of the boy's father. The two were so unalike. Catoris had been a cold, hard man, ambitious and deadly. His son was infinitely more likeable, loyal and steadfast. The only virtue he shared with his father was courage. 'Ah, Dagorian, what you should see is a man two years past seventy. But you are looking at what was, boy. Not what is. I will be honest with you, I am disappointed. Even so I do not believe the king is making a mistake. Like me the soldiers who first marched against the Ventrian Empire are growing old now. Eighteen hundred men over fifty. Two hundred of those will not even see sixty again. The king is only thirty-five, and he wants to cross the Great River and conquer Cadia. All reports suggest that such a war will last five years or more. The army will have to cross deserts and mountains, wade rivers thick with crocodiles, hack their way through jungles. Young men will be needed for such an enterprise. And some of the older men are yearning for home.'

Dagorian removed his black and gold helm, and absently brushed his hand over the white horsehair plume. 'I don't doubt you are right about the older men, sir. But not you. Without you some of the battles would have been . . .' The White Wolf raised his finger to his lips, the movement sharp and swift.

'All my battles have been fought. Now I will go home and enjoy my retirement. I will breed horses, and watch the sun rise over the mountains. And I will wait for news of the king's victories, and I will celebrate them quietly in my home. I have served Skanda, as I served his father. Faithfully and well, and to the best of my considerable abilities. Now I need a little fresh air. Walk with me in the garden.'

Swinging a sheepskin cloak around his shoulders

Banelion pushed open the doors and strode through to the snow-covered garden. The paved path could no longer be seen, but the statues that lined it pointed the way. Crunching the snow underfoot the two men walked out past the frozen fountain. The statues were all of Ventrian warriors, standing like sentries, spears pointed towards the sky. The older man took Dagorian's arm and leaned in close. 'It is time for you to learn to curb your tongue, young man,' he said, keeping his voice low. 'Every whisper spoken inside the palace is reported to the king and his new advisers. The walls are hollow, and listeners write down every sentence. You understand?'

'They even spy on *you*? I cannot believe it.'

'Believe it. Skanda is no longer the boy-king who charmed us all. He is a man, ruthless and ambitious. He is determined to conquer the world. And he probably will. If his new allies are as trustworthy as he thinks.'

'You doubt the Prince Malikada?'

Banelion grinned and led the young man around the frozen lake. 'I have no reason to doubt him. Or his wizard. Malikada's cavalry are superbly disciplined, and his men fight well. But he is not Drenai, and the king puts great faith in him.' On the far side of the lake they came to a stone arch, beneath which was a bust of a handsome man, with a forked beard, and a high sloping brow. 'You know who this is?' asked Banelion.

'No, sir. A Ventrian noble of some kind?'

'This is the general, Bodasen. He died three hundred and fifty years ago. He was the greatest general the Ventrians ever had. He it was – with Gorben – who laid the foundations of their empire.'

The old man shivered and drew his cloak more tightly

about him. Dagorian stared hard at the white stone of the bust. 'I have read the histories, sir. He is described as a plodding soldier. Gorben was said to have led the army to victory.'

Banelion chuckled. 'As indeed has Skanda. And in the months to come you will hear the same of me. That is the way of the world, Dagorian. The victorious kings write the histories. Now let us go back, for this cold is eating into my bones.'

Once back inside Dagorian banked up the fire and the general stood before it, rubbing his hands. 'So tell me,' he said, 'have they found Bison yet?'

'No, sir. They are scouring the whorehouses. The man with the cracked skull has regained consciousness. The surgeons say he will not die.'

'That is a blessing. I would hate to hang old Bison.'

'He's been with you from the first, I understand.'

'Aye, from the first, when the old king was merely a young prince, and the kingdom was in ruins. Days of blood and fire, Dagorian. I would not want to live them again. Bison is – like me – a relic of those days. There are not many of us left.'

'What will you do when we find him, sir?'

'Ten lashes. But don't tie him to the post. That'll hurt his dignity. He'll stand there and hold to it. His back will bleed, and you'll not hear a sound from him.'

'I take it you like the man.'

Banelion shook his head. 'Can't stand him. He has the strength of an ox, and the brains to match. A more irritating, undisciplined wretch I have yet to see. But he symbolizes the strength, the courage and the will that has brought us across the world. A man to move mountains, Dagorian. Now you best get some rest. We'll finish in the morning.'

'Yes, sir. Can I fetch you some mulled wine before you retire?'

'Wine does not sit well with me these days. Warm milk and honey would be pleasant.'

Dagorian saluted, bowed and left the room.

Chapter Two

Regimental discipline was observed in ritual fashion. Every one of the 2000 men of the regiment, in their armour of black and gold, stood in a giant square around the barracks ground. At the centre the twenty senior officers waited, and, seated on a dais behind them was the White Wolf. He wore no armour, but was dressed in a simple tunic of grey wool, black leggings and boots. Around his shoulders was a hooded sheepskin cloak.

The morning was bright and clear as Bison was led out. The lumbering giant had been stripped to the waist, and Dagorian suddenly understood the man's bizarre nickname. His head was totally bald, but thick, curling hair grew from his neck and over his massive shoulders. More like a bear than a bison though, thought Dagorian. The young officer's dark gaze flickered to the men walking with Bison. One was Kebra, the famed bowman, who had once saved the king's life, sending a shaft through the eye of a Ventrian lancer. The other was the blue-eyed black man, Nogusta, swordsman and juggler. Dagorian had once watched the man keep seven razor sharp knives in the air, then, one by one send them flashing into a target. They walked straight and tall. Bison cracked a joke with someone in the first line.

'Silence!' shouted an officer.

Bison approached the whipping-post and stood beside

the lean, hawk-faced soldier who had been ordered to complete the sentence. The man looked ill at ease, and was sweating despite the morning cold.

'You just lay on, boy,' said Bison, amiably. 'I'll hold no grudge for you.' The man gave a weak, relieved smile.

'Let the prisoner approach,' said the White Wolf. Bison marched forward and saluted clumsily.

'Have you anything to say before sentence is carried out?'

'No, sir!' bellowed Bison.

'Do you know what is special about you?' asked the general.

'No, sir!'

'Absolutely nothing,' said the White Wolf. 'You are an undisciplined wretch and the clumsiest man ever to serve under me. For a copper coin I'd hang you and be done with it. Now get to the post. This cold is chilling my bones.' So saying he lifted the sheepskin hood over his head and pulled the cloak around him.

'Yes, sir!' Bison spun on his heel and marched back to the post, reaching up and taking hold of the wood.

The man with the whip untied the thong binding the five lashes and cracked it into the air. Then he shrugged his shoulders twice and took up his position. His arm came back.

'Hold!' came a commanding voice. The soldier froze. Dagorian turned to see a small group of men striding onto the barracks ground. They were all Ventrian officers wearing golden breastplates and sporting red capes. At the centre was the Prince Malikada, the king's general, a tall, slender nobleman, who had been chosen to replace the White Wolf. Beside him was his champion, the swordsman, Antikas Karios. A fox and a cobra, thought Dagorian. Both men were slim and graceful, but

41

Malikada's power was in his eyes, dark and brooding, gleaming with intelligence, while Antikas Karios radiated a physical strength, built on a striking speed that was inhuman.

Malikada strode to the dais and bowed to the general. His hair was jet black, but his beard had been dyed with streaks of gold, then braided with gold thread. Dagorian watched him closely.

'Greetings, my lord Banelion,' said Malikada.

'This is hardly the time for a visit,' said Banelion. 'But you are most welcome, Prince.'

'It is *exactly* the time, General,' said Malikada, with a wide smile. 'One of my men is about to be disciplined incorrectly.'

'One of *your* men?' enquired the White Wolf, softly. Dagorian could feel the tension in the officers around him, but no-one moved.

'Of course one of my men. You were present when the king – glory be attached to his name – named me as your successor. As I recall you are now a private citizen of the empire about to head for home and a happy retirement.' Malikada swung round. 'And this man has been accused of striking one of my officers. That, as I am sure you are aware, under Ventrian law, is a capital offence. He shall be hanged.'

An angry murmur sounded throughout the ranks. Banelion rose. 'Of course he shall hang – if convicted,' he said, his voice cold. 'But I now change his plea to not guilty and – on his behalf – demand trial by combat. This is *Drenai* law, set in place by the king himself. Do you wish to deny it?' Malikada's smile grew wider, and Dagorian realized in that moment that this was exactly what the Ventrian wanted. The swordsman, Antikas, was already removing his cloak and unbuckling his breastplate.

'The king's law is just,' said Malikada, raising his left arm and clicking his fingers. Antikas stepped forward, drew his sword and spun it in the sunlight. 'Which of your ... former ... officers will face Antikas Karios? I understand your aide, Dagorian, is considered something of a swordsman.'

'Indeed he is,' said Banelion. Dagorian felt fear rip into him. He was no match for the Ventrian. He swallowed down the bile rising in his throat, and fought to keep his emotions from his face. Glancing up he saw Antikas Karios staring at him. There was no hint of a sneer, or mockery of any kind. The man simply stared. Somehow it made Dagorian feel even worse. Rising from his seat Banelion gestured for Nogusta to come forward. The black man approached the dais, saluted, then bowed. 'Will you defend the honour of your comrade?' asked the White Wolf.

'But of course, my general.'

Dagorian's relief was intense, and he reddened as he saw a slight smile appear on the face of the Ventrian swordsman.

'This is not seemly,' said Malikada, smoothly. 'A common soldier to face the finest swordsman alive? And a black savage to boot? I think not.' He turned to a second Ventrian officer, a tall man with a long golden beard, crimped into horizontal waves. 'Cerez, will you show us your skills?'

The man bowed. Wider in the shoulder than the whip lean Antikas, Cerez had the same economy of movement and catlike grace found in all swordsmen. Malikada looked up at Banelion. 'With your permission, General, this student of Antikas Karios will take his place.'

'As you wish,' said Banelion.

Nogusta stepped forward. 'Do you wish me to kill the

man, or merely disarm him, General?'

'Kill him,' said Banelion. 'And do it swiftly. My breakfast is waiting.'

Both men removed their armour and upper clothing and strode out bare-chested into the centre of the barracks ground. Nogusta lifted his sword in salute. Cerez attacked immediately, sending out a lightning thrust. Nogusta parried it with ease. 'That was discourteous,' whispered Nogusta, 'but I will still kill you cleanly.'

Their blades clashed as Cerez charged forward, his curved sword flashing with bewildering speed. But every thrust or cut was parried by the black man. Cerez dropped back. Dagorian watched the contest closely. The Ventrian was younger by thirty years, and he was fast. But there was not an ounce of fat on Nogusta's powerful frame, and his vast experience enabled him to read his opponent's moves. Dagorian flicked a glance at Antikas Karios. The champion's dark, hooded eyes missed nothing, and he leaned in to whisper something to Malikada.

The two warriors were circling one another now, seeking an opening. The action had been fast, and the black man, though skilful, was visibly tiring. Cerez almost caught him with a sudden riposte, the blade slashing close to Nogusta's cheek. Suddenly Nogusta appeared to stumble. Cerez lunged – and in that moment realized he had been tricked! Nimbly spinning on his heel, all signs of fatigue vanished, Nogusta swayed away from the blade, his own sword slicing through his opponent's golden beard and biting deep into his throat. Cerez stumbled forward, falling to his knees, blood gushing from the wound. Dropping his sword he tried to stem the rush of life from his severed jugular. Slowly he toppled forward, twitched once, then was still. Nogusta strode back across the barrack-square and bowed to the White Wolf. 'As you commanded, Lord, so was it done.'

Ignoring the furious Malikada the White Wolf rose. 'The prisoner is not guilty,' he said, his voice clear and firm. 'And since this is my last moment among you all, let me thank you for the service you have given the king, while under my command. Those among you chosen to retire will find me camped on the flat ground to the west of the city. We will be ready for departure in four days. That is all. Dismissed!'

As he stepped from the dais Malikada moved in close. 'You have made an enemy this day,' he whispered. The White Wolf paused, then met the prince's hawk-eyed gaze.

'An infinitely better prospect than having you for a friend,' he said.

The king's birthday was always celebrated with extravagant displays; athletics competitions, boxing matches, horse races, and demonstrations of magic to thrill the crowds. Spear-throwing, archery, sword bouts, and wrestling were also included, with huge prizes for the winners in all events. This year promised even greater extravagances, for it was the king's thirty-fifth birthday, a number of great mystical significance to Drenai and Ventrian alike. And the event was to take place in the Royal Park at the centre of Usa, the ancient capital of the old Ventrian Empire. The city was older than time, and mentioned in the earliest known historical records. In myth it had been a home for gods, one of whom was said to have raised the royal palace in a single night, lifting mammoth stones into place with the power of his will.

Hundreds of huge tents had been pitched in the meadows at the centre of the thousand-acre Royal Park, and scores of carpenters had been working for weeks building tiered seating for the nobility.

The tall towers of the city were silhouetted against the eastern mountains as Kebra the Bowman leaned on a new fence and stared sombrely out towards where the archery tourney would be held. 'You should have entered,' said Nogusta, passing the bowman a thick wedge of hot pie.

'To what purpose,' answered Kebra, sourly, placing the food on the fence rail and ignoring it.

'You are the champion,' said Nogusta. 'It is your title they will be shooting for.'

Kebra said nothing for a moment, transferring his gaze to the snow-topped peaks away to the west. He had first seen these mountains a year ago, when Skanda the king, having won the Battle of the River, had ridden into Usa to take the emperor's throne. Cold winds blew down now from these grey giants and Kebra shivered and drew his pale blue cloak closer about his slender frame. 'My eyes are fading. I could not win.'

'No, but you could have taken part.' The words hung in the cold air. A team of thirty workers moved to the king's pavilion and began to raise wind-shields of stiffened crimson silk around it. Kebra had seen the pavilion constructed on many occasions, and recalled, with a stab of regret, the last time he had stood before it, receiving the Silver Arrow from the hand of the king himself. Skanda had given his boyish grin. 'Does winning ever get boring, old lad?' he had asked.

'No, sire,' he had answered. Turning to the crowd he had raised the Silver Arrow, and the cheers had thundered out. Kebra shivered again. He looked up into the black man's pale, unreadable eyes. 'I would be humiliated. Is that what you want to see?'

Nogusta shook his head. 'You would not be humiliated, my friend. You would merely lose.'

Kebra gave a tired smile. 'If I had entered most of the Drenai soldiers would have bet on me. They would lose their money.'

'That would be a good reason to decline,' agreed Nogusta. 'If it were truly the reason.'

'What is it you want from me?' stormed Kebra. 'You think there is a question of honour at stake here?'

'No, not honour. Pride. False pride, at that. Without losers, Kebra, there would be no competitions at all. There will be more than a hundred archers taking part in the tourney. Only one will win. Of the ninety-nine losers more than half will know they cannot win before they draw the first shaft. Yet still they will try. You say your eyes are fading. I know that is true. But it is distance that troubles you. Two of the three events require speed, skill and talent. Only the third is shot over distance. You would still be in the top ten.'

Kebra stalked away from the fence. Nogusta followed him. 'When the day comes that you don't wish to hear the truth from me,' he said, 'you merely have to say.'

The bowman paused and sighed. 'What is the truth here, Nogusta?'

The black man leaned in close. 'You demean the championship by refusing to take part. The new champion will feel he has not earned the title. In part, I fear, this is why you have declined.'

'And what if it is? He will still earn a hundred gold pieces. He will still be honoured by the king, and carried shoulder high around the Park.'

'But he will not have beaten the legendary Kebra. I

seem to recall your delight fifteen years ago when you took the Silver Arrow from the hands of Menion. He was as old as you are now when he stood against you in the final. And you beat him finally only when it came to the distant targets. Could it be that his eyes were fading?'

Bison strolled over to where they stood. 'Going to be a great day,' he said, wiping crumbs from his white moustache. 'The Ventrian sorcerer, Kalizkan, has promised a display no-one will ever forget. I hope he conjures a dragon. I've always wanted to see a dragon.' The bald giant looked from one man to the other. 'What is it? What am I missing here?'

'Nothing,' said Nogusta. 'We were just involved in a philosophical debate.'

'I hate those,' said Bison. 'I never understand a word. Glad I missed it. By the way I've entered the wrestling. I hope you two will be cheering for me.'

Nogusta chuckled. 'Is that big tribesman taking part this year?'

'Of course.'

'He must have thrown you ten feet last year. It was only luck that you landed head first, and thereby avoided injury.'

Bison scowled. 'He caught me by surprise. I'll take him this year – if we're matched.'

'How many times have you entered this competition?' asked Kebra.

'I don't know. Almost every year. Thirty times, maybe.'

'You think you'll win this time?'

'Of course I'll win. I've never been stronger.'

Nogusta laid his hand on Bison's massive shoulder. 'It doesn't concern you that you've said the same thing for more than thirty years? And yet you've never even reached the quarter-finals.'

'Why should it?' asked Bison. 'Anyway, I did reach the quarters once, didn't I? It was during the Skathian campaign. I was beaten by Coris.' He grinned. 'You remember him? Big, blond fellow. Died at the siege of Mellicane.'

'You are quite right,' said Nogusta. 'Coris was beaten in the semifinal. I remember losing money on him.'

'I've never lost money on the king's birthday,' said Bison, happily. 'I always bet on you, Kebra.' His smile faded and he swore. 'This will be the last year when you pay off all my winter debts.'

'Not this year, my friend,' said Kebra. 'I'm not entered.'

'I thought you might forget,' said Bison, 'so I entered you myself.'

'Tell me you are joking,' said Kebra, his voice cold.

'I never joke about my debts. Shouldn't you be out there practising?'

The crowds were beginning to gather as Dagorian strolled out onto the meadow. He was uncomfortable in full armour, the gilded black and gold breastplate hanging heavy on his slim shoulders. Still, he thought, at least I don't have to wear the heavy plumed helm. The cheek guards chafed his face and, despite the padded cap he wore below it, the helm did not sit right. Once when the king called out to him Dagorian had turned sharply and the helm had swivelled on his head, the left cheek guard sliding over his left eye. Everyone had laughed. Dagorian had never wanted to be a soldier, but when your father was a hero general – and, worse, a dead hero general – the son was left with little choice.

And he had been lucky. The White Wolf had taken him on to his staff, and spent time teaching the youngster tactics and logistics. While Dagorian did not enjoy soldiering he had discovered he had a talent for it, and that made a life of campaigning at least marginally tolerable.

The preparations for the king's birthday were complete now, and within the hour the crowds would begin to surge through the gates. The sky was clear, the new day less cold than yesterday. Spring was coming. Only in the evenings now did the temperature drop below freezing. Dagorian saw the three old warriors talking by the fence rail. He strolled across to where they stood. As he approached, Kebra the Bowman strode away. He looks angry, thought Dagorian. The black swordsman saw Dagorian approach and gave a salute.

'Good morning to you, Nogusta,' said the officer. 'You fought well yesterday.'

'He does that,' said Bison, with a wide, gap-toothed grin. 'You're the son of Catoris, aren't you?'

'Yes.'

'Good man,' said Bison. 'You could always rely on the Third Lancers when he was in command. He was a hard bastard, though. Ten lashes I got when I didn't salute fast enough. Still, that's the nobility for you.' He swung to Nogusta. 'You want more pie?' The black man shook his head and Bison ambled away towards one of the food tents.

Dagorian grinned. 'Did he just praise my father, or insult him?' he asked.

'A little of both,' said Nogusta.

'An unusual man.'

'Bison or your father?'

'Bison. Are you entered in any of the tournaments?'

'No,' said the black man.

'Why not? You are a superb swordsman.'

'I don't play games with swords. And you?'

'Yes,' answered Dagorian. 'In the sabre tourney.'

'You will face Antikas Karios in the final.'

Dagorian looked surprised. 'How can you know that?'

Nogusta lifted his hand and touched the centre of his brow. 'I have the Third Eye,' he said.

'And what is that?'

The black man smiled. 'It is a Gift – or perhaps a curse – I was born with.'

'Do I win or lose?'

'The Gift is not that precise,' Nogusta told him, with a smile. 'It strikes like lightning, leaving an image. I can neither predict nor direct it. It comes or it . . .' His smile faded, and his expression hardened. Dagorian looked closely at the man. It seemed he was no longer aware of the officer's presence. Then he sighed. 'I am sorry,' he said. 'I was momentarily distracted.'

'You saw another vision?' asked Dagorian.

'Yes.'

'Did it concern the sabre tourney?'

'No, it did not. I am sure you will acquit yourself well. Tell me how is the White Wolf?' he asked, suddenly.

'He is well, and preparing plans for the return home. Why do you ask?'

'Malikada will try to kill him.' The words were spoken softly, but with great authority. The black man was not venturing an opinion, but stating a fact.

'This is what you saw?'

'I need no mystic talent to make that prediction.'

'Then I think you are wrong,' said Dagorian. 'Malikada is the king's general now. Banelion does not stand in his way. Indeed he will be going home in three days, to retire.'

'Even so his life is in danger.'

'Perhaps you should speak to the general about this?' said Dagorian, stiffly.

Nogusta shrugged. 'There is no need. He knows it as well as I. Cerez was Malikada's favourite. He believed him to be almost invincible. Yesterday he learned a hard lesson. He will want revenge.'

'If that is true will he not seek revenge against you also?'

'Indeed he will,' agreed Nogusta.

'You seem remarkably unperturbed by the prospect.'

'Appearances can be deceiving,' Nogusta told him.

As the morning wore on Nogusta's words continued to haunt the young officer. They had been spoken with such quiet certainty that the more Dagorian thought of them, the more convinced he became of the truth they contained. Malikada was not known as a forgiving man. There were many stories among the Drenai officers concerning the Ventrian prince and his methods. One story had it that Malikada once beat a servant to death for ruining one of his shirts. As far as Dagorian knew there was no evidence to support the tale, but it highlighted the popular view of Malikada.

Such a man would indeed nurse a grudge against Banelion.

With at least another two hours before the start of his duties Dagorian decided to seek out the general. He loved the old man in a way he had never learned to love his own father. Often he had tried to work out why, but the answer escaped him. Both were hard, cold men, addicted to war and the methods of war. And yet with

Banelion he could relax, finding words easy and conversation smooth. With his father his throat would tighten, his brain melt. Clear and concise thoughts would travel from his mind to his mouth, appearing to become drunken on the way, spilling out – at least to himself – as stuttering gibberish.

'Spit it out, boy!' Catoris would yell, and the words would dry up, and Dagorian would stand very still, feeling very foolish.

In all his life he could only recall one moment when his father had shown him affection. And that was after the duel. A nobleman named Rogun had challenged Dagorian. It was all so stupid. A young woman had smiled at him, and he had returned the compliment. The man with her stormed across the street. He slapped Dagorian across the face, and issued a challenge.

They had met on the cavalry parade-ground at dawn the following day. Catoris had been present. He watched the fight without expression, but when Dagorian delivered the killing stroke he ran forward and embraced him clumsily. He remembered the incident now with regret, for instead of returning the embrace he had angrily pulled clear and hurled his sword aside. 'It was all so stupid!' he stormed. 'He made me kill him for a smile.'

'It was a duel of honour,' said his father, lamely. 'You should be proud.'

'I am sick to my stomach,' said Dagorian.

The following day he had entered the monastery at Corteswain, and pledged his life to the Source.

When his father died at Mellicane, leading a charge that saved the king's life, Dagorian had known enormous grief. He did not doubt that his father loved him, nor indeed that he loved his father. But – apart from that one embrace – the two of them had never been able to show their affection for one another.

Shaking off the memories Dagorian approached the gates, and saw the crowds waiting patiently outside. They parted and cheered as the Ventrian sorcerer, Kalizkan, made his entrance. Tall and dignified, wearing robes of silver satin, edged with golden thread, the silver-bearded Kalizkan smiled and waved, stopping here and there to speak to people in the throng. Six young children stayed close by him, holding to the tassels of his belt. He halted before a young woman, with two children. She was wearing the black sash of the recently widowed, and the children looked thin and under-nourished. Kalizkan leaned in close to her, and lifted his hand towards the cheap tin brooch she wore upon her ragged dress. 'A pretty piece,' he said, 'but for a lady so sad it ought to be gold.' Light danced from his fingers, and the brooch gleamed in the sunlight. Where it had sat close to the dress the sheer weight of the new gold made it hang down. The woman fell to her knees and kissed Kalizkan's robes. Dagorian smiled. Such deeds as this had made the sorcerer popular with the people. He had also turned his vast home into an orphanage in the northern quarter and spent much of his free time touring the slum areas, bringing deserted children to his house.

Dagorian had met him only once – a brief introduction at the palace, with twenty other new officers. But he liked the man instinctively. The sorcerer gave a last wave to the crowd and led his children into the park. Dagorian bowed as he approached.

'Good morning to you, young Dagorian,' said Kalizkan, his voice curiously high pitched. 'A fine day, and not too cold.'

The officer was surprised that Kalizkan had

remembered his name. 'Indeed, sir. I am told you have prepared a wondrous exhibition for the king.'

'Modesty forbids me to boast, Dagorian,' said Kalizkan, with a mischievous grin. 'But my little friends and I will certainly attempt something special. Isn't that right?' he said, kneeling down and ruffling the blond hair of a small boy.

'Yes, uncle. We will make the king very happy,' said the child.

Kalizkan pushed himself to his feet and smoothed down his silver satin robes. They matched the colour of his long thin beard, and highlighted the summer sky blue of his eyes. 'Well, come along, my children,' he said. With a wave to Dagorian the tall sorcerer strode on.

Dagorian moved out through the gates, and along the highway to where the horses of the officers were stabled. Saddling his chestnut gelding he rode out to where the White Wolf was camped, west of the city walls. The camp itself was largely deserted, since most of the men would be at the celebrations, but there was a handful of sentries, two of whom were standing outside Banelion's large, black tent. Dagorian dismounted and approached the men.

'Is the general accepting visitors?' he asked. One of the sentries lifted the tent flap and stepped inside. He returned moments later.

'He will see you, Captain,' he said, saluting.

The sentry lifted the flap once more and Dagorian ducked into the tent. The White Wolf was sitting at a folding table, examining maps. He was looking frail and elderly. Dagorian hid his concern and gave a salute. Banelion smiled. 'What brings you here today, my boy? I thought you had duties in the Park.'

Dagorian quietly told him of the conversation with

Nogusta. The White Wolf listened in silence, his expression unreadable. When the young man had finished he gestured him to a chair. Banelion sat quietly for a moment, then leaned forward. 'Do not take this amiss, Dagorian, but I want you to forget about the warning. And let us make our goodbyes now, for you must not come close to me again.'

'You think it is true, sir?'

'True or false it must not affect you. You are remaining behind, and will serve Malikada as you served me – with loyalty and honour.'

'I could not do that if he was responsible for your death, my general.'

'I am no longer *your* general. Malikada is!' snapped Banelion. His face softened. 'But I am your friend. What is between Malikada and myself is for me to concern myself with. It has no bearing on your dealings with the king's general. We are not talking friendship here, Dagorian, we are talking politics. More than this we are talking survival. I can tolerate an enemy like Malikada. You cannot.'

Dagorian shook his head. 'You talk of honour, sir? How could I honour the man who murdered my friend?'

'Try to understand, boy. Two years ago Malikada was leading an army that killed Drenai soldiers. He faced the king in two battles and did his best to kill him. When the last city fell we all expected Malikada to be executed. Skanda chose to make him his friend. And he has proved a remarkable ally. That is Skanda's great talent. Half the army he leads used to be his enemies. That is why he took the empire, and why he will hold it. Three of Skanda's closest friends were killed by Malikada and his men – including your father. Yet Skanda honours him. If Malikada manages to have me killed it will not matter to the king, for I am yesterday,

Malikada is today. Let it not matter to you either.'

The White Wolf fell silent. Dagorian reached out and took the old man's hand. 'I am not the king. I am not even a soldier by choice. And I cannot think as you would wish me to. All I want is to see you live.'

'Many men have tried to kill me, Dagorian. I am still here.' Banelion rose. 'Now go back to the celebrations.'

Dagorian moved to the tent entrance and turned. 'Thank you, sir, for all you have done for me.'

'And you for me,' said Banelion. 'Farewell.'

Outside the tent Dagorian summoned the sentries to him. Both were older men, their beards flecked with silver. 'The general's life is in danger,' he told them, keeping his voice low. 'Watch carefully for strangers. And if he leaves the camp for any reason make sure someone is close to him.'

'We know, sir. They'll not get to him while we live,' said the first.

Dagorian stepped into the saddle and rode back through the city. Leaving his horse at the stables he joined the last of the crowd surging through the open gates. He had been gone for more than an hour, and many of the events had already begun. Threading his way through the throng he made his way to the king's pavilion and rejoined the guards.

The wrestling was under way. More than forty pairs of fighting men were grappling, and the crowd was cheering loudly. Dagorian saw the giant Bison hurl an opponent out of the circle. Far to the left the archery tournament had also begun. Two hundred bowmen were shooting at straw-filled targets.

Dagorian glanced at the nobles seated around the king. Malikada was sitting beside Skanda. The king

57

looked magnificent in his armour of polished iron. Unadorned it gleamed like silver. Skanda laughed and gestured towards one of the wrestling bouts. Dagorian's eyes did not follow where the king pointed. His gaze remained fixed on Skanda's profile. The king was a handsome man, his golden hair, streaked now with silver, shone in the sunlight like a lion's mane. This was the man who had conquered most of the world. Beside the powerful figure of Skanda the Ventrian prince Malikada seemed almost frail. Both men were laughing now.

Two rows behind the king sat the pregnant queen, Axiana. Serene and exquisitely beautiful she seemed to have no interest in the proceedings. The daughter of the Ventrian emperor deposed by Skanda she had been taken in marriage to cement Skanda's claim to the throne. Dagorian wondered if the king loved her. A ridiculous thought, he chided himself. Who could not love Axiana? Dressed in white, her dark hair braided with silver thread, she was – despite the advanced state of her pregnancy – an arresting vision of beauty. Her gaze suddenly turned to Dagorian, and he looked away, guiltily.

The smell of roasting meats drifted out from the huge tent behind the pavilion. Soon the tourneys would be suspended for an hour for the nobles to eat and drink. Dagorian moved back to check the guards around the tent. Sixty spearmen were waiting there. They stood to attention as the young officer approached. 'Take your places,' he commanded. All but four of the men filed out around the tent. Dagorian led the last group to the entrance behind the pavilion.

'Tie your chin strap,' he ordered one of the men.

'Yes, sir. Sorry, sir.' Passing his spear to a comrade the man hastily tied the thongs.

'Remain silent and at attention until the last of the guests return to the pavilion. You are the King's Guards. Your discipline is legendary.'

'Yes, sir!' they chorused.

Dagorian stepped into the tent. Food tables had been set all around the huge enclosure, and a score of servants waited, bearing trays on which goblets of wine had been set. Dagorian gestured the servants forward, and they moved in two lines to flank the entrance. Trumpets sounded from the Park. Dagorian moved behind the first line of servants and waited. Within moments the king and queen entered, followed by Skanda's generals and nobles.

Immediately the silent tension within the tent disappeared, as wine was served and the guests made their way to the food tables. Dagorian relaxed, and allowed himself to gaze on the wonder that was Axiana. Her eyes were dark blue, the colour of a sunset sky, just after the sun had fallen. They are sad eyes, he thought. In his young life Dagorian had never given much thought to the status of women, but now he wondered just how the queen had felt when ordered to marry the man who took her father's empire. Had she and her father been close? Had she sat upon his knee as a child and tugged his long beard. Had he doted upon her? Pushing such thoughts from his mind Dagorian was about to leave when a young Ventrian officer approached him. The man gave a slight, almost contemptuous, bow. 'The Prince Malikada would like a word with you, sir,' said the man.

Dagorian eased his way to where Malikada waited. The Ventrian prince was dressed in a black tunic, embroidered with a silver hawk at the shoulder, and his beard was now braided with silver wire to match it. He gave a friendly smile as Dagorian approached and

59

extended his hand. His grip was firm and dry. 'You were Banelion's aide, and I understand you accomplished your tasks with dedication and efficiency.'

'Thank you, sir.'

'I have my own aide, Dagorian, but I wanted you to know that I appreciate your talents, and that I will bear you in mind for promotion when a suitable position arises.'

Dagorian bowed, and was about to step away when the prince spoke again. 'You were fond of Banelion?'

'Fond, sir? He was my general,' replied Dagorian, carefully. 'I respected him for his great talents.'

'Yes, of course. In his time he was a formidable foe. But now he is old and spent. Will you serve me with the same dedication?'

Dagorian found his heart beating faster. He looked into Malikada's dark, cold eyes, and saw again the fierce intelligence there. There would be no point in trying to lie to this man directly. He would read it immediately. Dagorian's mouth was dry, but his words when they came were spoken steadily. 'I am dedicated to the king's service, sir. You are the king's general. Any order you give me will be carried out to the best of my ability.'

'That is all one can ask,' said Malikada. 'Now you may go. Antikas Karios will take over your duties here.' With that he smiled and swung away.

Dagorian turned, and almost collided with the heavily pregnant queen. 'My apologies, my lady,' he stuttered. She gave him a distant smile and moved past him. Feeling like a dolt Dagorian left the tent and wandered back to the open park.

Thousands of people were wandering across the grass, or sitting on blankets and eating prepared lunches. Soldiers and athletes were practising for their events, horse trainers were running their mounts, stretching them for the races ahead. Dagorian looked around for the king's horse, Starfire. It was always entered in the races, and never failed. But, as he scanned the horses he saw that the giant black gelding was not among the mounts being exercised. He strolled to one of the handlers and enquired of the horse.

'Lung rot,' said the man. 'It's a damn shame. Still he's getting old now. Must be eighteen if he's a day.'

Dagorian was saddened to hear it. Every Drenai child knew of Starfire. Bought by the king's father for a fabulous sum it had carried Skanda into all his major battles. Now it was dying. Skanda must be heartbroken, he thought.

Relieved to be free of his duties he wandered back to the officers' rest area and stripped off his armour, ordering a young Cul to return it to his quarters. Then he strolled out to enjoy the festivities. The prospect of becoming Malikada's aide had been an odious one, and he was grateful that the task had been taken from him. I should have gone home with the White Wolf, he thought, suddenly. I hate soldiering. While his father had been a living hero Dagorian had attended the Docian Monastery at Corteswain, studying to become a priest. He had been happy there, his lifestyle humble and almost serene.

Then his father had died, and the world changed.

Moving through the crowd he saw Nogusta sitting on the grass, Bison stretched out beside him. The bald giant had a swollen eye and a purple bruise on his cheekbone. Dagorian joined them. 'How are you faring?' he asked Bison.

'Quarter-finals,' said the giant, sitting up and stifling a groan. 'This is my year.'

Dagorian saw the vivid bruises and the man's obvious fatigue, and masked his scepticism. 'How long before your next bout?'

Bison shrugged and looked to Nogusta. 'An hour,' said the black man. 'He's fighting the tribesman who beat him last year.'

'I'll take him this time,' said Bison, wearily. 'But I think I'll take a nap first.' Lying back the giant closed his eyes. Nogusta covered him with a cloak and rose.

'You saw the general?' he asked Dagorian.

'I did.'

'He advised you to stay away from him.'

'You have a great gift.'

Nogusta smiled. 'No, that was just common sense. He is a wise man. Malikada is not so wise. But that is often the way with ambitious men. They come to believe in tales of their own destiny. Everything they desire, so they believe, is theirs by right. Chosen by the Source.'

'The Source is given credit and blame for many deeds,' said Dagorian. 'Are you a believer?'

'I would like to be,' admitted Nogusta. 'It would certainly make life more complete if one could believe in a grand plan for the universe. If we could be certain that evil men would receive judgement. However, I fear that life is not so simple. Wise men say that the universe is in a state of constant war, a battle between the Source and the forces of chaos. If that is true then chaos commands the most cavalry.'

'You are a cynic,' said Dagorian.

'I think not. I am just old and have seen too much.'

The two men sat down beside the sleeping Bison. 'How is it that a black man serves in the army of Drenan?' asked Dagorian.

'I am a Drenai,' answered Nogusta. 'My great-grandfather was a Phocian seaman. He was captured at sea and the Drenai made a slave of him. He was freed after seven years and became an indentured servant. Later he returned to his homeland and took a wife, bringing her back to Drenan. Their first son did the same, bringing my grandmother back to our estates in Ginava.'

'Estates? Your family have done well.'

'My people had a talent with horses,' said Nogusta. 'My great-grandfather bred war mounts for the old king's cavalry. It made us rich at the time.'

'But you are rich no longer?'

'No. A Drenai nobleman became jealous of our success, and fostered stories about us among the local villagers. One night a child went missing. He told them we had taken her for an obscene sacrifice. Our house was burned to the ground, and all my family slaughtered. The child, of course, was not there. It transpired she had wandered into the mountains and fallen down a steep slope. Her leg was broken.'

'How is it you were not killed with your family?'

'I went out to find the child. When I got back with her it was all over.'

Dagorian looked into Nogusta's strange blue eyes. He could read no emotion there. 'Did you seek justice?' he asked. Nogusta smiled.

'Twelve villagers were hanged.'

'And the nobleman?'

'He had friends in very high places and was not even arrested. Even so he fled to Mashrapur, and hired four swordsmen as his permanent bodyguards. He lived in a house behind high walls, and rarely came out in public.'

'So he was never brought to justice?'

'No.'

'What became of him? Do you know?'

Nogusta looked away for a moment. 'Someone scaled his walls, slew his guards and cut his heart out.'

'I see.' For a while both men sat in silence. 'Are you pleased to be going home?' asked Dagorian.

The black man shrugged. 'I am tired of constant war. What does it achieve? When the old king took arms against the emperor we all felt the cause was just. But now . . . ? What has Cadia ever done to us? Now it is about glory and building an everlasting name. The Ventrian Empire once boasted a thousand universities, and hospitals for the sick. Now it is bled dry and all the young men want to fight. Yes, I am ready to go home.'

'To breed horses?'

'Yes. Many of my father's horses escaped into the high country. There will be a sizeable herd by now.'

'And will Bison go with you?'

Nogusta laughed aloud. 'He will sign on with a mercenary regiment somewhere.' His smile faded. 'And he will die in a small war over nothing.'

The winter sun was high now, its pale warmth melting the patches of snow.

'I wanted to be a priest,' said Dagorian. 'I thought I heard the call. Then my father was killed and my family informed me it was my duty to take his place. From a priest to a soldier . . . there's a leap!'

'Once there were warrior priests,' said Nogusta. 'The Thirty. There are many legends of them.'

'There has been no temple since the War of the Twins,' said Dagorian. 'But the order had slipped a long way by then. One of my ancestors fought alongside the Thirty at Dros Delnoch. His name was Hogun. He was a general of the Legion.'

'I only know about Druss and the Earl of Bronze,' admitted Nogusta.

'That's all anyone remembers. I sometimes wonder if he even existed at all . . . Druss, I mean. Or was he just a combination of many heroes?'

'Don't say that to Bison. He swears he is of Druss's line.'

Dagorian gave a wry chuckle. 'Almost every soldier I know claims Druss as an ancestor. Even the king. But the simple fact is that most of the earliest stories tell us Druss had no children.' Trumpets sounded and Dagorian looked up to see the royal party moving back to their seats. Nogusta woke Bison.

'Almost time, my friend,' he said.

Bison sat up and yawned. 'That was all I needed,' he said. 'Now I'm ready. How's Kebra doing?'

'He didn't take part in the elimination event,' said Nogusta. 'As reigning champion he can come in for the final stages, the Horse, the Hanging Man, and the Distance.'

'He'll win,' said Bison. 'He's the best.'

'Place no money on him, my friend,' said Nogusta, lightly touching the centre of his forehead.

'Too late,' said Bison.

Dagorian strolled to a food tent and purchased a wedge of meat pie, which he ate swiftly, then returned to the meadow. He saw Bison engaged in a furious contest with a massive opponent. Bison was bleeding from cuts above both eyes, and seemed to be suffering. His opponent charged in, ducking to grab Bison's leg and up-end him. But the Drenai warrior skipped back, then dived onto the tribesman's back. Both men rolled, but Bison had a neck lock in place. Robbed of air the tribesman was forced to submit. Bison rose, staggered, then sat down. Nogusta ran to his side, helping Bison from the circle. Men were cheering now, and clapping Bison on the back.

Dagorian moved forward to offer his congratulations when a giant of a man stepped in front of him. 'You will be easy meat, old man,' he told Bison. 'Look at you! You're exhausted.' Dagorian saw anger in Bison's eyes, but Nogusta half dragged him away. The young officer followed them.

'Who was that?' he asked Nogusta.

'The Ventrian champion, Kyaps,' said the black man.

'I'll . . . whip . . . him too,' muttered Bison.

Dagorian moved to Bison's left and between them he and Nogusta half carried Bison to a bench seat. The big man slumped down. 'Semifinals, eh?' he said, spitting blood to the grass. 'Just two more and I'll be champion.'

'When is the next bout?' asked Dagorian.

'They are preparing for it now,' said Nogusta, massaging Bison's huge shoulders.

'I think he should withdraw,' said the officer.

'Don't worry about me,' said Bison, forcing a grin. 'I'm just acting like this to fool them all.'

'It's certainly fooling me,' said Nogusta, drily.

'Have faith, black man,' grunted Bison, heaving himself to his feet. The Ventrian champion was waiting for them. He tied his long dark hair into a pony-tail and gave a wide smile as the older man entered the circle. At the sound of the drum Bison surged forward, to be met with a kick to the chest that halted him in his tracks. A chopping elbow opened a huge cut on his cheek, then Kyaps ducked down, threw an arm between Bison's legs and heaved him high, hurling him out of the circle. The old man landed hard. He lay still and did not move. Nogusta and Dagorian moved to his side. He

66

was out cold. Nogusta felt for a pulse. 'Is he alive?' asked Dagorian.

'Yes.'

After some minutes Bison stirred. He tried to open his eyes, but one was swollen shut. 'I guess I didn't win,' he mumbled.

'I guess you didn't,' agreed Nogusta. Bison smiled.

'Still, I earned some money,' he said. 'I only bet myself to make the semis. Ten to one they offered.'

'It'll cost you what you won to have your face mended,' Nogusta told him.

'Nonsense. You can stitch the cuts. They'll be fine. I'm a fast healer.' He sat up. 'I should have entered the boxing,' he said. 'I would have won that.'

The two men helped him to his feet. 'Let's go see Kebra win,' said Bison.

'I think you should have another nap,' advised Nogusta.

'Nonsense. I feel strong as an ox.'

As they were about to move off Kyaps strolled across to where they stood. He was a full head taller than Bison. 'Hey, old man,' he said. 'The next time you see me you kiss my boots. Understand?'

Bison chuckled with genuine humour. 'You have a big mouth, child,' he told him.

Kyaps leaned forward. 'Big enough to swallow you, you Drenai scum!'

'Well,' said Bison, 'swallow this.' His fist smashed into Kyaps' chin, and Dagorian winced as he heard the snapping of bone. The Ventrian champion hit the grass face first and did not move. 'See,' said Bison. 'I should have entered the boxing. I'd have won that.'

Chapter Three

Kebra the bowman was relaxed, his mind focused, his emotions suppressed, all thoughts of Bison's actions forgotten. Anger would not be an ally now. Archery required calm concentration and great timing.

He had entered the tourney in the fifth stage with only twenty archers left. The target, thirty paces away, was a straw man, with a round red heart pinned to the chest. Kebra had struck the heart ten times with ten shafts, giving him 100 points. The Ventrian bowman standing to his right had hit nine, and two other men had seven.

These four alone moved on to the sixth stage.

The crowd among the competitors was swelling now, and once again Kebra could feel the old excitement coursing through him. He had watched the other three competitors, and only the stocky Ventrian posed any real danger. But the man was being unsettled by the mainly Drenai crowd, who jeered and shouted as he took aim.

The next event was one of Kebra's favourites. He had always enjoyed the Horse, for it was the closest the tourney could offer to combat shooting. Led by running soldiers four ponies bearing figures of straw tied to the saddle, would pass before the bowmen. Each archer was allowed three shafts. There was a larger element of luck in this event, as the horses would swerve, causing the straw figures to sway in the saddle. But the crowd loved it. And so did the Drenai champion.

Kebra stood waiting, one shaft notched to the string, two others stuck in the ground before him. He glanced at the four ostlers, watching them eke out the guide ropes. A trumpet sounded. The men ran forward, exhorting the ponies to follow them. Three obeyed immediately, the fourth hanging back. Kebra drew back on the string, sighting carefully, allowing for the speed of the first horse. He loosed the shaft. Without waiting to see it strike home he ducked down and notched a second arrow. Coming up smoothly he shot again at the second target. An angry roar went up from the crowd. Kebra ignored the impulse to see what had caused it and brought his bow to bear. The last pony, an arrow jutting from its flank had reared up and was fighting the rope. It broke loose and galloped towards the king's pavilion. Kebra loosed his last shaft, and watched as it arced towards the panic-stricken pony. The arrow punched home in the back of the straw man.

Angry jeers turned to a roar of applause at the strike. Several men ran out onto the meadow and gathered the wounded pony, which was led away. The man whose arrow caused the wound was disqualified.

Only then did Kebra have a chance to check his score. All three shafts had scored. Another thirty points.

The Ventrian archer, a small, chubby man, turned to him. 'It is an honour to see you shoot,' he said. He held out his hand. 'I am Dirais.' Kebra accepted the handshake. He glanced at the scoreboard, held aloft by a young cadet. The Ventrian was ten points behind him. The other archer, a slim, young Drenai, was a further twenty points adrift.

A dozen soldiers moved out onto the meadow, dragging a wheeled, triangular scaffold, 20 feet high, across the grass. As they were setting it into place Kebra saw the king and Malikada striding out from the pavilion, coming towards them.

Skanda gave a wide grin and clapped Kebra on the shoulder. 'Good to see you, old lad,' he said. 'That last shot reminded me of the day you saved my life. A fine strike.'

'Thank you, sire,' said Kebra, with a bow. Malikada stepped forward.

'Your legend is not exaggerated,' he said. 'Rarely have I seen better bowmanship.' Kebra bowed again. Skanda shook the young Ventrian's hand.

'You are competing with the finest,' he told Dirais. 'And you are acquitting yourself well. Good luck to you.' Dirais gave a deep bow.

Malikada leaned in close to the Ventrian. 'Win,' he said. 'Make me proud.'

The king and his general moved back and the last three archers faced the Hanging Man.

A figure of straw was hung from the scaffold. A soldier dragged the figure back, then released it to swing like a pendulum between the supports. The young Drenai stepped up first. His first shaft struck the straw man dead centre, but his second hit a support pole and glanced away. His third missed the Hanging Man by a whisker.

Next came Dirais, and the Hanging Man was swung back once more. It seemed to Kebra that it was given an extra push by the Drenai soldiers, and was moving at greater speed. And the Drenai soldiers in the crowd began again to jeer and shout in an effort to unsettle the Ventrian. Even so the chubby archer hammered his first two shafts into the dummy. His third also struck a support pole.

Kebra stepped up. The figure was swung again, this

time more sedately. For the first time anger flared in the bowman. He did not need this advantage. Even so he did not complain, and, calming himself, sent three arrows into the target. The applause was thunderous. He glanced towards Dirais, and saw the fury in the man's dark eyes. It was bad enough for him to be facing the Drenai champion without such partisan efforts from the officials.

The young Drenai archer was eliminated, and now came the final test. Two targets were set up thirty paces distant. They were the traditional round targets, with a series of concentric circles, each of a different colour, surrounding a gold circle at the centre. The outer rim was white, and worth two points. Within this was blue, worth five, then silver worth seven, and lastly gold for ten.

Kebra shot first, and struck gold. Dirais equalled him. The targets were moved back ten paces. This time Kebra only managed blue. Dirais, despite the increased jeering struck gold once more.

With only two shafts left Kebra was leading by 175 points to 160. Keep calm, he told himself. The targets were lifted and carried back another ten paces. The colours were a distant blur to Kebra now. He squinted hard and drew back on the string. The crowd was silent. He loosed, the shaft arcing gracefully through the air to thud home into the white. There were no cheers from the crowd now. Dirais took aim and struck gold once more – 177 points to 170, with only one shaft left.

The targets were moved back again. Kebra could only dimly make out the outline. He rubbed his eyes. Then, taking a deep breath he took aim at the target he could barely see – and let fly! He did not know where the shaft landed, but heard one of the judges shout: 'White!' He was relieved to have hit the target at all – 179 points to 170.

Dirais would need gold to win. Kebra stepped back. The crowd were shouting now at the top of their voices.

Please miss, thought Kebra, wanting the championship more than he had ever wanted anything in his life. His chest felt tight and heavy, and his breathing was shallow. He glanced at the crowd, and saw Nogusta. Kebra tried to force a smile, but it was more like a death's head grin.

Dirais stood up to the mark, and drew back on the string. He stood, rock steady. Kebra's heart was pounding now. What were the odds on a man striking three golds in a row? A minor fluctuation in the breeze, a slight imperfection in the shaft or the flights. The gold was no bigger than a man's fist, and the distance was great: sixty paces. During his best days Kebra would have hit only four in five at this distance. And this Ventrian was not as skilled as I once was, he thought. What, three in five? Two in five? Sweet Heaven, just miss!

Just as Dirais was about to loose his final shaft a white dove flew up out of the crowd in a frantic flurry. His concentration momentarily lost he shot too quickly, his arrow punching home into silver. Kebra had won.

Strangely there was no joy. The crowd was cheering wildly but Kebra looked at Nogusta. The black man was standing very still. Dirais turned away, offering no congratulation. Kebra took him by the arm. 'Wait!' he commanded him.

'For what?' asked the Ventrian.

'I want you to shoot again.' Dirais looked puzzled, but Kebra drew him to the line.

'What is happening here?' asked one of the judges.

'Someone released that dove deliberately,' said Kebra. 'I have asked Dirais to shoot again.'

'You cannot ask this,' said the judge. 'The last shaft has been fired.' The king moved through the crowd, and the judge explained what had happened. Skanda approached Kebra.

'Are you sure this is what you want?' he asked, his good humour vanished, his face hard and cold. 'It makes no sense.'

'I have been champion for fifteen years, sire. I have beaten every man who stood beside me at the line. I beat them with skill. The jeering was unpleasant, but a true champion rises above that. The dove, however, is a different matter. Such a sharp and flurried movement would have unsettled anyone. It was a deliberate act to sabotage the man's chances. And it succeeded. I ask you, sire, to let him shoot again.'

Suddenly Skanda grinned, and for a moment he looked like the boy-king again. 'Then let it be so,' he said.

The king climbed to a fence rail and stood above the crowd. 'The champion has requested that his opponent be allowed to shoot one more arrow,' he bellowed. 'And there will be silence when he does so.' He leapt down and signalled Dirais.

The young Ventrian notched his shaft and sent it unerringly into the gold.

Kebra's heart sank. Ventrian soldiers swarmed forward and hoisted Dirais into the air. Kebra stood by silently. The king approached him. 'You are a fool, man,' he whispered. 'But the deed was not without merit.'

Skanda handed him the Silver Arrow, and Kebra waited until the celebrations had died down. The Ventrians lowered Dirais and the small archer stepped up and bowed deeply before Kebra. 'This is a day I shall remember all my life,' he said.

'As shall I,' Kebra told him, presenting the arrow. The little man bowed again.

'I am sorry your eyes let you down.' Kebra nodded and swung away.

No-one approached him as he stalked from the meadow.

Stunned and disbelieving Bison watched him go. 'Why did he do that?' he asked, dabbing at his wounded cheek with a blood-soaked cloth.

'He is a man of honour,' said Nogusta. 'Come, it is time that wound was stitched.'

'What has honour to do with paying my debts?'

'I fear it would take too long to explain,' the black man told him. Taking him by the arm he led the bewildered Bison to a medical tent. Nogusta borrowed a sickle shaped needle and a length of thread and carefully drew the folds of the cheek wound together. Altogether ten stitches were needed. Blood slowly seeped between them. The cuts above Bison's eyes were shallow, and needed no stitches. Already scabs were forming there and the trickle of blood had ceased.

'He really let me down,' grumbled Bison. 'He let us all down.' Dagorian, who had stood by in silence moved alongside the giant.

'You are not being fair on him,' he said, softly. 'It was an act of greatness. The Ventrian was being barracked and jeered. And someone did release that dove in order to throw his aim.'

'Of course he did,' said Bison. 'I paid him to do it.'

Dagorian's expression changed, becoming cold. 'You make me ashamed to be a Drenai,' he said. Turning away Dagorian left the two warriors.

'What's wrong with him?' enquired Bison. 'Has the world gone mad?'

'You are an idiot sometimes, my friend,' said Nogusta. 'Perhaps you should go back to the barracks and rest.'

'No. I want to see Kalizkan's magic. There might be a dragon.'

'You could ask him,' said Nogusta, pointing to a section of open lands between the tents. The silver garbed wizard was sitting on a bench, surrounded by children.

'I don't think so,' said Bison, doubtfully. 'I don't like wizards much. I think I'll collect my winnings and get drunk.'

'What about your debts?'

Bison laughed. 'We're leaving next week. They'll never follow me back to Drenan.'

'Is the word *honour* just a sound to you?' asked Nogusta. 'You have built up credit on trust. You gave your word to repay. Now you will become a thief whose word cannot be trusted.'

'What's put you in such a foul mood?' asked Bison.

'You would not understand if I carved the answer on your simian forehead,' snapped the black man. 'Go and get drunk. A man should always stick to what he does best.' Leaving Bison he walked across the meadow, threading his way through the crowd.

Antikas Karios approached him as he passed the king's pavilion. The swordsman gave a thin smile. 'Good morning to you,' he said. 'That was a clever trick you used against Cerez. I had warned him in the past about arrogance. I will not have to warn him again.'

Nogusta was about to move on, but the Ventrian stepped into his path. 'The king would like you to entertain his guests before the races.' Nogusta nodded

75

and followed the officer towards the front of the pavilion. Skanda saw him coming and gave a broad smile, then turned to say something to Malikada. Nogusta approached the king and gave a deep bow. 'My congratulations on your birthday, sire,' he said.

Skanda leaned forward. 'I have told Prince Malikada of your skill with knives. I fear he doubts my word.'

'Not at all, majesty,' said Malikada, smoothly. Skanda clapped him on the shoulder, then rose. 'What can you show us today, my friend?' he asked Nogusta. The black man called for one of the archery targets to be brought up. While this was being done a sizeable crowd began to gather. Nogusta removed five throwing knives from the sheaths stitched to his baldric, then spread the blades in his left hand.

'Is the target large enough?' asked Malikada, as the 6 foot high target was placed within 10 feet of the black man. The Ventrian officers around him laughed at the jest.

'I will make it smaller, my lord,' said Nogusta. 'Perhaps you would care to stand in front of it?' Malikada's smile froze in place. He glanced at the king.

'Either you or me, old lad,' said Skanda.

Malikada rose and walked to the front of the pavilion, where a soldier opened the gate for him. He strode out to the target and turned, his dark eyes staring intently at Nogusta. 'Do not move, my lord,' said Nogusta.

The black man spun a razor sharp knife in the air, then caught it. He repeated this with the other blades, throwing each one higher than the last. Then, while one was still in the air, he sent up another, then another, until all five were spinning and glittering in the sunlight. There was absolute silence now as the crowd waited in tense expectation. Still spinning the knives Nogusta slowly backed away until he was ten paces from where Malikada stood at the target.

The Ventrian prince watched the whirling blades. He seemed relaxed, but his eyes were narrowed and unblinking. Suddenly Nogusta's right arm shot forward. One of the knives slashed through the air, punching home in the target no more than an inch from Malikada's left ear. The Ventrian jerked, but remained where he was. A bead of sweat began at his temple, trickling down his right cheek. Nogusta was juggling once more with the four remaining blades. Another knife thudded home alongside Malikada's left ear. The third and fourth slammed into the target alongside his arms.

Nogusta caught the last knife then bowed deeply to Skanda. Led by the king the crowd burst into applause.

'You want to risk the blindfold?' asked Skanda, 'or is that the end of the display?'

'Let it be as you desire, sire,' said Nogusta.

The king looked across at Malikada. 'What do you think, my friend? Would you like to see him throw blindfolded?'

Malikada gave an easy smile but stepped away from the target. 'I accept that his skills are remarkable, majesty, but I have no wish to stand before a blind man with a throwing knife.' The crowd laughed and applauded the prince, who returned to the pavilion.

'I'd like to see it,' said Skanda, moving down the steps and vaulting the gate. He strode to the target and stood before it. 'Don't let me down, old lad,' he told Nogusta. 'It's bad luck for a king to be killed on his birthday.'

Antikas Karios moved alongside Nogusta. He was holding a black silk scarf, which he folded to create a blindfold. This he tied over Nogusta's eyes. The black man stood for a moment, statue still. Then spun on his heel, making a complete circle. The throwing knife flashed through the air. The crowd gasped. For just a moment they believed it had slammed into the king's throat. Skanda lifted his hand, touching his finger to the ivory hilt which was nestling alongside his jugular. Nogusta pulled clear the blindfold. Skanda stepped up to him. Applause and cheers rang out.

'Just for a moment there you had me worried,' said the king.

'You take too many chances, sire,' Nogusta told him.

Skanda grinned. 'That is what makes life worth living.' Without another word he turned back to the pavilion. Nogusta gathered his knives and sheathed them, then made his way back through the crowd.

Three men followed him at a discreet distance.

As Nogusta had predicted Dagorian won his way through to the final of the sabres, and there met Antikas Karios. The Ventrian was faster in the strike than any man Nogusta had ever seen, his blade a shimmering blur. Three times in swift succession he pierced Dagorian's defences, lightly touching his sabre to the padded chest guard. The contest was short, and embarrassingly one sided.

With the contest over Dagorian waited courteously while Antikas Karios received the Silver Sabre then faded back into the crowd. Nogusta tapped him on the shoulder. 'You fought well,' said the black man. 'Your arm is swift, your eye good, but your narrow stance let you down. Your feet were too close together. When he attacked you were off balance.'

'Even so he is the most formidable swordsman I have ever seen,' said Dagorian.

'He is deadly,' agreed Nogusta.

'Do you think you could have beaten him?'

'Not even at my best.'

Dusk was closing in and the crowd began to mill at the meadow. Kalizkan strode out alone to the centre of the field. As the sky darkened he raised his slender arms. Bright light shone from his fingers, spraying up into the air in vivid parallel flashes. The crowd applauded. In the sky the lights became a sea of stars, flowing together to form a male face, crowned with horns. This was the Bat-god, Anharat. Other divine faces glowed into view, gods and goddesses from Ventrian mythology. The faces spun in the air, creating a colossal circle of light that filled the sky. Lastly a white horse and rider could be seen, galloping between the stars. It came closer and closer. The rider was a handsome man, his armour glowing, his sword held high. He rode to the centre of the circle of gods, and reared his horse. Then he pulled off his helm, and the crowd roared to see it was Skanda. The king of kings to whom even the gods showed obeisance. Applause rang out. The image shimmered for several seconds, then the eldritch stars broke up once more, flowing over the heads of the crowd, and lighting the way to the three exit gates.

The carriages of the nobles had been drawn up outside the pavilion. The king and Malikada rode together, Skanda waving to the people as the carriage made its slow way to the gates. Then the crowd was allowed to leave. Nogusta bade farewell to the young Drenai and wandered away.

Night fell upon the meadow, and workmen moved in to dismantle the tents and the pavilion.

A lone wagon pulled up outside the tent of Kalizkan, and four men climbed from it. Furtively they glanced around, to be sure they were not overlooked. Then they entered the tent, and removed the blood-drenched bodies of six young children.

Nogusta was troubled as he made his way through the city streets. The crowd was thinning now, many stopping at ale houses and taverns, or moving through to the lantern lit night markets and the whores who plied their trade there. Nogusta was uneasy – and it was not the three men following who made him so. He had become aware of them earlier in the day. No, it was the talisman he wore. Sometimes a year could pass without a vision. Yet today he had experienced three, bright, vivid scenes. The first he had outlined to Dagorian. The second he had withheld, for it showed the young man fallen and bleeding upon a bridge of stone. But the third was altogether more mysterious; he was facing someone wearing black armour. His enemy was not human, and when their swords clashed lightning leapt up from the blades. And there was something else. The shadow of huge wings descending towards him. Nogusta shivered. He had experienced the vision during Kalizkan's magical display, and wondered if somehow the sorcery had affected the talisman, causing a false vision. He hoped so.

He glanced up into the night sky and shivered. The last of the winter could be felt now that the sun had gone down, and the temperature was barely above freezing. Lifting his head he scented the night, the city smells, hot food, spicy and rich, smoke from wood fires, the musty human scents left by the crowd. The last vision had left him on edge. It was like the night before a battle, when the air is charged with tension.

Pausing in the Lantern Market he stopped at a stall and examined the wares, glazed pottery and necklaces of jade. He glanced back the way he had come. Two of the assassins were engaged in conversation. The third he could not see. Swiftly he scanned the crowd. Then he saw him, some way ahead, in a shadowed doorway.

Nogusta had no wish to kill these men. They were merely obeying the orders of their commander. But it would not be easy to evade them. A woman approached him. She was young and blonde, her face and lips painted. He smiled at her and she took his arm, leading him into an alley. A narrow flight of stairs led to a small room and a grimy bed. Nogusta paid her, then opened the window and stared down. The three assassins were waiting in the shadows.

'Is there another way out of here?' Nogusta asked the girl.

'Yes.' She pointed to a curtain. 'Through there, along the corridor, and down into the back streets. Why?'

'Thank you,' he said, opening his pouch and tossing her a silver coin. He was about to leave when she opened her dress and lay back on the bed, moonlight gleaming from her full breasts, her ivory belly and her pale thighs. Nogusta chuckled. Let them wait in the cold, he thought.

And moved to the girl.

An hour later he slipped through the curtain, along the corridor and out into the night.

The feeling of unease was still strong upon him, and he had long ago learned to trust his instincts. He smiled as he remembered the lion. It had been a night like this, cold and bright. He had awoken, nostrils flaring, aware of danger. Armed with only a knife the fourteen-year-old Nogusta had slipped from his room and out into the night. His father's horses had been uneasy, and they stood in a tight group, watching warily. The lion had burst from the undergrowth, and leapt the paddock fence. In one movement Nogusta had hurled his knife. It slammed into the lion's side. With a startled roar it turned on the boy. Nogusta had sprinted towards the barn, knowing the lion would catch him. But then Palarin, the lord of the herd, a huge black stallion of seventeen hands charged the lion, rearing up and lashing out with his hooves. The sudden attack made the lion swerve, but then he continued after the boy. Nogusta made it to the barn, grabbed a pitchfork, and turned just in time. The lion leapt, impaling itself on the twin blades. In its dying rage it lashed out, snapping the pitchfork and slashing Nogusta's chest, breaking three ribs.

He smiled at the memory. Never as good with horses as his brothers he had, for a time at least, been the hero who saved the herd. It was a good memory. Palarin had sired many fine warhorses, and from his line came the king's great war mount, Starfire.

Yet, like me, even he is getting old now, thought Nogusta, with a sigh. And he had been missing from the afternoon races. The rumour was that Starfire was ill. Nogusta decided to seek out the horse tomorrow, and see what treatment had been recommended.

He moved off into the back streets, enjoyed a meal at a small tavern, then headed for the barracks. He had no doubt the men, having lost him, would be waiting there. How he would handle the situation would depend entirely on their skill. If they were clumsy he would disable them, but if they were skilful he would have to kill them. This thought was not a happy one. In truth Nogusta had seen enough killing in his life, and wanted nothing more than to return to the high mountains and find the descendants of the herd. It would, he thought, at least make some sense of the remainder of his life. His thoughts turned to Skanda. The man was brave and adored by his troops. He was charismatic and intelligent.

Yet there was something missing in him, some cold empty place untouched by human warmth. Despite this Nogusta liked him. Who could not? The man was capable of immense generosity. Yet equally he could be suddenly vain and jealous, and act with incredible malice. Perhaps all kings are this way, thought Nogusta. Perhaps it is the nature of powerful men.

The sky was clear, the moon and stars bright as he made his way through the back streets. The smell of freshly baked bread from the barracks kitchens wafted to him on the breeze, and he slowed his walk. Some thirty paces ahead the street intersected the Avenue of Light. Across the avenue, past the statues of the emperors was the old barracks building. Nogusta halted. Three men, armed with knives or short swords, were waiting somewhere ahead. Three men he had never met, who had been ordered to kill him. He did not hate them. They were merely soldiers obeying orders.

Yet neither was he prepared to die. Taking a deep breath he strode out onto the Avenue of Light. Lanterns were placed on tall poles along both sides of the Avenue, the bronze statues of the emperors gleaming like gold.

Nogusta moved out into the open and walked across the broad paved road. As he skirted the statue of the ancient king, Gorben, two men sprinted from the shadows. Both carried knives. Nogusta let them come. As the fastest man approached him Nogusta spun to one side, then launched a kick into the man's kneecap. The strike was not perfect, but the assassin was hurled from his feet. Nogusta ignored him and leapt to meet the second man, knocking aside the knife arm and hammering a right hook to the man's chin. He too spun to the ground, but rolled to his feet immediately. The first man was sitting in the road, unable to stand on his twisted knee.

But he hurled his knife. Nogusta swayed aside from the blade, which flashed harmlessly by to clatter against the base of Gorben's statue. The second assassin attacked again, this time more warily. Nogusta stood very still, encouraging the man to move in close. He did so with a sudden rush. Nogusta grabbed his wrist and dragged him into a savage head butt which smashed the man's nose. He groaned and sagged against the black warrior. Nogusta spun him then slammed the edge of his palm against the assassin's neck. The man fell without a sound. The third man had not shown himself.

Nogusta walked on. The barracks gate was only thirty paces ahead now. Nogusta glanced back. The Ventrian with the injured knee had hobbled to his comrade and was sitting beside him. The black man moved into the shadow of the gate arch. A whisper of movement! Nogusta dived forward just as a knife sliced the air above him. The assassin was fast and leapt upon Nogusta before he could rise. Nogusta's elbow slammed back into the man's ribs, bringing a grunt of pain. The black man swivelled and sent a straight left into the Ventrian's face. The man lashed out, his fist cracking against Nogusta's cheek. Nogusta's head thumped against the stone walkway. Bright stars exploded before his eyes and Nogusta felt a wave of dizziness threatening to engulf him. For a while the two men grappled, and the older warrior felt his strength draining away. The assassin drew a second knife. With the last of his strength Nogusta hit him in the throat with stiffened fingers. The man gagged and reared up. Nogusta grabbed him by his shirt and threw him to one side. Rolling to his feet the black warrior kicked the assassin under the chin, catapulting him backwards. He moved in for a second strike, but his opponent was unconscious.

Breathless and exhausted Nogusta slumped to a bench seat under the arch. It would have been less effort to kill them all, he thought.

Hooded and cloaked against the night winds Ulmenetha walked slowly up the winding path towards the white marble temple that crowned the hill. She was tired, her calves burning as she reached the open gates. There was a time, back in Drenan, when she would have run this hill for the sheer pleasure of it. In the days of her youth she had been slim and fast, and physical exertion had been a joy that lifted her spirits. Not now. Now it was a chore to drag her overweight frame up such an incline. Panting she sat herself down on the steps of the temple entrance and waited for her hammering heart to slow down.

A young priest in white robes walked by her, bowing as he passed.

Heaving herself to her feet she entered the building, curtsying towards the High Altar. Dipping her finger into a stone bowl full of holy water she traced a circle upon her brow then walked to the back of the temple, seating herself in an alcove beneath a wreath of elegantly carved vines.

Another priest, a tall, balding young man with a prominent nose and a weak chin, saw her there and approached. 'What do you seek, mother?' he asked her. 'The Oracle Voice is not present.'

'I need no Voice,' she told him.

'Then why are you here at this late hour?' He was wearing the grey robes of a Senior Brother and his blue eyes looked world-weary and bored.

'Are you a Seer?' she asked him.

'Sadly, no, mother. I am still a student in such matters.

But I have hopes that one day the curtain will part for me. What encouragement do you seek?'

'I seek a place without demons,' she told him. Instantly his face changed, and he made the sign of the Protective Horn.

'Such a word should not be used here,' he admonished her, his voice less friendly.

She smiled. 'If not here, then where? Never mind,' she added, seeing his confusion. 'Is there one among your order who is a Seer?'

'There was one,' he told her. 'Father Aminias. But he died last week. We were all saddened, for he was a fine man.'

'Was he ill?'

'No. He was attacked while out on his pastoral duties. A madman, it seems. He was screeching at the top of his voice, and he stabbed poor Aminias many times before he was dragged away.'

'And there is no-one else?'

'No, mother. Such Gifts are becoming increasingly rare, I think.'

'And yet they are ever more important,' she said, pushing herself to her feet.

'You spoke of . . . unholy beings. Why was that?' His blue eyes were suddenly fearful. Ulmenetha shook her head.

'You do not have the power to help me,' she said.

'Even so, mother, I would be grateful if you would enlighten me.'

Ulmenetha was silent for a moment. She looked at the grey robed priest. Her first impression had been of a weak man, but as she looked more closely she felt she might have mistaken sensitivity for weakness. And she desperately needed someone to confide in.

Ulmenetha took a deep breath, and sat down once more. 'Someone is summoning demons,' she said, at last. 'They are everywhere, and growing in number. I have the eyes to see them, but not the wit to discern their purpose.' The balding priest sat down beside her.

'Father Aminias said the same thing,' he told her. 'It was his belief that a great spell was being wrought. But I cannot see these . . . these creatures. And I know not how to combat them. Nor even if I should try.' He gave a wan smile. 'Who are you, mother?'

'I am the Priestess Ulmenetha, the companion of Axiana the queen.'

'And what did you hope to achieve here?'

'I sought answers. I have had three visions, and can make no sense of any of them.' She told him of the four warriors and the white crow, of the demon in the lake, and of the sacrifice of the emperor. He listened in silence.

'I have never been blessed with your Gift,' he said, 'but what I have been given is the Gift of Discernment. Your visions are true ones. This I know. You saw three scenes. Three is a number of great power among mystics, and your experience is not unique. What you saw is called a *kiraz*. The first scene concerns the *cause* of the problem. The second illuminates how the problem will *manifest* itself. The third is more complex. It always reveals the protagonists, but also often reveals a clue to the *solution* of the problem. Now let us examine them in detail. The Demon of the Lake – the *cause* – is more of a symbolic vision. It came out of the ice, you say. If I read it correctly the lake is a symbol for a gateway between its world and ours. You say it flowed like smoke into the body of a man. This is a man being possessed. But more than that it is a man being possessed after having been slain. What we have is a demon inhabiting a corpse. This demon must therefore be a most powerful creature. He now dwells in the world of men. He it is who has summoned the creatures you see over the city. It is his purpose that must be discerned.

'As to the emperor being sacrificed . . . this is not a symbol. There were many rumours when he was slain, and the body was never recovered. But the voice you heard was interesting. "The day of Resurrection is at hand. You are the first of the Three." Once again we have the number three. But what is to be resurrected? And who are the other two? This is the *manifestation* of the problem. Three are to be sacrificed in order for the Demon to achieve his purpose. One is already slain.

'Now to the scene in the forest. You and the queen stand protected by a few soldiers. Three old men and a youngster are all that stand between you and a terrible evil. The clue here, I believe is the person you are protecting. Axiana is obviously one of the Three. It makes sense, since her father was the first. Perhaps there is something in the bloodline that the Demon requires.' He smiled and spread his hands. 'I can tell you no more, Ulmenetha.'

'Should I try to find these soldiers?'

He shook his head. 'What you saw is what will be, whether you seek them out or not.'

'You did not mention the white crow,' she pointed out.

'No,' he said, sadly. 'Nor did I need to. You know what that means.'

'Aye, I know,' she said, wearily. She gazed around the temple, unwilling to leave its quiet sanctuary. On the wall above the High Altar was carved the symbol of Emsharas, the slender hand holding a crescent moon. 'I thought this to be a Source temple,' she said. 'It is unusual to find the crescent moon in such a place.'

'You perceive Emsharas to be a creature of evil?'

'Was he not, according to legend, a demon?' she asked.

'He was indeed one of the Windborn, a spirit being. The name "demon" is a description devised by man. We have here in this temple many of the oldest scrolls in existence, and even some legends engraved on gold foil. I have studied them over the years. I have come to admire Emsharas, and I believe he was Source driven. Did your studies include the legends of the Demon Wars?'

'Very briefly,' she told him. 'Thousands of years ago Emsharas and his brother, Anharat, were enemies. Emsharas joined the human armies of the Three Kings, and banished all demons from the world. That is the sum total of my knowledge.'

'In truth that is probably the sum total of all our knowledge,' he said. 'But you notice the figure three appearing again? It is of great mystical significance. However, he did not merely banish demons from the world. All the creatures of the Windborn vanished as a result of the Great Spell.'

'And now they are coming back,' she said.

'It would appear so,' he agreed.

Banelion summoned his twenty senior officers soon after dawn. All were veterans, many of them men who had served with him for more than thirty years. They were survivors, tough and lean, hard eyed and iron willed. They stood to attention around him, filling the tent. No-one could ever have accused the White Wolf of sentimentality, and yet, as he looked into their faces, he felt an acute sense of family. These men had been his brothers, his sons. He had raised them, and trained them, and led them across the world. Now he was taking them home, to a retirement few desired, but all deserved.

Banelion rarely looked into mirrors. He had lost that vanity at sixty. But now, looking at these men he felt the weight of his years. He could remember them all as they had been, bright eyed, fresh of face, their hearts burning to serve – aye and to save – the country of their birth.

'There will be no easing of discipline,' he told them. 'We will have eighteen hundred men with us, all private citizens now. But I will not lead an unruly mob back to Drenan. Every man who travels with us will sign on for the journey as a soldier, subject to my discipline and under my orders. Any who do not wish to do so will be turned away. The payment will be one half silver per man per month, to be paid out of my own treasury. Officers will receive five full silvers. The payment will be made upon landing at Dros Purdol. Any questions?'

There were many, and for more than an hour he discussed the logistics of the journey with the officers, then dismissed them.

Alone once more he sat down on his pallet bed and spent a further half-hour planning for the problems he expected upon the journey. Satisfied he had covered most of the areas of possible delay he finally allowed his mind to dwell on the immediate danger posed by the threat of Malikada.

Despite what he had told Dagorian about the king, and his lack of concern over the fate of his oldest general, the White Wolf knew that Malikada was unlikely to send Ventrian assassins to kill him. Such a move would cause uproar in the army, and affect the king's plan to march on Cadia. That march would begin in three days. If the White Wolf was murdered Skanda would be forced to call for an inquiry. No, Malikada's attempt would be more subtle. A Drenai might be paid to kill him, a man known to harbour resentment against Banelion. And there were plenty of those, common soldiers who had suffered under the lash for minor infringements of discipline, junior officers who felt they had been over-looked for advancement, senior officers who had suffered public rebuke. Then there were men stripped of their rank for incompetence. Banelion smiled. If Malikada offered enough money he could be trampled to death under a stampede of men anxious to earn it.

Banelion poured himself a goblet of water. But if the murderer was taken alive and questioned under torture such a payment would come to light, and that would throw suspicion back upon Malikada, no matter who he hired to make the transaction. The White Wolf dismissed the idea. It was too unsubtle for the Ventrian fox.

What then? Banelion lifted the goblet to his lips. He hesitated, and stared down at the clear liquid. Poison would be the likeliest answer. Not a cheerful prospect, he thought, putting down the goblet. From now on he would eat at the communal kitchen, standing in line with the rest of his men.

Satisfied he had considered every possibility for attack he relaxed.

He was wrong.

Chapter Four

The old barracks building was three hundred years old, built to house the Immortals, the Emperor Gorben's élite regiment. At the time of its construction it was one of the wonders of the world. Famous artists and sculptors had been summoned from all over the empire to paint its ceilings, and sculpt the masterpieces that surrounded it. Now most of the statues had been removed, and shipped to Drenan, or sold to collectors to raise money for the king's wars. The painted ceilings and walls were chipped, cracked and faded. Most of the Drenai soldiers of the king's new army were housed in the north of the city, in three new barracks.

Here, off the Avenue of Light, the old building was slowly surrendering to the ravages of time and lack of care. Already there were plans to demolish it, and erect a colosseum. But for now it remained the temporary quarters of the old men being sent home. Discipline was already non-existent, and there were no guards at the gates, no bugle call to announce the dawn, no officers to oversee drills or exercises.

Nogusta shivered as he walked across the deserted parade-ground and on into the east wing where he shared a room with Bison and Kebra.

Once upon a time architects from all over the world visited this barracks, to marvel at its design.

Now it was a dying place, full of decaying memories no-one wanted to share.

Wearily Nogusta climbed the stairs. There were no lanterns here now, the interior lit only by the shafts of moonlight spearing through the high windows of each landing. Slowly Nogusta made his way to the fourth floor.

Kebra and Bison were sitting in stony silence within the room. Nogusta guessed the question of winter debts had been discussed. He moved past his comrades towards a blazing fire in the hearth. Its warmth was comforting.

Nogusta removed his black shirt and allowed the heat to bathe his upper body. The gold and silver charm he wore glittered in the firelight. Something cold touched his back, like the whisper of a frozen wind. He stood and turned, expecting to see the door or the window open. But they were closed tight.

'Did you feel that breeze?' he asked the silent men. They did not answer him. Kebra was sitting on his bed, his face stony, his pale eyes glaring at Bison. Suddenly an icy chill enveloped the room, the heat from the fire dying away. Nogusta stared at the flames, which were high and bright. No warmth came from them. The only heat he could feel was radiating from the crescent moon charm upon his breast. It glowed with a bright light. In that moment a terrible fear settled on the black man, for he knew why the charm was glowing.

Bison surged to his feet with a menacing growl. 'You slagging traitor!' he shouted at Kebra. His huge hand snatched his sword from its scabbard. The slender bow-man drew a curved dagger and rose to meet him.

'No!' shouted Nogusta, leaping towards them. The

sound of his voice, deep and powerful, cut through the tension. Kebra hesitated. But Bison moved in for the kill. 'Bison!' yelled Nogusta. For a moment only the giant hesitated. His eyes were glittering strangely, and his mouth was frozen into a snarl.

'Look at me! Now!' bellowed Nogusta. Bison paused again. The cold was now almost intolerable, and Nogusta began to shiver uncontrollably. Bison turned towards him, his eyes distant. 'Take my hand,' said Nogusta, reaching out. 'Do it for friendship, Bison. Take my hand!'

Bison blinked, and his expression softened for an instant. Then his anger blazed again. 'I'm going to kill him!'

'Take my hand first, then do what you must,' urged Nogusta. For a fraction of a moment he thought Bison would refuse, but then the big man reached out. Their fingers touched, their hands gripped. Bison let out a long, shuddering sigh and fell to his knees. Kebra leapt at him. Nogusta caught the movement at the last moment. Dragging Bison back he leapt between them, his left hand snaking out to grab Kebra's wrist. The bowman's face was twisted into an evil grimace, his pale eyes bulging. Nogusta hung on to the knife wrist. 'Be calm, Kebra,' he said. 'Be calm. It is Nogusta. It is your friend, Nogusta.'

Kebra's twisted face relaxed, the madness ebbing away. He shuddered and dropped the knife. The room grew warmer. Nogusta released his grip on the two men. Kebra sagged to the bed.

'I . . . I don't know what came over me,' said Bison. He stumbled towards Kebra. 'I'm sorry,' he said. 'Truly.' Kebra said nothing. He merely sat and stared at the floor.

The glowing light of Nogusta's charm faded, leaving only the simple silver crescent and the golden hand which held it.

'We have been attacked,' he said, softly. 'You are not at fault, Bison. Nor is Kebra.'

The white-haired bowman glanced up. 'What are you talking about?'

'Sorcery. Did you not feel the cold in the room?' Both men shook their heads. Nogusta pulled up a chair and sat. Kebra and Bison were staring at him now. He touched the crescent charm. 'This is what saved us.'

'Have you gone mad?' asked Kebra. 'It was just rage, that's all. Bison kept on and on about me losing the tournament. We just got angry.'

'Can you really believe that?' asked Nogusta. 'You have been friends for thirty years. Never have you drawn weapons against each other. I urge you to trust me on this, my friends. Orendo told me the same thing. He said when they were in the merchant's house a terrible cold came upon the room, and they became full of rage and lust. That's when they killed and raped. He said there were demons in the air. I did not believe him. I believe him now. Do you remember how you felt when you ran at Bison?'

'I wanted to cut his heart out,' admitted Kebra.

'And you believe now that it was really what you wanted?'

'It felt real *then*,' said Kebra. He shook his head and wiped his hand across his face. 'What did you mean about the charm saving us?'

'Simply that. It is a "ward charm". A talisman. It has been in my family for generations.'

'It was glowing when you reached out for me,' said Bison. 'It shone like a huge diamond.'

'I saw that,' said Kebra. 'But, gods, man, who would want to use sorcery against us?'

'Malikada perhaps. Had I not been wearing the charm

95

my rage would have surged also. We could have killed each other.'

'Well, let's kill Malikada,' said Bison.

'Good idea,' said Kebra. 'Then we'll grow our magic wings and fly away free over the mountains.'

'Well, what then?' asked the giant.

'We leave the city,' said Nogusta. 'We won't travel with the White Wolf. We'll head south into the mountains until the army marches on the Cadian border, then we'll join the other returnees.'

'I don't like the idea of running away,' said Bison.

'As I recall,' said Kebra, drily, 'I once saw you racing like a sprinter to get out of the way of a flash flood. And are you not the man who had his arse scarred while fleeing from that lioness outside Delnoch?'

'That was different,' argued Bison.

'No it wasn't,' said Nogusta. 'Malikada is the king's general. We cannot fight him. It would be like fighting a storm or, indeed, a flash flood. Pointless. Added to which we do not know for sure that this was Malikada's work. No, the safest and most sensible plan is to leave the city. In two days the army marches and Malikada will have other problems to consider. He will forget about us.'

'What will we do in the mountains?' asked Bison.

'Hunt a little meat, pan for gold in the streams, perhaps,' Nogusta told him.

'Gold. I like the sound of that,' said Bison, tugging on his white walrus moustache. 'We could get rich.'

'Indeed we could, my friend. Tomorrow I will purchase horses and supplies.'

'And pans for the gold,' Bison reminded him.

The giant moved to his own bed and pulled off his boots. 'I still say you shouldn't have let that Ventrian shoot again,' he said.

Kebra looked up at Nogusta and shook his head. Then he smiled. 'I would feel a lot better if I didn't agree with him,' he said. 'I still can't believe I did it.'

'I can, my friend. It was noble,' said Nogusta, 'and no more than I would expect from you.'

Ulmenetha took hold of the iron chains, leaned back upon the swinging wicker chair and gazed out over the distant mountains. She could feel them calling to her, like a mother to a lost child. In the mountains of her home she had known great happiness. There was ancient wisdom there, and serenity radiated from the eternal peaks. These were not her mountains, but they called nonetheless. Ulmenetha resisted the pull and turned her attention to her immediate surroundings. The roof garden of the late emperor's palace was a wondrous place in summer, its terraces ablaze with colour, and filled with the scent of many perfumed flowers. High above the city it seemed an enchanted place. In winter it was less so, but now, with spring but days away, the yellow and purple polyanthuses were flowering, and the cherry trees were thick with blossom, gossamer thin petals of faded coral. Sitting here alone in the bright sunshine thoughts of demons seemed far away, like a child's dream in a darkened bedroom. Ulmenetha had enjoyed her early childhood. Wrapped in love, and full of joy, she had played in the mountains, living wild and free. The memory lifted her, and – just for a moment – she felt like a child again. Ulmenetha swung the chair around and around on its iron chains. Then she let go and watched the mountains spin before her eyes. She giggled and closed her eyes.

'You look foolish,' said Axiana, sternly. 'It does not become a priestess to play on a child's swing.'

Ulmenetha had not heard the queen's approach. She leaned forward, her feet thumping to the ground, halting the swing. 'Why do you say that?' she asked. 'Why is it that so many people believe that religion and joy have little in common?'

Ulmenetha eased her large frame upright and walked with the pregnant queen to a wide bench seat beneath the cherry trees. Already they were rich with blossom of coral and white. 'There is no dignity in such behaviour,' the young woman told her. Ulmenetha said nothing for a moment. Axiana settled herself down, her slender hands over her swollen belly. You never laugh, child, thought Ulmenetha, and your eyes radiate sorrow.

'Dignity is much overrated,' she said, at last. 'It is a concept, I think, devised by men to add gravitas to their strutting.' A flicker of a smile touched Axiana's beautiful face. But it passed as swiftly as a noonday shadow. 'Men are ridiculous creatures,' continued the priestess, 'arrogant and vain, insensitive and boorish.'

'Is this why you became a priestess? To avoid contact with them?'

Ulmenetha shook her head. 'No, dear heart. I had a jewel among men. When I lost him I knew there would never be another.' She took a deep breath and stared out over the southern mountains. She could just make out three riders heading into the high country.

'I am sorry, Ulmenetha,' said the queen. 'My question brought you sadness.'

'Not at all,' the priestess assured her. 'It brought me remembered joy. He was a fine man. He spent two years trying to woo me, and became convinced that if he could beat me to the top of Five Rise mountain I would marry him.' The queen looked mystified. 'I used to run through the mountains. I was slimmer then, and I could run for ever. No man could best me on the longer races. Vian tried for two years. He trained so hard. That's when I grew to love him.'

'And did he beat you?'

'No, but he won me. Good days.' They lapsed into silence for several minutes, enjoying the warmth of the morning sun.

'What is it like to be in love?' asked Axiana. Ulmenetha felt sadness swell in her, not for the love she had lost, but for the lovely young woman at her side. How sad it was that a woman only weeks from giving birth should still wonder about love.

'Sometimes it arrives like a flash flood, but at other times it grows slowly until it becomes a great tree. Perhaps it will be that way for you and the king.'

Axiana shook her head. 'He thinks nothing of me. I am an ornament of no more worth than any of the other ornaments he owns.'

'He is a great man,' said Ulmenetha, aware of the shallowness of her response.

'No, he is not. He is a great killer and destroyer. Men worship him as if he were a god, but he is not. He is a plague, a cancer.' The words were not spoken with passion, but with a quiet resignation that somehow added to their power.

'He has a good side,' said Ulmenetha. 'His people love him, and he is often generous. And I have seen him weep. When he was younger and it was thought that Starfire was lame, he was inconsolable.'

'Inconsolable?' queried Axiana. 'He did not appear inconsolable when Starfire went to the tannery. I understand they use the hides for furniture, the meat for food, and the hoofs and bones for glue. Is that right?'

'You must be mistaken, my pet.'

'I am not mistaken. I heard him on his birthday. All the older horses – including Starfire – were sold. The money received went into the war chest. The man is without a soul.'

'Do not speak this way, dear heart,' whispered Ulmenetha, feeling a sudden chill.

'No-one can hear us. There are no secret passages in the garden, no hollow walls for clerics to hide behind with their quill pens. Skanda cares only for war, and he will never be satisfied. The world could fall to him and he would know only despair, for there would be no more battles to fight. So, tell me, Ulmenetha, about love.'

The priestess forced a smile. 'There is an old legend. I am rather partial to it. In the beginning the old gods created a herd of perfect animals. They had four legs, four arms and two heads. And they were blissfully happy. The gods looked upon this perfection of happiness and grew jealous. So one day the Chief of the Gods cast a mighty spell. And in an instant all the animals were ripped in half and scattered across the world. Now each of the beasts only had one head, two arms and two legs. And they were destined for ever to search the earth for their other halves, seeking that perfect fit.'

'That is a vulgar story,' chided Axiana.

A young, female servant approached them and curtsied deeply. 'You have a visitor, my lady,' she said. 'The Lord Kalizkan.' Axiana clapped her hands together in delight.

'Send him out to us,' she said.

Moments later the tall wizard made his entrance. He was wearing robes now of sky blue satin, and a matching wide-brimmed hat of stiffened silk. Sweeping off the hat he made an elaborate bow. 'And how is the queen today?' he asked, with a wide, enchanting smile.

'I am well, sir. All the better for seeing you.' Ulmenetha rose and offered the wizard her seat. He gave her a dazzling smile and sat beside the queen. Ulmenetha moved back to allow them privacy and returned to her seat in the swinging chair. It was a pleasure to see Axiana in such high spirits. Kalizkan was good for her, and Ulmenetha liked him. The wizard leaned in close to the queen and the two talked for some time. Then Axiana called out. 'Come here, Ulmenetha, you must see this!'

The priestess obeyed and stood before the white-bearded wizard. 'What is your favourite flower?' he asked her.

'The high mountain lily,' she told him.

'The white lily with blue stripes?'

'Yes.'

Kalizkan reached down and lifted a handful of dirt. Then his pale eyes narrowed in concentration. A tiny stem appeared in the dark earth, then grew, putting out slender leaves. A bud appeared and opened slowly, exposing long white petals, striped with the blue of a summer sky. Reaching out he offered her the flower. Ulmenetha's fingers touched it, and it became smoke, dispersing on the breeze. 'Is that not wonderful?' said Axiana.

Ulmenetha nodded. 'You have a great talent, sir,' she said.

'I have studied long and hard,' he told them. 'But it pleases me to bring pleasure to my friends.'

'Is your orphanage prospering, Kalizkan?' asked the queen.

'It is, dear lady, thanks to the kindness of the king and your good wishes. But there are so many more children living on the streets, close to starvation. One wishes one could help them all.'

As the two talked on, oblivious to Ulmenetha, the priest-ess found herself once more thinking of the demons in the air. Quietly she made her way back to the swinging chair and settled her back against the cushions. The sun had reached noon and was shining down with painful bright-ness. She closed her eyes – and a thought came to her.

Demons had no love of bright light. Perhaps now she could soar unobserved.

With a last look at the chatting couple she took a deep breath, reaching for the inner calm that precipitated flight. Then she released her spirit and fled towards the sun like an arrow. High above the city she floated, and gazed down. The roof garden was tiny now, the size of her thumbnail, the river flowing through the city no more than a thin web-thread of glistening blue and white. No demons were flying now, but she could see them in the shadows, under the eaves of buildings. There were hundreds of them. Perhaps thousands. They were writhing over the city like white maggots on rotting pork.

Three detached themselves from the shadows of the palace, and swept up towards her, their talons reaching out. Ulmenetha waited, frozen in terror. They closed upon her, and she could see their opal eyes and their sharp teeth. There was nowhere to run. They were between her and the safety of her flesh.

A shining figure of bright light appeared alongside her, a sword of flame in his hands. Ulmenetha tried to look into his face, but the brilliance of the light forced her to turn away. The demons veered away from him. A voice whispered into her mind. It was strangely familiar. 'Go now, swiftly!' he urged her.

Ulmenetha needed no urging. With the demons fallen back she fled for the sanctuary of her flesh.

She swept over the roof garden and saw the queen sitting beside . . . sitting beside . . .

The eyes of her body flared open, and a strangled cry burst from her lips. Axiana and Kalizkan moved swiftly to her side. 'Are you well, Ulmenetha?' asked Axiana, reaching out to stroke her friend's cheek.

'Yes, yes. I had a bad dream. So stupid. I am sorry.'

'You are trembling,' said Kalizkan. 'Perhaps you have a fever.'

'I think I will go inside,' she said, 'and lie down.'

She left them there and returned to her own room alongside the queen's apartments. Her mouth was dry and she poured a cup of water and drank deeply. Then she sat down and tried to picture what she had seen in the roof garden.

The image had been fleeting, and she found that the more she concentrated upon it the less clear it became.

Silently she returned to the roof garden, pausing in the doorway, unseen. From here she could see the kindly wizard and the queen sitting together. Closing the eyes of her body she gazed upon them both with the eyes of spirit.

Her heart hammered, and she began to tremble once more.

Kalizkan's face was grey and dead, his hands only partly covered in flesh. Bare bone protruded from the ends of his fingers. And as Ulmenetha looked more closely she saw a small maggot slither out from a hole in the wizard's cheek and drop to the shoulder of his blue satin robes.

Backing away she returned to her room, and prayed.

Dagorian stood in the centre of the small room. Blood had splashed to the white walls, and the curved dagger that caused the terrible wounds had been tossed to the floor, where it had smeared a white goatskin rug. The body of the old woman had been removed before Dagorian arrived, but the murderer was still sitting by the hearth, his head in his hands. Two Drenai soldiers stood guard over him.

'It seems fairly straightforward,' Dagorian told Zani, the slender Ventrian official. 'In a rage this man killed his mother. There are no soldiers involved. No threat to the king. I do not see why you called me to the scene.'

'You are the Officer of the Watch for last night,' said Zani, a small man, with close cropped dark hair and a pronounced widow's peak. 'We are to report all cases of multiple killings.'

'There was more than one body?'

'Yes, sir. Not here, but elsewhere. Look around you. What do you see?'

Dagorian scanned the room. Shelves lined the walls, some bearing jars of pottery, others bottles of coloured glass. On the low table beside the hearth he saw a set of rune stones, and several papyrus charts of the heavens. 'The woman was a fortune-teller,' he said.

'Indeed she was – and a good one, by all accounts.'

'This is relevant?' asked Dagorian.

'Four such people were killed last night in this quarter of the city alone. Three men and a woman. Two were murdered by customers, a third by his wife, and this woman by her son.'

Dagorian crossed the room and opened the back door, stepping out into the narrow garden beyond. The Ventrian followed him. The sun was bright in the sky, the warmth welcome. 'Did the victims know one another?' asked Dagorian.

'The son told me he knew one of the dead.'

'Then it remains coincidence,' concluded Dagorian.

The Ventrian sighed and shook his head. 'Twenty-seven in the last month. I do not think coincidence will stretch that far.'

'Twenty-seven fortune-tellers?' Dagorian was astonished.

'Not all were fortune-tellers. Some were mystics, others priests. But their talent was the common factor. They could all walk the path of Spirit. Most could read fragments of the future.'

'Not very well, apparently,' Dagorian pointed out.

'I disagree. Come, let me show you.' Dagorian followed the small Ventrian back to the door. Zani pointed to recent scratches upon the wood, in the shape of an inverted triangle, with a snake at the centre. 'All the entries to the room bear this sign. It is part of a ward spell, protective sorcery. The old woman knew she was in danger. When we found her she was clutching an amulet. This too was a protective piece.'

'Protection against *sorcery*,' said Dagorian, patiently. 'But she wasn't killed by sorcery, was she? She was murdered by her son. He admits to the crime. Does he claim he was demon possessed? Is that his defence?'

'No,' admitted Zani. 'But perhaps it ought to be. I have spoken to the neighbours. He was devoted to his mother. And even he no longer knows why his rage exploded.'

Dagorian approached the distraught young man sitting by the hearth. 'What do you recall of the crime?' he asked him. The man looked up.

'I was sitting in my room, and I just got angrier and angrier. The next thing I knew I was here . . . in this room. And I was stabbing, and stabbing . . .' He broke down and hid his face in his hands.

'What made you angry?'

It seemed at first that the young man had not heard the question, but the sobbing subsided and he wiped his eyes with the sleeve of his shirt. 'I can't remember now. I really can't.'

'Why did your mother make the ward signs on the doors?'

'She was frightened. She wouldn't see any customers and she wouldn't come out of the room. We were running out of money. I think, maybe, that's why I got angry. We couldn't afford fuel, and my room was so cold. So terribly cold.' He began to sob once more.

'Take him away,' Dagorian told the soldiers. They lifted the man to his feet and marched him from the house. A small crowd had gathered outside. Some of them shouted abuse at the prisoner.

'There is something very wrong here,' said Zani.

'Send me the details of the other crimes,' Dagorian told him. 'I will look into them.'

'You think you will solve the mystery in a day?' asked Zani. 'Or will you not be marching with the army tomorrow?'

'I leave tomorrow,' said Dagorian. 'But still I wish to see the reports.'

Leaving the house he mounted his horse and rode back to the new barracks. Once there he waited for the reports, read them carefully, then requested a meeting with his immediate superior, the Ventrian swordsman Antikas Karios.

He was kept waiting outside the Ventrian's office for an hour, and when he was at last ushered inside, he saw Antikas walk in from the garden beyond, where he had been exercising. Stripped to the waist he was sweating heavily. A servant brought him a towel. Antikas sat down behind the broad desk and drank a cup of water. Then he towelled his dark hair. The servant moved behind him with a brush and a jar of oil. Lightly he massaged the Ventrian's scalp, before brushing his hair back and tying it in a pony-tail. With a flick of his hand Antikas dismissed the man, then turned his dark eyes on Dagorian.

'You wished to see me?'

'Yes, sir.' Swiftly he told the officer of the spate of murders, and the concerns of the official Zani that some orchestrated campaign of killing might be under way.

'Zani is a good man,' said Antikas. 'He has been a city official for fourteen years, and served with distinction. He has a fine mind. What is your opinion?'

'I have read the reports, sir. In each case the killers have been apprehended, and confessed, without torture. But I do share Zani's concern in one respect.'

'And that is?'

'Twenty-seven mystics in sixteen days. And, according to the reports, every one of them was living in fear.'

Antikas rose from his desk, crossed the room and took a fresh shirt from a drawer. Shaking the rose petals from it he pulled it over his head. Then he returned to the desk. 'You are a good swordsman,' he said. 'Your moves are well executed.'

'Thank you, sir,' said Dagorian, confused by the change of subject.

'It is your footwork that lets you down.'

'So Nogusta told me, sir.'

'Yes,' said Antikas, with a cold smile. 'If he were twenty years younger I would challenge him. He is exceptional.' Antikas sat down and took a second drink from the water cup. 'I see from your dossier that you were training for the priesthood.'

'I was, sir. Until my father died.'

'Yes, a man must uphold family honour. Did your teaching incorporate mysticism?'

'Only briefly, sir. But no sorcery.'

'I think you will find that these crimes are based on rivalry among petty wizards. Even so, such actions cannot be tolerated. Find out which mystics are still alive. The true source of the murders will be one of those.'

'Yes, sir, I will try, but I cannot do this in a day.'

'Indeed so. You will remain here. I will send for you when we have crossed the Great River.'

'Yes, sir. Is this a punishment, sir?'

'No. Merely an order.' Antikas began to shuffle papers on his desk, but Dagorian stood his ground. 'There was something else?' he asked.

'Yes, sir. I was wondering if the Lord Kalizkan could help us. His powers are great, and it would save time.'

'The Lord Kalizkan is busy preparing spells to aid the king in his coming battle with the Cadians. But I will convey your request to him.' Dagorian saluted crisply and took one step back, before spinning on his heel and marching to the door. The Ventrian's voice halted him. 'Trust me, Dagorian, you will never need to *ask* if I am punishing you. You will *know*.'

Dagorian and Zani rode to three addresses in the north of the city, each said to be the home of an astrologer or seer. All were empty. Neighbours were unable to supply information. The fourth address was a house in a rich area called Nine Oaks. The houses here stood in several acres of landscaped gardens, with fountains and walkways meandering through cultivated woodland.

The two men rode their horses through the woods, coming at last to a tall house, the outer walls faced with blocks of green marble. No servant moved out to greet them as they made their way to the front of the building. Dagorian and Zani dismounted and tied the reins of their mounts to a hitching rail.

The main doors were locked and barred, the green wooden shutters of the windows closed tight. A one-eyed old man wearing a green patch and pushing a wheel-barrow came into sight, moving slowly across the garden. He stopped as he saw them. Dagorian approached him. 'We are looking for the master of the house,' he said.

'Gone,' the old man told him.

'Gone where?'

'Just gone. Had all his valuables packed into three wagons and left.'

'When was this?'

'Four days ago. No . . . five now.'

Zani moved alongside the old man. 'What is your name?'

'I am Chiric, the head gardener. The only gardener now, come to think of it.'

'Did your master seem troubled?' asked Dagorian.

'Aye, that would be one word to describe it. Troubled.'

'What other words might you use?' put in Zani.

The old man gave a crooked grin. 'I might say terrified.'

'Of what?' queried Dagorian. Chiric shrugged.

'Don't know and don't care. Spring's coming and I've too much planting to do to worry about what frightens the likes of him. Can I go now?'

'In a moment,' the Ventrian told him. 'Do you live in the house?'

'No. Got a small cabin back in the woods. Warm and snug. Suits me, anyway.'

'Has anything strange happened here recently?' asked Dagorian.

The old man gave a dry, rasping laugh. 'Strange things happen here all the time. That's the way with wizards. Coloured lights, flashes of fire. Groups of them used to come round. They'd chant late into the night. Then he asks me why the hens have stopped laying. Asked me to join in one night. Said they were one short of some mystic number. No thank you, said I.'

'What was it that terrified him?' persisted Dagorian.

'Do I get paid for all this information?' asked Chiric. 'If not I've got better things to do than stand around jawing all day.'

Zani's anger overflowed. 'You could spend a few weeks in the Watch dungeons,' he said, 'for obstructing officers of the king. How does that sound?'

Dagorian stepped in swiftly, dipping his hand into his money pouch and producing a small silver coin. The old man pocketed it with incredible speed, then cast a surly glance at Zani. 'Labourers get paid,' he said. 'That's why they labour. Anyway, you were asking about his fear. Well I was away for a few days last month. My youngest got wed to a farmer from Captis. When I got back some of the servants had gone. And the master had bought three big black wolfhounds, teeth like knives. Hated the bastards, I did. I asked Sagio about it . . .'

'Sagio?' put in Zani.

'My under gardener. Good lad. He quit too – afterwards! Anyways, he said that the master wouldn't come out of the house. Claimed someone had put a death spell on him. He spent days and days in his library poring over scrolls and the like. And always the dogs were padding around the house. Then, last week, the dogs attacked him. Went mad by all accounts. He managed to lock himself in the library. When he came out the dogs had torn each other to pieces. Blood everywhere. I had to clear it up. Well, me and Sagio had to clear it up. Still, horrible it was. But then if you're going to keep wild dogs you've got to expect trouble, haven't you. I reckon it was the cold got to 'em. Marble houses, pah! Can't keep them warm, can you? Room they were in was freezing.'

'And he left the city?'

'The same day. You should have seen him.' Chiric chuckled. 'He was covered in charms and talismans. And he was chanting all the way to the coach and four. You could still hear him as it drove through the gates.'

Dagorian thanked the man and walked back to his horse. Zani came alongside. 'What now, Drenai?'

'We break in,' said Dagorian, moving to one of the shutters on the ground floor and drawing his sword.

'Hey, what are you doing?' shouted the old man.

'We are officers of the king,' Zani told him. 'You are welcome to observe our investigation. But if you seek to hinder us I will keep my promise about that dungeon.'

'It was only a question,' grumbled Chiric, grasping the handles of his wheelbarrow. Clearing his throat the old man spat on the path, then trundled the wheelbarrow off towards the woods.

Dagorian slid his sabre between the shutters and lifted the bar beyond. It fell clear with a hollow thud. Opening the shutters Dagorian sheathed his blade and climbed inside. The interior was gloomy and he opened two other windows. Zani clambered into the building. 'What are we looking for?' he asked. Dagorian spread his hands.

'I have no idea.' They were standing now in a beauti-fully decorated sitting-room, with seven sofas and a splendid mosaic floor and painted walls. Passing through it they entered a hall, and searched the rooms beyond. The furniture throughout was expensive. The library was shelved from floor to ceiling, the shelves bent under the weight of books, scrolls and parchments. The north wall was still blood-stained, as was the pale green carpet.

'I hope Chiric is a better gardener than a cleaner,' said Zani.

A door at the back of the library led to a study. This too had shelves on all four walls, most of them bearing glass jars, filled with viscous liquids. In one floated a human hand, in another a small, deformed foetus. Others contained organs. There was a large cupboard set into the western wall. Dagorian opened it. More jars were stored here, this time filled with herbs. The Drenai officer scanned them, finally selecting one and carrying it to a narrow desk, upon which was a human skull, re-sculpted into a container for two ink wells. Dagorian placed the jar on the desk and broke the wax seal around the lid.

'What is it?' asked Zani.

'*Lorassium* leaves. They have great healing powers, but *lorassium* is essentially a heavy narcotic used by mystics to aid their visions.'

'I have heard of it. It is very expensive.'

The young Drenai officer sat down, dipped his hand into the jar, pulling two leaves from it. They were a dark, lustrous green, and a heady scent filled the air. 'What are you doing?' asked Zani.

For a moment Dagorian said nothing, then he looked up at the Ventrian. 'There is a force working here that is outside the realm of normal human senses. We could stumble around the city for days and never find the answer. Perhaps it is time to use the eyes of the spirit.'

'Are you versed in these things?'

'Not entirely. But I know the procedure.'

Zani shook his head. 'I know nothing of sorcery – nor do I wish to. But there have been a lot of deaths, Drenai. I think the risk is too great for one who only – as you openly admit – knows the *procedure*. I think it might be wiser to take the problem to the Lord Kalizkan. There is no greater wizard than he.'

'I have already set that in motion, Zani,' said the officer. 'But arrogance compels me to try to solve this mystery myself.'

As he finished speaking he rolled the two leaves and placed them in his mouth.

Bright colours flashed before his eyes, and a sharp pain lanced from his neck, down his arms and into his fingers. Calming himself Dagorian began to recite in his mind the Mantra of Dardalion, the simplest of the Three Levels. He felt as if he were floating inside his own body, twisting and turning. But there was no release, and he did not soar free as he had hoped. Slowly he opened his eyes. Zani's blue tunic was shining now with ethereal lights and dancing colours. A bright aura flickered around the man. Dagorian realized that it was not the tunic which was shining, but the man himself. Over his heart there was violet light, tinged with red, which deepened into maroon over his belly. This then was the aura mystics spoke of. How beautiful it was. He looked at Zani's round face. Honesty, loyalty and courage shone there, and he had a vision of the Ventrian sitting in a small room, three children playing at his feet. A young woman was close by, plump and raven haired. She was smiling.

Transferring his gaze he glanced at the walls. Ward

spells had been placed over the windows and the doors, and these he could see now, glowing faintly red. Turning in the chair he looked out of the east window at the shadowed garden. He blinked. A face was staring in, a ghost white face, with large dark, protruding eyes and a lipless mouth. The skin was scaled like a fish, the teeth sharp as needles. Other faces clustered around it, and a long skinny arm pushed into the room. The ward spell flared and the arm was hastily withdrawn.

'There are demons at the window,' he said, huskily, his words echoing inside his head.

'I see no demons,' said Zani, his voice trembling.

'Yet they are there.'

'It is getting cold in here,' said Zani. 'Can you feel it?'

Dagorian did not answer. Rising from the desk he walked to the inner door and looked out into the library and the stairs beyond. White forms were floating close to the ceiling, others were huddled together away from the sunlight lancing through the western windows.

Fear touched the officer. There were scores of them.

They flew at him, their talons lashing out. The pain was great and he stumbled back. 'What is it?' shouted Zani.

In panic Dagorian ran for the front door. The demons were covering him now, tearing at him. He screamed aloud, blundered into the door, then scrabbled for the handle. It was locked. He fell to his knees, the pain indescribable. Zani grabbed his arm, hauling him to the western window. Bright light bathed him, and the demons withdrew. Zani helped him climb out into the garden. Dagorian stumbled out to the grass, then fell and rolled to his back under the shadows of the trees.

White, translucent forms dropped from the branches above, talons and teeth ripping at his face. Wildly he thrashed his arms at them, but his fingers passed through them.

A shining sword of fire swept out. The demons fell back. A voice whispered to him. 'The Prayer of Light! Recite it you fool, or you will die here.'

Pain and terror were blocking Dagorian's memory. The voice spoke again. 'Say it with me: Oh Lord of Light, Source of All Life, be with me now in this hour of peril and darkness . . . Say it aloud!'

Dagorian began to recite the prayer. The demons withdrew, but hovered close by, their dark malevolent eyes glaring at him.

Rising to his knees Dagorian watched them. Slowly the power of the *lorassium* began to fade, and with it his spirit sight. The demons became more and more translucent, until, at last, they appeared no more than shapeless wisps of wood smoke. Then they were gone.

Safe now he stared down at his arms and hands, amazed that there was no blood. The talons had ripped into him so many times. He slumped back exhausted. 'What happened here?' whispered Zani. 'What were you struggling against?'

Dagorian did not answer. The *lorassium* did not merely increase visual powers, but also enhanced perception and cognitive skills. As the effects faded he fought to hold to the impressions he had gained, even during his panicked flight.

The demons were not sentient – at least not in a way any human could understand. They were . . . the word 'Feeders' came to his mind. Yes, that was it. Like a hungry pack they sought to devour . . . what? What was the source of his pain? It was not physical, and yet it would have killed him. The *lorassium* was almost gone now, and he struggled to hold to the knowledge he had gained.

Though not sentient the creatures had a purpose that was *beyond* their own desires. Their violence was *directed*.

The sun was setting behind the mountains. Soon the dark would come. Fear rose again in Dagorian. 'We must get away from here,' he said.

Chapter Five

Moonlight glistened on the outer skin of the White Wolf's tent, turning its flanks to silver. Inside the old man opened the map casket, and began searching through it. A brazier full of hot coals filled the tent with warmth, and two glowing lanterns cast flickering shadows on the inner walls.

Finding the map he was looking for the old man straightened. His lower back ached, and he stretched his arms high, trying to loosen his muscles. The cold struck him then, bitter as a winter blizzard. With a groan he turned towards the brazier of coals. No heat came from them now. He sat on the pallet bed, suddenly weary, dropped the map upon the thin mattress and reached out his hands towards the fire. The hands were old and liver spotted, the knuckles large with rheumatism.

Depression grew in him. Once I was young, he thought. He remembered his first battle in the old king's re-formed army. He had fought all day, with never a hint of fatigue. And that night he had bedded two of the camp women, one after the other. He glanced down at his thin, wrinkled legs, the loose skin slack over withered muscles. You should have died years ago, he said to himself.

The cold grew more intense, but he had ceased to feel it.

The depression deepened into a bleak despair, formed

of regret for what had passed, and a chilling fear of all that was to come; incontinence and senility. What would he do back in Drenan? Hire servants to change his soiled bed linen, and to wipe away the drool that dripped from his mouth. Perhaps he would not see the disgust on their faces. Then again, perhaps in moments of clarity, he would.

The old man drew his dagger and laid the blade upon his wrist. Clenching his fist he saw the arteries stand out. Swiftly he sliced the dagger blade across them. Even the blood that flowed was weak and thin, pumping out to stain the leather cavalry kilt, flowing on over his thighs and down into his boots.

He sat very still, remembering the glory days, until at last he toppled from the bed.

The fire flared, and heat began once more to permeate the tent.

After some minutes the tent flap was opened and two men stepped inside.

The first man ran to the body and knelt beside it. 'Sweet Heaven,' he whispered. 'Why? He was in good spirits when you sent him for the map, my lord. And he won heavily on the king's birthday. He was talking about his home near Dros Corteswain, and his plans for the farm. This makes no sense.'

The White Wolf stood silently, his pale gaze scanning the interior of the tent. Upon the folding table was a goblet and a jug, that had contained water. Now it was filled with melting ice. Condensation had also created a sheen of ice on the tent walls.

Banelion masked his anger. The possibility of a sorcerous attack had not occurred to him, and he cursed himself for his stupidity.

'I don't understand,' said the grey-bearded officer,

kneeling by the corpse. 'Why would he kill himself?'

'Why does anyone kill themselves?' countered Banelion. 'Have the body removed.'

Dagorian and Zani stabled their mounts. The ride had been a silent one, and now, as they walked through the dusk shadowed streets, the little Ventrian moved in close to the taller officer. 'I think you should tell me what happened back there,' he said.

The Drenai warrior nodded, then led Zani to a small tavern just off the Market Square. It was almost empty and they took a window table. Dagorian ordered wine, added a little water, then sipped the drink. 'There were demons,' he said, at last, keeping his voice low. 'Scores of them. Perhaps hundreds. They filled the house – all except for the room with the ward spell. They tore at me with talons and teeth. I thought my flesh was being ripped from my bones.'

'But there were no wounds. Perhaps it was just the drug.'

Dagorian shook his head. 'There were wounds, Zani. I can still feel them. They were tearing at my spirit – my soul, if you like. They were even outside, in the trees. Worse, I sensed they were everywhere. They are probably here even now, in the shadows of the ceiling, by the walls.'

Zani glanced around nervously. But he could see nothing. 'What were they like?' Dagorian described them, their bone-white faces and bulging eyes, their sharp teeth and talons. Zani shivered. It sounded like the ravings of a madman – which Zani would have infinitely preferred to be true. But they were investigating more than a score of bizarre murders, and everything Dagorian described had the ring of truth to it. Even so it was wildly beyond Zani's understanding. The Drenai officer fell silent. Zani spoke again, keeping his voice low. 'What does all this mean, Drenai?'

'I do not know. It is far beyond what I was taught. But there was something else. I was rescued by a shining figure with a sword of fire. He it was who made me recite the holy verses.'

'A shining figure,' repeated Zani. 'An angel, you mean?'

Dagorian saw scepticism swell once more in the Ventrian's expression. 'I am sorry, Zani. Were I you I would also be deeply suspicious. Is the man mad? Did the *lorassium* merely swell his delusions?' Zani relaxed and smiled. 'Well, the man is not mad. But he is frightened. And he does have a theory, of sorts.'

'That, at least, sounds promising,' said Zani.

'All the people killed – or fled – were seers. They could *see* the demons.'

'Which means?'

'Think of an army on the march in enemy territory. The scouts are the eyes. Therefore the first objective is to kill the scouts. The army is now blind.'

'But these demons cannot kill. They did not attack me. And once the drug wore off you were also safe.'

'They cannot kill *directly*. But they can influence emotions. That much I was taught back at the Temple. If their malevolence is directed by a power magus they can inspire great malice and hatred. That is the key to the killings. The boy who killed his mother, the dogs who attacked their master. All of them.'

'I know little of demons – and I wish I knew less,' said Zani. 'But what I do know is that this is far beyond my talents. We must consult Kalizkan.'

'Before this morning I would have agreed with you,' said Dagorian. 'I will think on it.'

'What is there to think about? He is the greatest sorcerer in the empire.'

'I know. That is what worries me.'

'You make no sense.'

'I have read stories about sorcerers summoning demons. In ones or twos. Here we have hundreds. Only the greatest of the magi could even consider such a spell. A sorcerer of such power would not be unknown. He would be famous, rich and powerful. Is there another such sorcerer in Usa?'

Zani's face darkened. 'I have met Kalizkan many times,' he said, coldly. 'He is a fine man, and much admired. He rescues children from the streets. He is kind and greatly loved. To speak of him summoning demons is a slander. And I'll hear no more of it. I think the drug addled your senses, Drenai. I suggest you return to the barracks and rest. Perhaps tomorrow you will be clear headed again.'

The Ventrian pushed back his chair and strode for the door. Dagorian made no attempt to call him back. If the situation were reversed he too would be sceptical. Zani reached the door, pulled it open and stepped outside. Dagorian heard him scream. The Ventrian officer stumbled back into the tavern, blood pumping from a terrible wound in his throat. Three dark-clad warriors moved inside. They were hooded and masked. The first thrust a sword deep into Zani's belly. The other two ran at Dagorian. The Drenai warrior up-ended the table in their path, slowing them, then drew his own blade. A sword lunged for his throat. Dagorian swayed aside and launched an overhand cut that chopped deep into his opponent's neck, slicing through the bone beneath. He was dead before he hit the floor. As his sabre came clear Dagorian leapt backwards. The second assassin's sword sliced air. Bringing up his sabre in a reverse cut Dagorian slashed the blade into the assassin's arm. It cut deep. The man screamed and dropped his sword. The killer who had stabbed Zani threw a knife, which missed Dagorian and clattered against the far wall.

The man with the wounded arm scrambled back and ran for the door. His companion hesitated – then joined him, and the two escaped into the night. Dagorian ran to Zani, but the little Ventrian, lying in a spreading pool of blood, was dead.

Anger rose in the Drenai officer, and he ran from the tavern, trying to catch the killers.

The streets were dark now, and there was no sign of them. Sheathing his sabre he returned to where the bodies lay. The tavern keeper approached him. 'I have sent for the Watch,' he said. Dagorian nodded and moved to the rear of the room, where the dead assassin lay. Flipping the body with his foot he knelt down and wrenched away the mask and hood. The man was unknown to him. He heard a soft curse from the tavern keeper and swung round.

'You know this man?'

The tavern keeper nodded dumbly. 'He has been in here several times – usually in uniform.'

'Who is he?'

'I don't know his name. But he's an aide to Antikas Karios.'

For the third time that afternoon Nogusta signalled a halt to rest the horses. The two mares ridden by Kebra and Bison did not need rest, but Nogusta's huge black gelding was breathing heavily and sweat bathed its flanks. Nogusta stroked its sleek neck. 'Do not be down-hearted, Great One,' he whispered, soothingly. 'You have been ill, and you need time to regain your strength.' The black man led him through the stand of pine and up the last rise. On the crest he paused and gazed down at the verdant valley below.

'I still can't believe it,' said Bison, moving alongside Nogusta. 'Sold for his hide! There must have been a mistake.'

'No mistake. He has a lung infection, and the king decided he was no longer of use.'

'But this is Starfire. He's been the king's warhorse for years. The king loves this horse.'

'Beware the love of kings,' said Nogusta, coldly. 'Starfire is like us, Bison. He's at least eighteen years old, and not as strong and fleet as once he was. Skanda had no more use for him. So he was sold for hide and meat and glue.'

'If he's useless why did you buy him?'

'He deserved better.'

'Maybe he did, but what will you do when he drops dead?' argued Bison. 'I mean . . . look at the state he's in! Horses don't survive lung rot.'

'The diagnosis is wrong. There is no wasting of the muscles. It is just an infection and he will improve in the mountain air. But if he does die it will be under the sky, free and proud, among friends who care for him.'

'He's just a horse,' persisted Bison. 'Do you really think he cares?'

'I care.' Taking up the reins Nogusta started the long walk down into the valley. Bison and Kebra rode ahead and by the time the black warrior led the warhorse to level ground his two companions had made camp beside a stream. Bison had collected dry wood for a fire and Kebra had unpacked pots and plates for the evening meal.

Nogusta unsaddled the black gelding, let him roll, then groomed him. The horse was huge, almost eighteen hands, with a strong, arched neck and a beautiful back. A white blaze, in the shape of a star, adorned his brow. 'Rest now, my friend,' said Nogusta. 'The grass here is good.' The weary gelding plodded onto the meadow and began to crop grass.

'This is a fine place,' said Kebra. 'Good farming land. If I was twenty years younger I'd build here.'

As dusk deepened jack rabbits began to appear. Kebra shot two, skinned and cleaned them, adding the fresh meat to the broth.

Nogusta wrapped himself in his cloak and sat with his back to a tree. It was peaceful here, and the view was majestic. Snow-crested mountains broke the line of the horizon, and folds of hills and valleys lay before them. Away to the east he could see a deep forest part bathed in mist. To the west a lake glimmered blood red in the dying sunlight. Kebra was right. It was a place to build on, and he imagined a wide, low house, with windows that looked out on the mountains. Horses and cattle would prosper here. He gazed lovingly upon the mountains. What were the works of Man, when set against these giants of nature, he wondered? Man's evil seemed small here, tiny and insubstantial. The mountains cared nothing for the whims of kings and princes. They were here before Man, and they would outlast him, surviving perhaps even when the sun failed and eternal darkness fell upon the planet.

Kebra brought him a plate of food and the two men sat in companionable silence, eating their meal. Bison finished his swiftly, then took a flat pan and headed off upstream to search for gold.

'He'll find nothing,' said Kebra. 'There is no gold here.'

'It will keep him occupied,' said Nogusta, sadness in his voice.

'You still expect us to be followed?'

Nogusta nodded. 'Malikada is not a forgiving man. He will send men, and I will kill them. And for what? One man's arrogance.'

'We might be able to avoid them,' offered Kebra. Nogusta took a deep breath and pushed himself to his feet.

'Maybe. I have had no fresh visions to tell me otherwise. But death is coming, Kebra. I can smell it.' Kebra did not reply. Nogusta was rarely wrong about these things.

Starfire moved closer to the two men. His breathing was still ragged. Nogusta moved smoothly to his feet and stroked the gelding's long neck. 'Bison could be right,' said Kebra. 'Trying to escape pursuit upon a sick horse does not seem to make a great deal of sense.'

'He has been poorly stabled,' said Nogusta. 'My father knew about these things. He always soaked the straw, and ensured the stables were clean. And Starfire has not been exercised.'

'That's not my point,' said Kebra, softly.

'I know, my friend. It is not sensible.' He grinned. 'But I would do it again.'

Ulmenetha watched from the roof gardens as the army marched from the city. Four thousand Drenai foot soldiers, in ranks of threes, and three thousand Ventrian cavalry in columns of twos. Behind them were the wagons, bearing supplies, or dismantled siege engines and ballistae. Word had reached Usa that the Cadian army was on the march and Skanda was eager to meet them.

The king had not bothered to visit Axiana, but had sent a farewell message via Kalizkan. Ulmenetha had avoided the wizard, keeping to her rooms until he had gone. Now she stood high above the cheering crowds as Skanda rode from the city. The populace were scattering rose petals before his horse, and he was waving and smiling.

Amazing, thought Ulmenetha. A few years ago he had been an invading foreigner, feared by all. Now, despite the endless battles and the destruction of empire, he was a hero to them. He was a god.

She wondered idly whether it would have been different had he been ugly. Could a man with an ugly face command such devotion? Probably not. But then Skanda was not ugly. He was handsome and tall, golden haired, with a winning smile and enormous charm. We are so stupid sometimes, she decided. Last year Skanda had donated 10,000 *raq* to the city orphanage – one hundredth of the amount he spent on his wars. Yet the people loved him for it. It was the talk of the city. In the same month a respected holy man had been accused of trying to seduce a young priestess. He was savagely condemned and banished from Usa. This also was the talk of the city. Such extremes, thought Ulmenetha. All the holy man's life work was dust following one misguided action. People scorned him. Yet the greatest killer in the empire could win love by giving away a tiny portion of the money he had plundered from the city treasury.

Ulmenetha sighed. Who could understand it?

As the last of the soldiers left the city she wandered back through the upper levels of the palace, and down to the long kitchens. Servants were sitting around with little to do and Ulmenetha helped herself to a second breakfast of cheese and eggs, followed by bread and a rich red strawberry preserve.

While eating she listened to the chatter among the servants. They were talking about a young Drenai officer who had gone insane, and stabbed to death a Ventrian official and an officer from the staff of Antikas Karios. Soldiers were scouring the city for him. Others had ridden south to see if he had tried to join the men marching home with the White Wolf. Returning to the upper levels she sought out Axiana. The queen was sitting on her balcony, a wide-brimmed hat shielding her face from the spring sunlight. 'How are you feeling today?' asked Ulmenetha.

'I am well,' answered Axiana. 'Kalizkan wants me to move into his home. He wishes to be close when the boy is born.'

Ulmenetha felt a sudden chill in her heart. 'What answer did you give him?' she asked.

'I said I would think on it. Did you hear about Dagorian?'

'Dagorian?'

'The handsome young officer who always stares at me. I told you about him.'

'I remember. What has he done?'

'They say he went mad and killed some people. I find it hard to believe. He has such gentle eyes.'

'Looks can be deceptive,' said Ulmenetha.

'I suppose so. I have been to Kalizkan's house. It is very comfortable. He has wonderful gardens. And he is so amusing. You like him too, don't you?'

'I have always enjoyed his company,' admitted Ulmenetha. 'But I think you should stay here.'

'Why?' asked Axiana, looking up. Ulmenetha was at a loss to explain her remark. She was not even tempted to tell the queen of what she had seen on the roof garden.

'His house is overrun by shrieking children,' she said, finally, 'and most of his servants are male. I think you would be more at your ease here.' She saw Axiana's expression harden. 'But it is your decision, my lady. Whatever you think best.'

Axiana relaxed and smiled. 'You are probably right. I shall consider your advice. Will you do something for me?'

'Of course.'

'Find out what happened with Dagorian.'

'It may be too gruesome,' argued Ulmenetha.

'Even so.'

'I shall do it immediately,' said Ulmenetha.

With Antikas Karios and his staff gone from the city Ulmenetha walked the two miles to the offices of the Militia who were seeking the renegade officer. There a thin cleric, with deep-set eyes, told her of the murder of Zani. She asked what investigation the two men were working on, and was told it involved a series of murders. She pressed for further details.

'What is your interest here, lady?' asked the cleric, suspiciously.

'I am the queen's midwife, and she herself asked me to ascertain the facts. The young officer is known to her.'

'I see.' The man's expression changed instantly, and he gave an oily smile. 'Can I fetch you a chair?'

'No, I am fine. You were about to tell me the details of their investigation.'

He leaned forward across the broad counter that separated them. 'The papers relating to their case are no longer here, lady,' he said, lowering his voice. 'They were transferred to the offices of Antikas Karios. But I can tell you that the investigation involved the killing of mystics.

I spoke to Zani about it myself. He was convinced there was more to the murders than was immediately apparent.'

'I see. And where was Zani killed?'

He gave her the address of the tavern, and once more Ulmenetha trekked across the city. It was noon before she reached the tavern, which was already full. Easing her way through the throng she sought out the innkeeper, but was told that he was visiting his family to the west of the city. Further inquiries were useless in the noise and the hustle. She found a seat at the back of the tavern, and ordered a lunch of roast chicken, followed by several pieces of freshly baked fruit pie and cream. Then she sat quietly, waiting for the midday rush to ease. She stayed in the tavern for almost two hours, and when the crowd dissipated she summoned a serving maid.

'Were you here when the murders took place?' she asked. The girl shook her head.

'Did you want more food?' she enquired.

'Yes. Another slice of pie. Were any of the serving maids here that night?'

'Yes. Dilian.'

'Is she here today?'

'No. She went away with Pavik.'

'Pavik?'

'The tavern keeper,' answered the girl, moving away.

Moments later a thick set woman in her early fifties strode to where Ulmenetha sat. 'Why are you pestering my staff?' she asked, belligerently, her large arms folded across her ample bosom. 'And why should you be interested in the whereabouts of my husband?'

'I am investigating the murders,' said Ulmenetha. The woman gave a scornful laugh.

'Oh, I see. Now the army has gone the city police have

turned power over to you, eh? Is that right, you fat cow?'

Ulmenetha gave a sweet smile. 'Perhaps you would prefer to answer my questions in the city dungeon, you raddled slut. One more foul word from you and I shall send the Watch to arrest you.' Ulmenetha spoke the threat softly, and with quiet confidence, and the power of the words lanced through the woman's bluster.

'Who are you?' she asked, licking her lips.

'Sit down,' ordered Ulmenetha. The woman sank to the seat opposite.

'I have been sent here by someone in a very high place – someone who could cause you great harm. Now tell me all you know of the killings.'

'I wasn't here. My husband saw it all.'

'What did he tell you?'

'This is not fair,' whined the woman. 'We've been told what to say. And we've said it. We've done our duty, Pavik and me. We don't want to be involved in . . . in politics.'

'Who told you what to say?'

'Someone in a very high place who could do me considerable harm,' spat the woman, regaining some of her courage.

Ulmenetha nodded. 'I understand your fear,' she said. 'And you are quite right in your desire to avoid becoming enmeshed in the intrigues of the nobility. But you have already told me much.'

'I've told you nothing.'

Ulmenetha looked into the woman's frightened eyes. 'You have told me that your husband lied about the murders. Therefore I must assume that the officer, Dagorian, did not commit them. This means that you have accused an innocent man of a crime. Whatever the intrigue you are now facing the death penalty.'

'No! Pavik told the truth to the first man. Absolutely the truth. Then this other man came and made him change his story. Then he told Pavik to leave the city for a few days.'

'This other man has a name?'

'Who are you?'

'I dwell at the palace,' said Ulmenetha, softly. 'Now, give me the name.'

'Antikas Karios,' whispered the woman.

'What really happened that night?'

'The policeman, Zani, was murdered as he left the tavern. Then three men tried to kill the Drenai. He slew one, wounded another, and they fled. That's all I know. But please, for pity's sake, tell no-one I told you. Say you heard it from someone in the tavern that night. Will you do that?'

'Indeed I will. You say your husband and the serving maid have left the city. Do you know where they went?'

'No. Antikas Karios sent a carriage for them.'

'I see. Thank you for your help.' Ulmenetha rose. The woman pushed herself to her feet and grabbed the priestess by the arm.

'You won't say. You promise!'

'I promise.'

Ulmenetha left the tavern. She glanced back once to see the woman's fearful face at the window.

She will never see her husband again, thought Ulmenetha.

When Dagorian left the tavern that night he ran back to his rooms at the new barracks, changed his clothing, leaving his armour, breastplate and greaves behind, gathered what money he had saved and walked away into the city night.

The death of Zani had been shocking enough, but to discover that the assassins had been sent by Antikas Karios was a bitter blow. Dagorian knew that his life was in far greater peril than he had feared. Antikas Karios had no reason to order him killed, and this meant that the order must have come from Malikada himself. And, as Banelion had pointed out, Dagorian did not have the power to withstand such an enemy.

Worse, the whole poisonous business was undoubtedly linked to the deaths of the mystics, and the demons over Usa. It was therefore likely that he would be hunted on two fronts, on one side by swords, on the other by sorcery.

Dagorian had never been more frightened. He had no plan, save to make his way to the oldest quarter of the city. Here he could hide among the multitudes of the poor and the dispossessed, the beggars and thieves, the whores and the urchins. It was the most densely populated quarter, with narrow streets and twisting lanes, dark alleyways and shadowed arches.

It was close to midnight as Dagorian lay down in the doorway of an old warehouse. He was desperately tired and close to despair.

A figure emerged from the moon shadows. Dagorian pushed himself to his feet, his hand on his knife hilt.

In the moonlight he could see the man was not an assassin, but a beggar, dressed in rags. The man approached him cautiously. He was painfully thin, and his skeletal face was pitted with old sores. 'Spare a copper coin, sir, for an unfortunate victim of the war?'

Dagorian relaxed and was about to reach into his money pouch, when the man sprang forward, a rusty knife in his hand. Dagorian swayed aside, blocking the knife arm and sending a right cross to the beggar's chin.

The man fell heavily against the warehouse door, striking his head on the wooden frame. Dagorian wrestled the knife from his grasp, and flung it to one side. The man sank to his haunches.

'Give me your clothes,' said the officer, removing his own cloak and shirt.

The man blinked in the moonlight, and stared up at the Drenai with a look of incomprehension. 'Your clothes, man. I need them. In return you get this fine cloak.'

Slowly the beggar peeled off his wretched coat and the soiled shirt he wore beneath it. 'And your footwear,' said Dagorian. 'You may keep your breeches. I think I'd rather hang than wear them.' The man's body was fish white in the moonlight, his chest and back criss-crossed with old scars – the marks of many whips.

The officer donned the clothing and the coat, then sat down and pulled on the man's boots. They were of cheap hide, the soles as thin as paper.

'You're the one they seek,' said the beggar, suddenly. 'The killer Drenai.'

'The first part is right,' Dagorian told him.

'You won't pass for a beggar. You're too clean. Well scrubbed. You need to lie low for a few days, let your hair get greasy, and get some dirt under your fingernails.'

'A pleasant thought,' responded the Drenai. Yet he knew the man was right. He looked at the beggar, who had made no attempt to clothe himself, despite the chill of the night. He is waiting for me to kill him, thought Dagorian, suddenly. And that is what I should do. 'Get dressed and be on your way,' he said.

'Not very bright, are you?' said the beggar, pulling on the fine blue woollen shirt, and giving a gap-toothed grin.

'You'd prefer it if I slit your throat?'

'It's not about preference, boy. It's about survival. Still, I'm grateful.' The beggar rose, and swung the black cloak around his thin shoulders. 'You'd better start thinking about a hiding place. If you can stay clear of them for a couple of days they'll believe you escaped from the city. Then you can make a move.'

'I do not know the city,' admitted Dagorian.

'Then good luck to you,' said the beggar. Holding the boots in his left hand he moved to where his knife lay and picked it up. Then he was gone.

Dagorian moved away, ducking down a dark alley. The man was right. He needed a place to hide. But where could a man hide from the powers of sorcery?

He felt the rising of panic, and quelled it. The White Wolf had taught him much, but the most valuable lesson was that, when in peril, keep a cool head. 'Think fast if you have to – but always think!' Dagorian sucked in a deep, calming breath, and leaned against a wall. Think! Where can the powers of sorcery be held at bay? In a holy temple. He considered travelling to one of the many churches, but that would mean asking for sanctuary. The building may be holy, but he would be putting his life in the hands of the monks. And – even if they did not betray him – he would be risking their lives. No, that was not an option. Where else then? At the home of a friendly sorcerer, who could place ward spells around him. But he knew no sorcerers – save Kalizkan.

Then a thought struck him. The old woman who had been killed by her son. She had laid ward spells on all the doors of the inner room.

Dagorian carried on walking, trying to get his bearings. The old woman had lived in the northern section of the old quarter. He glanced at the sky, but there were thick clouds and he could see no stars. He walked on for an hour. Twice he saw soldiers of the Watch, and ducked into the shadows.

At last he reached the woman's house. Moving to the rear he scaled a wall and entered the building. There were no windows in the back room and Dagorian lit a lantern. Blood still stained the walls, and the rune stones remained scattered on the table. He glanced at the two doors. Both bore the carved triangle and the snake.

Hoping that the ward spells were still active he blew out the lantern and moved to a narrow bed in the corner.

Sleep came instantly.

He was sitting in a cave, and a fire was burning. He felt hot and confused. 'Be calm, child,' came a familiar voice. He tried to place it, and remembered the shining figure who had rescued him at the wizard's house.

'What am I doing here?' he asked, sitting up and looking around. The cave was empty, and when the voice spoke again, he realized it was coming from the blazing fire.

'You are not here. There is no here. This is a place of spirit. Your body lies in the woman's hovel. It was a good choice. They will not find you.'

'Why do you not show yourself?'

'All in good time, child. Have you put together the clues? Do you even begin to understand what is happening?'

'No. All I know is that Malikada wishes me dead.'

'Malikada cares nothing for you, Dagorian. You are an incidental in a great design. Kalizkan – or the creature that calls itself Kalizkan – is a Demon Lord, of enormous power. He seeks to cast the Spell of the Three Kings. If he succeeds the world will be changed beyond the recognition of man. It will become as it once was. The demons

135

will be flesh once more, and the two worlds will become one.'

Dagorian raised his hand. 'Stop for a moment. This is making my head spin. The two worlds? What is the meaning?'

'Aeons ago the creatures we call demons lived among us. Shape-Shifters, blood-drinkers, were beings. We were at war with them for a thousand years. Then three kings came together, and with the aid of a mighty wizard they changed the world, banishing the demons to another place, a grey realm of spirit. Sorcerers can still summon demons using blood magic, opening the gateways for fleeting heartbeats. But when the spell is done the demons return to the grey. Kalizkan seeks to repeat the Spell of the Three Kings.'

'And he can do this?'

'It has already begun, child. The Ventrian emperor was the first to be sacrificed. But the spell requires three deaths, each of kings, and each king to be mightier than the last. When the final death blow is delivered the world will be cursed as it was in time past. The drinkers of blood will return.'

'Three kings? Then they will try to kill Skanda. I must get to him.'

'You cannot. His death is but hours away, and on the fastest horse you could not reach the army within a day. By this time tomorrow the Drenai army will be destroyed, and Skanda will be strapped to the altar.'

'Sweet Heaven! There must be something I can do.'

'You can save the third king.'

'There is no king greater than Skanda.'

'There is his unborn son. If destiny allows him to live he will be a greater man than his father. But Kalizkan plans to destroy him.'

'I could not get into the palace. They are searching for me everywhere.'

'If you do not then all is lost.'

Dagorian awoke in a cold sweat. As he saw the solid walls of the house relief swelled within him. It was a dream. He laughed at his foolishness, and fell asleep once more.

Wrapped in his cloak against the night cold Nogusta leaned back against the tree and fed another stick to the fire. Bison was snoring softly, the sound strangely comforting in the quiet of the night. Nogusta drew one of his ten diamond-shaped throwing knives from the black baldric draped across his chest and idly twirled the blade through his fingers. The silver steel gleamed in the moonlight.

Ushuru would have loved this place of high, lonely beauty, the vast expanse of the mountains, the wildness of wood and forest. She would have been happy here. *We* would have been happy here, he corrected himself.

Time had not eased the grief. Perhaps he had not wished it to.

His mind flew back, ghosting over the years, seeing again the huge living-room. They had all been laughing and joking, sitting around the hearth. His father and his two brothers had just returned from Drenan, where they had negotiated a new contract with the army for a hundred horses, and the celebrations were in full flow. He could still see Ushuru sitting on the couch, her long legs drawn up beneath her. She was crafting a dream-deceiver for Nogusta's youngest nephew. A web of twisted horse hair, woven around a sapling circle that would hang over his bed. Nightmares were said to be drawn to the deceiver, and trapped in the web, leaving the sleeper free of torment. The twenty-year-old Nogusta moved to her side, placing his arm over her shoulder. Lightly he kissed her cheek.

'It is a fine piece of work,' he told her.

She smiled. 'It will confuse the sleep demons.'

He grinned. She had learned the western tongue well, but her translations were always too literal. 'Do you miss the lands of Opal?' he asked her, in the ancient tongue.

'I would like to see my mother again,' she told him. 'But I am more than content.'

She continued to weave the web. 'Of what does Kynda dream?' he asked her.

'Fire. He is surrounded by fire.'

'He burned his fingers last week at the forge,' Nogusta told her. 'Children learn by such painful mistakes.' Even as the thought came to him a bright picture formed in his mind. A small child tumbling down a steep slope. As she fell her foot became trapped under a jutting tree root, snapping her leg. Nogusta stood.

'What is it, my love?' asked Ushuru.

'A child hurt in the hills. I'll find her.'

He kissed her once more, this time upon the lips, then left the house. The memory burned at him now with exquisite pain. He had been twenty years of age, and would never kiss her again. The next time he saw her, less than ten hours distant, she would be a corpse, her beauty destroyed by knives and fire. Kynda's nightmares would have come true, flames roaring through his bedroom.

But this he did not know as he set out to find the village child. When he came upon her she was unconscious. Freeing the child he splinted the leg then carried her back to the village. He had been surprised to find no search parties, and it was just after dawn when he entered the village from the north.

A crowd surged out from the meeting hall as he approached. The girl was awake now. Her father – Grinan the baker – ran forward. 'I fell down, daddy,' she said. 'I hurt myself.' Nogusta saw that the baker's shirt was smeared with soot. He thought it strange. Grinan took his daughter from Nogusta's arms. Then he saw the splint.

'I found her by Sealac Hollow,' said Nogusta. 'Her leg is broken, but the break is clean. It will mend well.'

No-one spoke. Nogusta knew the villagers had little love for his family, but even so their reaction was strange, to say the least. Then he saw that a number of the men in the crowd also had scorch marks upon their clothes.

From the back of the crowd came Menimas, the nobleman. He was a tall thin man, with deep-set dark eyes, and a moustache and beard trimmed to a perfect circle. 'Hang him!' he said. 'He is a demon worshipper!'

At first the meaning of the words did not register. 'What is he saying?' Nogusta asked Grinan. The man avoided his eyes. He looked down at his daughter.

'Did this man take you away, Flarin?' he asked her.

'No, daddy. I fell down in the woods. I hurt my leg.'

Menimas stepped forward. 'He has bewitched the child. Hang him, I say!' For a moment no-one moved, then several men ran at Nogusta. He downed two of them with a left and right combination, but weight of numbers overpowered him and he was wrestled to the ground. They bound his arms and dragged him to the oak on the market square. A rope was thrown over a high branch, and a noose fastened around his neck.

He was hoisted up, the rope burning into his throat. He heard Menimas scream: 'Die, you black bastard!' Then he passed out.

Somewhere within the darkness he became aware of sensation; warm air being forced into his lungs. He could feel the flow of it, his chest rising to accommodate it. Then he felt the warmth of a mouth upon his own, pushing more air into his starved lungs. Gradually other sensations followed; a burning pain on the skin of his throat, the cool of the ground beneath his back. Strong hands pushed down upon his chest, and he heard a commanding voice. 'Breathe, damn you!'

The warm air had stopped flowing now, and Nogusta, growing short of oxygen, sucked in a huge, juddering, breath.

He opened his eyes to find himself lying on the ground, staring up at the leaves of the oak. The rope still hung from a thick branch, but it had been hacked in two. The face of a stranger swam into sight. Nogusta tried to speak, but his voice was a croak. 'Say nothing,' said the grey-eyed man. 'Your throat is bruised, but you will live. Let me help you stand.' Nogusta struggled to his feet. There were soldiers in the square, and twelve villagers were standing by under guard.

Nogusta touched his throat. The noose still hung there. He lifted it clear. The skin below was raw and bleeding. 'I . . . rescued . . . a child,' he managed to say. 'And . . . they attacked me. I . . . don't know why.'

'I know why,' said the man. Turning to Nogusta he laid a slender hand on his shoulder. 'Last night these people burned your home. They killed your family.'

'My family? No! It cannot be!'

'They are dead, and I am sorry for your loss. I cannot tell you how sorry. The killers believed . . . were led to believe . . . that your family kidnapped the child for . . . some blood rite. They are simple and stupid people.'

The pain in his throat was forgotten now. 'They didn't kill them all? Not all of them?'

'Yes. All of them. And though it will not bring them back you will see justice now. Bring the first!' he ordered. It was the baker, Grinan.

'No, please!' he shouted. 'I have a family. Children. They need me!'

The pale-eyed soldier stepped in close to the pleading man. 'Every action a man takes has consequences, peasant. This man also had a family. You have committed murder. Now you will pay for it.' A woman outside the ring of soldiers screamed for mercy, but a noose was placed over Grinan's head and he was hauled into the air, his feet kicking out.

One by one the twelve villagers with fire-blackened clothes were brought forward and hanged.

'Where is Menimas?' asked Nogusta, as the last man died.

'He fled,' said the soldier. 'He has friends in high places. I doubt he will be convicted.'

Leaving the village to bury its dead the soldiers and Nogusta returned to the burnt-out estate. Nogusta was in deep shock now, his mind swimming. The seven corpses had been wrapped in blankets and laid out in a row before the ruins. One by one he went to them, opening the shrouds, and staring down at the dead. The child Kynda was unmarked by fire, and his tiny hand was clutching the dream-deceiver made by Ushuru. 'Smoke killed him,' said the officer.

One by one Nogusta dug the graves, refusing all offers of help.

When they were all buried the pale-eyed officer returned. 'We have rounded up some of your horses. The rest escaped into the mountains. The tack room was largely intact and I have had a horse saddled for you. I need you to come with me to the garrison to make a report on the . . . incident.'

Nogusta did not argue. They rode for most of the day, and camped that night at Shala Falls. Nogusta had spoken to no-one during the ride. Now he lay within his blankets, his emotions numbed. It was as if he could feel nothing. He kept seeing Ushuru's face, and her smile.

Two of the soldiers were talking nearby, their voices low. 'Did you see it?' said one. 'It was horrible. I've never seen the like. Don't want to again. Made me feel sick.'

Even through the numbness Nogusta felt grateful for the sympathetic reaction in the soldier.

'Yes, it was gross,' said his companion. 'The White Wolf blowing air into a black man's mouth! Who'd believe it?'

Even now – more than thirty years later – Nogusta felt a cold anger rising in him at the memory. Still, anger is a better emotion than sorrow, he thought. Anger is alive and can be dealt with. Sorrow is a dead creature and sits like a weight that cannot be released.

He rose and wandered away into the trees, gathering more dead wood for the fire. You should sleep, he told himself. There will be killers coming. You will need all your strength and skill.

Returning to the fire he fed it then settled down under his blanket, his head resting on his saddle.

But sleep would not come, and he rose again. Bison groaned and woke. Pushing back his blanket the giant pushed himself to his feet and stumbled to a nearby tree, where he urinated noisily. Retying his leggings he turned and saw Nogusta sitting by the fire.

'Didn't find any gold today,' he said, squatting down beside the black man.

'Maybe tomorrow.'

'You want me to keep watch?'

Nogusta grinned. 'You never could keep watch, Bison. By the time I lie down you'll be asleep.'

'I do find it easy to sleep,' admitted Bison. 'I was dreaming about the Battle at Purdol. You, me and Kebra on the wall. Have you still got your medal?'

'Yes.'

'I sold mine. Got twenty *raq* for it. Wish I hadn't now. It was a good medal.'

'You can have mine.'

'Can I?' Bison was delighted. 'I won't sell it this time.'

'You probably will, but it doesn't matter.' Nogusta sighed. 'That was the first great victory. It was on that day we realized the Ventrians could be beaten. I remember it rained all that day, lightning in the sky, thunder over the sea.'

'I don't remember much about it,' admitted Bison. 'Except that we held the wall and the White Wolf supplied sixty barrels of rum for the army.'

'I think you drank most of it.'

'That was a good night. All the camp whores gave it away for free. Have you slept?'

'Not yet,' said Nogusta.

Bison tugged at his white walrus moustache. He could see his friend was unhappy, but did not have the courage to broach the subject. Nogusta and Kebra were both *thinking* men, and much of what they spoke of sailed high above Bison's head. 'You ought to sleep,' said Bison, at last. 'You'll feel better for it.' At the thought of sleep he yawned. Then he wandered back to his blankets. Nogusta settled down again and closed his eyes.

In that moment he experienced a sudden vision. He saw ten riders moving slowly across green hills, white-topped mountains behind them. Nogusta looked at the riders. The sun was high, the ten riders hooded against its glare. They rode into a wood. One of them pushed back his hood and removed a helm of black iron. His hair was long, and ghost white, his face grey, his eyes blood red. An arrow flashed from the trees. The rider threw up his hand, and the shaft sliced through it, driving on to pierce the flesh of his face. He dragged it clear. Both wounds healed instantly.

The vision changed. Suddenly it was night, and two moons hung in the sky, one a crescent, the other full. And he saw himself standing by the tree line on a hillside beneath alien stars. A woman was walking towards him. It was Ushuru. And she was smiling.

This vision also faded, and Nogusta found himself floating high above a plain. He saw the Drenai infantry commit themselves to an attack on the Cadian centre. Skanda was leading the charge. As the Cadians reeled back a trumpet sounded and Skanda signalled to Malikada for the cavalry to attack the right. But Malikada did not move, and the cavalry remained, holding to the hill.

Nogusta could see the despair in Skanda's eyes; the disbelief and the dawning realization of betrayal and defeat.

And then the slaughter began.

Nogusta awoke in a cold sweat, his hands trembling. Bison and Kebra were asleep, and the dawn light was creeping above the mountains. Pushing aside his blankets the black warrior rose soundlessly. Kebra stirred and opened his eyes.

'What is wrong, my friend?'

'Skanda is dead. And we are in peril.'

Kebra pushed himself to his feet. 'Dead? That cannot be.'

'He was betrayed by Malikada and the Ventrians. They stood by while our comrades were slaughtered.' Slowly, remembering every image, he told Kebra of his visions.

The bowman listened in silence. 'The betrayal and the battle I can understand,' he said, when Nogusta had finished. 'But demonic riders with eyes of blood? What is that supposed to mean? It can't be real, can it? Any more than walking with Ushuru beneath two moons.'

'I do not know, my friend. But I think the riders will come. And I will face them.'

'Not alone you won't,' said Kebra.

Chapter Six

All her life Ulmenetha had known many fears. Her mother's sickness and death had filled her with a terror of cancer that caused awful nightmares, and left her trembling in her bed, her face and body bathed in cold sweat. Small, scurrying rodents inspired a sense of dread in her, leaving her incapable of movement. But most of all the death of her beloved Vian had made her fear love itself, and to run for the sanctuary of the convent.

She sat now in her room, staring up at the stars, contemplating the nature of fear.

For Ulmenetha terror began the moment control was lost. She had been powerless when her mother was dying. She could only watch in silent anguish as the flesh shrivelled away and the spirit fled. As a consequence Ulmenetha had worried over Vian, making sure he ate well, and was always dressed in warm clothes when the winter winds blew. He had laughed at her coddling. Ulmenetha had been preparing an evening meal when word reached her he was dead. While searching for a lost sheep he had slipped on the ice and fallen from the high ridge. There was nothing she could have done to prevent it, but that did not stop the guilt from eating its way into her soul. It was she who had urged him to find the sheep. Guilt, remorse and sorrow had overwhelmed her.

So she had run from her fears, and even taken the extra precaution of becoming fat, in order that men would no longer find her attractive. All this so that she would never again suffer the true terrors of life.

Yet here she was, sitting in a palace bedroom, with the demons closing in.

What can I do, she asked herself? The first answer, as always, was to run, to leave the palace and make the long journey back to Drenan and the convent. The thought of running, putting these fears behind her, was immensely seductive. She had money, and could book passage on a caravan to the coast, and then take a ship to Dros Purdol. Sea air on her face. The thought of flight brought calm to her mind.

Then she pictured Axiana's face, the large, childlike eyes, and the sweet smile. And with it the memory of Kalizkan's rotting, maggot-ridden flesh.

I cannot leave her! The panic began again. What can you do against the power of demons, whispered the voice of flight. You are a fat priestess with no arcane skills. Kalizkan is a sorcerer. He could blast your soul from your overweight body. He could consign you to the Void. He could send assassins to plunge their knives into your obese belly!

Ulmenetha rose from her chair and moved to the table by the window. From a drawer she took a silver-rimmed oval mirror and held it up to her face. For years she had avoided mirrors, hating the bloated image they portrayed. But now she looked beyond the flesh, and deep into the grey eyes, recalling the girl who had run the mountain paths – the girl who had run for joy and not for fear.

At last calm, her mind set, she returned the mirror to the drawer. First she must tell Axiana of her discoveries concerning Dagorian. The officer was innocent, and the true villain, she was sure, was Kalizkan. Then realization struck her. Kalizkan was not the enemy. Kalizkan was dead! Something had taken over the body; something powerful enough to cast a sweet and reassuring spell, enchanting all who came into contact with it.

If she were to tell Axiana the simple truth the queen would think her mad. How then to convince her of the perils that lay in wait?

You must walk with care down this road, she warned herself.

Gathering her thoughts she was about to find Axiana when a servant tapped at her door. Ulmenetha called for her to enter. The girl stepped inside and curtsied.

'What is it, child?'

'The queen wishes you to prepare your belongings. They will be taken to Kalizkan's house in the morning.'

Ulmenetha fought for calm. 'Is the queen in her apartments?'

'No, my lady. She left this afternoon. The Lord Kalizkan came for her.'

At noon on the second day Dagorian found his hunger overriding his caution. Leaving his sabre behind, but hiding his hunting knife beneath the beggar's rags, he left his hiding place and risked the short walk to the market. The sun was bright in a clear sky, the market square packed with people. Easing his way through the crowd he stopped at a meat stall, where a spit of beef was being turned over a charcoal grill. The cook looked at him sourly, but Dagorian produced two copper coins and the man cut several thick slices, placing them on a wooden platter. The smell of the roasting meat was divine. It was almost too hot to hold and Dagorian burned his fingers. He blew on the meat, then tore off a chunk. It was exquisite. Juices ran down his stubbled chin. The cook's expression softened. 'Good?' he enquired.

'The best,' agreed Dagorian.

A commotion began at the far end of the market place. Instantly alert Dagorian prepared to run. Had he been spotted? Were they coming for him? The crowd milled, and word spread like a fire through dry brush. An old man pushed his way through them, coming to the stall.

'The army's been crushed,' he told the cook. 'The king is dead.'

'Dead? The Cadians are coming here?'

The old man shook his head. 'Apparently Prince Malikada forced them back across the river. But all the Drenai perished.'

The crowd surged around Dagorian, everyone talking. Skanda dead? It was unthinkable.

His hunger gone he felt sick with anguish. Turning from the stall he stumbled back into the crowd.

Everywhere people were talking, theorizing, wondering. How had Malikada repulsed the Cadians? How could all the Drenai have been wiped out, and yet Malikada's force remain intact? Dagorian was a soldier – albeit a reluctant one – and he knew the answer.

Treachery.

The king had been betrayed.

Sick at heart he made it back to the seer's home and slumped down in a chair.

The dream came back to him. Two kings slain. The third – the unborn child – in terrible danger.

What can I do, he thought? I am alone, trapped at the centre of a hostile city. How can I get to the queen? And even if I can how do I convince her of the danger she is in. He recalled trying to tell Zani of his fears concerning Kalizkan. The little man had rounded on him instantly. The sorcerer was probably the most popular man in the city, loved by all for his good works.

Dagorian took a deep breath. A phrase his father used came to his mind. 'If a man has a boil on his arse, you don't heal it by lancing the foot.'

Strapping his sabre belt to his waist Dagorian opened the back door, walked through the small garden, and out onto the crowded streets.

Kalizkan's house was an old one, originally built for Bodasen, the general who had led the Immortals in the time of Emperor Gorben. The façade was of white marble, inlaid with statues, and fronted by four tall columns. The building was three storeys high, with more than a hundred rooms, the grounds around it beautifully landscaped, with flowering trees and willows clustered on the banks of a small lake.

A high wall surrounded the estate, and a wrought-iron double gate ensured privacy for the master of the house.

Ulmenetha's carriage drew up outside the gate, and a soldier climbed down to open it. The carriage moved on, coming to a halt before the marble steps leading to a high, arched doorway. A second soldier opened the door of the carriage and Ulmenetha stepped down.

'Stay with me until I have spoken to the queen,' Ulmenetha told the two soldiers. Both bowed. They were strong men, tall and broad shouldered, and the priestess felt more comfortable knowing they were to be close.

She strode up the marble steps and was about to knock when the door opened. A hooded man stood in the shadows beyond. She could not see his face clearly.

'What is it you want?' he asked her, his voice deep, and curiously accented.

Ulmenetha was unprepared for such a cold greeting, and she bridled. 'I am the queen's companion, and here at her invitation.' The hooded man said nothing for a moment, then he stepped aside. Summoning the soldiers Ulmenetha walked inside. Curtains were drawn everywhere, and the interior was gloomy.

'Where is the queen?' she demanded.

'Upstairs ... Resting,' replied the man, after a moment's thought.

'Which rooms?'

'Go to the top of the stairs and turn right. You will find them.'

Turning to the soldiers she said: 'Wait here. I will be down presently.'

There was the smell of strong perfume in the air, cloying and strangely unpleasant, as if it masked some dank, underlying odour. Ulmenetha began to climb the wide, red-carpeted staircase. Her footfalls raised dust on the carpet and she shivered. Fear was strong in her now. This gloomy, shadow-haunted place was cold and unwelcoming. Glancing back she saw the soldiers standing by the open door, sunlight streaming through and shining on their armour. Fortified by the sight she walked on. Ulmenetha was breathing heavily by the time she reached the top of the stairs. There was a gallery here, the walls covered with old paintings, most of them landscapes. She noticed one of them was torn. She shivered again. This was no place for Axiana!

Reaching the first of the doors she found it was locked. A large key was still in the lock and she turned it. The door opened, the dry hinges creaking.

Dressed in a gown of blue and white satin Axiana was sitting on a couch in front of a barred window. She looked startled as Ulmenetha entered.

'Oh!' she cried, running to Ulmenetha and throwing

her arms around the priestess's shoulders. 'Take me away from here! Now. This is an awful place!'

'Where are your servants?' asked Ulmenetha.

'He sent them away. The hooded man. He locked me in! He locked me in, Ulmenetha! Can you believe it?' The priestess stroked the queen's hair.

'There are soldiers downstairs to bring you home. I shall send them to you to fetch your belongings.'

'No. Never mind them. Leave them. Let us just go!'

Taking the queen by the hand Ulmenetha returned to the gallery.

She glanced down. One of the soldiers was leaning against the far wall, the other sitting in a chair. The hooded man was standing by the door, which was now closed.

'The queen wishes her clothes to be packed, and the chests taken to the carriage,' said Ulmenetha, supporting Axiana to the first of the steps. Her words hung in the dusty air. The soldiers did not respond.

'The queen must remain here,' said the hooded man. 'It is the will of my lord.'

'You men! Come here!' called Ulmenetha. Still there was no movement. It was not that they had ignored her, she realized with horror. They had not heard her. Both remained still and silent. Axiana gripped her arm.

'Get me away from here!' she whispered.

Ulmenetha continued to walk down the stairs. Halfway down she saw a glint of metal in the standing soldier's throat. It was a knife hilt and it had pinned him to the wooden panelling beyond. Transferring her gaze to the seated man, she saw that he too was dead. The queen saw it too.

'Sweet Heaven,' whispered Axiana. 'He has killed them both.'

The hooded man advanced to the foot of the stairs. 'Take the queen back to her room,' he ordered. Ulmenetha's right hand, hidden until now in the folds of her voluminous white dress, came into sight. Even in the gloomy half-light the blade of the hunting knife shone bright.

'Get out of my way,' she told the hooded man. He laughed and continued to climb the stairs.

'You think to frighten me, woman? I can taste your fear. I will feed upon it.'

'Feed on this!' said Ulmenetha. Her hand shot up in an underarm throw which sent the blade slamming into the hooded man's throat. He stumbled, then righted himself, dragging the knife clear. Black blood gushed to the front of his dark tunic, streaming down his chest. He tried to speak, but the words were drowned in a bubbling dark froth. Ulmenetha waited for him to fall.

But he did not. He continued to advance. Axiana screamed. Ulmenetha pushed her back up the stairs, then swung to meet the threat from below. The flow of blood from his ruined throat had now drenched the man's dark leggings, but still he came on.

In that moment the priestess knew what she was facing. A demon clothed in human flesh. And yet there was no fear in her, no rising panic. For this was no disease, to slip past her guard and kill her mother, no icy ledge to rob her of her husband. This was flesh and bone, and seeking to harm a girl that she loved like a daughter.

She was calmer than at any time she could remember, her mind focused, her senses sharp.

Closer and closer he climbed. Ulmenetha waited until he raised the knife, then leapt forward, hammering her foot into his chest. He was catapulted back, his body arching in the air. His head struck the stair, his neck snapping. The body crashed to the floor.

Ulmenetha was not surprised as he struggled to his feet, his head flopping grotesquely to his shoulder. The hood had fallen away to reveal a pale, ghostly face, with a lipless mouth and protruding, blood-red eyes.

'Run, Axiana!' shouted the priestess, pointing to the gallery on the left and the far door. Axiana stood rooted to the spot. Tearing her gaze from the advancing man Ulmenetha moved swiftly to the queen, grabbing her arm and hauling her along the gallery. The far door was locked, but, as with Axiana's rooms, there was a key. Opening the door she pulled the key clear, pushed Axiana through, then locked the door behind them. A fist thundered against the door panel, causing it to vibrate. Twice more it struck, and a long, narrow crack appeared in the panelling.

'How do we get out?' asked Axiana, the tremble of panic in her voice.

Ulmenetha had no idea. The house was like a warren, and the corridor in which they stood had many doors, but no obvious stairway to take them back to ground level. 'This way,' said Ulmenetha, moving along the darkened corridor, and through two more doors. There were no keys here, and from far behind them the women heard a splintering crash.

Ulmenetha looked around. They were in a dormitory, a dozen beds on both sides of the room. All the beds were empty. The priestess moved to a window and dragged back the heavy curtains. The window was barred. Light filled the room now, and she could see several toys on the dusty floor, and by the far wall was a straw-filled doll, looking forlorn against the bare, dusty boards. 'Keep moving,' she told the queen. At the far end of the dormitory was another door. It was held shut by a locking bar between two brackets. Ulmenetha lifted the bar clear and pulled open the door. Within was a second dormitory.

Three children sat huddled against the far wall. A red-headed boy of around fourteen or fifteen stepped in front of the two girls, a small knife in his hand. He was painfully thin, and Ulmenetha could see open sores on his skinny arms. One of the girls moved forward. Perhaps a year older than the boy she was also waif thin, and dressed in rags, but she held a long piece of jagged wood, torn from one of the beds. Together they formed a protective shield in front of the youngest child, a small blonde girl of around four.

'Come any closer and we'll kill you,' said the waif with the jagged wooden spear.

There was no other exit from the room.

A floorboard creaked behind them. Ulmenetha swung to see the broken-necked man moving, knife in hand, across the dormitory.

Reaching down she took up the long wooden bar that had secured the door. As the demonic creature approached she rushed at him, swinging the wood like a club. He took the force of the blow on his shoulder. His arm snapped up, his fist cannoning into Ulmenetha's face. Thrown back she lost control of the wooden club and it clattered to the floor. The demon was upon her. Leaping back she avoided his first thrust, and scrambled over a bed. His red eyes stared at her, but as he moved forward the head lolled on the broken neck. He staggered. Then gripped the head with his left hand, dragging it by the hair until the eyes focused once more on the priestess. Then he advanced.

The young red-headed boy leapt at the creature,

slashing at his face with the knife blade. The demon swatted him aside. As he did so the waiflike girl crept up behind him and thrust the splintered wood into his back. He arched up. Ulmenetha crouched down, swept up the wooden bar, and charged forward, using it as a ram which hammered into his chest, hurling him into the far wall. As he struck the wall it seemed to Ulmenetha that his chest exploded. She blinked – and saw that the makeshift spear used by the girl had been driven through his back, tearing a huge hole in his chest. The body slid down the wall, then pitched forward to the boards.

Immediately the room was filled with the stench of rotting meat, and Ulmenetha saw maggots writhing through the dead flesh. The waif girl put her hand to her mouth and gagged.

'Let us get out of here,' said Ulmenetha. 'Quickly.'

Despite her revulsion Ulmenetha gathered her knife from beside the rotting corpse and, taking the shocked queen by the arm, led her back along the corridor, out onto the gallery, and down the stairs. The red-headed boy picked up the four-year-old and followed.

Not knowing where to go Ulmenetha moved down a set of stairs to what she thought must be the ground floor. A locked door barred her way at the bottom. A large key was hanging on a rusted hook. Lifting it clear she opened the door and stepped inside. Light was streaming in from two windows on the far side of the chamber, and shining down onto a sea of small bodies, carelessly heaped around a blood-drenched altar. The sight froze her blood. Though never having been blessed with the gift of a child Ulmenetha's maternal instincts were powerful, and the sight of so many murdered children filled her with an aching sadness.

Closing her eyes against the horror Ulmenetha stepped

backwards, just as the pregnant queen was about to enter. 'There is no way through,' said Ulmenetha. 'We must go back the way we came.'

A cold and terrible fury grew in her as she led the group back up the stairs. There must have been over a hundred children in that chamber, a hundred lives ended in torment and terror. This was evil on a scale Ulmenetha could scarcely imagine.

Moving back to the landing she came to the broken door and emerged onto the gallery above the front door. A tall figure stepped from the shadows. Axiana screamed, and Ulmenetha swung round, the knife flashing up and stabbing out. The blade was parried, then a calm voice spoke. 'I am no danger, lady. I am Dagorian.'

Ulmenetha looked into his face, recognizing it from her *lorassium* vision. Fear surged again in her. The scene in the woods, four men – three old, one young – protecting the queen from a hidden evil. Dagorian was the young man from the dream. 'Why are you here?' demanded Ulmenetha.

'I came to kill Kalizkan.'

'He is with the army,' said Ulmenetha. 'Now let us get out of this dreadful place.'

The sun was shining outside and the queen's carriage was still there, the driver stretched out asleep on the grass. Ulmenetha looked up at the bright, clean, blue of the sky with a gratitude she could scarce believe.

As the group approached the coachman yawned and stretched. Seeing the queen he scrambled to his feet and bowed.

'At your bidding, your highness,' he said.

'Take us to the palace,' ordered Ulmenetha.

Helping the queen into the carriage she glanced back at the two girls and the boy. All three were badly undernourished, clothed in rags. 'Get in,' she ordered them.

'Where you taking us?' asked the boy, suspiciously.

'Somewhere safer than this,' Ulmenetha replied.

They crowded in, followed by Dagorian. As the carriage moved away the young officer leaned in close to Ulmenetha. 'There is nowhere safe in the city,' he said, keeping his voice low.

'What do you suggest?'

'We must get to the coast, and find a ship. And we must do it before Malikada returns. We should head for the mountains.'

'There are forests there,' whispered Ulmenetha.

'You fear forests?' he asked, surprised by her reaction.

'The white crow will be there,' she told him. He was confused, but she turned away from him.

As the carriage made its way along the broad avenues Axiana saw the crowds milling. 'What is happening?' she asked. 'Why is everyone gathering so?'

'They have heard the news, highness. They are wondering what will happen to them now,' Dagorian explained.

'The news? What news?' she asked, mystified. Dagorian blinked, and transferred his gaze to Ulmenetha. She too was none the wiser.

The officer rubbed his hand over his stubbled jaw. 'I am truly sorry, your highness. But word has reached the city that our army was defeated by the Cadians.'

'That is not possible,' said Axiana. 'Skanda is the greatest warrior alive. You must be mistaken. This is just a rumour.'

Dagorian said nothing, but his gaze met that of Ulmenetha. The queen was looking out of the window again. Ulmenetha mouthed a question.

'The king?'

Dagorian shook his head. 'Then we must brave the forest,' said Ulmenetha.

Irritation crept into Malikada – a small, dark cloud in the clear blue sky of his joy. He stood on the hillside gazing down on the Drenai dead. Stripped now of armour and weapons, gone was their arrogance and their might. They were merely pale corpses, ready to be rolled into the huge pit being dug by Ventrian soldiers.

It was Malikada's moment of triumph. The army which had destroyed the empire of his ancestors was now ruined. He had always known revenge would be sweet, but had never guessed just how exquisite the taste would be.

Yet it was marred.

He swung to the swordsman, Antikas Karios. 'Now we will rebuild Ventria,' he said. 'And we will burn away the Drenai presence.'

'Yes, my lord,' replied Antikas, dully.

'What is wrong with you, man? Do you have the toothache?'

'No, my lord.'

'Then what?'

'They fought well and bravely, and it does not sit well with me that we betrayed them.'

Malikada's irritation flared into anger. 'How can you talk of betrayal? That would be their perspective. We fought them, you and I. We risked our lives to prevent Skanda's victories. The old emperor was weak and in-decisive, and yet we stood by him. We served him faithfully and well. At the last Skanda conquered us. We had two choices, Antikas. You remember that? We could have died, or we could have gone on fighting a different kind of war. We both chose the latter. We have remained true to our own cause. We are not traitors, Antikas. We are patriots.'

'Perhaps so, Lord. But this leaves a bad feeling in my stomach.'

'Then take your stomach elsewhere,' stormed Malikada. 'Go! Leave me to my pleasure.' Antikas bowed and walked away. Malikada watched the swordsman. He moved with such grace. The deadliest bladesman Malikada had ever seen, and yet, beneath it all, it now transpired, he was soft and weak! He had always envied Antikas, yet now he felt only contempt.

Malikada forced the image of the man from his mind, picturing again the moment when Skanda had signalled the charge. Oh, how he wished he could have been closer, to see the expression on the bastard's face, to witness the realization that he was doomed, that Malikada was ending his dreams of empire. Oh, how that must have eaten into Skanda's soul.

Irritation flared again within him. When Skanda had been dragged unconscious from the battlefield Kalizkan had refused permission for Malikada to witness the sacrifice. He would like to have seen that; to see the living heart cut from the body. A truly magnificent moment it would have been to stand over the king, their gaze locked together, watching the death agony, feeling Skanda's dying hatred. Malikada shivered with pleasure at the thought.

But then Kalizkan was a secretive man. Malikada had not been allowed to watch the old emperor's sacrifice either.

The corpses were being tumbled into the pit now, and covered with oil and dry wood. As the flames spread and black smoke spiralled up Malikada turned away. It was almost noon, and he needed to see Kalizkan. This was only the beginning. There were other Drenai garrisons along the coast, and there was still the problem of the White Wolf.

Also there was the question of Malikada's coronation.

Emperor Malikada! Now that had a fine sound. He would order Kalizkan to create an even greater illusion in the night skies over Usa – something that would dwarf the display Skanda had enjoyed.

He strolled back through the Ventrian camp towards the cliffs beyond. Red dust rose up around him as he walked, staining his highly polished boots. The cave entrance was dark, but he could see lantern light further inside. Stepping into the cave he felt a momentary fear. Kalizkan had become so withdrawn lately, and had ceased to treat him with his customary respect. Malikada had allowed the discourtesy, for he needed the man. His spells and his wizardry had been vital.

Had been vital.

The thought struck him that he no longer needed Kalizkan.

I need no-one, he realized. But I shall keep him with me. His skills will be more than useful when it comes time to invade the lands of the Drenai. But first there is Axiana. I shall wait until she has birthed the child, see it strangled, and then wed her myself. Who can then deny me the crown?

His good humour restored he continued on his way.

The body of Skanda was laid on a stone altar, the chest cut open. A linen cloth had been laid over his face. Kalizkan was sitting by a small fire, his blue satin robes stained with blood.

'Did he scream as he died?' asked Malikada.

Kalizkan rose. 'No, he did not scream. He cursed you with his last breath.'

'I would like to have heard that,' said Malikada.

There was a foul odour in the cave, and Malikada pulled a perfumed handkerchief from his pocket, holding it to his nose. 'What is that smell?' he asked.

'It is this form,' said Kalizkan. 'It has served its purpose, and is now rotting. And I have no wish to waste my enhanced powers sustaining it any longer.'

'Form? What are you talking about?'

'Kalizkan's body. It was already dying when I inhabited it. That was why he summoned me. To take away his cancer. I took him instead. His arrogance was overwhelming. How could he think to control Anharat, Lord of the Night?'

'You are making no sense, wizard.'

'On the contrary, Malikada. It all makes perfect sense, depending, of course, upon your perspective. I listened to your conversation with the swordsman. You were quite right. It is all a question of perspectives. Skanda believed you betrayed him, whereas you and I know you remained true to the one cause you believed in, the restoration of the Ventrian throne. Naturally with you to sit upon it. I, on the other hand, have no interest in the throne. And I have also remained true to my cause – the restoration of my people to the land which was once theirs by right and by force of arms.'

Malikada was suddenly frightened. He tried to back away, but found that his legs would not obey him. The perfumed handkerchief dropped from his fingers, and his arms fell uselessly to his sides. He was paralysed. He tried to shout for help, but, as his mouth opened, no sound came forth.

'I don't suppose,' said the creature within Kalizkan, 'that you are interested in my cause, save that to tell it will extend your life by a few moments.' The body of the wizard seemed to shimmer, and Malikada found himself gazing upon a rotting corpse. Half the flesh of the face had disappeared, the other half was grey-green and maggot infested. Malikada tried to shut his eyes, but even that was lost to him. 'My people,' said Kalizkan, 'lost a war. We were not killed. We were banished, to a grey, soulless world alongside your own. A world without colour, without taste, without hope. Now, thanks in small part to you, Malikada, we have the chance to live again. To feel the cold, heady night winds upon our faces, to taste the sweet joys that spring from human fear.'

Kalizkan came closer, and reached out his hand. Talons sprouted from the fingers. 'Oh yes, Malikada, let your terror flow. It is like wine, soft upon the tongue.' With an agonizing lack of speed the talons slowly pierced Malikada's chest.

'And now you can help me complete my mission. The queen, you see, has escaped from my home, and I need your form in order to use your men to hunt her down.'

The fierce pain of fire flowed through Malikada, searing its way across his chest, down into his belly, and up the spinal cord, exploding into his brain. It was an agony beyond enduring, and Kalizkan shivered with pleasure at it.

The talons ceased their probing as they closed around Malikada's heart. 'If I had more time,' said Anharat, 'I would hold you like this for some hours. But I have no time. So die, Malikada. Die in despair. Your world is ruined, and soon your people will be food for the Windborn.' The Ventrian's corpse twitched. The rotting body of Kalizkan fell to the floor.

Within Malikada now the demon stretched out his new arms. Kalizkan's body burst into flames.

Stepping back the new Malikada strode to the cave entrance. Lifting his hand he focused his concentration on the rocks above him. Dust filtered down, the rocks groaned. Malikada stepped into the sunlight.

And the cave ceiling crashed down behind him, blocking the entrance.

He strode down to where his men were waiting, pausing only to sniff the smoke rising from the great pyre. There was a delicious sweetness to it.

Back at his tent he summoned Antikas Karios. The swordsman bowed low.

'Go to the city and find the queen,' said Malikada. 'Protect her until my arrival.'

'Yes, my lord. Protect her from whom?'

'Just make sure she is there when I arrive.'

'I shall leave immediately, my lord.'

'Do not fail me, Antikas.'

An angry look came into the swordsman's deep, dark eyes. 'When have I ever failed you, cousin?'

'Never,' replied Malikada, 'and now is not the time to start.'

Antikas said nothing for a moment, but the demon within Malikada felt the swordsman's piercing gaze. Coolly he cast a small spell, which radiated from him, surrounding Antikas. The swordsman relaxed.

'It will be as you command,' he said.

'Take spare horses and ride all night. Be there before the dawn.'

The carriage moved slowly through the city streets. Crowds were everywhere now, and as dusk deepened, the riots began in the poorer quarters of the city. Several buildings were set afire. 'Why do they do this?' asked Axiana, watching the distant smoke, and hearing the far-off screams. 'What purpose does it achieve?'

Dagorian shrugged. 'That is hard to explain, your highness. Some people are in a state of panic. They fear the Cadians will descend on them with fire and sword.

Others know that with the army destroyed they are free to commit crimes they would otherwise have been punished for. They see the disaster as an opportunity to obtain wealth they could not hope to earn. I do not know all the reasons. But there will be many deaths tonight.'

The carriage pulled into the palace grounds, where it was stopped by an officer of the guards, and a squad of spear men. The man opened the door, saw the queen, and bowed low.

'Thank the Source you are safe, your highness,' he said. She gave him a wan smile, and the carriage moved on.

Inside the queen's apartments Axiana sank to a couch, resting her head on a satin pillow, and fell asleep. Ulmenetha began to gather clothes for the queen, packing them carefully into an ornate wooden chest. Then she went with the children to the deserted kitchens, where she gathered food: sides of ham, some hard cheese wrapped in muslin, and several small sacks of flour, sugar and salt. The children sat close by, gorging themselves on bread and preserves, washed down with fresh milk. Ulmenetha paused and watched them.

'What happened in that orphanage?' she asked the red-headed boy.

His bright blue eyes were suddenly fearful, but his expression remained set and hard. 'Children died,' he said. 'Everybody said Kalizkan was kind. You could be sure of a meal there. Lots of my friends had already gone. We went there ten days ago.' The boy closed his eyes and took a deep breath. 'Most of my friends were dead by then, but I didn't know. They used to take them underground, but you could still hear the screams.' He opened his eyes. 'I don't want to talk about it.'

'I understand,' said the priestess. Moving opposite the children she sat down. 'Listen to me. We are leaving the city. Tonight. You can come with us if you wish, or you can stay in Usa. It is up to you.'

'Where are you going?' asked the older girl, her deep, dark eyes holding to Ulmenetha's gaze.

'We will try to find a way to the coast, and then a ship to Drenan. It is a long way, and I think it will be a perilous journey. You may be safer here.'

'I am Drenai,' said the girl. 'Or at least my father was Drenai. I will come with you. There is nothing here for me. I do not want to stay.'

'You won't leave me here!' wailed the small blonde child, taking hold of the girl's hand.

'I won't leave you, little one. You can come with us.'

'Why should we go?' asked the boy. 'I can steal food for all of us.'

Reaching out she ran her fingers through his tangled red hair. 'Maybe in Drenan you won't have to steal food. We could live in a house.'

The boy swore. 'Who's going to give us a house, Pharis? Nobody *gives* anyone anything. You get nothing for nothing. That's the way of it.'

'You found food for me, Conalin. And you looked after Sufia when she was sick. You got nothing in return.'

'You're my friends and I love you. That's different. How do you know you can trust this fat woman?'

The girl looked up again into Ulmenetha's eyes. 'She came to rescue her friend. And she fought the beast. I trust her.'

'Well, I don't want to go,' said the boy, stubbornly.

'If you don't come, who will protect little Sufia?' she said.

'Oh, please come with us, Con,' pleaded Sufia. 'Please!'

He sat silently for a moment, then stared up at Ulmenetha, his eyes angry. 'Why should we trust you?' he asked her.

'I can offer no reason, Conalin. Save that I never lie. And I promise you this: If we reach Drenan safely the queen will buy you a house.'

'Why should you? You owe us nothing.'

'That is not true. Your bravery, and that of your sister, helped to kill the . . . beast, as you call it. Had you not helped me I would have been killed.'

'She's not my sister. She's Pharis, my friend. And if she and Sufia are going, I'll come too. But I don't believe you about the house.'

'Wait and see,' said Ulmenetha. 'Now let's find some sacks for supplies, and fill them. We don't want to be hungry when we reach the mountains.'

Back in the apartments the queen was asleep on the couch, and Dagorian had swapped his beggar's rags for one of Skanda's grey woollen tunics. It was emblazoned with a rearing white horse at the shoulder. He stood now on the balcony, watching the glow from the fires in the western quarter.

The rioting would die down during the night, and their best chance of escape lay in the hour before dawn, when the rioters were asleep, and the soldiers of the Watch were busy with the aftermath of the chaos.

Escape?

How long before the pursuit began? And how fast could they travel? The queen was heavily pregnant, the child due within days. She could not ride a horse at speed. The threat of miscarriage was too great. That meant taking a wagon. Hard-riding horsemen would catch them within hours.

Perhaps it would be wiser to try to reach Banelion. The White Wolf and his men could not be further than a few days' ride to the west.

He dismissed the idea. That would be the enemy's first thought. And anyway what could a few hundred old men do against Malikada's Ventrian army? Joining Banelion would merely serve a death warrant on more Drenai soldiers.

What then?

Some deception was necessary. Something that would give them time.

He heard the queen give out a soft moan in her sleep and moved back into the apartment. Sitting down beside her he gently took her hand. 'I will defend you with my life,' he whispered.

Ulmenetha watched him from the doorway. He was holding her hand with great tenderness and she realized, in that moment, that the young man was in love with Axiana. Sadness touched her. In a just world they would have met two years ago, when both were free. Even if she returned his love Axiana was carrying the heir to the throne of two nations. Her life would remain ruled by men of power. And they would never sanction a marriage to a junior officer like Dagorian.

Clearing her throat she stepped into the room, the children following her, bearing sacks of supplies.

'What now?' she asked Dagorian.

Releasing the queen's hand he rose. 'Are the children coming with us?' Ulmenetha nodded. 'Good,' he said. 'We will need a wagon and extra horses. I will find them. The queen must be disguised. No silks nor satins. No jewellery. We will leave the city as a poor family, fleeing from the riots. There will be many such over the next few days. With luck we will pass unnoticed among them. This will slow down the pursuit.'

'What can I do while you are fetching a wagon?'

'Find maps of the mountains. There will be many box canyons, broken trails, and treacherous areas. It would be helpful if we could plan a route, and not move blindly on faith alone.'

Swirling a dark cloak around his shoulders Dagorian left them. The youngest child, Sufia, was exhausted, and Pharis led her to a couch, where she lay down and fell asleep. Leaving the children in the apartment Ulmenetha took a lantern and made her way to the Royal Library on the ground floor. There were thousands of books here, and hundreds of scrolls. She searched for some time through the index, locating three ancient maps of the mountains, and also a traveller's diary that told of the trek from Usa to Perapolis in the south. If the Source was with them they would be following this route for at least part of the way.

Returning to the apartment she found the red-headed boy, Conalin, sitting on the balcony. Pharis and Sufia were cuddled together on the couch, fast asleep. She covered them with a blanket then moved to Axiana. The queen stirred, opened her eyes, and smiled sleepily. 'I had a terrible dream,' she said.

'Rest, my lady. You will need your strength in the morning.' Axiana closed her eyes.

Ulmenetha walked out onto the balcony. The western quarter of the city was ablaze, and she could hear distant screams. 'Are you not tired?' she asked Conalin.

'I am strong,' he said.

'I know that. But even the strong need sleep.'

'They are killing one another,' he said, gesturing

towards the distant flames. 'Robbing, looting, raping. Slaughtering the weak.'

'Does it sadden you?'

'It is what the weak are for,' he said, solemnly. 'That is why I shall never be weak.'

'How did you come to meet Pharis and the child?'

'Why do you want to know?' he demanded.

'I am making conversation, Conalin. If we are to be friends we need to know one another. That is the way of things. What is Pharis's favourite food?'

'Plums. Why?'

She smiled. 'That is part of knowing a friend. When you go out to steal food you will look for a plum for Pharis, because you know she likes them. Knowing is good among friends. So where did you meet?'

'Her mother's a whore who worked Merchant Alley. I first saw Pharis there. Two summers ago. Her mother was drunk, and lying in the gutter. Pharis was trying to lift her, to get her home.'

'And you helped?'

'Yes.'

'Why did you do that?'

'What do you mean?'

Ulmenetha shrugged. 'You were helping the weak, Conalin. Why did you not just rob her and walk away?'

'That's what I was going to do,' he snapped. 'I saw her lying there and I knew she'd have coin from the men she'd doxied. But then Pharis came along. She saw me standing there and she said, "Take her arm." So I did. Anyway, that's how we met.'

'What happened to the mother?'

Now it was his turn to shrug. 'She's still around. She sold Pharis to a whorehouse. Where rich men like to fondle young girls. I took her away from that. I climbed through the rear window one night, and I got her out.'

'That was very brave of you.' He seemed pleased at the compliment and his hard face relaxed. As it did so he looked younger, and terribly vulnerable. Ulmenetha wanted to reach out and stroke his tangled red hair, to draw him to her. He spoke again.

'Had to pick the lock on her room. And all the while the Breaker was asleep in a chair next to it.'

'The Breaker?' she enquired.

'The leg-breaker. The man who watches out for the girls. Well, they say he watches out for them, but if a girl won't do what she's told he bashes them.' He grinned suddenly. 'I bet he was in real trouble the following morning.'

'And what about Sufia?'

'We found her in that wizard's house. She was hiding under a bed. She was the last of them. Why was he killing children?' he asked her.

'He was, I believe, making blood magic,' said Ulmenetha. 'It is a vile practice.'

'There's a lot of them,' he said, softly. 'Vile practices.'

'Tell me about you,' she said.

'No,' he said, simply. 'I don't talk about me. But you are right, I am tired. I think I'll sleep now for a while.'

'I'll wake you when Dagorian gets back.'

'You won't have to,' he assured her.

Out on the streets the rioting continued unabated. Dagorian had avoided the guards by climbing over the palace wall, and dropping down onto the broad Avenue of Kings. From here he could see several bodies, sprawled in death. Rioters moved into sight, swilling looted wine. Keeping to the shadows he moved down the Avenue, then darted across it to one of the wide roads leading to the Merchants' Acre. Here, he knew, were the hauliers who daily distributed the merchants' wares to shops, homes and market stalls in the city.

He reached the first to find the buildings engulfed by flames, and could see wagons burning on the open ground beyond. Anger swept through him, threatening to engulf his mind. He wanted to draw his sword and run at the rioters, hacking and slashing. His fingers closed around the hilt of his sabre. A voice whispered into his mind, cold and calm, dispelling the fury.

'Do not let them possess you, Dagorian. They are everywhere.'

Dagorian leaned back against a wall, his hands shaking with the aftermath of rage. 'Who are you?' he whispered.

'A friend. You remember me? I came to you when the demons were rending your soul. And again at the home of the murdered seer.'

'I remember.'

'Know this, then, child: The city is possessed, and the demons are feasting on rage and murder. Every hour they grow stronger. By tomorrow no-one will be able to resist them. Do not succumb. Think clearly and coolly. I will be with you, though I will not speak again. Now find a wagon!'

The officer moved away from the wall, and ducked down a narrow alley. Smoke, thicker than any fog, hung in the air, burning his lungs. Holding his cloak over his face Dagorian ran on. The sounds of screaming came from all around him now, from the burning buildings where people were trapped, from the alleyways, where victims had been cornered.

Anger touched him again, but he fought it down.

He came to the wide gates of a second haulier. They had been burst open and a group of men and women carrying torches were running around the yard, setting the wagons ablaze. Others had thrown torches into the stables, igniting the straw inside. Horses were whinnying in terror. Cutting across the yard Dagorian opened the stable doors, ran inside, freeing all but two of the horses. Panic stricken the freed beasts galloped into the yard, scattering the rioters.

Moving to the remaining two horses Dagorian calmed them as best he could and led them from the stable. Fear was strong upon them, but they were used to the sure touch of their handlers, and they accepted Dagorian's authority. In the yard he tethered them to a wagon untouched by the rioters. The traces and brasses used to hitch the horses were laid over the back of the wagon. Dagorian moved to them.

A rioter ran forwards, tossing a torch to the wagon seat. Dagorian spun on his heel and sent a thundering right cross to the man's jaw. He fell without a sound. Hurling the torch aside he moved to the traces. A whoosh of burning air seared across the yard as flames burst through the stables' wall. The horses reared. Once more Dagorian tried to calm them, stroking their long necks, whispering soothing words. The heat was intense and the rioters moved away. Dagorian hitched the horses and climbed to the driver's seat. Releasing the brake he took up the whip and cracked it. The horses surged into the traces and the wagon moved forward. But to exit the yard they had to drive past the burning stables and the horses faltered, unwilling to face the flames again.

In the back of the wagon were several empty sacks. With his dagger he sliced two strips from one of them. Leaping to the ground he blindfolded the horses. Back in the driver's seat he cracked the whip. Reluctantly the team moved on. He could feel them faltering again as the heat swelled, but lashed them both with the whip and shouted at the top of his voice. The horses powered into the traces and the wagon rolled past the burning building and out into the road beyond.

Swinging them to the right he took them at speed down towards the Avenue of Kings.

Another mob was gathered there, but they scattered as the wagon bore down on them. One man ran forward and leapt at him. His face was a twisted mask of hatred, his eyes staring wide. Dagorian lashed out with his foot, kicking the attacker in the chest, and pitching him to the street. Up ahead a group of men tried to block his way, but the horses were galloping now, and would not be stopped. A hurled knife thudded into the backrest behind him, but then he was clear of them, and the palace gates were in sight.

They were open. And no guards could be seen.

Dagorian drove through, then dragged on the reins, hauling the horses to a stop.

Jumping down he struggled with the wrought-iron gates, pulling them closed.

They would not hold firm against a mob, he knew. Mounting the wagon again he drove it to the main doors.

The sky was lightening as he ran into the building, and up the long, winding staircase. The queen was awake now, and dressed in a simple woollen gown of blue, edged with white cotton.

'We must go quickly,' said Dagorian. 'The mob will soon be here.'

'Go? Where should I go? I am the queen. They will not harm me,' said Axiana. 'They are my people and they love me.' Her slender fingers touched the sleeve of her gown. 'And I will not wear this revolting outfit. It scratches my skin.'

'A mob does not know of love,' said Dagorian. 'They are outside killing each other, raping and looting. It will not be long before they realize that true riches can be found here.'

'My cousin Malikada will be back soon. He will protect me,' said Axiana.

'Please, my dove,' urged Ulmenetha, 'trust me! Your life is in danger, and we must flee the city.'

'The nobility are not given to panic, Ulmenetha. And certainly not in the face of peasant unrest.'

'It is not merely *unrest*,' Dagorian told her. 'The mobs are possessed.'

'Possessed? That cannot be!'

'It is true, highness. I swear it. I discovered the demons while investigating a series of murders. I believe Kalizkan summoned them. I have seen mobs before, and I have been out there among those demented people. There is a difference, believe me.'

'You are saying this to frighten me,' insisted Axiana.

Ulmenetha approached the queen. 'What he says is true, my dove. I have known about these demons for some time. I also know that Kalizkan is a walking corpse. He too is possessed. You saw the creature at his house. It was a *zhagul*. A dead man. I think we should listen to Dagorian and follow him to the mountains.'

'I will not!' insisted Axiana, drawing back, her eyes fearful. 'Malikada will protect me. I will tell him of Kalizkan's evil and he will punish him.'

Ulmenetha stepped in close and put her hands on Axiana's shoulders. 'Be calm,' she said, softly. 'I am here. All will be well.' Her right hand lifted, as if to stroke the queen's brow. Dagorian saw a blue light radiate from her palm. Axiana fell forward into Ulmenetha's arms. The priestess lowered her to a couch. 'She will sleep for several hours,' she said.

'You are a sorceress?' whispered Dagorian.

'I am a priestess!' she snapped. 'There is a difference. The little magic I know is used for healing. Now carry her down – and be careful with her.'

Dagorian lifted Axiana to his arms. Despite her pregnancy she was not heavy and he carried her to the wagon, lifting her to the tailboard. Ulmenetha settled her down, rolling an empty sack for a pillow, and covering her with a blanket. Pharis and Sufia scrambled aboard, and Conalin climbed to the driver's seat. Dagorian stepped up to sit beside him.

Dagorian drove the wagon to the royal stables, and there saddled a warhorse of some seventeen hands. 'Can you drive the wagon?' he asked Conalin. The boy nodded.

'Good. Then I will clear a way to the East Gate. If I go down do not stop. You understand?'

'Oh, I won't stop,' said Conalin. 'You can count on that.'

'Then let's go.'

The Avenue of Kings was deserted now, and eerily quiet. Dagorian led the way, the sound of his horse's hoof beats like slow beating war drums. He drew his sabre and scanned the Avenue. There was not a sign of life.

The dawn sun cleared the mountains.

The wagon moved on. After half a mile they saw a group of men sitting quietly by the roadside. They were blood smeared, their clothing stained by smoke. They looked up at the wagon, but made no hostile moves. Their eyes were dull, and they seemed weary beyond reckoning.

Dagorian sheathed his sabre.

They reached the gate and found themselves waiting in a line of some twenty wagons and coaches, all filled with fleeing families and their possessions. The gate arch was narrow, and it was taking time to manoeuvre the wagons through. A group of riders arrived from outside the city, but could not pass, and Dagorian heard the beginnings of an angry exchange.

Dismounting he tethered his horse and was about to climb onto the wagon when he heard the voice of Antikas Karios, ordering a wagon driver to draw his vehicle aside. Ducking down below the wagon he waited until the group cleared the gate, and thundered their mounts towards the palace.

The wait now to leave the city seemed interminable. Two impatient drivers moved forward at the same time. One of the horses reared, and lashed out at the opposing team. Both drivers leapt down and began a heated argument. Dagorian's patience snapped. Vaulting to the saddle he rode to the shouting men. Drawing his sabre he held the blade to the neck of the first. 'Back off,' he said, 'or I'll gut you like a fish!' The argument died instantly. The man scrambled back to his wagon and hauled on the reins, reversing his team. Swinging in the saddle Dagorian shouted to Conalin. 'Drive through!'

And then they were out onto open ground.

Conalin headed the horses up the long slope towards the mountains. Dagorian rode alongside, constantly looking back, expecting at any moment to see pursuers galloping after them. 'Give them a touch of the whip!' he ordered Conalin. The boy did so and the horses broke into a run. In the back of the wagon Ulmenetha was thrown to one side. The child Sufia began to cry. Ulmenetha gathered her close. 'There is nothing to fear,' she said, soothingly. The horses were breathing heavily as they reached the crest of the hill, dropping down on the other side. Out of sight of the city Dagorian ordered Conalin to slow down and continue following the road south and west.

The officer rode back to the rise and dismounted. Minutes later he saw Antikas Karios and his men leave the city. For one dreadful moment he thought they were heading in pursuit, but they turned due west along the merchant road.

How long before they realized their mistake? An hour? Less?

Back in the saddle he caught up with the wagon. Axiana was conscious now, and sitting silently, staring out over the mountains. Dagorian hitched his horse to the wagon and climbed aboard. 'We have lost them for now,' he told Ulmenetha. 'Where are the maps?'

Ulmenetha passed him the first. It was an old, dry scroll, which he carefully unrolled. The city depicted was vastly smaller than the metropolis Usa had become, but the mountain roads were clearly marked. They formed part of a trade route to the ghost city of Lem, 200 miles south. Built around the wealth of nearby silver mines – which had failed more than 200 years ago – Lem was now an abandoned series of ruins. Dagorian studied the map carefully. They would travel south for just over a hundred miles, then swing to the west for another 70 miles, crossing the Carpos mountains and picking up the coast road to Caphis. It was not the nearest of the ports, but the route was less well travelled, and should help them avoid the dangers of bandits and rebel tribesmen. Merchants were constantly harassed by such bands around the closest port, Morec.

A secondary factor in choosing Caphis, but nonetheless important, was that Malikada was likely to expect them to head for Morec, the intended destination of the White Wolf and his men.

He showed the route to Ulmenetha. She peered at the map. 'What do the symbols mean?' she asked him, tapping the scroll with her finger.

'They are a form of shorthand taken from High Ventrian. This one, which looks like the head of a ram, is a pictorial representation of three letters, N.W.P. It stands for no winter passage.'

'And the figures?'

'Distance between set points, using not the mile, but the Ventrian league. These will not be precise.'

'How far must we travel?' asked Pharis.

'Perhaps two hundred and fifty miles, much of it over rough country. We have no spare horses, so we will have to move with care, conserving the animals as best we can. With luck we will be in Caphis within a month. It is but a short trip then across the sea to Dros Purdol – and home!'

'Whose home?' asked Axiana, suddenly. Dagorian looked across at the queen. Her face was pale, her dark eyes angry. 'It is not my home. My home was raided by Drenai savages from across the sea. These same savages saw my father slain, and forced me to wed their leader. Is Axiana going home? No, she is being kidnapped and taken *from* her home.'

The officer was silent for a moment. 'I am sorry, your highness,' he said, at last. 'I am one of those Drenai savages. But I would willingly give my life for you. I have brought you from the city because you are in danger. Kalizkan is a monster. And, for purposes which I do not fully understand, desires to kill the child you carry. He and Malikada are in league. Of that I have no doubt.

Malikada delivered your father to him. Kalizkan killed him. Now Malikada's treachery has seen Skanda similarly murdered. If it is in my power to bring you safely to Drenan then I shall. After that you will be free. You will be fêted as the queen, and, if it is possible, an army will bring you back to Ventria and establish you once more upon the throne.'

Axiana shook her head. 'How can you be so naive, Dagorian? You think the Drenai nobility will care about me? I am a foreigner. You think they will support my child? I think not. He will die, poisoned or strangled, and some other *Drenai* nobleman will take the throne. That is the way it will be. You say Malikada delivered up my father. I can believe that. He loathed him, thought him weak, and blamed him for the losses against Skanda. You say he betrayed Skanda. This I can also believe, for he hated him. But he has always loved me. He is my cousin and would do nothing to harm me.'

'And the babe you carry?' asked Ulmenetha.

'I care nothing for him. He is a poisoned gift from Skanda. Let them take him. And as for you, Dagorian, return to your horse. I find your company repulsive.'

The words hurt him, but he stood, untied the reins of his mount and stepped into the saddle. Ulmenetha gathered up the map. 'You are wrong, highness,' she said, softly.

'I need to hear no words from you, traitress.'

A dry chuckle came from Conalin. He glanced back at Ulmenetha. 'You save her from the beast and she calls you names. Gods, how I hate the rich.'

Axiana made no reply, but stared out over the snow-capped mountains, her face set, her expression unreadable. She wanted to apologize to Ulmenetha, to say that the words were spoken in anger. Ingratitude was not one of Axiana's weaknesses. She knew that the priestess had risked her life to save her from the undead creature in Kalizkan's house. More than this, she knew that Ulmenetha loved her, and would never willingly see her come to harm.

But Axiana was frightened. Raised at court, her every whim catered to instantly, the events of the past two days had been deeply shocking to her. In the space of forty-eight hours she had been locked in a dank room, witnessed violent death, heard of her husband's murder, and was now in a creaking wagon, heading into the wild lands. She felt as if her mind was unravelling. Kalizkan, whom she had trusted and been fond of, was now revealed as a mass murderer, a child-killing beast. The Source alone knew what he had planned for her. She shuddered.

'Are you cold, my dove?' Ulmenetha asked her. Axiana nodded dumbly. The priestess moved to her, laying a blanket over her shoulders. Tears welled in Axiana's eyes. The wagon lurched over a rut in the road and Axiana half fell into Ulmenetha. The priestess caught her. Axiana rested her head against Ulmenetha's shoulder.

'I'm sorry,' she whispered.

'I know, child.'

'The baby is due soon. I am very frightened.'

'I will be here. And you are strong. Everything will be all right.'

Axiana took a deep breath, then sat upright. She could see Dagorian riding ahead, scanning the trail. They were heading towards a forest that covered the flanks of the hills like a buffalo robe. Axiana glanced back. The city of Usa could no longer be seen behind them.

The dark-haired Pharis took a red apple from a food sack, and offered it to Axiana. The queen accepted it with a smile, then looked at the girl. She was terribly thin and undernourished, but her face was pretty, her eyes large and brown. Axiana had never been this close to a commoner. She studied Pharis's thin dress. It was impossible to say what colour it had once been, for it was now a drab, lifeless grey, torn at the shoulder, the hip and the elbow, and badly frayed at the wrists and the neck. It would not have been used as a cleaning rag in the palace. Reaching out she touched the material. It was rough and dirty. Pharis drew back, and Axiana saw her expression change. The girl swung away and moved back to sit with Sufia.

At that moment the child within her moved. She gave a little cry. Then she smiled. 'He kicked me,' she said. Ulmenetha gently placed her hand over Axiana's swollen belly.

'Yes, I can feel him. He's lusty and anxious for life.'

'Can I feel him?' asked little Sufia, scrambling back on her hands and knees. Axiana gazed down into her bright blue eyes.

'Of course,' she said. Taking the child's small, grimy hand, she placed it over her stomach. For a moment there was no movement, then the baby kicked again. Sufia squealed with delight.

'Pharis, Pharis, come feel!' she cried.

Pharis looked up and met the queen's gaze. Axiana smiled and held out her hand. Pharis moved to her, and the baby obediently kicked once more.

'How did it get in there?' asked Sufia. 'And how will it get out?'

'Magic,' said Ulmenetha, swiftly. 'How old are you, Sufia?' she added, changing the subject. The child shrugged.

'I don't know. My brother Griss said he was six. And I'm younger than Griss.'

'Where is your brother?' asked Axiana, stroking Sufia's greasy blond hair.

'The wizard man took him away.' She was suddenly frightened. 'You won't let him take me away, will you?'

'Nobody will take you away, little one,' said Conalin, fiercely. 'I'll kill any who try.'

This pleased Sufia. She looked up at Conalin. 'Can I drive the wagon?' she asked.

Pharis helped her clamber over the backrest, and Conalin sat her on his lap, allowing her to hold the reins.

Axiana bit into the apple. It was sweet, wondrously sweet.

They had just reached the trees when they heard the sound of thundering hoof beats. Axiana glanced back. Five horsemen were cresting the rise behind them.

Dagorian galloped back to the wagon, his sabre gleaming in his hand.

Chapter Seven

Vellian had been a fighting man for fifteen of his twenty-nine years, and had served Malikada and Antikas Karios for twelve of them. He had joined the Ventrian army for the Great Expedition; the invasion of Drenan, and the righting of ancient wrongs. Every Ventrian child knew of Drenai infamy, their broken treaties, their territorial impudence, and their killing, centuries before, of the Great Emperor Gorben.

The invasion was to have put right all past wrongs.

That, at least, was how it was sold to the fourteen-year-old Vellian when the recruiting officers arrived at his village. There was no greater honour, they said, than serving the emperor in a just cause. They made extravagant promises about wealth and glory. The wealth did not interest Vellian, but thoughts of glory swept through him like a powerful drug. He signed that day, without seeking permission from his parents, and rode away to smite the savages and seek his fame.

Now he rode a weary horse on the Old Lem road, and all his dreams were dust.

He had watched the Drenai army in their hopeless battle against the Cadians and had felt the enormous weight of shame. None of the junior officers had known of Malikada's plan, and they had waited, swords drawn, for the signal to attack. The Drenai centre had fought bravely, driving a wedge into the Cadian ranks. The battle was won. Or it would have been, had the Ventrian cavalry moved in on the signal and attacked. Every man saw the signal, and some even began to move forward. Then Malikada had shouted: 'Hold firm!'

Vellian had at first believed it to be part of some subtle, superior plan worked out between Skanda and Malikada. But as the hour wore on, and the Drenai died in their thousands, the truth revealed itself. Malikada, a man he had served loyally for almost half his life, had betrayed the king.

There was worse to come. Skanda was taken alive, and delivered to a cave high in the mountains, where the wizard Kalizkan waited. He was taken inside and sacrificed in some foul rite.

For the first time Vellian considered desertion. He had been raised to value honour and loyalty and the pursuit of the truth. He believed in these things. They were at the heart of any civilized nation. Without them there was anarchy, chaos, and a rapid descent into the dark.

There was no honour in betrayal.

Then Antikas Karios had come to him, ordering him to gather his Twenty and follow him to Usa to protect the queen. This duty, at least, was honourable.

They had found the city in flames, bodies on the streets, and the palace deserted. No-one knew where the queen was hiding. Then Antikas questioned a group of men on the Avenue of Kings. They had seen a wagon leave the palace. A red-headed boy was driving it, and a soldier was riding beside it. There were women in the wagon, and it was heading towards the west gate.

Antikas had split the Twenty into four groups, and sent Vellian to the south.

'I may not come back, sir,' he told him. 'I have a desire to leave the army.'

Antikas had pondered the statement, then he gestured Vellian to follow him, and rode away from the other soldiers. 'What is wrong?' Antikas had asked him.

'I would say just about everything,' Vellian told him, sadly.

'You are referring to the battle.'

'To the slaughter, you mean? To the treachery.' He expected Antikas to draw his blade and cut him down, and was surprised when the officer laid a hand upon his shoulder.

'You are the best of them, Vellian. You are brave and honest, and I value you above all other officers. But you betrayed no-one. You merely obeyed your general. The weight of responsibility is his alone. So I say this to you: Ride south and if you find the queen bring her back to Usa. If you do not find her then go where you will with my blessing. Will you do this? For me?'

'I will, sir. Might I ask one question?'

'Of course.'

'Did you know of the plan?'

'I did – to my eternal shame. Now go – and do this last duty.'

An hour of hard riding followed, and then Vellian saw the wagon. As the men had said it was being driven by a youth with red hair. A child was sitting on the seat with him, and in the rear of the wagon were three women.

And one was the queen.

The soldier with them had drawn his sabre.

Keeping his hands on the reins Vellian rode his horse down the slope, and halted before the rider. His men rode alongside him. 'Good morning,' he said. 'I am Vellian, sent by the General Antikas Karios to fetch the queen back to her palace. The city is quiet now and the army will be returning before tomorrow to fully restore order.'

'An army of traitors,' said Dagorian, coldly. Vellian reddened.

'Yes,' he agreed. 'Now return your sabre to its scabbard and let us be on our way.'

'I don't think so,' said Dagorian. 'The queen is in great danger. She will be safer with me.'

'Danger from whom?' asked Vellian, unsure as to how to proceed.

'The sorcerer, Kalizkan.'

'Then put your fears at rest, for he is dead, killed in a rock fall.'

'I don't believe you.'

'I am not known as a liar, sir.'

'Neither am I, Vellian. But I have pledged my life to protect the queen. This I will do. You ask me to turn her over to you. Did you not pledge your life to protect her husband the king?' Vellian said nothing. 'Well,' continued Dagorian, 'since you failed in that I see no reason to trust you now.'

'Do not be a fool, man. You may be as skilled as Antikas himself with that sabre, but you cannot beat five of us. What is the point then of dying, when the cause is already lost?'

'What is the point of living without a cause worth dying for?' countered Dagorian.

'So be it,' said Vellian, sadly. 'Take him!'

The four riders drew their sabres. Dagorian gave out a yell and slapped the flat of his sabre on his horse's flanks. The beast leapt forward, straight into the group. One horse went down, two others reared. Swinging his mount Dagorian slashed his sabre across the shoulder of the nearest rider. The blade sank deep, then sang clear. Vellian stabbed at him, but Dagorian parried the thrust, sending a counter strike that sliced across Vellian's chest, cutting through his tunic and opening a shallow wound.

A rider moved in behind Dagorian, his sabre raised.

An arrow pierced the man's temple, pitching him from the saddle.

Then Nogusta came galloping into sight. Dagorian saw his arm go back, then snap forward. A shining blade flashed through the air, sinking deep into the throat of a second rider. Vellian attacked Dagorian, but his blade was parried. Dagorian's return cut missed him, but in swaying back Vellian almost lost his balance. His horse reared, hurling him to the ground. He landed heavily, and was stunned for a moment. Struggling to his knees he gathered his sabre and looked around him. All four of his men were dead.

Dagorian dismounted and approached him. Vellian stood his ground. From the trees came two other warriors, a bald giant with a white moustache, and an archer Vellian recognized as Kebra, the former champion. 'It seems,' said Vellian, 'that the roles are now reversed.'

'I have no wish to kill you,' said Dagorian. 'You may travel with us as our prisoner. You will be released when we reach the coast.'

'I think not,' said Vellian. 'How could I fail to follow so bold an example.'

Leaping forward he launched an attack. Their blades clashed, again and again. Just for a moment he felt he could win, but then a murderous riposte from Dagorian sent a spasm of fire through Vellian's chest. The sabre slid clear and the Ventrian sank to the ground.

He was lying now on the grass, looking up at the blue sky. 'I would also have protected the queen with my life,' he heard himself say.

'I know.'

* * *

For Axiana the rest of the day had a dreamlike quality, both real and unreal. The lurching of the wagon over the narrow forest trail, and the smell of damp earth, and green leaves, were strong and vital. But as she gazed about her at the faces of her companions she felt a curious sense of detachment. Apart from little Sufia they all seemed so tense, their movements sharp, their eyes frightened. Well, not all, she realized, her gaze settling on the black warrior. There was no fear in those strange blue eyes.

Dagorian rode silently alongside the wagon, occasionally swinging in the saddle to study the back trail. There was little to be seen, for they were deep in the forest now, the trail snaking through the trees. Yet still he looked. The other three also rode silently. Twice the black man left the group, riding the huge gelding back along the trail. The other two had placed themselves on either side of the wagon, only dropping back when the trail narrowed, and the trees closed in.

Axiana remembered the bowman, Kebra. He it was who had lost the tournament, and caused Skanda such anger. And the other fellow – Kebra called him Bison – was a hulking brute with a drooping white moustache.

The queen had never before been in a forest. Her father had often hunted here. He had killed lion and bear, deer and elk. She recalled seeing the trophies from her window. The bodies had looked so sad, slung upon the back of the wagon.

Bear and lion.

The thought did not frighten her. All fear had gone now. She was floating in harmony, living in the moment.

'How are you feeling?' asked Ulmenetha, placing her hand on the queen's arm. Axiana looked down at the hand. It was an impertinence to touch her, and yet she felt no anger.

'I am well.' Sunlight broke through the clouds, and speared through a gap in the trees ahead, slanted columns of gold illuminating the trail. 'How pretty,' said Axiana, dreamily. She saw the concern in Ulmenetha's eyes, but did not understand it. 'We should be getting back to the city,' she said. 'It will be dark soon.'

Ulmenetha did not reply, but moved in, drawing her close and cuddling her. She settled her head on Ulmenetha's shoulder. 'I am very tired.'

'You rest, my dove. Ulmenetha will look after you.'

Axiana saw the five horses tied to the rear of the wagon, and her body tensed. Ulmenetha held her close. 'What is wrong?' asked the priestess.

'Those horses . . . where did we get them?'

'We took them from the soldiers who attacked us.'

'That was just a dream,' said Axiana. 'No soldiers would attack me. I am the queen. No soldiers would attack me. No-one would lock me away. There are no walking dead men. It is all a dream.' She began to tremble and felt Ulmenetha's hand touch her face. Then she slid gratefully into darkness.

When she opened her eyes she saw bright stars in the sky. She yawned. 'I dreamt I was in Morec,' she said, sitting up. 'I grew up there. In the spring palace overlooking the bay. I used to watch the dolphins there.'

'Was it a nice dream?'

'Yes.' Axiana looked around. The trees were shadow-haunted now, and the temperature was dropping. Here and there, in sheltered hollows, the snow still lay on the ground. 'Where are we?'

'I'm not sure,' replied Ulmenetha. 'But we will be making camp soon.'

'Camp? Are we camping?'

'Yes.'

'Is there no house close by?'

'No,' said Ulmenetha, softly. 'No house. But it will be safe.'

'From bears and lions,' said Axiana, trying to sound authoritative.

'Yes, highness.'

Dagorian rode alongside the wagon and climbed to the driver's seat. 'Hold tight,' he said, taking the reins from Conalin. 'We are leaving the trail.' The wagon lurched to the right and down a shallow slope. Ulmenetha held on to Axiana. Dagorian drove the wagon down to a shallow stream. Kebra and Bison rode their horses across to where the black man waited. There was a fire burning against the cliff wall. The weary horses splashed into the stream and Dagorian cracked the whip twice as the wagon was slowly hauled across. Once on the other side he turned the team and applied the brake.

Ulmenetha helped the queen to climb down, and led her to the fire. There were flat rocks close by and Axiana sat upon one of them. Kebra lit a second fire and began to prepare a meal. The children gathered firewood. Everyone seemed so busy. Axiana gazed up at the towering cliff wall. There had been cliffs like this in Morec. She had climbed one once, and her mother had scolded her dreadfully. Suddenly she remembered the Royal Guards who had ridden up to the wagon earlier. What had happened to them? Why had they gone away? She was about to ask Ulmenetha, but then she caught the aroma of meat and spices coming from the pot on the camp-fire. It smelt delicious!

Rising she walked to the fire. The bowman, who was kneeling beside the pot, glanced up. 'It will be ready soon, your highness.'

'It smells wonderful,' she said. She wandered to the

moonlit stream, then along the banks, captivated by the glittering lights on the smooth stones beneath the water. They shone like gems. Alone now she sat down by the waterside, and remembered sitting on the beach in Morec, her feet in the water. Her nurse used to sing a song to her there, a song about dolphins. Axiana tried to remember it. She laughed as the lines came back to her, and began to sing.

> 'How I long to be,
> such a queen of the sea,
> to follow the ocean, always in motion,
> and always so wonderfully free.'

The bushes rustled alongside her and a huge form reared up, towering over her. Axiana clapped her hands and laughed happily. The bear was so large, and, unlike the sad carcasses her father had brought back, so full of life. The bear gave a deep, rumbling growl.

'Do you not like my song, Bruin?' she said.

She felt a strong hand upon her arm, and looked up to see the black warrior beside her. He was holding a burning torch in his left hand. Gently he drew her to her feet. 'He is hungry, highness, and in no mood for song.'

Slowly he backed away, drawing the queen with him. The bear spread his paws wide and lumbered through the bushes towards them. 'He is coming with us,' said Axiana, brightly. The black man moved carefully in front of her, holding out the burning torch. To her left she saw Kebra the Bowman, a shaft notched to the bow string.

'Do not shoot,' said Nogusta.

Bison and Dagorian moved in from the right. Bison was also holding a torch. The bear's great head moved from side to side. 'Be off with you!' shouted Bison, darting forward. Surprised by the movement the bear dropped to all fours and ambled away into the darkness.

'He was so big,' said Axiana.

'Indeed he was, highness,' the black man told her. 'Now let us return to the fire.'

The stew was served upon pewter plates and Axiana ate with relish. She asked for wine, and Ulmenetha apologized for forgetting to bring any. Instead she drank a cup of water from the stream. It was cool and pleasant. Ulmenetha prepared a bed for her beside the fire. Dagorian made a small hollow for her hip beneath the blankets. Resting her head on a rolled blanket pillow Axiana lay quietly listening to the conversation around the fire. She heard the words. The child, Sufia, was asleep beside her, the boy Conalin sitting watching over her.

'I saw a bear today,' Axiana told him, sleepily.

'Go to sleep,' said the boy.

Bison added a log to the fire as Kebra collected the pewter plates and carried them to the stream for cleaning. The giant cast a furtive glance at Nogusta, who was sitting quietly, his back to the cliff wall. Dagorian and Ulmenetha were whispering to one another, and Bison could not make out the words. Bison was confused by the events of the day. Nogusta had woken them early, and they had set off back towards the city. 'The queen is in danger,' was all the black man had said, and the ride had been fast, with no time for conversation. Bison was not a rider. He hated horses. Almost as much as he hated sleeping on the ground in winter, he realized. His shoulder ached, and he had a deep, nagging pain in his lower back.

Bison glanced towards where the queen was sleeping, the children stretched out alongside her. None of this made any sense to the giant. Skanda was dead – which served him right for putting his faith in Ventrians and sending all the best soldiers home. But this talk of wizards and demons and sacrifices made Bison uncomfortable. It was a known fact that men couldn't fight demons.

'What are we going to do?' he asked Nogusta.

'About what?' countered the black man.

'About all this!' said Bison, gesturing towards the sleepers.

'We'll take them to the coast and find a ship bound for Drenan.'

'Oh, really? Just like that?' snapped Bison, his anger growing. 'We've probably got the entire Ventrian army on our heels and demons to boot. And we're travelling with a pregnant woman who's lost her mind. Oh . . . and did I mention the fact that we're also saddled with the slowest wagon in Ventria?'

'She hasn't lost her mind, you oaf,' said Ulmenetha, icily. 'She is in shock. It will pass.'

'She's in shock? What about me? I was kicked out of the army. I'm not a soldier any more. That was a shock I can tell you. But I haven't started singing to bears yet.'

'You are not a sensitive seventeen-year-old girl, heavily pregnant,' said Ulmenetha, 'who has been torn from her home.'

'I didn't tear her from her home,' objected Bison. 'She can go back for all I care. So can you, you fat cow.'

'What do you suggest, my friend?' asked Nogusta, softly.

The question threw Bison. He was not used to being asked for opinions, and he didn't really have one. But he was angry at the fat woman for calling him an oaf. 'We ought to ride on. She's not Drenai, is she? None of them are.'

'I am,' said Ulmenetha, her voice edged with contempt. 'But then that is not the issue, is it?'

'Issue? What's she talking about?' Bison demanded.

'This isn't about nationalities,' said Dagorian. 'The demons desire to sacrifice the queen's child. You understand? If they succeed the world will slide down into horror. All the evils we know from legends, the Shape-Shifters, the Hollow Tooths, the Krandyl . . . all will return. We must protect her.'

'Protect her? There are four of us! How are we going to protect her?'

'The best way we can,' said Nogusta. 'But you do not have to stay, my friend. Your life is free. You can ride away. You are not held here by chains.'

The conversation was heading along a path Bison didn't like. He had no wish to leave his friends, and was surprised that Nogusta would even suggest it. 'I can't read maps,' he objected. 'I don't even know where we are now. I want to know *why* we should stay with her.'

Kebra returned to the fire, and carefully stowed away the clean plates. Then he sat down beside Bison. He said nothing, but his expression was one of amusement.

'*Why* we should stay?' stormed Dagorian. 'What kind of a question is that from a Drenai warrior? Evil threatens to kill a child. Never mind that the child is the heir to the throne, and that his mother is the queen. When evil threatens good men stand against it.'

Bison hawked and spat into the fire. 'Just words,' he said, dismissively. 'Just like all that high sounding bull that Skanda used to spout before battles. Justice and right, forces of Light against the Dark tyranny. And where did it get us, eh? Army's gone, and we're sitting in a cold forest waiting to be struck down by demons.'

'He is quite right,' said Kebra, with a wink to Nogusta. 'There is no point in arguing the issue. I don't much care about wealth and glory. Never did. The thought of getting back to Drenan and attending parades and banquets in my honour means nothing to me. And I do not need to live in a palace, surrounded by beautiful women. All I require is a simple farm on a nice plot of land. And I'll best achieve those dreams by heading for the coast on a fast horse.'

'My point exactly,' said Bison, triumphantly. Then he faltered. 'What was that about wealth?'

Kebra shrugged. 'Meaningless baubles. But you can imagine the kind of reception given to the small band of heroes who rescued the queen? Showered with gold and praise. Probably given a commission in the avenging army that would return to Ventria. Who needs it? You and I will head for Caphis tomorrow. We'll sail home quietly and retire. You can have a place on my farm.'

'I don't want to live on a farm,' insisted Bison. 'I want to be in the . . . what did you call it? . . . the avenging army.'

'You probably can,' Kebra assured him. 'You could dye your moustache black and pretend to be forty again. Now I'm for bed. It's been a long and tiring day.'

Rising from the fire he strolled to his blankets. 'Would they really give us riches and fame?' Bison asked Dagorian.

'I fear so.'

'They'd probably write songs about you,' said Nogusta.

'A pox on songs! Can't buy a whore with a song. But can we fight demons, Nogusta? I mean, can we actually beat them?'

'Have you ever seen me lose?' countered Nogusta. 'Of course we can beat them.'

'Then I think you are right,' said Bison. 'Can't let evil get its own way. I'm with you.' Pushing himself to his feet he walked back to his blankets and lay down. Within moments he was snoring softly.

'Sweet Heaven, he makes me sick,' said Dagorian.

'Don't judge him so harshly,' Nogusta told him. 'Bison is not a complex man, but he has a little more depth than you give him credit for. He may have trouble with the concepts, but the realities are different. You will see. Now you get some sleep. I'll take the first watch. And I'll wake you in around three hours.'

When Dagorian had gone Ulmenetha moved alongside Nogusta. 'Do you believe we can make it to the coast?' she asked him.

'Do you believe in miracles?' he countered.

Nogusta sat alone, enjoying the solitude. There was no real need to keep watch. They could do nothing if attacked here, save fight and die. But he had always enjoyed forest nights, the wind whispering in the leaves, the filtered moonlight, and the sense of eternity emanating from the ancient trees around him. Forests were never silent. Always there was movement; life. Bison's gentle snoring drifted to him and he smiled. Dagorian and Ulmenetha had gazed at the giant scornfully when he decided to travel with them for the wealth and the glory. Nogusta knew better. Bison needed an excuse for heroism. Like all men of limited intelligence he feared being tricked or manipulated. There was never any doubt that he would journey with them. Kebra had known this, and had given Bison the excuse he needed. The giant would stand beside his friends against any foe.

Do you believe in miracles, Nogusta had asked Ulmenetha?

Well, a miracle would be needed, he knew. Lifting Dagorian's map he turned it towards the fire. The symbols stood out well in the flickering light. Some 20 miles to the south was the line of the River Mendea. Three fords were marked. If they could reach the first by late tomorrow they would have a chance to cross the water and lose themselves in the high country. After that there was another 70 miles of rugged terrain. Old forts were indicated along the southern route, but these would be deserted now. There might be villages along the way, from which they could obtain supplies. But probably not. This was inhospitable land. Then they would reach the plains, and face a further 150 miles west to the coast. Even with the five spare horses it would be a month of hard, slow travel. We cannot make such a journey undetected, he realized. Despair struck him.

Ruthlessly he suppressed the emotion. One step at a time, he cautioned himself. First the river.

'Why are you doing this for us?' Ulmenetha had asked him.

'It is enough that I do,' he told her. 'It needs no explanation.'

He thought about it now, recalling the dread day he had arrived home to find his family murdered, seeing their bodies, carrying them to graves he dug himself. He had buried them, and with it had buried his dreams and theirs. All their hopes and fears had been consigned to the earth, and a part of him had remained there with them, in the cold, worm-filled ground.

He glanced around the camp. Ulmenetha was asleep in the wagon. Nogusta liked the priestess. She was a tough woman, and there was no give in her. Rising he walked round the fire and stood over the sleeping children. Conalin was a sullen boy, but there was steel in him. The two girls were cuddled together under one blanket. The child, Sufia, had her thumb in her mouth, and was sleeping peacefully.

Nogusta walked to the edge of the camp. Through a break in the trees the black silhouette of the mountains could be seen against the dark grey of the sky. He heard Kebra approach.

'Can you not sleep?' he asked the bowman.

'I slept for a while. But I am getting too old to enjoy cold nights on bare earth. My bones object.'

The two men stood in silence, breathing in the cold, clean air of the night. Then Kebra spoke. 'The riders we killed were carrying around three days of supplies. They may not be missed for a while.'

'Let us hope so.'

'I'm not afraid of dying,' said Kebra, softly. 'But I am afraid.'

'I know. I feel it too.'

'Do you have a plan?' asked the bowman.

'Stay alive, kill all enemies, reach the coast, find a ship.'

'Things always look brighter when you have a plan,' said Kebra.

Nogusta smiled, then his expression hardened. The black man ran his hand over his shaved head. 'The forces of evil are gathering, and all hope rests in the hands of three old men. It almost makes me believe in the Source. The sense of humour here is cosmic.'

'Well, my friend, I *do* believe. And if I had to pick three old men to save the world I'd make the same choice He did.'

Nogusta chuckled. 'So would I, but that just makes us *arrogant* old men.'

* * *

For two days Antikas Karios searched to the west. Now he and his fifteen men rode weary horses into Usa. The men were no less tired and sat slumped in their saddles. They had removed their bronze helms and hung them from the pommels of their saddles. Their clothes were travel stained, their white cloaks grimy. Antikas was faced with two unpalatable truths. First that the fleeing group must have headed south, and secondly that Vellian had either betrayed him, or was dead. The latter was surely unlikely. Dagorian was a highly skilled swordsman, but he could not have defeated five veteran soldiers.

Antikas recalled the notes he had read concerning the young officer. The son of a hero general Dagorian had never wished to be a soldier. In fact he had trained for two years to be a priest. According to the reports pressure from his family had led him to enlist in his father's regiment. These facts alone would have meant little to most men, but to the sharp mind of Antikas Karios they revealed a great deal. To become a priest required not only immense commitment and belief, but a willingness to put aside all desires of the flesh. Such a decision could not be taken lightly, and once taken would clothe a man in chains of iron. But Dagorian had shrugged off those chains following 'pressure from his family'. His commitment to his god, therefore had been less than his commitment to his kin. This showed either a weak personality, or a man destined always to put the needs of others before his own desires. Or both.

Antikas had not been concerned when Malikada ordered the officer's death. Nor had he been unduly surprised when Dagorian bested the assassins. But his actions since were mysterious. Why had he kidnapped the queen? And why had she, apparently, gone willingly with him?

The tall chestnut he was riding stumbled on the wide avenue, then righted itself. Antikas patted its neck. 'Soon you can rest,' he said.

It was nearing dusk as they approached the palace gates. A pall of smoke hung over the western quarter of the city, and there was no-one on the streets. Sending his riders to the barracks to tend their mounts and get some rest Antikas rode through the gates of the palace. Two sentries were standing to attention as he passed. Guiding his horse to the stable he dismounted. There were no stable hands in sight. This irritated Antikas and he unsaddled the gelding and rubbed him down with a handful of dry straw. Then he led him to a stall. Antikas filled the feedbox with grain, drew a bucket of water from the stable well and covered the gelding's back with a blanket. He deserved more, and Antikas was irritated that no ostlers were present. But then why should they be, he thought? There are no other horses in the stables.

Antikas was tired, his eyes gritty through lack of sleep, but he went in search of Malikada. Rather than face the long walk back to the main doors he cut in through the kitchen entrance, thinking to order a meal sent to his rooms. Here too there was no sign of life. The place was deserted. As he moved on he saw piles of unwashed, food-encrusted dishes and noticed that the pantry door was open, the shelves empty. It made no sense. At dusk the kitchens should have been bustling with servants preparing the evening meal.

Climbing the narrow winding stair to the first floor he emerged into a wide, richly carpeted corridor, and walked on, past the library, to the ornate staircase leading to the royal apartments. After his experience at the stables and kitchens he was not surprised to find no sign of servants, and none of the lanterns had been lit. The palace was gloomy, and lit only by the fading light of the dying sun streaming through the tall windows.

He had just begun to believe Malikada was staying at the barracks when he saw two sentries at the door of what had been Skanda's apartments. Antikas strode towards them. Neither offered him the customary salute. He paused to admonish them, then heard Malikada's voice call out from beyond the door. 'Come in, Antikas.'

Antikas entered and bowed. Malikada was standing at the balcony, his back to him. The swordsman was momentarily confused. How had Malikada known he was outside?

'Speak,' said Malikada, without turning.

'I am sorry to report that the queen has gone, my lord. But I will find her tomorrow.'

Antikas expected an angry outburst, for Malikada was a volatile man. He was surprised, therefore, when his cousin merely shrugged. 'She is on the Old Lem road,' said Malikada. 'She is travelling with four men, her midwife, and three youngsters. One of the men is the officer, Dagorian. I will send men after her tomorrow. You need not concern yourself further.'

'Yes, Lord. And what of the other matters?'

'Other matters?' asked Malikada, dreamily.

'Getting messages to our garrisons on the coast, dealing with the White Wolf, rooting out Drenai sympathizers. All of the plans we have been discussing for months.'

'They can wait. The queen is all important.'

'With respect, cousin, I disagree. When the Drenai learn of Skanda's death they could mount a second invasion. And if the White Wolf is allowed to escape . . .'

But Malikada was not listening. He stood on the balcony, staring out over the city. 'Go to your room and rest, Antikas. Go to your room.'

'Yes, Lord.'

Antikas left the room. Once more there was no salute from the guards, but he was too preoccupied now to take issue with them. He needed a change of clothing, a meal, and then rest. His own apartment was small, a tiny bedroom and a modest sitting-room with two couches and no balcony. He lit two lanterns then stripped off his armour and the dust-stained tunic beneath, filled a bowl with water from a tall jug and washed his upper body. He would have preferred a hot, perfumed bath, but, without servants, it was unlikely that the bath-house boilers were working.

Where had the servants gone? And why had Malikada not gathered more?

Clothing himself in a fresh tunic and leggings he sat down and, out of habit, polished his breastplate, helm and greaves, which he then hung on a wooden frame. The room began to grow cold. Antikas strode to the window, but it was tightly shut. He thought of lighting a fire, but hunger was gnawing at him. The temperature dropped even further. Antikas swung his sword belt around his waist and left the room. The corridor was infinitely warmer. How curious, he thought.

Behind him, within the room, the water in his washing bowl froze, and ice patterns formed on the windows.

Leaving the palace he crossed the Avenue of Kings. Canta's Tavern was but a short walk, and the food there was always good.

When he arrived he found the doors locked, but he could hear signs of movement within. Angry now he hammered his fist on the wood. All movement inside ceased. 'Open up, Canta! There is a hungry man out here,' he called.

He heard the bolts being drawn back. The door swung open. Within were two men. One, the owner, Canta, a short, fat, balding man with a heavy black moustache, had a kitchen knife in his hand, the other man was holding a hatchet. 'Come in quickly,' said Canta. Antikas stepped inside. They slammed shut the door and bolted it.

'What are you afraid of?' asked Antikas. The men looked at one another.

'How long have you been back in the city?' asked Canta.

'I just rode in.'

'There have been riots,' said the tavern keeper, dropping his knife to a table and slumping down. 'Riots like you've never seen. People hacking and stabbing their neighbours. Last night the baker murdered his wife and ran along the street with her head in his hands. I saw it with my own eyes, Antikas, through the window slats. There is madness everywhere. Tomorrow I'm getting out.'

'And what of the Militia?' asked Antikas.

'They're out there with them, burning and looting. I tell you, Antikas, it beggars belief. By day everything is quiet, but when the sun goes down the nightmare begins again. There is a great evil at work here. I feel it in my bones.'

Antikas rubbed his weary eyes. 'The army is back now. They will restore order.'

'The army is camped a mile from the city,' said the other man, a stocky figure with a greying beard. 'The city is defenceless.'

The tavern was gloomy and dark, lit only by a fading log fire in the hearth. 'Do you have any food?' asked Antikas. 'I have not eaten since yesterday.'

Canta nodded and moved away to the kitchen. The other man sat opposite the swordsman. 'There is sorcery here,' he said. 'I think the city is dying.'

'Nonsense,' snapped Antikas.

'You haven't seen it, man. Outside. After dark. I have. I'll not forget it. The mob becomes possessed. You can see it in their eyes.'

'That is the way with mobs,' said Antikas.

'Maybe it is, soldier. But yesterday . . .' his voice tailed away. The man rose and walked away to the fire, slumping down beside it and staring into the flames. Canta returned with a plate of cold beef and cheese and a jug of watered wine.

'It is the best I can offer,' said Canta. Antikas reached for his money pouch. 'Don't concern yourself with that,' said Canta. 'Take it as a gift.'

The sound of sobbing came from the hearth. Antikas looked at the weeping man with distaste. Canta leaned in close. 'Last night he killed his wife and daughters,' whispered the innkeeper. 'And he loved them dearly. He came to me this morning, covered in blood. He could not believe what he had done.'

'He will be arrested and hanged,' said Antikas, coldly.

'Wait until you've lived through the night before making judgements,' advised Canta.

Antikas did not reply. Slowly he ate the meal, savouring the taste of the cold beef and the texture of the smoked cheese. At last replete he sat back. A stair board creaked. Antikas glanced up and saw a tall, thin priest, in robes of white, moving down the stairs. 'He has been here two days,' said Canta. 'He says little, but he is mightily afraid.'

The priest acknowledged Antikas with a curt nod and moved past him to sit at a table at the far wall.

'What is he doing at a tavern?' asked Antikas.

'He says that this place was built on the ruins of a shrine, and that demons will avoid it. He is leaving with us tomorrow.'

Antikas rose and moved across the room. The priest glanced up. He had a thin, ascetic face, with a prominent nose and a receding chin. His eyes were pale and watery. 'Good evening to you, Father,' said Antikas.

'And to you, my son,' answered the priest.

'What is it you fear?'

'The end of the world,' said the priest, his voice dull and toneless.

Antikas leaned forward on the table, forcing the man to meet his gaze. 'Explain,' he ordered him.

'Words are useless now,' said the priest, once more averting his gaze. 'It has begun. It will not be stopped. The demons are everywhere, and growing stronger each night.' He lapsed into silence. Antikas found it hard to suppress his irritation.

'Tell me anyway,' he said, sitting down on the bench seat opposite the man.

The priest sighed. 'Some weeks ago Father Aminias, the oldest of our order, told the Abbot he had seen demons over the city. He maintained the city was in great danger. Then he was murdered. A few days ago a woman came to me in the temple. She was a priestess, and midwife to the queen. She had been blessed with a *kiraz* – a three-fold vision. I spoke with her, and tried to interpret it. After she had gone I began to study the ancient scrolls and grimoires in the temple library. There I came upon a prophecy. That prophecy is being fulfilled now.'

'What are you saying?' persisted Antikas. 'You think the sun will fall from the sky, that the oceans will rise up and destroy us?'

'Nothing so natural, my son. Both the old emperor and Skanda were, I believe, descended from the line of three ancient kings. These kings, and a wizard, fought a war long ago. It was not a war against men. There are few details of it now, and those that remain are hopelessly distorted, and full of bizarre imagery. What is clear, however, is that it was a war against non-humans – demons, if you like. All the ancient tomes tell of a period when such creatures walked among us. The three kings ended that period, banishing all demons to another world. There are no details now of the spell that was wrought, but one of the tomes tells of the patterns of planets in the sky that awesome night. A similar pattern is in the heavens now. And I believe – with utter certainty – that the demons are returning.'

'Tomes, stars, demons – I understand none of this, priest,' snapped Antikas. 'Offer me proofs!'

'Proofs?' The priest laughed aloud. 'What proofs would be sufficient? We are in a city being torn apart every night by those possessed. The prophecy talks of the Sacrifice of Kings. The priestess told me her vision showed the old emperor was killed in such a manner. Now Skanda is dead. You are a soldier. Were you there when his army was destroyed?' Antikas nodded. 'Was he slain on the battlefield, or taken to a secret place, and then killed?'

'It is not my place to discuss these things,' said Antikas. 'But, for the sake of argument, let us assume he was. What do you take it to mean?'

'It means the fulfilment of prophecy. Two of three kings sacrificed. When the third dies the gateways will open, and the demons will be back among us. In the flesh.'

'Pah!' snorted Antikas. 'And there your argument falters, for there is no third king.'

'Not so,' said the priest. 'In the words of the prophecy the sacrifices will consist of an owl, a lion and a lamb. The owl represents wisdom and learning. The old emperor was, as you will recall, a learned man, who founded many universities. Skanda, may his soul burn, was a ravening lion, a destroyer. The third? A lamb is a newborn creature. A child, therefore, or a babe. I am not a seer. But I do not need to be, for I saw Queen Axiana recently, and her child is soon due. He will be the third king.'

Antikas leaned back in his chair and drew in a long breath. 'You speak of spells and grimoires, but only one man had such power. Kalizkan. And he is dead. Killed in a rockfall.'

'I do not speak of men,' said the priest. 'No *man* could summon such magic. I knew Kalizkan. He was a caring man, thoughtful and sensitive. Two years ago he came to the temple to be healed of a terrible cancer. We could not help him. He had but days to live. He spent two of those days studying ancient texts in our library. After the visit of the priestess I studied those same texts myself. One of the spells contained there was of a merging. If a sorcerer had enough power – so it maintained – he could draw a demon into himself for the purposes of prolonging his life. Shared immortality.' The priest fell silent, then sipped water from a pewter tankard. Antikas waited patiently. The priest spoke again. 'We were all surprised when Kalizkan continued to survive. But he did not come to the temple again, nor visit any holy place. It is my belief – though I can offer you no further proofs – that Kalizkan, in a bid to heal himself, allowed his body to be possessed. But either the promise of the spell was a lie, or Kalizkan was not powerful enough to withstand the demon. Whatever, I think Kalizkan died long ago. And, if I am right, no rockfall would have killed him.'

'And yet it did,' insisted Antikas.

The priest shook his head. 'The Demon Lord would merely have found another host. You say he died in a rockfall. Was there one survivor who walked away unscathed?'

Antikas pushed back his chair and rose. 'I have heard enough of this nonsense. Your brains are addled, priest.'

'It is my sincere hope that you are right,' the priest told him.

From outside came the sound of wailing. Scores of voices joined in. Antikas shivered, for the sound was unearthly.

'It begins again,' said the priest, closing his eyes in prayer.

Despite his apparent dismissal of the priest Antikas was deeply troubled. He had served Malikada for more than fifteen years, and had shared his hatred of the Drenai invaders. And while he had never fully condoned the treachery that led to the destruction of the Drenai army, he had seen it as the lesser of two great evils. However, the events of the past few days had concerned him, and now, with the added weight of the priest's words, doubt began to gnaw at him.

Malikada had escaped the rockfall which killed Kalizkan, and from that moment had seemed changed. He was colder, more controlled. That, in itself, meant nothing. Yet he had also lost interest in strengthening his grip on the empire. Killing Skanda was but a step towards freeing Ventria from the grip of the Drenai. There were garrisons all over the land, many of them containing Drenai units. And the sea lanes were patrolled by Drenai ships. Both he and Malikada had planned this coup for months, and both had been acutely aware of the dangers of Drenai reprisals. Yet now Malikada showed complete disinterest in the grand design. All he seemed to want was Axiana.

Antikas crossed to the fire. The wife-killer was sitting silently, staring at the flames through eyes red-rimmed from weeping. Outside they could hear hundreds of people moving through the streets. Canta crept across the room. 'Stay silent,' he whispered. 'Make no movement.'

Antikas moved to the shuttered window, and listened. People were gathering together, and he could hear a babble of voices. There were no words to be understood, though they seemed to be speaking to one another in strange tongues. Antikas shivered.

Suddenly a spear smashed through the shutters, passing inches from Antikas's face. He leapt back. An axe blade smashed the wood to shards and he found himself staring at a sea of faces, all twisted into fearsome grimaces, their eyes wide and staring. At that moment Antikas knew the truth of the priest's words. These people were possessed.

Behind him Canta screamed and fled for the stairs. Antikas drew his sabre and stood his ground. The axe-man grabbed the window-sill and began to haul himself across the threshold. His face changed, his expression softening. He blinked. 'In the name of Heaven, help me!' he shouted, dropping his axe to the floor. A knife was plunged through his back and the body was dragged from the window. The mob did not advance, but stood, staring with hatred at the lone swordsman standing inside. Then they drew back and moved away down the street.

The priest approached Antikas. 'A long time ago there

was a shrine here. The remains of the altar can still be found at the rear of the cellar. Great and holy spells were once cast here. They cannot enter.'

Antikas sheathed his sabre. 'What are *they*?'

'The Entukku. Mindless spirits who live to feed. Some say they are born from the souls of the evil dead. I do not know whether that be true. But they swim in the air all around us now, like sharks, feasting on the dark emotions of the possessed. Usa is a feeding ground, and faces extinction.'

'What can be done, priest?'

'Done? Nothing.'

Antikas swung on the man, grabbing his white robes at the neck and hauling him close. 'There is always something!' he hissed. ' So think!'

The priest sighed. Antikas released him. 'Are you a believer?' asked the priest.

'I believe in my skills and my sabre.'

The priest stood for a moment, staring out into the darkness. 'You cannot kill the Demon Lord,' he said, 'for he is immortal. You could destroy the host body, but he would find another. And his strength is growing. You saw the mob. A few days ago the Entukku could merely inspire men to acts of violence. Skanda's death gave them the ability to possess hosts utterly. How can you fight such power with a sabre? Were you to step outside this door the demons would descend upon you and then the great Antikas Karios would be running with the mob, screaming and killing.'

Antikas considered his words. 'That may be so, priest,' he said, at last, 'but you say his power is derived from the murder of kings. What happens if he fails to kill the third?'

'How can he fail? Who can withstand demons?'

Antikas stepped in close to the man. The words he used were softly spoken, but the priest blanched. 'If I hear another negative phrase from you I will hurl you from this window, and out into the night. Do you understand me?'

'In the name of mercy . . . !' wailed the priest. Antikas cut him short.

'I am not known as a merciful man, priest. Now answer the question. What if the third king eludes the demons?'

'I am not sure,' answered the priest. 'The power he is using is derived from the previous sacrifices. Such power, though great, is finite. If he does not complete the third sacrifice in time then he will – I believe – be drawn back into his own world.'

'What do you mean, in time?'

'The pattern of the heavens is the clue. There are times when the strength of a spell is made immeasurably more powerful if cast with the right conjunction of planets. I believe this to be the case now.'

'And how long does that give us?'

'That is hard to estimate, for I am no astrologer. But no more than a month. That is for sure.'

Canta returned from his hiding place upstairs. He and the man by the fire up-ended a table, lifting it into place against the shattered window. Antikas lit several lanterns. 'What are you doing?' asked Canta, fearfully.

'They cannot pass the portals of the tavern,' said Antikas, 'so let us have some light.' He gestured to the priest to join him and returned to the table. 'I need to get to my horse before dawn,' he said. 'Have you a spell to aid me?'

The priest shook his head. 'My skills were not suited to magick.'

'What then, pray, are your skills?'

'I am a healer.'

Antikas cursed, then lapsed into thought. They were silent for several minutes. Then the swordsman glanced up. 'You say this place is holy. What makes it so?'

'I told you. It was once a shrine.'

'Yes, yes. But what remains here to keep it holy. Was a spell cast?'

'Yes, many spells. They are held in the stone of the walls, and the wood of the beams.'

'Therefore, if we were to move the shrine to another place, that would also be holy?'

'I believe so.'

'Come with me,' ordered Antikas, rising and lifting one of the lanterns from its wall bracket. Together the two men moved through to the back of the tavern. Finding the door to the cellar Antikas moved down the steps. It was cold below ground, and he threaded his way past barrels of beer, wine and spirit. 'Where is the altar?' he asked.

'Over here,' said the priest, leading him to a block of stone some 3 feet high. The shape of a bull had been carved on the front of the stone, the image all but weathered away. On each side was a sculpted hand, holding a crescent moon. These too had been eroded by time. Antikas left the priest holding the lantern and returned upstairs.

Gathering the axe dropped by the first of the mob he moved back to the cellar.

'What are you going to do?' asked the priest. Antikas swung the axe, bringing it crashing down on the altar. Twice he struck, then a fist-sized section broke away. Dropping the axe he took up the stone.

'You say that spells are held in the stone. Perhaps this will shield me from the demons.'

'I cannot say that for sure,' said the priest. 'What you have is a tiny fragment.'

'I have no choice but to try, priest. The queen is in the mountains, guarded by only four men.'

'And you think a fifth will make a difference?'

'I am Antikas Karios, priest. I always make a difference.'

Tucking the rock into his tunic Antikas returned to the upper room. Moving to the upturned table which blocked the window he peered out into the street. All was silent. His mouth was dry, his heart beating fast. Antikas Karios feared no living man, but the thought of the demons waiting threatened to unman him. Placing his hand on the table he prepared to draw it aside.

'Don't go out there!' pleaded Canta, echoing the voice in Antikas's own heart.

'I must,' he said, wrenching the table aside and climbing to the sill.

The night breeze was cool on his skin, and he leapt lightly to the ground. Behind him the others hastily drew back the table. Antikas ran across the street, ducking into an alley. He had gone no more than a hundred paces when the attack came. The temperature around him plummeted, and he heard whispers on the breeze. They grew louder and louder, filling his ears like angry hornets. Pain roared inside his head. Inside his tunic the rock grew warmer. Antikas staggered and almost fell. Anger surged – but as it did he felt the cold seep into his brain. Voices were hissing at him now in a language he had never heard, and yet he knew what they were saying. 'Give in! Give in! Give in!'

He lurched against the side of a building and fell to his knees. The pain from striking the cobbles cut through the discordant shrieking inside his mind. He focused on it – and on the heat from the rock against his skin.

He wanted to rage against the invasion, to scream. But some deeper instinct overrode his emotions, urging him to stay calm, to fight coolly. Yet he felt like he was drowning in this sea of voices – at one with them, sharing their hunger for blood and pain and death.

'No,' he said, aloud. 'I am . . .' For a moment there was panic. Who am I? Scores of names surged through his mind, shouted by the voices within. He fought for calm. 'I am . . . Antikas Karios. I am ANTIKAS KARIOS!' Over and over, like a mantra, he said his name. The voices shrieked louder still, but with less power, until they receded into dim, distant echoes.

Antikas pushed himself to his feet and ran on. The shrieking of human voices could be heard now, some distance to his left. Then to his right. Then ahead.

Unable to possess him the demons were gathering their human forces to cut him off.

Antikas paused and looked around. To his left was a high wall, and, close by, a wrought-iron gate. He ran to it, and climbed the gate, stepping out onto the wall some 15 feet above the ground. Nimbly he moved along it, to where it joined the side of a house. There was an ivy covered trellis here and Antikas began to climb. Below him a mob gathered, shouting curses. A hurled hammer crashed against the wall by his head. He climbed on. A piece of rotten wood gave way beneath his foot, but he clung on, drawing himself towards the flat roof. He heard the creaking of the iron gate below, and glanced back. Several of the mob were climbing the wall.

Easing himself onto the roof Antikas gazed around in the moonlight. There was a door to the building. Moving swiftly to it he forced it open. As he entered the stairwell beyond he heard the sound of boots upon the stairs. With a soft curse he backed out onto the roof, and ran to the edge of the building.

Some 60 feet below was a narrow alleyway. He glanced at the roof opposite, gauging the distance. Ten feet at least. On the flat he could make the jump with ease, but there was a low wall around the rooftop.

Pacing his steps he moved back to the door then turned and ran at the wall. He leapt, his left foot striking the top and propelling him out over the alleyway. For one terrifying moment he thought he had misjudged his leap. But then he landed and rolled on the opposite rooftop. The hilt of his sabre dug into his side, tearing the skin. Antikas swore again. Rising he drew the blade. The golden fist guard was dented, but the weapon was still usable.

The door on the second roof burst open and three men ran out. Antikas spun towards them, the sabre slicing through the throat of the first. His foot lashed out into the knee of the second, spinning the man from his feet. The third died from a sabre thrust to the heart. Antikas ran to the doorway and listened. There was no sound upon the stairs, and he moved down into the dark, emerging into a narrow corridor. There were no lanterns lit, and the swordsman moved forward blindly, feeling his way. He stumbled upon a second stair and descended to the first level. Here there was a window with the curtains drawn back, and faint moonlight illuminated a gallery. Opening the window he clambered out, and dropped the 10 feet to the garden below.

Here there was a lower wall, no more than 8 feet high. Sheathing his sabre he leapt, curling his fingers over the stone and hauling himself to the top. The street beyond was empty.

Antikas silently lowered himself to the cobbles and ran on.

Emerging onto the Avenue of Kings he raced across the street towards the palace. The mob erupted from alleyways all around him, shrieking and baying. Ducking he sprinted for the gates. The two sentries stood stock still as he approached, showing no sign of alarm. Antikas reached them just ahead of the mob, and realized he could go no further. Angry now he spun to face them.

But they had halted just outside the gates and were now standing silently, staring at him.

The sentries still had not moved, and Antikas stood, breathing heavily, his sabre all but forgotten.

Silently the mob dispersed, moving back into the shadows on the opposite side of the Avenue.

Antikas approached the first of the sentries. 'Why did they not attack?' he asked.

The man's head turned slowly towards him. The eyes were misted in death, the jaw hanging slack. Antikas backed away.

Reaching the stable he moved to the stall where he had left his horse. The beast was on its knees. He noticed someone had changed the blanket with which he had covered the beast. His had been grey, this was black. Opening the stall door he stepped inside.

The black blanket writhed, and scores of bats fluttered up around him, their wings beating about his face.

Then they were gone, up into the rafters.

And the horse was dead.

Angry now Antikas drew his sword and headed for the palace. The priest had said he could not kill the Demon Lord, but, by all the gods in Heaven, he would try. The rock grew warm against his skin, and a soft voice whispered into his mind.

'Do not throw away your life, my boy!'

Antikas paused. 'Who are you?' he whispered.

'You cannot kill him. Trust me. The babe is everything. You must protect the babe.'

'I am trapped here. If I leave the palace the mob will hunt me down.'

'I will guide you, Antikas. There are horses outside the city.'

'Who are you?' he repeated.

'I am Kalizkan, Antikas. And all this pain and horror is of my making.'

'That is hardly a recommendation for trust.'

'I know. I am hoping that the power of truth will convince you.'

'My choices appear limited,' said Antikas. 'Lead on, wizard!'

High in the palace the Demon Lord raised his arms. Over the city the Entukku, in ecstasy and bloated with feeding, floated aimlessly above the buildings. The Demon Lord's power swept over them, draining their energies. They began to wail and shriek, their hunger increasing once more.

Stepping back from the window the Demon Lord began to chant. The air before him shimmered. Slowly he spoke the seven words of power. Blue light lanced from floor to ceiling, and a pungent odour filled the room. Where a moment before had been a wall, decorated with a brightly coloured mural, there was now a cave entrance, and a long tunnel.

Faint figures of light moved in the tunnel, floating towards him. As they came closer the Demon Lord held out his hands. Black smoke oozed from his fingers and drifted down the tunnel. The light figures hovered and the smoke rose up around them. The lights faded, but the smoke hardened, taking shape.

Ten tall men emerged, wearing dark armour and full-faced helms. One by one they strode into the room. The Demon Lord spoke a single harsh word and the tunnel disappeared.

'Welcome to the world of flesh, my brothers,' said the Demon Lord.

'It is good to feel hunger again,' said the first of the warriors, removing his helm. His hair was ghost white, his eyes grey and cold. His face was broad, the lipless mouth wide.

'Then feed,' said the Demon Lord, raising his hands. This time a red mist flowed from his hands, and floated across the room. The warrior opened his mouth, displaying long, curved fangs. The red mist streamed into his open mouth. The others removed their helms and moved in close. One by one they absorbed the mist. As they did so their bone-white faces changed, the skin blushing red. Their eyes glittered, the grey deepening to blue and then, slowly, to crimson.

'Enough, my brother,' said the first warrior. 'After so long the taste is too exquisite.' Moving to a couch he sank down, stretching out his long, black-clad limbs.

The Demon Lord's arms dropped to his side. 'The long wait is almost over,' he said. 'Our time has come again.' The others seated themselves and remained silent.

'What is it you require of us, Anharat?'

'In the mountains to the south there is a woman. She carries the child of Skanda. It will be born soon. You must bring it to me. The Spell of Three must be completed before the Blood Moon.'

'She is guarded well?'

'There are eight humans with her, but only four warriors, and three of these are old men.'

'With respect, brother, such a mission is demeaning. We are all Battle Lords here. The blood of thousands has stained our blades. We have feasted on the souls of princes.'

'It was not my intention,' said the Demon Lord, 'to offer insult to the Krayakin. But if we do not take the babe then all will be lost for another four thousand years. Would you rather I entrusted this task to the Entukku?'

'You are wise, Anharat, and I spoke hastily. It will be as you order,' said the warrior. Raising his hand he made a fist. 'It is good to feel the solidity of flesh once more, to breathe in air, and to feed. It is good.' His blood-filled eyes gazed on the body of Malikada. 'How long before you can let fall this decaying form? It is ugly to the eye.'

'Once the sacrifice is complete,' Anharat told him. 'For now I need this obscenity around me.'

A shimmering began in the air around Anharat, and the hissing of many voices. Then it faded.

'These humans are so perverse,' said Anharat. 'I ordered one of my officers to rest in his room. Now he is fleeing the city in a bid to save the queen and her child. It seems he went to a tavern and a priest spoke to him.'

'He understands magick, this officer?' asked the warrior.

'I do not believe so.'

'Then why have the Entukku failed to seize him?'

'There are spells around the tavern, ancient spells. It is not important. He will afford you some pleasure, for he is the foremost swordsman in the land. His name is Antikas Karios, and he has never lost a duel.'

'I shall kill him slowly,' said the warrior. 'The taste of *his* terror will be exquisite.'

'There is one other of the group to be considered. His name is Nogusta. He is the last of the line of Emsharas the Sorcerer.'

The warrior's eyes narrowed, and the others tensed at the sound of the name. 'I would give up eternity,' said the warrior, 'for the chance to find the soul of Emsharas the Traitor. I would make it suffer for a thousand years, and that would not be punishment enough. How is it that one of his line still lives?'

'He carries the Last Talisman. Some years ago one of my disciples inspired a mob to destroy him and his family. It was a fine night, with great terror. Pleasing to the eye. But he was not there. Many times I have tried to engineer his death. The Talisman saves him. That is why he must be considered with care.'

'He is one of the old ones guarding the woman?'

'Yes.'

'I do not like the sound of it, Anharat. It is not a coincidence.'

'I do not doubt that, at all,' said Anharat. 'But does it not show how far the enemy has fallen in power that his only defence is a group of old men? All but one of his priests here are slain, his temples deserted, his forces routed. He has become to this world a pitiful irrelevance. Which is why it will pass to us before the Blood Moon.'

'Is this tavern far?' asked the warrior.

'No.'

The warrior rose and put on his helm. 'Then I shall go and feast myself upon the heart of this priest,' he said.

'The spells are strong,' warned Anharat.

The warrior laughed. 'Spells that would drain the

Entukku are as wasp stings to the Krayakin. How many other humans are there?'

'Only two.'

The warrior gestured and two of his fellows stood. 'The milk of the Entukku was good, but flesh tastes sweeter,' he said.

The wagon lurched as one of the rear wheels hit a sunken rock. The weary horses sagged against their traces. Conalin tried to back up the team, but the horses stood their ground. Bison swore loudly and dismounted. Moving to the rear of the wagon he grabbed two spokes of the wheel. 'Give them a touch of the whip,' he ordered. Conalin cracked it above the horses' backs. They surged forward. At the same time Bison threw his weight against the wheel and the wagon bumped over the rock. The giant fell sprawling to the trail, the wheel narrowly missing his arm.

The women in the wagon – save Axiana – laughed as he rose, mud on his face. 'It's not funny!' he roared.

'It is from where I'm sitting,' said Ulmenetha. Bison swore again and trudged back to where Kebra was holding the reins of his mount.

'This trail is too narrow,' he said, heaving himself into the saddle. 'I don't think we've made more than twelve miles today. And already the horses are exhausted.'

'Nogusta says we'll change the team again when we reach the flatlands.'

Bison was not mollified. He glanced back to the spare mounts they had taken from the dead lancers. 'They are cavalry mounts. They're not bred to pull wagons and they tire easily. Look at them! They were ridden hard even before we took them, and they are exhausted also.'

It was true, and Kebra knew it. The horses were all

weary. Somewhere soon they would have to rest them. 'Let's move on,' he said.

The wagon finally crested a high hill and emerged from the forest. Far off to the south they could see the glittering ribbon of the River Mendea, and beyond it soaring mountain peaks, snow crested and crowned by clouds. 'We'll not make the river by dark,' said Kebra.

'I could carry the cursed wagon faster than these horses can pull it,' said Bison.

'You are in a foul mood today,' observed Kebra.

'It's this damned horse. Every time I go up, he goes down. He goes up, I come down. He's treating my arse like a drum.' Another squeal of laughter came from the wagon, this time from little Sufia, who repeated the phrase in a sing-song voice.

'His arse is a drum! His arse is a drum!'

Ulmenetha scolded her, gently, but was unable to keep the smile from her face.

'I'll ride your horse if you drive the wagon,' said Conalin.

'Done!' said Bison, happily. 'Heaven knows I'm no rider.'

Dagorian came riding up the trail. 'About a mile further the road widens,' he said. 'There is even a paved area. It is overgrown now, but it will help us earn back a few miles.'

Bison climbed to his place at the driving seat and sat upon a folded blanket. 'Ah, but that is good,' he murmured, settling himself down and taking up the reins. Kebra saw the boy was having difficulty reaching the stirrup of Bison's mount and edged closer, holding out his hand. Conalin spurned it and clumsily hauled himself up. Kebra dismounted and adjusted the stirrups.

'Have you ever ridden, lad?' he asked.

'No, but I am a fast learner.'

'Grip with your thighs, not your calves. And trust the horse. He knows what he's doing. Come, I'll give you a lesson.' Swinging into the saddle he moved out over the rise and slowly rode down to the flat land below. Glancing back he saw Conalin holding the reins at chest level as the horse picked its way down the slope. At the base of the hill Kebra drew alongside Conalin, showing him the basics of guiding the mount.

'We'll try a trot,' he said. 'You must get in rhythm with the horse. Otherwise you'll end up like Bison, and it will play a tattoo on your buttocks. Let's go!'

Kebra's mount moved smoothly into a trot. Behind him Conalin was being bounced around in the saddle. His horse slowed. 'Don't haul on the reins, lad. That's his signal to stop.'

'I'm no good at this,' said the red-head, his face flushing. 'I'll go back to the wagon.'

'Nothing good ever comes easy, Conalin. And I think you are doing fine. A born horseman.'

'Truly?'

'You just need to get used to the horse. Let's try again.'

As the wagon trundled down the slope the two riders set off once more. For a while Conalin felt his spine was being bruised, but then, suddenly and without warning, he found the rhythm and the ride became a delight. The sun broke through the clouds, and the tightness in his stomach faded away. He had lived his life in the squalor of the city, and had never before seen the glory of the mountains. Now he rode a fine horse, and the breeze was fresh against his skin. He found in that moment a joy he had never known. He gave Kebra a wide grin. The bowman smiled and rode in silence beside him. At the tree line they swung their mounts.

'Now for a little canter,' said Kebra. 'Not too much, for the horses are tired.'

If trotting had been a joy, the ride back to the wagons was a delight Conalin would treasure all his life. The rags he wore were forgotten, as were the sores on his back. Today was a gift no-one could take away from him.

'You ride so well – like a knight!' Pharis told him as he drew alongside the wagon.

'It's wonderful,' he told her. 'It's like . . . it's like . . .' He laughed happily. 'I don't know what it's like. But it's wonderful!'

'You won't be saying that by this evening,' warned Bison.

Dagorian rode with them for the next hour, then headed off towards the south to find a place to camp.

As the sun began to slide towards the western mountains Nogusta came galloping up from the rear. 'There is no sign of pursuit yet,' he told Kebra. 'But they are coming.'

'We won't reach the river by tonight. The horses are tired,' said the bowman.

'As am I,' admitted Nogusta.

They rode on, and as dusk deepened they came across Dagorian, camped beside a small lake. He had lit a fire and the weary travellers climbed down from the wagon to sit beside it. Kebra and Conalin unsaddled the horses, wiping their backs with dried grass. Kebra showed the boy how to hobble the mounts, then they left them to graze and unhitched the wagon team. Conalin was moving stiffly and Kebra grinned at him. 'The muscles on the inside of your thighs have been stretched,' he said. 'You'll get used to it. Did you enjoy the ride?'

'It was all right,' said Conalin, nonchalantly.

'How old are you, lad?'

The boy shrugged. 'I don't know. What does it matter?'

'At your age I don't think it does. I am fifty-six. *That* matters.'

'Why?'

'Because my dreams are all behind me. Do you swim?'

'No. And I don't want to learn.'

'It is almost as fine a feeling as riding a horse. But it is up to you.' Kebra strolled away to the lake side and stripped off his clothing. The water was cold as he waded out. Then he dived forward and began to swim with long easy strokes. Conalin wandered to the water side and watched him in the fading light. After a while Kebra swam back and climbed out of the water. He shivered and dried himself with his tunic, which he then stretched out on a rock. Pulling on his leggings he sat down beside the boy.

'I don't dream,' said Conalin, suddenly. 'I just sleep and then wake up.'

'Those are not the dreams I spoke of. I meant the dreams we have for life, things we wish for ourselves, like a wife and family, or riches.'

'Why are they behind you? You could have these things,' said the boy.

'Perhaps you are right.'

'My dream is to wed Pharis, and to fear nothing.'

The sky darkened to crimson as the sun dropped behind the western peaks. 'It would be nice to fear nothing,' admitted Kebra. Bison strolled up and draped a blanket around Kebra's shoulders.

'Old men like you should beware of the cold,' said Bison, walking on and dipping a cup into the water. He drank noisily.

'Why did he say that?' asked Conalin. 'He looks old enough to be your father.' Kebra chuckled.

'Bison will never be old. You look at his bald pate and his white moustache and you see an old man. Bison looks in a mirror and sees a young man of twenty-five. It is a gift he has.'

'I don't like him.'

'I agree with you. I don't like him much either. But I love him. There's no malice in old Bison, and he'd stand by your side against all the armies of the world. That's rare, Conalin. Believe me.'

The boy was unconvinced, but he said nothing. Out on the lake the splintered reflection of the moon lay broken upon the water, and to the west the lake gleamed blood red in the dying sun. Conalin glanced up at the silver-haired bowman. 'Will I ride tomorrow?' he asked him.

Kebra smiled. 'Of course. The more you ride the better you'll get.'

'It feels safer on a horse,' said Conalin, gazing out over the lake.

'Why safer?'

'The wagon is so slow. When they catch us we'll not be able to escape in a wagon.'

'Maybe they won't catch us,' said Kebra.

'Do you believe that?'

'No. But there's always hope.' Conalin was pleased that the man had not tried to lie to him. It was a moment of sharing that made the boy feel like an equal.

'What will you do when they come?' asked Conalin.

'I'll fight them. So will Nogusta and Bison. It's all we can do.'

'You could ride away on your fast horses,' Conalin pointed out.

'Some men could, but we're not made that way.'

'Why?' asked the boy. It was such a simple question, yet, at first, Kebra was unable to answer it. He thought about it for a while.

'It is hard to explain, Conalin. You start by asking yourself what makes a true man. Is it his ability to hunt, or to farm, or to breed stock? In part the answer is yes. Is it his capacity to love his family? In part the answer is also yes. But there is something else. Something grand. It seems to me that there are three instincts which drive us on. The first is self-preservation – the will to survive. The second is tribal. We have an urge to belong, to be a part of a greater whole. But the third? The third is what counts, boy, above all things.'

Ulmenetha moved silently alongside them and removed her shoes. Sitting down she rested her feet in the water.

'What is the third thing?' asked Conalin, angry that they had been interrupted.

'That is even harder to explain,' said Kebra, who was also disconcerted by the arrival of the priestess. 'The lioness would willingly give her life to save her cubs. That is her way. But I have seen a woman risk her life for someone else's child. The third instinct compels us to put aside thoughts of self-preservation for the sake of another life, or a principle, or a belief.'

'I don't understand,' said Conalin.

'You should ask Nogusta. He would explain it better.'

Ulmenetha turned towards them. 'You don't need it explained, Conalin,' she said, softly. 'When you rescued Pharis it was that third instinct which came into play. And when you stood in that room in Kalizkan's house and fought against the beast.'

'It is not the same. I love Pharis and Sufia. But I do not

love the queen. I would not risk death to save her.'

'It is not about her,' said Kebra. 'Not specifically, anyway. It is about many things: honour, self-worth, pride . . .' he lapsed into silence.

'Would you die for me?' asked Conalin, suddenly.

'I'm hoping not to die for anyone,' said Kebra, embarrassed. Swiftly he rose and walked back to the camp.

'Yes, he would,' said Ulmenetha. 'He is a good man.'

'I don't want anyone dying for me,' the boy told her. 'I don't want it!'

Chapter Eight

Nogusta and Dagorian were sitting by the fire, studying the maps Ulmenetha had supplied. Bison was stretched out alongside them, his head resting on his arm. 'When are we going to eat?' he grumbled. 'My stomach thinks my throat's been cut.'

'Soon,' promised Nogusta. He turned back to Dagorian, and spread a second map on the ground beside the fire. The map was of etched leather, the hide stained white. Once there had been many colours, denoting woods, mountains and lakes. But these were badly faded now, and some of the etching had worn away. Even so the scale was good and both men could just make out the symbols showing the positions of forest roads and river crossings. 'I would think we are close to here,' said Nogusta, indicating an etched spear on the top right-hand corner of the map. 'The outer edge of the Forest of Lisaia. According to the map there are three bridges. Two questions arise: Are they still there, and, if they are, what effect will the spring floods have upon them? I have seen bridges under water at this time of year in the mountains.'

'I'll ride ahead and scout them tomorrow,' said Dagorian. The young man stared down at the map. 'Once we reach the high country beyond we will have to leave the wagon.' Nogusta nodded. The only other route was to journey all the way to the ghost city of Lem, and then take the coast road. This would add 80 miles to the journey. In the distance a wolf howled. The sound hung eerily in the air. Dagorian shivered.

Nogusta smiled. 'Contrary to popular belief wolves do not attack men,' he said.

'I know. But it chills the blood nonetheless.'

'I was bitten by a wolf once,' said Bison. 'On the arse.'

'One can only pity the wolf,' said Nogusta.

Bison chuckled. 'It was a she-wolf and I got too close to her cubs, I guess. She chased me for half a mile. You remember? It was back at Corteswain. Kebra did the stitching. I had a fever for four days.'

'I remember,' said Nogusta. 'We all drew lots and Kebra lost. He says the sight haunts him to this day.'

'Left a nasty scar,' said Bison. Rolling to his knees he dropped his leggings. 'Look at that!' he said, pointing his buttocks towards Dagorian. The officer laughed aloud.

'You are quite right, Bison. That's one of the ugliest things I've ever seen.' Bison hauled up his leggings and buckled his belt. He was grinning broadly.

'I tell all the whores it's a war wound from a Ventrian spear.' He swung towards Kebra. 'Are we going to eat or starve to death?' he bawled.

Some way back, sitting with her back to a tree, Axiana accepted a cup of water from Pharis. The slim, dark-haired girl squatted down before the queen. 'Are you feeling better now?' she asked.

'I am hungry,' said Axiana. 'Fetch me something from the wagon. Some fruit.'

Pharis was delighted to obey. The order made her a servant of the queen, an honourable role, and she was determined to fulfil it well. She ran to the wagon and rummaged in the food sacks. Little Sufia was sitting there, unmoving, her eyes staring up at the sky.

'What are you looking at?' asked Pharis.

The little girl took a deep breath. 'Fetch Nogusta,' she said, her voice cool and distant.

'He's talking to the officer. I'd better not disturb him.'

'Fetch him now,' said Sufia. Pharis looked hard at the little girl.

'What is wrong?'

'Do it now, child, for time is short.' Pharis felt goose-flesh upon her arms, and backed away.

'Nogusta!' she called. 'Come quickly!' The black warrior ran across to the wagon, followed by Dagorian and Kebra.

'What is it?' he asked. Pharis simply pointed to the small blonde child. She was sitting cross-legged facing them, her face serene, her blue eyes bright.

'The wolves are coming,' said Sufia. 'Draw your swords! Do it now!' Although the voice was that of the child, the words were spoken with great authority.

Suddenly the queen screamed.

A huge grey wolf padded from the trees, then another. And another.

One raced forward, straight at Bison, who was sitting beside the fire. The giant reared up and, as the gleaming fangs darted towards his throat, hammered a blow to the wolf's face. The beast spun away, rolled, and attacked again. As it leapt Bison grabbed it by the throat and hurled it at the pack. Nogusta grabbed Pharis and threw her onto the wagon, then drew his sword as a wolf leapt for him. The blade flashed in the moonlight, slashing through the beast's neck. Kebra was hurled to the ground as another beast lunged at him. One of the horses screamed and went down. Dagorian lanced his blade through the chest of a huge grey male, then swung towards Axiana. She was sitting by the tree, and not one of the beasts approached her. Conalin and Ulmenetha had waded into the lake, and one of the beasts was swimming out towards them. Another wolf leapt. Dagorian jumped backwards, the fangs snapping at his face. Thrusting up his sword he plunged it into the wolf's belly. On the ground beside him, his left hand gripping the fur of a wolf's throat, Kebra plunged his dagger again and again into the side of the beast. The wolf slumped down over him.

On the back of the wagon Sufia stood and raised her arms over her head, bringing her hands slowly together. She was chanting as she did so. Blue fire formed around her fingers. Her right arm snapped forward, pointing to the lake. A ball of fire flew from her hand, exploding against the back of the swimming wolf. It thrashed about, flames licking over its fur. Then it swam away.

Her left hand dropped and the fire flew down into the earth beside the wagon, flaring up with a tremendous flash. The wolf pack scattered and ran back into the forest.

Dagorian felt a pain in his arm. He glanced down to see blood dripping from a bite to his left forearm. He could not recall being bitten. Bison walked over to where he stood. His left ear was sliced open, blood streaming to his thick neck.

Five wolves were dead in the campsite.

Kebra pushed the body of the dead wolf to one side and rose unsteadily. For a moment no-one spoke. 'Wolves don't attack people, you said,' Bison pointed out to Nogusta. Lifting his hand to his blood-covered ear he swore.

'They do if the Entukku inspire them,' said the voice of Sufia. Ulmenetha and Conalin waded ashore and approached the wagon. Pharis was sitting against the food sacks, her knees drawn up. She was staring fearfully at the child.

'Who are you?' asked Nogusta. Sufia sat down, her little legs dangling over the tailboard.

'I am a friend, Nogusta. Of that you can be sure. I helped Dagorian back in the city, when the demons were upon him. And I rescued Ulmenetha when she sat upon the palace roof and saw the monster. I am Kalizkan the Sorcerer.'

For a moment no-one spoke. 'You are the cause of this terror,' said Nogusta, coldly.

'Indeed I am. But it was done unwittingly, and no-one feels more grief than I. But time is too short to explain. I cannot stay in this child's form for long, for it would damage her mind. So listen to me now. The enemy has sent a force against you the like of which you will never have seen. They are called the Krayakin. They are supreme warriors, but they are not immortal. Blades can cut them, but not kill them. They fear only two things, wood and water.' The child turned to Kebra. 'Your arrows can kill them, if you pierce heart or head. The others of you must fashion weapons of wood, stakes, spears, whatever you can.'

'How many are there?' asked Nogusta.

'There are ten, and they will be upon you before you reach the river.'

'What more can you tell us?' asked Dagorian.

'Nothing now. The child must return. I will help you where I can. But death calls me and the power of my spirit is fading. I cannot remain among the living for much longer. But trust me, my friends. I will return.'

Sufia blinked and rubbed her eyes. 'Why is everyone staring at me?' she said, her eyes filling with tears.

'We were wondering if you were hungry, little one,' said Kebra. 'What shall I cook for you?'

Bakilas, Lord of the Krayakin, reined in his mount. The five men lay sprawled in death, and the parallel lines of the wagon tracks could be seen disappearing into the forest. Bakilas dismounted and examined the ground around the dead men. Removing his black, full faced helm he winced as sunlight speared against his skin. Swiftly he scanned the tracks. Replacing his helm he moved to his horse and stepped into the saddle.

'The soldiers caught up with the wagon here, and were met by a single rider. They spoke to him, and then there was a fight. At this point other men joined in, having ridden from the forest. The battle was brief. One of the soldiers fought a hand to hand duel and was killed cleanly.'

'How do you know they spoke first, brother?' asked Pelicor, the youngest of the Krayakin. As well as the black armour and helm he was hooded against the sunlight.

Bakilas swung in the saddle. 'One of the soldiers' horses urinated on the grass. You can still see the stain. It was standing still at the time.'

'It is still conjecture,' muttered Pelicor.

'Then let us see,' said Bakilas. They rode their horses in a circle around the dead men, then Bakilas pointed to one of the corpses. 'Rise!' he commanded. The body of Vellian twitched and slowly rose from the grass. The ten riders focused upon it. The body spasmed, the air around it shimmering.

Images formed in the minds of the Krayakin; scenes drawn from the decaying brain of the slain soldier. They saw, through the dead man's eyes, the wagon and its occupants, and watched as the young officer rode to meet them. The conversation they heard was fragmented, and they honed their concentration.

'Good *morning, I am Vellian, sent* ... *Karios* ... *palace. The city* ... *restore order*.'

'*An army* ... *traitors*.'

'*Yes. Now* ... *sabre* ... *scabbard and let* ... *way*.'

'*I don't think so* ... *great danger* ... *safer with me*.'

There followed a sudden fracture in the image and the Krayakin saw a brief intrusion of other memories, of a young woman running on the grass.

'The corruption has gone too far,' said Pelicor. 'We cannot hold the line.'

'We can,' said Bakilas, sternly. 'Concentrate!'

Once more they saw the young officer facing the soldiers. The man Vellian was speaking. '*Do not be a fool, man. You may be as skilled as Antikas himself with that sabre, but you cannot beat five of us. What is the point then of dying, when the cause is already lost?*'

'*What is the point of living without a cause worth dying for?*' countered the officer.

The Krayakin sat silently as the scene played itself out, the young officer attacking, then being joined by a black rider and a silver-haired bowman. As Bakilas had already said the battle was brief, and the Krayakin analysed the skills of the victors.

The body slumped back to the grass. 'The young man is fast, and sure,' said Bakilas. 'But the black man is a master. Speed, subtlety and strength, combined with cunning and ferocity. A worthy opponent.'

'Worthy?' snapped Pelicor. 'He is human. There are no worthy opponents among them. Only sustenance. And he will supply little.'

'So angry, brother? Are you not enjoying this return to the flesh?'

'Not yet,' said Pelicor. 'Where are my armies? Where is the glory to be found here, on this miserable mountain?'

'There is none,' admitted Bakilas. 'The days of Ice and Fire are long gone. But they will return. The volcanoes will spew their ash into the sky, and the ice will return. It will be as it was. But first we must bring the mother and babe to Anharat. Be patient, brother.'

Bakilas touched spurs to his horse and rode for the forest.

The sunlight was less harsh in the shelter of the trees and Bakilas once more removed his helm, his white hair flowing free in the slight breeze, his grey eyes scanning the trail. Pelicor was not alone in lusting after the days of Ice and Fire. He too longed for them. Marching with the armies of the Illohir, scattering the humans, feasting on their terror and sucking their souls from their skulls. Heady days!

Until Emsharas had betrayed them.

It remained a source of pain that would never ease. Yet even with Emsharas's treachery the Battle of the Four Valleys could have been won, should have been won. The Krayakin had led the counter charge, and had smashed the enemy right. Bakilas himself had almost reached the Battle Standard of the human king, Darlic. Above the battle Anharat and Emsharas had fought on the Field of Spirit, and, just as Bakilas breached the spear wall around Darlic, Anharat had fallen. The dark cloud of ash shielding the Illohir from the harsh, deadly light of the sun, had been ripped apart. Illohir bodies withered in their tens of thousands, until only the Krayakin remained. Ten thousand of the greatest warriors ever to stride the earth. The humans had turned on them with renewed ferocity, their Storm Swords – enchanted by the traitor, Emsharas – had ripped into Krayakin flesh. By the end of the day only 200 Krayakin remained in the flesh to flee the field. The rest were Windborn once more.

The days of Illohir dominance on earth were over.

In the weeks that followed the Krayakin were harried and tracked down, until only ten survivors remained.

Then Emsharas had evoked the Great Spell, and all the remaining creatures of the Illohir, demons and sprites, wood nymphs, trolls and warriors, were cast into the grey hell of Nowhere. Existing without substance, immortal without form, the Illohir floated in a soulless sea. Only memory survived, memories of conquest and glory, of the sweet wine of terror, and the sustenance it supplied.

Nothing in all of existence could surpass the joys the Krayakin had known. Bakilas himself had once adopted human form, and had partaken of all the pleasures known to Man. Food and drink, drugs and debauchery. All were pitiful when compared to the tasting of souls. A faint memory stirred, and he remembered Darela. What he had felt for her was frightening. They had touched hands, then lips. Unused to human frailty Bakilas had been drawn into a relationship with the woman that left his senses reeling. With the last of his strength he had returned to the caverns of the Illohir and resumed his Krayakin form. Then he journeyed back to the village and drank Darela's soul. He had thought that would end her spell over him.

But he had been wrong. The memory of their days together came back again and again to haunt him.

The Krayakin rode in silence for several hours. The

smell of death was strong upon the wind as they rode down a short slope and emerged by the shores of a glittering lake. Keeping to the shadows of the trees Bakilas took in the campsite. There were five dead wolves upon the ground, and a sixth body by the water-line. Bakilas dismounted and lifted his hood into place. Then he walked out into the sunshine. Pain prickled his skin, but he ignored it. At the centre of the camp the grass was singed in a circle of around five feet in diameter. Removing his black gauntlet he reached out and touched the earth. His hand jerked back. Pulling on his gauntlet he returned to the shadows.

'Magick,' he said. 'Someone used magick here.'

Tethering their mounts the Krayakin sat in a circle. 'Anharat did not speak of magick,' said Mandrak, at just under 6 feet tall, the smallest of the warriors. 'He spoke only of three old men.'

'How strong was it?' asked Drasko, next to Bakilas the eldest of the group.

'By the power of four,' he answered. 'The wolves must have been possessed by the Entukku and the wizard used the light of *halignat*. Only a master could summon such power.'

'Why should the wolves have been possessed?' asked Pelicor.

Bakilas felt his irritation rise. 'Study was never a strength of yours, brother. Had they been merely wolves then any bright flash of light would have dispersed them. *Halignat* – the Holy Light – is used only against the Illohir. It would have hurled the Entukku back to the city – and perhaps beyond. Those closest to the flash might even have died.'

'If there is such a wizard,' said Drasko, 'why did we not sense his presence before now?'

'I do not know. Perhaps he is using a mask spell unknown to us. Whatever, we must proceed with more caution.'

'Caution is for cowards,' said Pelicor. 'I have no fear of this wizard, whoever he may be. His spells may vanquish the Entukku, but they are little more than mind-maggots. What spells can he hurl against the Krayakin?'

'We do not know,' said Bakilas, struggling to remain patient. 'That is the point.'

Bakilas strode to his horse and stepped into the saddle. Mandrak rode beside him as they set out after the wagon. 'He has always been impatient,' said Mandrak.

'It is not his impatience which offends me – but his stupidity. And he is a glutton. I have always abhorred that trait.'

'His hunger is legendary,' admitted Mandrak.

Bakilas did not reply. They had reached the end of the tree line, and the bright sun scorched his face. Putting on his helm he pulled up his hood and spurred his mount onwards. The brightness hurt his eyes, and he longed for the onset of night, the freshness of the breeze, the dark, cold beauty of the star-filled sky.

Their mounts were tired as they reached the base of a tall hill. Bakilas examined the trail. The fugitives had stopped here to change the horses, and the occupants of the wagon had walked up the hill. Two women and a child. He rode on. One of the women had picked up the child and carried it. A heavy woman, whose imprints were deeper than the rest.

Spurring his mount up the hill he rode over the crest, and saw the tracks wending away into another wood. He was grateful for the promise of shadow.

Did they know they were being followed? Of course

they did. No-one could hope to spirit away a queen without pursuit. Did they know they were being followed by the Krayakin? Why should they not, since a wizard was amongst them? Bakilas thought hard about the wizard. Drasko's point had been a good one. Why could they not sense the presence of his magick? The air should be thick with it. Closing his eyes Bakilas reached out with his senses.

Nothing. Not a trace of sorcery could be detected. Even a mask spell would leave a residual taste in the air. It was worrying. Anharat had always been arrogant. It was his arrogance that led to the defeat of the Illohir at the Battle of the Four Valleys. What had he said? How far had the enemy fallen that he could rely on only three old men. It could be viewed quite differently. How mighty was the enemy that all he *needed* were three old men. He thought of the black warrior. Such a man was not built for retreat. Somewhere along this trail he would seek to attack his pursuers. It was the nature of the man.

They approached the trees with caution, swords drawn, then entered the wood.

There was no attack. For another hour they followed the wagon tracks. They were fresher now, the edges of the wheel imprints clean and sharp.

Bakilas drew back on the reins. The wagon tracks turned off from the road and vanished into the trees. There was thick undergrowth beyond the tree line, and the wagon had crushed bushes and saplings beneath it. Why would they take such a difficult trail? Bakilas removed his helm and sniffed the air.

Mandrak moved alongside his leader. 'Can you smell it?' he asked. Bakilas nodded. Humans could never surprise the Krayakin, for human glands secreted many scents, oozing from their pores in the disgusting sweat that bathed them. Of all of his brothers Mandrak's sense of smell was the most keen. Bakilas drew rein and scanned the tree line and the bushes beyond, careful not to let his gaze dwell on two of the hiding places he had identified.

'Three men are hidden there,' said Mandrak.

'I have identified two,' whispered Bakilas.

'One is behind the large oak overhanging the rise, another is crouched behind a bush just below it. The other one is further back. Yes . . . with the horses.'

'Why are we stopping?' asked Pelicor.

'Remove your helmet, and you will know,' Bakilas told him, his voice low.

Pelicor did so. Like his brothers his hair was white, but his face was broad and flat, the eyes small and set close together. His nostrils flared, and he smiled. 'Let me take them, brother. I am hungry.'

'It might be wiser to circle them,' offered Mandrak. 'Cut off their means of escape.'

'There are three of them!' snapped Pelicor. 'Not thirty. How can they escape us? Come let us put an end to this dismal mission.'

'You wish to take them alone, Pelicor?' asked Bakilas.

'I do.'

'Then by all means charge. We will await your victory.'

Pelicor replaced his helm, drew his longsword and slashed his spurs into the horse's flanks. The beast reared then galloped into the trees. Just beyond the trail the black warrior stepped from behind a tree. Pelicor saw him and dragged on the reins. The warrior was holding a slim knife by the blade.

'You think to hurt me with that?' yelled Pelicor, spurring the horse once more.

The warrior's arm came back, the knife flashed forward, missing the charging rider. The blade slammed into a small wedge of wood, beside the trail, slicing through a length of stretched twine. A young tree, bent like a bow, snapped upright. Three pointed stakes lashed to it slammed into Pelicor's chest, smashing through his black armour, breaking his ribs and spearing his lungs. The horse ran on. The body of the Krayakin warrior hung in the air twitching.

Bakilas heard a whisper of movement. Flinging up his arm he took the arrow through his gauntleted hand. The arrow head sliced through the limb and buried itself in the pale flesh of his face, cutting his tongue. The wood of the shaft burned like acid. At first he tried to pull the arrow loose from his cheek, but the barbs caught against the inner flesh. With a grunt he pushed the shaft through his other cheek, snapped off the head, then drew the arrow clear of his face and hand. The wounds began to heal instantly. But where the wood had touched him the soreness continued for some time.

'They have run,' said Mandrak. 'Do we give chase?'

'Not through the woods. There will be other traps. We will catch them upon the road . . . very soon.'

Bakilas rode to where Pelicor hung from the stake. His eyes were open, his body in spasm.

'Help me,' he whimpered.

'Your body is dying, Pelicor,' said Bakilas, coldly. 'And soon you will be Windborn again. We can taste your fear. It is most exquisite. Drasko, Mandrak and myself fed only recently. Therefore our brothers shall draw sustenance from what remains of your form.'

'No . . . I . . . can . . . heal.'

Bakilas shivered with pleasure at the increase in fear emanating from the impaled warrior. Like the others

243

Pelicor had endured thousands of years in the torment that was Nowhere. The thought of returning to it filled him with horror. 'Who would have thought you could be capable of such intense terror, Pelicor. It is almost artistic,' said Bakilas.

Bakilas drew back, and the remaining six Krayakin moved in with daggers drawn.

Dagorian moved out onto the old bridge, testing each step. The ancient boards beneath his feet were 10 feet long, 18 inches wide, and 2 inches thick. They creaked ominously as he moved out upon them. Less than 12 feet wide the bridge spanned just over 100 feet. Below it the swollen river rushed on down the mountains, white water surging over massive rocks, and sweeping on to a rumbling fall some 2 miles down river. If he fell through he would be swept to his death. No man could swim in such a torrent.

The boards were nailed to huge cross beams set every 9 feet, and gaping cracks showed between them. Dagorian was sweating heavily as he moved out over the river. Since the attack by the wolves his fears had been growing, preying on his mind. Doubt had crept in, and with it a fierce longing to live. To be free of his duty. Only his sense of honour held him to this doomed quest, and even this was fraying. You should have stayed in the temple, he thought, as he moved carefully out over the rotting boards. Nogusta had ordered him to get the wagon across, if possible. He glanced back to where the others waited. They were all looking at him, including the queen. Carefully he moved on to the safety of the far bank.

There was still no way to be sure the bridge would take the weight of the wagon.

Moving swiftly back to where the others waited he instructed them to walk with care, keeping to the stone reinforced rail. Ulmenetha took Axiana by the arm and led her out onto the bridge. Pharis followed with Sufia. Conalin remained with the wagon.

'Get across, boy,' ordered Dagorian.

'I can drive it,' insisted Conalin.

'I don't doubt your skill. I just don't want to see you die.' The boy was about to argue, but Dagorian shook his head. 'I know you have courage, Conalin, and I respect it. But if you want to help me then lead the spare horses across. I will follow when you are safe on the far bank.'

Conalin climbed down and moved to the rear of the wagon. Dagorian took his place, gathered up the reins, and waited. The boy moved out past him. 'Talk to them as you walk,' advised Dagorian, 'for the rushing water will frighten them.'

The boy was halfway across when one of the boards suddenly moved. A horse reared, but Conalin stepped in close, whispering to it, stroking its long neck. Dagorian looked on admiringly. Conalin continued on his way. Upon reaching the far side he turned and waved. Dagorian flicked the reins and the team moved out onto the bridge. The horses were nervous and, keeping his voice low and even, Dagorian encouraged them. Underneath the wagon the boards groaned. One split, but did not give way. Dagorian was sweating as they reached the centre of the bridge. The rushing of the water below sounded thunderous now. One of the horses slipped, but righted itself.

Then a board cracked, and the wagon lurched. For a sickening heartbeat Dagorian thought he was about to be pitched into the river. He sat very still for a moment, his heart thudding in his chest, then carefully climbed down. The left rear wheel was halfway through the boards, being supported only by the jutting axle head. Dagorian let out a soft curse. Putting both hands under the tailboard he struggled to lift it clear. It did not move a hair's breadth.

'They're coming!' shouted Conalin. Dagorian swung to see Nogusta, Kebra and Bison. They were galloping their horses, riding hard and fast. Nogusta reached the bridge first, dragging on the reins. Then he leapt from the saddle and led the giant black gelding out onto the bridge. Kebra and Bison followed his lead. There was no room for them to pass.

Bison tossed his reins to Kebra and strode to where Dagorian stood at the rear of the wagon. 'Get back in the driver's seat,' said the giant, ' and give them a lash when I call.'

'It won't move,' said Dagorian.

'Riders!' yelled Conalin.

The warriors of the Krayakin breasted the slope, and, swords drawn, rode for the bridge. Dagorian scrambled up to the wagon. Bison grabbed the wheel. 'Now!' he shouted. The giant heaved, and the wagon rose. At the same time Dagorian lashed the reins across the backs of the team. The wagon lurched forward. Bison was hurled from his feet, but rolled clear of the iron shod wheel.

Dagorian lashed the backs of the team and the wagon picked up speed. Nogusta and Kebra came running behind.

The child Sufia climbed into the wagon as it reached the bank. In a high-pitched voice she chanted something in an alien tongue.

The Krayakin had reached the bridge, and two of them set off across it.

A ball of flame flew from Sufia's hand, striking the bridge. A column of fire reared up, and the bridge began to blaze. One of the Krayakin backed his horse to safety, but the second spurred his mount, riding through the blaze. Bison ran at the charging horse, waving his arms and shouting at the top of his voice. The beast reared. Bison hurled himself forward, ducking under the flailing hoofs. Throwing up his arms Bison clamped his hands to the horse's chest and pushed with all his strength. The horse toppled back hurling its rider into the flames. The boards gave way. Horse and warrior crashed through to the roiling river below. Fingers of fire swept along the boards. Bison's leggings caught alight. Spinning on his heel the giant ran, panic stricken, to the bank. Nogusta and Kebra leapt upon him, hurling him to the ground. They tried to beat out the flames on Bison's burning clothing, but to no avail. Then Sufia stepped forward and held out her hand. The fire leapt from Bison to the child's waiting fingers, where it vanished. Bison tore off his leggings. His flesh was badly burned on the left thigh. Sufia moved to him, dropping to her knees. Her tiny hand reached out. Bison winced as her fingers touched the blistered flesh of his thigh. Then, as if a cool breeze was whispering over the burn, all pain ceased. She lifted her hand. The burn was gone.

'Such small magick is still left to me,' said the voice of Kalizkan. The body of the child settled down against Bison, her blond head resting on his chest. 'Let her sleep,' said Kalizkan. Bison carefully lifted the sleeping child and carried her to the wagon, where he laid her down and covered her with a blanket.

Ulmenetha approached the giant warrior. 'That was a brave act,' she said, 'to charge a mounted knight. I must say you surprised me.'

Bison turned to her and gave a wide, gap-toothed grin. 'If you'd like to thank me properly we could move further back into the bushes.'

'Now, that reaction *doesn't* surprise me,' she said. With a withering glance at his naked lower body she added: 'And find some fresh leggings. There are ladies present.'

'That's when I normally need it,' he said, still grinning.

Swinging away the priestess walked back to where Axiana and Pharis were sitting together. From the wagon Conalin grinned at the old man. 'Women,' said Bison, 'who can understand them?' Conalin shrugged.

'I don't,' he admitted. 'But I know enough to realize that she doesn't like you.'

'You think so?' asked Bison, genuinely surprised. 'What makes you believe that?'

Conalin laughed aloud. 'Perhaps I'm wrong.'

'I think you might be,' agreed Bison.

Black smoke was rising from the blazing bridge, and Nogusta strode to the bank, staring across the river to where the eight remaining Krayakin warriors waited. Dagorian joined him. 'There are other bridges,' he said. 'But we have gained a little time.'

The Krayakin divided into two groups. Four warriors rode down river towards the west, the other four heading east.

'We have had more luck than we deserve,' said Nogusta, softly.

'What happened back in the forest?'

'We killed one. But only because the leader wanted him dead. They are deadly foes, Dagorian. More terrible than any I have faced before.'

'And yet two are dead, and we have suffered no losses.'

'Not yet,' whispered Nogusta.

Dagorian shivered suddenly. He glanced at the black warrior. 'What have you seen with that Third Eye of yours?'

'Do not ask,' advised Nogusta.

Ulmenetha's spirit rose above the campsite, hovering in the night air. The moon was bright, the sky clear over the mountains. From here she could see Nogusta, sitting alone on a hillside. Close by Kebra was talking to Conalin. Axiana, Pharis and Sufia were asleep in the wagon. Bison sat alone by the camp-fire, finishing the last of the stew prepared by Kebra.

There was freedom here in this astral solitude, and Ulmenetha gloried in it. There were no demons over the forest, no Entukku with their slashing talons. She allowed herself to rise further, the moonlit forest shrinking below her. Ulmenetha flew north, over the ruined bridge, intending to seek out the Krayakin.

A glowing form materialized in the air alongside her. This time she could make out a face. It was that of a young man, golden haired and handsome. 'It is not wise,' he said, 'to journey far. The Krayakin will be able to see you, and they can summon the Entukku to attack you.'

'I need to know how close they are,' said Ulmenetha.

'The group heading east will lose two days. Those heading west will cross the river at Lercis, forty miles from here. They will not catch up with you by tomorrow.'

'Why is this happening to us, Kalizkan? What did you do?'

'It is not safe here, lady. Return to your body and sleep. We will talk again in a place of sanctuary.'

The figure vanished.

Ulmenetha flew back to the campsite, and there hovered for a while, enjoying a last taste of freedom.

Back within her body she settled down, covering herself with a blanket. Sleep came easily, for she was very tired.

She became aware of the smell of honeysuckle, and opened her eyes to see a small garden. A latticework arch was close by, red and cream honeysuckle growing up and through it. There were flower beds full of summer plants, blazing with colour in the sunlight. Ulmenetha looked around, and saw a small cottage, with a thatched roof. She recognized it instantly. It was her grandmother's house.

The door opened, and a tall man stepped out. He was silver-haired and silver-bearded, and dressed in a long robe of silver satin. Kalizkan bowed. 'Now we can talk,' he said.

'I preferred you as the golden-haired young man,' said Ulmenetha.

Kalizkan chuckled. 'I must admit to you, lady, that he is a conceit. I never was golden haired, nor handsome . . . save in the spirit form. Were you ever as you appear now? So slim and innocent.'

'Indeed I was. But those days are long gone.'

'Not here,' said Kalizkan.

'No, not here,' she agreed, wistfully.

'So what would you have me tell you?'

'All of it.'

Kalizkan led her to a wooden bench beneath the honeysuckle arch, and they sat down in the shade. 'I was dying,' he said. 'Cancer was spreading through me. For more than ten years I used my magick to hold it at bay, but as I grew older my powers began to fade. I was frightened. Simply that. I studied many ancient grimoires, seeking spells to prolong my life, but always avoiding blood magick. Finally I sank to that. I sacrificed an old man. I told myself he was dying anyway – which he was – and I was only robbing him of a few days of life. He came willingly for I offered to create a pension for his widow.' Kalizkan lapsed into silence. Then he spoke again. 'The deed was an evil one, though I tried to convince myself otherwise. I thought of all the good I could still do if I lived. I reasoned that a small evil was acceptable, if it led to a greater good.' He smiled ruefully. 'Such is the path to perdition. I summoned a Demon Lord and sought to control him, ordering him to heal me. Instead he possessed me. With the last of my strength I hurled my spirit clear. From that day to this I have watched all the good I have done in my life eroded and stained by the evils he used my form to commit. All my children were sacrificed. And now thousands are dead, and the city of Usa is in torment.

'There is little I can do now to set matters right. My powers are limited – aye, and fading. Death calls me and I will not be here to see the end.

'But what I can do in the time that remains is teach you, Ulmenetha. I can instruct you in the magick of the land. I will teach you to use *halignat* – the holy fire. I will show you how to heal lesser wounds.'

'I have never been adept at such skills,' she said.

'Well now you must learn,' he told her. 'I can no longer use the child. She is malnourished and her heart is weak. It almost failed when I burned the bridge. I will not have another innocent life upon my hands.'

'I cannot do it,' said Ulmenetha. 'I cannot learn in a day!'

'Where we sit is not governed by *time*, Ulmenetha. We are floating in the open heart of eternity. Trust me. What

251

you take from here will be vital to the safety of the child and the future of the world.'

'I do not want such responsibility. I am not . . . strong enough.'

'You are stronger than you think!' he said, forcefully. 'And you will need to be stronger yet.'

Angry now, Ulmenetha rose from the bench. 'Bring Nogusta here. Teach him! He is a warrior. He knows how to fight!'

He shook his head. 'Yes, he is a warrior. But I do not need someone who knows how to kill. I need someone who knows how to love.'

The night air was cold, but Conalin, a blanket round his shoulders, sat in quiet contentment alongside Kebra. The bowman did not speak, and this, in itself, pleased Conalin. They were together in silence. Companions. Conalin flicked a glance at Kebra's profile, seeing the moonlight glinting on the old man's white hair.

'What are you thinking?' asked the boy.

'I was remembering my father.'

'I didn't mean to disturb you.'

'I'm glad you did,' said Kebra. 'They were not pleasant memories.' He turned to the boy. 'You look cold. You should sit by the fire.'

'I am not cold.' The open sores on his arms and back were troubling him. Pushing up his sleeve he scratched at the scabs on his arm. 'What will you do if you reach Drenan?'

'I'll try my hand at farming. I own a hundred acres in the mountains close to the Sentran Plain. I'll build a house there. Maybe,' he finished, lamely.

'Is that what you really want?'

Kebra gave a rueful smile. 'Perhaps not. It is a dream.

My last dream. The Sathuli have a blessing which says: May all your dreams – but one – come true.'

'Why is that a blessing? Would not a man be happier if all his dreams came true?'

'No,' said Kebra, shaking his head, 'that would be awful. What would there be left to live for? Our dreams are what carry us forward. We journey from dream to dream. At this moment your dream is to wed Pharis. If that dream comes true, and you are happy, you will want children. Then you will dream for them also. A man without dreams is a dead man. He may walk and talk, but he is sterile and empty.'

'And you have only one dream left? What happened to all the others?'

'You ask difficult questions, my friend.' Kebra lapsed into silence. Conalin did not disturb it. He felt a great warmth within, that all but swamped the cold of the night. My friend. Kebra had called him, my friend. The boy stared out over the silhouette of the mountains and watched the bright stars glinting around the moon. There was a harmony here, a great emptiness that filled the soul with the music of silence. The city had never offered such harmony, and Conalin's life had been an endless struggle to survive amid the cruelty and the squalor. He had learned early that no-one ever acted without selfish motives. Everything had a price. And mostly Conalin could not afford it.

Nogusta strolled towards where they sat. Conalin felt his irritation rise. He did not want this moment to be disturbed. But the black warrior moved silently past them and down to the camp-site.

'Is he your best friend?' asked Conalin.

'Best friend? I don't know what that means,' Kebra told him.

'Do you like him better than Bison?'

'That's easier to answer,' said Kebra with a smile. 'After all, nobody *likes* Bison. But no, he's not a *better* friend.' Reaching down he plucked two grass stems. 'Which of these stems is better?' he asked Conalin.

'Neither. They are just grass.'

'Exactly.'

'I don't understand.'

'Neither did I when I was young. In those days I thought that anyone who smiled at me was a friend. Anyone who offered me food was a friend. The word had little real meaning. But true friendship is rarer than a white raven, and more valuable than a mountain of gold. And once you find it you realize there is no way to grade it.'

'What did he do to become your friend? Did he save your life?'

'Several times. But I can't answer that question. I really can't. No more, I think, could he. And now my tired old bones need sleep. I will see you in the morning.'

Kebra rose and stretched his back. Conalin stood and they walked back to the camp-site. Bison was asleep by the fire, and snoring loudly. Kebra nudged him with his foot. Bison grunted and rolled over.

Conalin added sticks to the dying fire and sat watching the flames flicker as Kebra settled down alongside Bison. The bowman spread his blanket over his lean frame, then came up on one elbow. 'You are a bright lad, Conalin,' he said. 'You can be whatever you want to be, if your dreams are grand enough.'

For a while Conalin sat quietly by the fire. Dagorian emerged from the bushes and strolled to the wagon. The young officer looked tired, his movements heavy with weariness. Conalin watched him take an apple from a food sack and bite into it. Seemingly unaware of the boy Dagorian strolled back to the fire, pausing to gaze down on the sleeping figure of Axiana. Pharis was lying beside her, little Sufia cuddled in close. Dagorian stood silently for a moment, then sighed and joined Conalin by the dying blaze. Bison began to snore again. Conalin rose and prodded the giant with his foot, exactly as Kebra had done. Obligingly Bison rolled over, and the snoring ceased.

'Neatly done,' said Dagorian, reaching out and adding the last of the fuel to the fire. Conalin did not reply. Rising he left his blanket and wandered to the tree line, gathering dry sticks and twigs. He was not tired now, for his mind was full of questions, and the only man he would trust to answer them was asleep. He made several trips back to the fire, and was pleased to see Dagorian settle down in his blankets.

Conalin walked to the nearby stream and drank, then moved out away from the camp, strolling through the moonlit woods. The night breeze rustled in the leaves, but there was no other sound. The day's drama seemed far away now, an incident from another life. Then he remembered the big man running at the mounted knight, ducking under his horse and hurling the enemy back into the flames. He knew what Ulmenetha had meant when she said she was surprised. Conalin had not expected such a rare display of courage from the obscene old man. Yet the others had not been surprised. Conalin walked on, oblivious to his surroundings. The night air was full of new scents, fresh and vibrant and utterly unlike the musty stink of the city. He came to a break in the trees, and saw a moonlit meadow. Rabbits were feeding on the grass, and he paused to watch them. It seemed strange to see these creatures so full of life. His only previous experience of them was to see them hanging by their hind legs in the market place. Here, like him, they were free.

A dark shadow swept over the meadow, and a great bird swooped low over the feeding rabbits. They scattered, but the bird's talons slashed across the back of one fleeing rabbit, bowling it over. Before it could rise the bird was upon it, gripping it tight, its curved beak tearing the life from its prey.

Conalin watched as the hawk fed.

'That is unusual,' said a voice. Conalin leapt like a startled deer, and swung round, fists raised. Nogusta was standing beside him. The boy's heart was pounding. He had not heard the black man approach. Nogusta appeared not to notice Conalin's reaction. 'Hawks usually feed on feather,' he said. 'They need to be wedded to fur by a falconer.'

'How can they survive on feathers?' asked Conalin, anxious to seem unperturbed by the warrior's silent approach.

Nogusta smiled. 'Not literally feathers. It means they generally feed on other birds, pigeon and – if the hawk is clever enough – duck. This hawk probably escaped his handler and returned to the wild.'

Conalin sighed. 'I thought the rabbits were free here,' said Conalin.

'They are free,' said Nogusta.

'No. I meant really free. Free from danger.'

'Nothing that walks, flies, swims or breathes is ever free from danger. Speaking of which you should not stray too far from the camp.'

Nogusta turned and walked away into the darkness. Conalin caught up with him. 'If you do save the queen,' he said, 'what reward will you get?'

'I don't know. I haven't given it any thought.'

'Will you become rich?'

'Perhaps.'

They reached the edge of the camp and Nogusta paused. 'Go and get some rest. We will have to push hard tomorrow.'

'Is that why you are doing this?' persisted Conalin. 'For the reward?'

'No. My reasons are far more selfish.'

Conalin took a step towards the camp. Then another question occurred to him and he swung round. But Nogusta was nowhere to be seen.

Gathering his blankets Conalin lay down beside Pharis. There was so much here that he didn't understand. What could be more selfish than labouring for a personal reward?

Life in the city had been brutally hard, and Conalin had been alone for much of his young life. Even so he felt he understood the nature of human existence. Happiness was a full belly, joy was having enough food for a full belly tomorrow, and love was a commodity mostly associated with money. Even his love of Pharis was ultimately selfish, for Conalin gained great pleasure from her company. It was that pleasure, he believed, which led him to yearn for her. Like the men and women who gathered at the Chiatze House, and smoked the long pipe, paying for pleasure dreams, and returning again and again, with haunted eyes and shrinking purses.

Conalin had no recollection of his parents. His first memories were of a small room, packed with children. Some of them were crying. All of them were filthy. Conalin had been tiny then, perhaps three or four years of age. He recalled the baby, lying on a soiled blanket. He remembered prodding it with his finger. It did not move. The lack of movement had surprised him. A fly had landed on the baby's open mouth, and slowly walked over the blue lips. Some time later a tall man had removed the baby.

Conalin couldn't remember the man's face. It had seemed so high and far away. But he remembered the legs, long and thin, encased in loose-fitting black leggings. His time in the house of gloom had not been happy, for his belly was rarely full, and there were many beatings.

After that there had been several homes. One, at least, had been warm and comfortable. But the price of that warmth had been too high, and he pushed the memories away.

Life on the streets had been better.

Conalin had even begun to think of himself as a wise man. He knew where to steal his breakfast, and could always find a warm, safe place to sleep, even in the depths of harsh winters. The soldiers of the Watch could never catch him, and his troubles with the street gangs had largely ended when he had killed Cleft-tongue. The gangs avoided him then, for Cleft-tongue had been feared, and anyone who could kill him in one-to-one combat was not to be trifled with. Conalin remembered the fight without any pleasure. He hadn't wanted to kill anyone. All he desired was to be left alone. But Cleft-tongue would have none of it. 'You steal on my patch, you pay rent,' he had said. Conalin had ignored him. Then, one night, the burly youth had come at him with a knife. Conalin was unarmed and had run. He recalled the laughter which followed him on his flight. Angry he had stolen a butcher's cleaver, and returned to where the gang had settled down for the night, in a deserted alleyway. He had walked up to where Cleft-tongue sat, called his name, and, as the youth turned, hit him in the temple with the cleaver. The blade had sunk deep, far deeper than Conalin had intended. Cleft-tongue died instantly.

'Now leave me alone,' Conalin told the others.

They had done so.

Unable to sleep Conalin pushed back his blanket and rose, walking to a nearby tree and urinating. Then he moved to the remains of the fire and added some of the twigs he had gathered earlier. With a stick he located the last glowing area of coals and, for some minutes, tried to blow them to fresh life. Finally admitting that the fire had died he sat back.

That was when he noticed the glow on the far side of the camp, a soft white light that was bathing the body of the sleeping priestess. Conalin watched it for some time, then he moved to Kebra's side and woke the bowman.

'What is it, lad?' asked Kebra, sleepily.

'Something is wrong with the priestess,' said Conalin. Kebra sat up, then pushed back his blankets. Dagorian awoke, saw the glowing light, and, with Conalin and Kebra, walked over to where Ulmenetha lay. The light was stronger now, almost golden. It was radiating from her face and hands. Kebra knelt beside her.

'She is burning up,' said the bowman. Conalin looked closer. Sweat was running from the woman's fat face, and her silver and blond hair was drenched. Kebra tried to wake her, but to no avail. The light around her grew brighter, and small white flowers blossomed around her blankets, writhing up through the grass. A heady scent filled the air, and Conalin could hear far-away music, whispering in his mind. Kebra drew back the blanket that covered the priestess. Only then did they see that she was floating some inches above the ground.

Nogusta moved alongside them, kneeling down and taking Ulmenetha's hand. The glowing light swelled, and flowed up along Nogusta's arm, bathing him in light. Releasing her hand he leapt backwards.

'Is she under attack?' asked Dagorian.

'No,' said Nogusta. 'This is not blood magick.'

'What should we do?' put in Kebra.

'Nothing. We will cover her and wait.'

Conalin peered down at the priestess's glistening face. 'She is getting thinner,' he whispered. It was true. Sweat was coursing over her body, and her flesh was receding.

'She'll die if this carries on,' said Kebra.

'What is happening to her is not of an evil origin,' said Nogusta. 'If it were I would sense it through my talisman. I do not think she will die. Cover her.'

Conalin lifted the blanket over Ulmenetha. As he did so his hand touched her shoulder. Once more the light flowed, bathing him. An exquisite feeling of warmth and security filled him. His back itched and tingled, and he moaned with pleasure. Dizziness overcame him and he fell back to the grass. Pulling off his filthy shirt he gazed down at his arms. The open sores had vanished, and his skin glowed with health. 'Look!' he said to Kebra. 'I am healed.'

The bowman said nothing. Reaching out he also touched the priestess. The light flowed over him. Bright lights danced behind his eyes, and it seemed, at first, as if he was looking through a sheen of ice, distorting his view. Slowly the ice melted, and he found himself staring at the distant mountains, their peaks sharp and clear against the new dawn. He too sat back. 'I can see!' he whispered. 'Nogusta, I can see! Clearly!'

As the dawn rose, streaking the sky with gold, the light around Ulmenetha faded away, and her body slowly settled down upon the carpet of white flowers.

Her eyes opened, the last of the golden light shining from them.

'We cannot reach the coast,' she said. 'The Demon Lord is marching his army across the mountains, and the way to the sea is closed to us.'

Nogusta knelt beside her. 'I know,' he said, wearily.

Ulmenetha tried to sit, but sagged back exhausted. Her lips were dry. Nogusta ran to the wagon, returning with a water skin and a cup. Helping her to sit he held the cup to her lips. She drank sparingly. 'We must try . . . to reach . . . the ghost city,' she said. 'Now let me rest.' Nogusta lowered her to the ground. She fell asleep instantly.

'What did she mean?' asked Kebra. 'The sea is our only hope.'

'We would never reach it. The Krayakin are less than a day behind us, and the Ventrian army is moving across the mountains. Three thousand men are on the march, and more than two hundred cavalry have been sent to cut us off from the coast.'

Kebra knew the strength of Nogusta's Third Eye and he sat silently for a moment, absorbing the information. 'What then can we do?' he asked. 'We cannot fight an army, and we cannot escape it. Is our plan merely to run until we are exhausted – like an elk tracked by wolves?'

'Who is being tracked by wolves?' asked Bison, rising from his blankets and walking across to join them. Before Nogusta could explain the situation to him the giant saw the sleeping priestess. 'Kreya's Tits!' he exclaimed. 'Look at her! She's thin as a spear. What have I missed?'

'A great deal, my friend,' said Kebra. Slowly he explained the events of the last few minutes, the glowing around the priestess, the healing of his eyes, and the sores on Conalin's back and arms, and lastly, the news of the march of the Ventrian army. Bison ignored the last news.

'She healed you? What about my ear? It hurts like the devil. You could have woken me up. What kind of a friend are you?' He dropped to his knees beside the priestess and shook her shoulder. Ulmenetha did not stir. 'Well, this is nice,' said Bison, glancing up at Kebra. 'So far I've been bitten by wolves, burnt by magick and kicked by a horse. And you get your eyes healed. Is that fair?'

'Life is not fair, Bison,' said Kebra, with a smile. 'As any one of your large number of wives would testify.' His smile faded. 'The question is what are we going to do?' At that moment Axiana cried out. Beside her Pharis awoke and moved to her side.

'What is it, my lady?' she asked.

'I think . . . the baby is coming,' said Axiana.

Axiana was frightened, and called for Ulmenetha. The black warrior, Nogusta, moved to her side. 'She cannot come to you now,' he said, taking the queen's hand. 'She is sleeping, and cannot be woken.' Fear turned to panic in Axiana.

'The baby is coming! I need her!' Her face spasmed as fresh pain seared through her.

'Move aside, man,' said Bison, dropping to his knees beside the frightened girl.

'I don't want you!' shouted Axiana, horrified. 'Not you!'

Bison chuckled. 'As I've just been told, life isn't fair. But I've birthed babes before, and a large number of horses, cows and sheep. So you'll just have to trust me.' He turned to Nogusta. 'I want you to make a screen around her. Give us some privacy. And you, girl,' he told Pharis, 'can help me.' Bison drew back the blanket covering the queen. Her gown was wet. 'The water's broken,' he said. He looked across at Nogusta. 'Could we get a little urgency going here?'

Nogusta nodded and rose. Nogusta and Dagorian cut long branches from nearby trees, then stripped them of leaves. Plunging them into the earth around the queen they tied blankets to them, creating a roofless tent around her. Several times she cried out. Pharis emerged and moved to the stream, filling a bowl with water, and returning to the tent.

Little Sufia sat in the doorway of the tent, staring wide eyed into the interior. Conalin walked over to her, lifting her into his arms and carrying her to the wagon. The child was nervous and frightened. 'They are hurting her,' she said, her eyes brimming with tears.

'No they are not,' said Conalin, soothingly. 'A baby is coming. It's inside her, and it is going to come out.'

'How did it get inside her?' asked Sufia.

'It grew from a very small seed,' said Conalin. 'And now it is ready to live.'

A long shriek came from the tent. Sufia jumped. 'Why is she hurting?' Sufia began to cry. Kebra walked to the wagon. 'It is all right,' he said, ruffling the child's blond hair.

'She wants to know why the queen is in pain,' said Conalin.

'Well,' began Kebra, uneasily, 'she's . . . slim in the hips and –' Sufia's bright blue eyes were locked to Kebra's gaze. '– and . . .' He swung and called for Nogusta. 'The child has some questions,' he said, brightly.

'Answer them,' said Nogusta, walking away towards the stream.

'Thank you so much,' Kebra called after him. He turned back to Sufia. 'I can't really explain,' he told the child. 'Childbirth is sometimes painful, but soon the queen will be well, and you will be able to see the baby boy. That will be nice, won't it?'

The queen shrieked once more, and Sufia dissolved into tears.

Kebra moved away and began to prepare breakfast. Sitting beside the stream Nogusta and Dagorian talked in low voices. 'Does Bison know what he's doing?' asked the young officer.

'Yes. Believe it or not many of the camp whores request Bison when they are ready to deliver.'

'I can't think why.'

'Maybe he fathered most of the children,' ventured Nogusta. 'But I believe she is in safe hands.'

'Safe hands? How safe are any of us?'

Nogusta heard the fear in the young man's voice. He was concerned, for he had noticed the growing tension in the officer ever since the wolf attack. 'Nothing has changed since you rescued the queen,' he said.

'I didn't rescue her – Ulmenetha did that. And the children. I just came later. And we would all have been killed had you not arrived to kill the lancers. I don't feel that I have been of any real use.' Dagorian sighed. 'I am not like you, Nogusta. Nor the others. You are tough men. The stuff of heroes. I . . .' he faltered. 'I am just a failed priest.'

'You do yourself a disservice,' said Nogusta. Dagorian shook his head.

'You remember when you warned me about an attempt on Banelion's life? I went to him, as I told you.'

'Yes. He advised you to stay away from him. That was good advice.'

'Maybe it was – but a hero would have disobeyed him. Don't you see? I was glad to be relieved of responsibility. I thanked him and I left. Would you have done so?'

'Yes,' said Nogusta.

'I don't believe you.'

'I wouldn't lie to you, Dagorian.'

'But would you have felt relief?'

'You are torturing yourself unnecessarily,' said the black man. 'What is really at the heart of this?'

'I am afraid.' He looked into Nogusta's face. 'What is it that you have seen? I need to know.'

'You do not *need* to know,' Nogusta assured him. 'And it would serve no purpose to tell you. This gift I have is like a sharp sword. It can save a life, or it can take it. At this moment you and I are alive, and we have a mission. All we can do is try to stay alive. What I have seen, or not seen, is irrelevant.'

'That is simply not true,' said Dagorian. 'The future is not set in stone. You could, for example, have seen me walking on a particular cliff top. The ground gives way and I fall to my death. But if you warn me I will not walk on that cliff top. Then I will live.'

Nogusta shook his head. 'I told you once before that the gift is not that precise. I do not choose what to see.'

'I just want to know whether I will survive,' said Dagorian. 'Have you seen that, at least?'

'Ultimately no-one survives,' hissed Nogusta. 'That is the way of life. We are born, we live, we die. All that counts is the manner in which we live. And even that does not count for long. History will forget us. It forgets all men eventually. You want certainty? *That* is certainty.'

'I fear I may be a coward,' said Dagorian. 'I might run from this mission.'

'You will not run,' said Nogusta. 'You are a man of

courage and honour. I know you are afraid. So you should be – for so am I. Our enemies are great in number, and our friends are few. Yet we will do what we must, for we are men, and the sons of men.'

The queen cried out again. Dagorian jerked at the sound, then pushed himself to his feet and walked from the camp.

For more than an hour the group waited, and there was little sound from within the roofless tent. Then Bison emerged, wandered to the fire and ate some of the hot oats Kebra had prepared for breakfast. The bowman approached him.

'What is happening?' asked Kebra.

'She is resting a little,' the giant told him.

'How soon will she have the child?'

Bison shrugged. 'The water sac has burst and the baby is on its way. How long? I don't know. Another hour. Perhaps two or three. Maybe more.'

'That's not very precise,' snapped Kebra. 'I thought you were an expert in this.'

'Expert? A few times doesn't make you an expert. All I know is that there are three stages to birthing. The first is under way. The baby is moving.'

'And the second?'

'The contractions will become more severe as the child enters the birth canal and on into the vagina.'

Kebra smiled. 'That's the first time I've ever heard you use the correct term.'

'I'm not in the mood for jokes at the moment,' said Bison. 'She's a slim girl, and this is the first child. There's likely to be a lot of torn flesh. And I know little of what to do if anything goes wrong. Has anyone tried again to wake the priestess?'

'I'll sit by her,' promised Kebra.

'You do that. Smack her face. Pour water on her. Anything.'

'As soon as she wakes I'll send her to you.'

Bison rose and ambled back to the tent. Kebra moved to the sleeping priestess. She was no longer bathed in sweat. Her skin was clear and firm, and Kebra was surprised to see how pretty she was now that the excess flesh was gone. And she looked so much younger. He had thought her to be in her forties, but now he saw she was – despite the grey in her blond hair – at least ten years younger. He took her hand and squeezed her fingers. 'Can you hear me, lady?' he said. But she did not stir.

The morning wore on, the sun climbing towards noon. Nogusta, normally so cool and in control, was pacing the camp. Once he approached the tent and called out to Bison. The response was short, coarse and to the point. Nogusta strode to the stream. Kebra, still unable to wake the priestess, joined him there.

'We are losing the time we gained at the bridge,' said Nogusta. 'If this goes on much longer the enemy will be upon us.'

'Bison doesn't know how long the labour will last. It could be hours yet.'

Nogusta suddenly smiled. 'Would you want Bison as the midwife to your first-born?'

'It is a ghastly thought,' admitted Kebra.

Chapter Nine

No nightmare ever suffered by Axiana had been worse than this. Her dress removed, her bare feet pressing into the damp earth, her lower back a rhythmic sea of pain, she squatted like a peasant beneath an open sky. Her emotional state had been fragile ever since the horror of the events at the house of Kalizkan, and everything since had conspired to fill her with terrible fear. Her husband was dead, her life as a royal princess a diminishing memory. All her life she had been pampered, never knowing hunger or poverty; the heat of summer kept from her by servants with peacock fans, the cold of winter barred from the palace by warm fires and fine clothes of wool.

Only days ago she had been sitting in a padded satin chair amid the splendour of the royal apartments, servants everywhere. And despite her husband's disdain of her, she had been the queen of a great empire.

Now, naked and frightened, she squatted in a forest, wracked with pain, and waiting to birth a king in the wet and the mud.

Beside her the giant, Bison, was supporting her weight. His ugly face was close to hers, and when she turned her head she could feel the coarseness of his bristling moustache against the skin of her face. His left hand was rubbing gently across the base of her spine, easing the pain there. Back in Usa Ulmenetha had showed her the

268

satin covered birthing stool, and quietly explained all the processes of birth. It had almost seemed an adventure then. Fresh pain seared through her and she cried out.

'Don't breathe too fast,' said Bison. His gruff voice cut through her rising panic. The contractions continued, the rhythm of pain rising and falling. The girl, Pharis, lifted a cup to Axiana's lips. The water was cool and sweet. Sweat dripped into Axiana's eyes. Pharis wiped it away with a cloth.

Cramp stabbed through her right thigh. She reared up against Bison and screamed. 'My leg! My leg!' Lifting her easily he turned her to her back, leaning her against a fallen tree. Kneeling beside her his huge hands began to rub at the muscles above her knee. Pharis offered her more water. She shook her head. The humiliation was colossal. No man but her husband had ever seen her naked, and on that one night she had bathed in perfumed water and waited in a room lit with the light of three coloured lanterns. The light now was harsh and bright, and the ugly peasant was rubbing her thighs with his huge calloused hands.

And yet, she thought suddenly, he cares! Which is something Skanda never did.

Axiana remembered the night the king had come to her. He cared nothing that she was a virgin, untutored and unskilled. He had made no attempt to ease her fears, nor even arouse her. There had been no pleasure in the act. It had been painful and – thank the Source – short lived. He had not said a word throughout, and when he had finished he rose from her bed and stalked from the room. She had cried for hours.

Axiana felt dizzy. She opened her eyes to see bright lights dancing before her vision. 'Breathe slowly,' advised Bison. 'You'll pass out else. And we don't want that, do we?'

Pain flared once more, reaching new heights. 'There's blood! There's blood!' wailed Pharis.

'Of course there's blood,' snapped Bison. 'Just stay calm, girl. Go and fetch some more water!'

Axiana moaned. Bison leaned in to her. 'Try to think of something else,' he said. 'One of my wives used to chant. You know any chants?'

Anger replaced the pain in Axiana, roaring up like a forest fire. 'You oaf! You stupid . . .' Suddenly she let fly with a stream of coarse and obscene swear words, in both Drenai and Ventrian, words she had heard but had never before uttered; would never have believed herself capable of uttering. It was, as she had always believed, the language of the gutter. Bison was completely unfazed.

'My third wife used to talk like that,' he said. 'It's as good as a chant,' he added, brightly.

Axiana sagged against him, exhausted. All the years of nobility, the education and the instilled belief that nobles were a different species to mere mortals, peeled away from her, like the layers of an onion. She was an animal now, sweating, grunting and moaning; a creature without pride. Tears welled as the pain soared to fresh heights. 'I can't stand it!' she whispered. 'I can't!'

'Course you can. You're a brave girl. Course you can.' She swore at him again, repeating the same word over and over.

'That's good,' he said, with a grin. Her head sagged against his shoulder. His hand pushed back the sweat-drenched hair from her brow. More than anything else this one small gesture restored her courage. She was not alone. The pain eased momentarily.

'Where is Ulmenetha?' she asked Bison.

'She'll be here when she wakes. I don't know why

she's still sleeping. Nogusta thinks it's magick of some kind. But I'm here. You can trust old Bison.'

Pharis leaned in and wiped her face, then offered her more water. Axiana drank gratefully.

The morning wore on, the sun passing noon and drifting slowly across the sky. For a time Bison lifted her once more to a kneeling position, but the cramps returned, and by mid-afternoon she was sitting once more with her back against the fallen tree. Her strength was almost gone, and she was floating in pain, semi-conscious. She remembered her mother, the wan young face, the eyes dark circled. She had died in childbirth. Her son born dead, her body torn, her life blood draining away. Axiana had been six years old. Her nurse had brought her in to say goodbye. But her mother had been delirious, and had not recognized her. She had called out a name, screamed it loud. No-one knew who she was calling for.

She had been buried on a bright summer afternoon, her son beside her.

'I am going to die like her,' thought Axiana.

'No, you're not,' said Bison.

'I didn't . . . mean to say that . . . aloud,' whispered Axiana.

'You're not going to die, girl. In a little while I'll lay your son on your breast, and the sunlight will touch you both.'

'My . . . son.' The thought was a strange one. For the duration of her pregnancy Axiana had thought only of the *baby* inside her. Skanda's baby. Skanda's child. An object created by a virtual rape which had changed her young life.

My son is waiting to be born.

'I can see the head,' said Pharis. 'The baby is coming!'

Bison wiped away the sweat from Axiana's face. 'Do not push,' he said. 'Not yet.'

She heard the advice, but the urge to propel the obstruction from her body was overpowering. 'I can't . . . stop myself!' she told him, taking a deep breath.

'No!' he thundered. 'The head is not engaged fully.' Her face reddened with the effort of pushing. 'Pant!' he ordered her. 'Pant. Like this!' Pushing out his tongue he made quick shallow breaths.

'I'm not . . . a . . . dog!' she hissed at him.

'You'll damage the child if you don't. His head is soft. Now pant, damn you!' Summoning Pharis to support the queen's shoulders Bison moved back to observe the birth. The head was almost clear, and one shoulder. Then he saw the umbilical cord, tight around the baby's neck like a blue-grey serpent, choking the life away. His fingers were too thick and clumsy to dislodge it. Fear touched him then. Twice before he had observed this phenomenon. The first time a surgeon had cut the cord. The baby had lived, but the woman had died, for the afterbirth had not come away cleanly, remaining inside to rot and poison the blood. The second time the cord had effectively strangled the infant. 'Don't push!' he told the queen. Taking a deep breath Bison supported the infant's head with his left hand then, as gently as he could eased the little finger of his right hand under the cord. Twice it slipped back into place, but the third time he hooked it, drawing it carefully over the head.

With the threat removed Bison called out. 'Now you can push! Push like the Devil!'

Axiana grunted, then cried out as the baby slid clear into Bison's hands. The babe's face and body were covered in grease and blood. Swiftly Bison tied the umbilical cord, then cut it. Then he wiped the child's nostrils and mouth, clearing its airways. The babe's tiny arm moved, then it drew in its first breath.

A thin wail sounded into the forest.

Bison heard the sound of running feet outside the roof-less tent. 'Stay back!' he yelled. He swung to Pharis. 'Get some fresh water.' Moving forward on his knees he laid the babe on Axiana's breast. Her arms went around it. Pharis was staring open mouthed at the tiny, wrinkled creature in the queen's arms. 'Get water, girl,' said Bison. 'You'll have plenty of time to gawp later.'

Pharis scrambled up and ran from the tent.

Axiana smiled at Bison. Then she began to sob. The old man kissed her brow. 'You did well,' he said, gruffly.

'So did you,' said Ulmenetha, from behind him.

Bison sucked in a deep breath and released his hold on the queen. Glancing up at the priestess he forced a grin. 'Well, if you really want to thank me . . .' he began.

Ulmenetha raised her hand to silence him. 'Do not spoil this moment, Bison,' she said, not unkindly. 'Go back to your friends. I will finish what you have done so well.' Bison sighed and pushed himself to his feet. He was tired now. Bone weary.

He wanted to say something to the queen, something to show how much these last few hours had meant to him; how proud he was of her, and how he would never forget what had happened here. He wanted to say he was privileged to have attended her.

But Ulmenetha had moved past him, and the queen was lying back with her eyes closed, her arms holding the infant king.

Bison walked silently from the tent.

Bakilas sat in the starlight, his pale body naked, the water burns on his ankles and feet healing slowly, the blisters fading. His three companions were sitting close by. Drasko's burns were more severe, but the bleeding had stopped. His horse had fallen as they forded the river, and only swift work by Lekor and Mandrak had saved him. They had hauled him clear, but the river water had penetrated the black armour, and was scorching the skin of his chest, belly and arms. Drasko's mood was not good as he sat with the group.

Pelicor's physical death, and return to the Great Void, had been amusing. The warrior had always been stupid and Bakilas had never felt any kinship with him. But the destruction of Nemor upon the bridge had cast a pall over the company. They had watched the huge old man charge the mounted warrior, and had felt their brother's terror as he fell through the flames and plummeted into the raging river. They had experienced the pain of his burns as the acid water ate away his skin and dissolved his flesh and bones.

Even with the probable success of Anharat's Great Spell bringing the Illohir back to the earth, it would still take hundreds of years for Pelicor and Nemor to build the psychic energy necessary to take form once more. Two of his brothers had become Windborn, and the enemy remained untouched. It was most galling.

Yet, at least, they now knew the source of the magick hurled against them. The blond-haired child. This, in itself, led to other questions. How could a child of such tender years master the power of *halignat*?

'What do we do now, brother?' asked Drasko.

'Do?' countered Bakilas. 'Nothing has changed. We find the child and return it to Anharat.'

Drasko idly rubbed at the healing wound on his shoulder. 'With respect, I disagree. We are all warriors here, and in battle can face any ten humans. But this is not a battle. Two of our number have returned to the Other Place, their forms lost to them. And we are no closer to completing our mission.'

'They will have to fight us,' said Bakilas. 'They cannot run for ever. And once we face them they will die.'

'I am not so sure,' said Mandrak. 'They may be old, but did you feel the power of their spirits? These men are warrior born. There is no give in them. Such men are dangerous.'

Bakilas was surprised. 'You think they can stand against the Krayakin?'

Mandrak shrugged. 'Ultimately? Of course not. But we are not invincible, brother. Others of us may lose our forms before this mission is done.'

Bakilas considered his words, then turned to the fourth of the group. 'What do you say, Lekor?'

The thin-faced warrior looked up. 'I agree with Mandrak,' he said, his voice deep as distant thunder. 'I too saw the spirits at the bridge. These men will not die easily. They will choose their own battleground, and we have no choice but to follow them. Then there is the question of the sorcery. Who is the power behind the child?'

The night breeze shifted. Mandrak's nostrils flared. With one smooth move he threw himself to his right, and rolled to his feet alongside where his armour lay. The others had moved almost as swiftly, and when the men emerged from the tree line the naked Krayakin were waiting for them, swords in hands.

There were a dozen men in the group, all roughly dressed in homespun clothing, and jerkins of animal skins. The leader, a large man with a forked black beard, wore a helm fashioned from a wolf's head. Three of the men had bows drawn, the others held knives or swords and one was hefting a curved sickle. 'Well, what have we here?' said the leader. 'Four naked knights on a moonlight tryst. Perverse, if you ask me.' His men chuckled obediently. 'Put down your swords, gentlemen,' he told the Krayakin. 'You are outnumbered, and once we have divested you of your horses and gold we will let you go.'

Bakilas spoke, but not to the man. 'Kill them all – save for the leader,' he said.

Instantly the four Krayakin warriors leapt at the startled men. One bowman loosed a shaft, but Bakilas's sword flashed in the night air, snapping the arrow in two. Then he was among the robbers, his sword cleaving left and right. One man died, his neck severed, a second fell to the ground, his chest gaping open. Mandrak blocked a savage cut from the leader's sword, then stepped inside and hammered a straight left to the man's face, breaking his nose. The leader staggered. Mandrak leaned back, then leapt, his right foot thundering against the leader's chin. The man went down as if poleaxed. Drasko killed two men, then lanced his sword through the back of another as the man turned to run.

Within moments the battle was over. Four survivors had fled into the forest, and seven men lay dead upon the grass. Bakilas moved to the unconscious leader, flipping the man with his foot. The leader grunted and struggled to sit up. Still dazed he rubbed his chin. Then, incongruously he cast around for his fallen helm. Setting it upon his head he pushed himself to his feet. He saw the dead men lying where they had fallen. He tried to run, but Mandrak was quicker, grabbing him by his jerkin and hurling him to the ground. 'What are you going to do with me?' he wailed.

Bakilas stepped up to the man, hauling him to his feet.

'We need to contact our leader,' he said, softly. 'You can help us with that task.'

'Anything,' said the man. 'Just ask.'

Bakilas took hold of the man's shirt and ripped it open, exposing his naked chest. He traced a line down the skin, locating the man's sternum. Slamming his fingers into the man's chest he split the skin beneath the breast bone. His hand drove in like a blade, then opened for his long fingers to encircle the still beating heart. With one wrench he tore the organ free. Letting the body sink to the grass he held up the dripping heart. 'Anharat!' he called. 'Speak to your brothers!'

The heart rose from Bakilas's hand and burst into a bright flame which soared up above the clearing. Then it coalesced into a ball and slowly dropped to hover above the warriors.

'I am here,' said a voice that whispered like a cold wind across a graveyard.

The Krayakin sat in a circle around the flame. 'Two of our company are Windborn once more,' said Bakilas. 'We would appreciate your guidance.'

'The child is born,' said the voice of Anharat. 'The route to the sea is cut off, and they must journey south. I am marching with the army to the city of Lem. There we will sacrifice the child. His blood will flow upon my own altar.'

'What of the wizard who is helping them?' asked Drasko.

'There is no wizard. The soul of Kalizkan possessed the child, but he is now gone to the Halls of the Dead. He will not return. Continue south. I have also returned a *gogarin* to the forest ahead of them. They will not pass him.'

'We need no help, brother,' said Bakilas. 'And a *gogarin* could kill them all – the babe included.'

'They will not be foolish enough to attempt to pass the beast,' said Anharat. 'Not once they know it is there. And I shall see that they do.'

'You are taking a great risk, Anharat. What if it does kill the babe?'

'I have already begun the Spell,' said the voice of the Demon Lord. 'It hangs in the air awaiting only the death of the third king. If the babe is killed before the time of sacrifice there will still be enough power released to bring back more than two-thirds of the Illohir. Now find them, and bring the babe to my altar.'

The flame faded, becoming thick, black smoke, which drifted in the air before slowly dispersing.

'The city of Lem,' said Drasko. 'Not a place of good omens.'

'Let us ride, brothers,' said Bakilas.

Nogusta drew rein at the mouth of the great canyon, and for several moments all his fears and tensions disappeared, swamped by the awesome beauty before him. The ancient map had shown a canyon here, and a trade road winding through it, but nothing etched on paper could have prepared Nogusta for the sheer majesty before him. Towering peaks, cloaked with trees and crowned by snow, deep valleys, full of lush grass and glittering streams and rivers, filled his field of vision.

The road continued along a wide ridge, steadily climbing and twisting around a mountain. At each curve a new panorama greeted him. The canyon was colossal.

Nogusta rode on, lost in the natural splendour of this high country. He felt young again, clean air filling his lungs, long-forgotten dreams rising from the dusty halls of his memory. This was a place for a man to live!

Starfire too seemed to be enjoying the ride. The great

black gelding had been increasing in strength for some days now and, though still a shadow of his former self, the horse was swiftly recovering from the lung infection that had condemned him to the slaughterhouse. Nogusta dismounted and walked to the rim, staring down at the forest and river below. What were the dreams of men when compared to this, he wondered?

The wagon was an hour behind him, and he found himself growing angry. How had he become chained to this doomed quest? The answers were obvious, but offered little comfort. For life to have meaning a man needed a code to live by. Without it he was just a small, greedy creature following his whims and desires to the detriment of those around him. Nogusta's code was iron. And it meant he could not ride away and leave his friends and the others to the fate that so obviously awaited them somewhere along the road.

He had told the boy, Conalin, his reasons for helping the queen were selfish – and so they were. He remembered the day his father had taken the family to the Great Museum in Drenan. They had viewed the exhibits, the ancient swords and statues, the gilded scrolls and the many bones, and at last his father had led them to the Sickle Lake, and there they had sat, eating a lunch of bread and cold roast meat. It was his tenth birthday. He had asked his father about the heroes, whose lives were celebrated at the museum. He had wondered what made them stand and die for their beliefs. His father's answer had been long-winded, and much of it had passed over the boy's head. But there was one, striking, visual memory. His father had taken his mother's hand mirror and placed it in Nogusta's hand. 'Look into it, and tell me what you see,' he said. Nogusta had seen his own reflection, and told him so.

'Do you like what you see?' his father had asked. It was a strange question. He was seeing himself.

'Of course I do. It's me!'

Then his father said: 'Are you proud of what you see?' Nogusta couldn't answer that. His father smiled. 'That is the true secret that carries a hero to deeds other men can only envy. You must always be able to look in a mirror and feel pride. When faced with peril you ask yourself, if I run, or hide, or beg or plead for life, will I still be able to look into a mirror and feel pride?'

Stepping into the saddle Nogusta rode on. The ridge road dipped steeply and Starfire's hoofs slipped on the stone. Riding with care the black warrior reached the canyon floor, and an old stone bridge that crossed the river. He was riding under the trees now, and stopped to examine the map once more. There was a second bridge marked, some 3 or 4 miles to the south-east. He decided to examine it before heading back to the wagon. There were still patches of snow upon the hillsides, and the air was cool as he heeled Starfire forward. The old road ran alongside a steep incline, then disappeared round the flanks of the hill.

Knowing he could see more of the land from higher ground Nogusta took hold of the pommel and ran the gelding up the slope. Starfire was breathing heavily as he crested the hill and Nogusta paused to allow the gelding to catch his breath.

Then he saw the cabin, set back in the trees, its walls built of natural stone, its roof covered with earth. Climbing ivy clung to the walls, and flowering shrubs had been set beneath the windows. The area around the cabin was well tended, and smoke drifted lazily from the stone chimney. Nogusta hesitated. He did not want to bring danger to any innocent mountain folk, but equally they would know the mountains and be able to advise him on the best route to Lem. Touching heels to Starfire he rode forward, but the horse grew nervous as they cleared the trees, and backed away.

Nogusta spoke soothingly to the animal, stroking the long black neck. Once in the clearing before the cabin he could see why Starfire was reluctant to approach the house. Partly hidden by a tall flowering shrub lay a blood-drenched body. He saw it was that of a man – or rather the remains of a man. The corpse was in two halves. Dismounting and holding on to the reins Nogusta approached it, kneeling to examine the tracks around it. The earth was hard, and little could be seen. The man was around twenty years of age. In his right hand there was a rusty sword. He had known then that he was under attack, and had faced his killer. Ragged talon marks showed across his chest and belly. He had literally been cut in half at the stomach by one violent slashing blow. Nogusta glanced to the right. Blood had spattered the ground at least 20 feet from the scene of death. No bear could have done this. Still holding on to the reins Nogusta moved to the cabin. The door had been caved in, the thick timbers smashed to shards. To the right the door frame had been torn away, and a section of wall caved in. Within the main room lay the partially consumed body of a woman.

Looping the reins over a fence rail Nogusta entered the cabin. He had seen great horror in his life, from the murder of his wife and family, to the victims of sacked cities, and the awesome, bloody aftermath of great battles. But there was here, in this grim tableau, a sadness that touched him deeply. The cabin was old, but had been lovingly restored by this young couple. They had turned a deserted ruin into a home. They had planted bright flowers, some of them inappropriate to forest soil, blooms that would never take root, but would wither and die here. This young couple were not expert, but they were romantic and hard working. Eventually they might have made a good living here. But something had come upon them. Something unexpected and deadly. The man had taken his sword and tried to defend his love. He had failed, and had died knowing his failure.

The woman had hidden behind a strong locked door, and had seen it smashed to shards. The beast had been too large to pass through the doorway, and had caved in the wall. The woman had tried to run through to the back of the house. Talons had swept across her back, ripping her apart. Death for both of them had been mercifully swift.

Nogusta returned to the sunlight and scanned the clearing. The blood was almost dry, but the attack on these people was very recent. He gazed at the tree line. There was a broken sapling there. Nogusta ran across the clearing. Here the earth was softer and he saw the footprint. Three times as long as that of a man, flaring wide at the toes. Talons had made deep gouges in the earth. The sapling, as thick as a man's arm, had been snapped cleanly, and a large bush had been uprooted by the charging beast. Back across the clearing Starfire whinnied. He pawed at the ground, his ears flat to his skull. Nogusta moved to the horse, unlooping the reins. The breeze shifted. Starfire reared suddenly. Taking hold of the pommel Nogusta vaulted to the saddle. He felt heat flare against his chest, and realized the talisman he wore was beginning to glow.

Beyond the cabin, to the north he saw tall trees swaying, and heard the splintering of wood. A hideous screeching began, and the ground trembled beneath the horse. Swinging Starfire he let the horse have its head. Starfire needed no urging, and launched himself into a run. Behind them something colossal burst from the undergrowth. Nogusta could not risk glancing back, as Starfire was galloping over rough ground towards the trees. But he could hear the beast bearing down upon them with terrible speed. Ducking under a low branch he headed for the road, urging the gelding on. Starfire was tired now, but his hoofs pounded the ground and he quickened. Nogusta rode down the incline at breakneck pace, Starfire slithering to his haunches. Only brilliant horsemanship kept Nogusta from being hurled from the saddle. Then they were on flat ground and riding towards the ridge road. Here Nogusta swung Starfire once more.

There was no sign of pursuit, and the talisman was no longer glowing.

What kind of an animal was strong enough to cut a man in half, fast enough to chase a horse as swift as Starfire, and evil enough to cause a reaction in his talisman?

Nogusta had no answer.

All he knew was that this beast stood between the wagon and the bridge.

And there was no other known route to safety.

Axiana was sleeping as the wagon slowly lumbered along the old road. Ulmenetha laid her now slender hand on the queen's brow. Axiana's life force was strong, radiating from her. The priestess leaned back against a pillow of empty sacks and stared up at the blue sky. The sensation of waking from her long life with Kalizkan had been disorientating in the extreme. The old wizard had told her that time had no meaning where they sat, but she had not understood it fully until she woke. It was as if she had slept for decades. The memories of the flight from the palace seemed to belong to another life, a distant existence. Ulmenetha had struggled to recall them. Equally she could not quite remember the fat, frightened woman she had been.

The girl, Pharis, was holding the infant, and the child Sufia was asleep beside her.

'Isn't he beautiful?' said Pharis. 'So small, so sweet.'

'He is beautiful,' agreed Ulmenetha. 'And so are you.' The girl glanced up, confused. Her face was thin, pinched and dirty, and her filthy hair hung in greasy rat's tails. Her clothes were rags and there were sores upon her bony shoulders. 'I am not mocking you, Pharis,' said Ulmenetha. 'You have great love within you, and that is a virtue of great beauty. Be sure to support the babe's head, for his neck is not strong.'

'I will,' she said, happily. 'I am holding a king!'

'You are holding an infant. Titles are bestowed by men, and no title would concern him now. What he needs is love and his mother's milk.'

Ulmenetha glanced back to where Kebra and Conalin were riding behind the wagon. The boy was riding close to Kebra, listening to the bowman. With the talent Kalizkan had inspired in her Ulmenetha could see so much more than the naked eye would allow. Conalin had been starved of affection all his life, and had never known the love of a father. Kebra was a quiet, lonely man, frightened to commit himself to a wife and family. The two were perfect for one another. She transferred her gaze to Dagorian. The young officer was well to the rear, leading the five spare horses. He was full of fear, and fighting to maintain his courage.

You should have remained a priest, thought Ulmenetha, for you are a gentle soul.

Rising she climbed across to sit beside Bison. He glanced at her and gave a crooked smile. 'How's my boy doing?' he asked.

'He is sleeping. Where did you learn to birth a child?'

'Here and there. The camp followers always used to call for me when a babe was due. Only ever had one die on me. Cord strangled it. Almost happened with our little prince. Apart from that, though, the camp whores thought I was a good-luck omen at a birth.'

The wagon emerged onto open ground and in the distance Ulmenetha could see the awesome majesty of the canyon. 'How did you get so thin?' asked Bison.

'It is a long story. How did you get so ugly?' She said it with a smile and Bison chuckled.

'I was born ugly,' he said, 'but I was also born strong. I'm still strong. Stronger than most men half my age.'

'How old are you?'

'Fifty,' he lied.

'You are sixty-six,' she said, 'and I see no reason to be ashamed of the fact. And you are quite right, you are stronger than most men half your age. You are also a better man than you like to admit. So let's have no more stupidity.'

'Well, I am stupid,' he said. 'Always have been. Nogusta and Kebra they talk about things I don't understand. Honour and such like. Philosophy. Goes over my head like a flight of geese. I'm just a soldier. I don't know anything else. I don't want to know anything else. I eat when I'm hungry, piss when my bladder's full, and rut when I can afford the price. That's all life is for me. And it's all I want.'

'That is just not true,' said Ulmenetha. 'You have

friends, and you stand by them. You have ideals, and you live by those. You are not terribly honest, but you are loyal.' She fell silent and studied his profile, then focused as Kalizkan had taught her. Vivid images appeared in her mind, bright with colour. Random scenes from Bison's life sped across her vision. Honing her concentration she slowed them. Most were what she would have expected, lust or violence, drunkenness or debauchery. But, here and there, she found more edifying scenes. She spoke again. 'Six years ago you came upon four men raping a woman. You saved her, and received two stab wounds which almost killed you.'

'How do you know that? Did Kebra tell you?'

'No-one needed to tell me. I know many things now, Bison. I can see more clearly than I ever have before. In fact, more clearly than I would wish to. What is your greatest dream?'

'I don't have dreams.'

'When you were a child. What did you dream of?'

'Flying like a bird,' he said, with a wide, gap-toothed grin. 'I'd spread my wings and soar through the sky, feel the wind in my face. I'd be free.'

The child, Sufia, came climbing over the backrest. 'Did you really have wings?' she asked Bison, as she scrambled onto his lap.

'I had great big wings,' he said. 'White wings, and I flew over mountains.'

'I'd like big wings,' said Sufia. 'I'd like white wings. Will you take me flying with you?'

'I don't fly any more,' he said, ruffling her blond hair. 'When you get old and fat you lose your wings.' He glanced at Ulmenetha. 'Isn't that right?'

'Sometimes,' she agreed.

Sufia snuggled up against Bison, holding on to his heavy, black woollen jerkin. He glanced at Ulmenetha. 'Children like me. They're not so bright, are they?'

'Children can make mistakes,' she agreed. 'But, in the main, they know a protector.' Ulmenetha gazed fondly down upon the child. Her heart was weak, and, under normal circumstances, she would be unlikely to reach puberty. Reaching out she laid her hand on Sufia's head, and, for the first time, released the power that Kalizkan had taught her. 'There is a force in all of us,' Kalizkan had told her. 'The Chiatze call it *tshi*. It is invisible, and yet terribly potent. It maintains our lives and our health. It helps us to repair damaged tissue.'

'Why did it not work for you?' she asked.

'Man is not intended to be immortal, Ulmenetha. The cancer came on too fast, and too powerfully. However, mastery of the *tshi* is an invaluable tool for a healer.'

Ulmenetha focused her energies, flowing her own *tshi* into the child.

'Your hand is very hot,' said Sufia. 'It's nice.'

Ulmenetha relaxed as she felt the child's fluttering heart grow stronger. It was not healed as yet, but it would be.

'I preferred you with more meat on you,' said Bison. 'But you do look younger.' He was about to speak again but Ulmenetha gave him a warning glance.

'Remember,' she said, 'no more stupidities.'

'If you don't ask you don't get,' he said, with a grin.

Up ahead she saw Nogusta walking his horse towards them. Ulmenetha could sense his concern. The black warrior was a powerful man, not given to despair and negative thoughts. But now his spirits were at a low ebb. Dagorian, Kebra and Conalin rode around the wagon to meet him. Bison hauled on the reins. Swiftly Nogusta told them of the killings at the cabin, and the beast that had pursued him.

'Did you get a look at it?' asked Bison.

'No,' said Nogusta. 'Had I waited a heartbeat longer I would have been as dead as the two lovers I found.'

'You're sure it wasn't just a bear?' said Bison.

'If so it is the mother of all bears. But no, I do not think it a creature of this world. Nothing I know of – or have heard of – could cut a grown man in half with one sweep.'

'What do we do then?' asked Dagorian. 'Find another way through?'

Nogusta drew in a deep breath. 'I do not see that we can. Firstly the maps do not show a second route. Secondly – even if there are other routes – if the beast was sent against us specifically there may be others of his kind guarding them. And last, but by no means least, we do not have the strength or the weapons to fight, on open ground, the warriors trailing us. And they must be getting close now.'

'Well, this is all very jolly,' snapped Bison. 'What more bastard luck can we expect? An outbreak of plague among us?'

'What choices do we have?' asked Kebra. 'We can't go back, we can't go forward, and if we stay here the Krayakin will kill us. For once I'm in agreement with Bison – luck seems to be running against us.'

'We are still alive,' said Nogusta. 'And we do have choices. The question is, which one gives us the best hope of success.'

'We cannot go back,' said Ulmenetha. 'Therefore we must face the beast.'

'With what?' queried Bison.

'With magick and with lances,' she said.

'I like the sound of the magick part,' said Bison.

'What do you have in mind, lady?' asked Kebra.

'Explanations will need to wait. One group of the Krayakin are less than two hours behind us. Ride back to the trees and fashion three long lances. Make sure the wood is stout and strong.'

Kebra swung his horse and rode back to the woods. Dagorian followed him, but Nogusta hesitated.

'Take the wagon on into the canyon, but do not leave the main road,' Ulmenetha ordered Bison. He glanced at Nogusta for confirmation. The black man nodded. Then he too rode to the woods.

'If you can kill it with magick,' said Bison, 'why do we need lances?'

'I cannot *kill* it,' she told him. 'What I can do is cast a spell that masks our scent and renders us almost invisible.'

'*Almost* invisible?'

'If the beast is close he will see a disturbance in the air around us – like a heat haze.'

'I don't want to go near any beasts,' wailed Sufia. Bison lifted her to his shoulder.

'No beast can get you while old Bison is here,' he said. 'I'll bite his head off.'

'You haven't got any front teeth,' she pointed out.

'No, but I've got tough old gums,' he said, with a chuckle.

The lances they cut were around 8 feet long, strong but unwieldy. Nogusta and Kebra strapped knives to the tips, and Nogusta added more twine around the lower haft, creating a hand grip. Dagorian's lance was more primitive, 7 feet in length the wood sharpened to a jagged point. As the wagon rolled slowly along the ridge road Nogusta and Kebra rode ahead, the bases of their lances resting on the saddle stirrups. There was little conversation. Axiana, Pharis and Sufia sat in the wagon, Conalin with them, his horse tied to the rear.

'I could have cut a lance,' said the boy.

'You don't have the skill with horses yet,' said Bison. 'When horses get frightened they take a deal of handling. You couldn't do that and wield a lance.' Conalin was unconvinced, but he said no more.

The light was fading as they neared the lower road. Nogusta and Kebra drew rein and the black warrior turned his mount and rode back to the wagon. He was about to ask when Ulmenetha needed to cast her spell, but she signalled him to silence. He was momentarily confused. Then she asked him. 'How is your chest?'

'My chest? It is fine.'

'No sensation of heat? How strange, for there should be.'

For a moment he thought she had lost her senses. Then he felt the talisman glowing. Ulmenetha touched her lips then her ear. Nogusta understood immediately. They were being observed, and overheard.

'I am feeling much better,' he said. 'I think it must have been a spring chill.'

'Spring chill?' said Bison. 'What the . . . ?' Ulmenetha's hand came down upon his in a sharp pinch.

'Do not speak,' she said, softly. Bison cast a glance at Nogusta and was about to disobey Ulmenetha when Kebra's horse suddenly reared, half pitching the bowman from the saddle. Dropping his lance Kebra clung to the pommel. The horse backed away.

Upon the road ahead a glowing figure had appeared, almost 7 feet high, black wings spreading from its shoulders, like a massive cloak fluttering in the breeze.

The face was dark, wide at the brow, narrow at the chin, an inverted black triangle with a wide gash of a mouth, and high slanted eyes, burning like coals.

'It is only an image,' whispered Ulmenetha. But Nogusta did not hear her. He drew a throwing knife and hurled it with all his might. The blade flashed through the dusk air, cutting through the apparition and clattering to the road beyond.

'You cannot harm me, human,' said the demon. The black wings spread wide and it rose into the air, floating close to the wagon. The creature peered inside, his gaze fixed to the babe carried by Axiana. Sufia screamed and buried herself under some blankets. The horses were growing uneasy. The demonic creature hovered for a moment, then drew back. 'It is not necessary for you all to die,' he said. 'What will it achieve? Can you stop me? No. Why then do you struggle on? Behind you – oh so close behind you – are my Krayakin. Ahead is a *gogarin*. Do you need me to explain the nature of such creatures? Or do the legends persist?'

'It was a beast with six legs,' said Nogusta. 'It was said to weigh as much as three tall horses.'

'Five would be closer,' said the apparition. He floated close to Nogusta, the burning eyes glittering. 'Yes, you look like him,' he said, and Nogusta could feel the hatred in the voice. 'The last of his mongrel line.' He moved away again. 'But I was speaking of the *gogarin*. It is a creature unlike all others upon this earth. Eternally hungry it will eat anything that lives and breathes. Nothing can approach it, for it radiates terror. Strong men fall to their knees at its approach, spilling their urine to drench their leggings. You cannot defeat it with your pitiful spears. I watched you flee from it earlier today. You, at least, understand what I am saying. Your heart was beating like a war drum – and that was without seeing the beast. Soon you will see it. And then you will all die.'

'What is the alternative you offer?' asked Nogusta.

'Merely life. For you have already lost. Had you the smallest chance of success I might offer riches, or perhaps even an extra hundred years of youth. I know that would appeal to your bald friend. But I need offer nothing more. The babe is mine. Leave it and its mother by the roadside. Then you can travel on to wherever you choose. My Krayakin will not harm you, and I will draw the *gogarin* back from this place. You also have my word that no harm will befall the queen.'

'I do not believe you,' said the warrior.

'I do not blame you for that,' the apparition told him, 'but it is the truth. I can also say that I will not be displeased should you reject my offer. You cannot stop me taking the babe, and it will give me great pleasure to see you die, Nogusta. Your ancestor – of cursed memory – visited a great evil upon my people, ripping their souls from the joys of this planet, and consigning them to an eternity of *Nothing*. No breath, no touch of flesh upon flesh, no hunger, no pain, no emotion – no life!' The apparition fell silent for a moment, and seemed to be struggling to contain his anger. 'Ride on,' he said, at last. 'Ride on and die for me. But do you really wish to take your friends to their deaths? They do not carry your blood guilt. They did not betray their race. Do they not deserve a chance to live?'

'My friends can speak for themselves,' said Nogusta.

The winged demon floated close to Bison. 'Do you wish to live?' he asked him. Ignoring the demon Bison lifted his buttocks from the driver's seat and broke wind thunderously.

'By Heaven, that's better,' he said. 'Are we moving on, or what?'

'I think we should,' said Ulmenetha, 'the stench is overpowering.'

'It was those wild onions,' said Bison, apologetically.

'Not from you . . . fool!' she snapped.

The demon drew back and hovered before Nogusta. Starfire whinnied and backed away. Nogusta calmed him. 'I would like to stay to watch you die,' said the apparition. 'But the body I have chosen waits for me some miles back – with the Ventrian army. Be assured, however, your passing will be painful. Not as painful, you understand, as I made it for your family. You should have seen them trying to flee the flames. Your wife was running along a corridor, her hair and her dress ablaze. Her screams were delightful. Her flesh burned like a great candle.'

There was a sudden gust of wind, and the apparition disappeared.

'That was Anharat, the Demon Lord,' said Ulmenetha. 'He it was who possessed Kalizkan, and brought such evil to the city.'

Nogusta did not respond at first. His face was streaked with sweat, and his face was set. When he did speak his voice was colder than the tomb. 'He killed my family. He watched them burn.'

'He has killed many families. Thousands upon thousands,' said Ulmenetha. 'His evil is colossal.' Nogusta took a deep, calming breath.

'What did he mean about my ancestor?'

'He was talking about Emsharas – his own brother. He it was who cast the first Great Spell.'

'His brother? Are you saying that my ancestor was a demon?'

'I have no answers for you, Nogusta. Little is known of Emsharas, save that he is considered the Father of Healers, and that his magick was holy. He was certainly of the Illohir, the Windborn.'

'Then I have demon blood in my veins?'

'Forget about demons!' she snapped. 'That is not important now. Why do you think he came to us? It was to instil fear, to cause torment and disquiet. You must overcome such thoughts. Any anger or rage you feel will only add to our danger, increasing the chances of the *gogarin* to sense our presence.'

'I understand,' said Nogusta. 'Let us move on.'

'When we reach the foot of the slope,' said Ulmenetha, 'you must ride close to the wagon. The spell will only extend a few feet. We must be as quiet as possible.' Nogusta nodded, then rode ahead and retrieved his lance and the thrown dagger.

'Can we kill this *gogarin* if necessary?' Bison asked Ulmenetha.

'I don't know.'

'Could he really give me another hundred years of youth?'

'I don't know that either. Does it matter?'

'Nice thought,' said Bison, lifting the reins and snapping them down to the backs of the waiting team. They lurched forward and the wagon moved slowly on down towards the canyon floor.

In the distance storm clouds were gathering, and a rumble of thunder echoed over the mountains.

At the foot of the slope Ulmenetha climbed down from the wagon and kicked off her shoes, feeling the soft earth beneath her feet. Relaxing she drew on the power of the land. The magick here was weak, and this surprised her.

It was as if the flow was being blocked. She wondered then if Anharat's power had affected the magick. Surely not. Squatting down she dug her hand into the earth. Her fingers struck something hard and flat. She smiled with relief. They were upon the old trade road. Over the centuries earth had covered the flagstones, and it was these buried stones that blocked her. Stepping from the old road she walked to a grove of nearby trees. The magick here was strong and ancient, and she drew upon it, feeling it flow through her legs, and up through the veins and arteries, swelling and surging. It was almost too strong, like fine wine, and she reached out to hold fast to the trunk of a tree.

Thunder rumbled to the south. Moving away from the trees she strode to the front of the wagon, and positioned herself to the left of the team. Nogusta, Kebra and Dagorian rode in close upon her command. Raising her hand she cast the spell. It was not especially difficult to create, but once created it needed to be held in place. The air around the wagon shimmered. Ulmenetha glanced back. She could no longer see the others. Reaching up she ran her hand along the sleek, near invisible, neck of the horse beside her, and curled her fingers around the bridle. 'Let no-one speak from now until I give the word,' she said. 'Let us go!'

She heard the reins slap upon the backs of the team, and, holding to the bridle she walked on towards the forest. The soft footfalls of the horses seemed as loud to her as the distant thunder, and the soft creaking of the wagon wheels swelled in her mind. Be calm, she warned herself, the thunder and the wind in the trees will mask the sounds.

The sky darkened, the storm moving over the forest. Lightning flashed, lighting up the forest road. A horse snorted in fear, and she heard Kebra soothe it with soft, whispered words. Ahead was the slope down which Nogusta had fled the beast. The wagon continued on, slowly.

Rain began to slash down from the heavy clouds above. Ulmenetha welcomed it. The sound covered them like a blanket.

Holding to the spell she walked on.

From above came the sound of splintering wood, and a high screeching cry that tore against Ulmenetha's ear drums, causing her knees to tremble. She dragged back on the bridle, halting the team. The screeching continued. One of the horses whinnied in terror. The screeching died away instantly, and a terrible silence followed. Ulmenetha glanced up the slope. Trees were swaying there. Fear threatened to swamp her, but she held fast to the spell.

Lightning flashed. Two of the horses snorted and stamped their hooves.

Some 30 feet above the wagon a huge, wedge shaped head emerged from the trees. Ulmenetha could see only the silhouette against the dark sky, but even above the lashing wind she could hear it snuffling, sucking in the scents of the forest, seeking out its prey.

The rain eased, and a break in the clouds allowed moonlight to bathe the scene. Ulmenetha stood very still, staring up at the great head. From the serpentine shape she had expected it to be scaled like a reptile. But it was not. Its skin was corpse white and almost translucent, and she could see the large bones of its neck pushing against the skin. The pale head twisted on its long neck, and she found herself staring into a slanted blue eye as large as a man's head. The pupil was round and black, and horribly human. The *gogarin* stared unblinking down towards the road. Then the head withdrew into the trees, and she heard again the splintering of wood as its enormous bulk crashed back through the forest. Tugging on the bridle she urged the wagon on, following the road around the base of the slope.

The storm swept on towards the north, the rain dying away. Breaks in the cloud cover came more often now, and the company kept moving towards the distant bridge and safety.

For an hour they plodded on. Ulmenetha was tired now, and finding it difficult to maintain the spell. The flagstones beneath the earth of the road did not allow her to replenish her power, and twice the spell faltered. She halted the team and softly called out to Nogusta.

'Does your talisman glow?'

'No,' came the response.

'I must draw power from the land. I need to leave the road.'

Releasing the bridle she ran to the roadside. Immediately the wagon and the surrounding riders became visible. Ulmenetha sank to her knees, pushing her hands into the earth. Unlike before the power seeped slowly, and she felt the tension rise in her. Her fear slowed the flow even more. She fought for calm, but it eluded her. 'Be swift!' called Nogusta. 'The talisman grows warm!'

Ulmenetha sucked in a deep breath, and sent up a swift prayer. The energy she sought had touched her blood, but it was not enough! Rising she ran towards the wagon and took hold of the bridle once more. She could hear the beast's approach now, as it crashed through the undergrowth. Fear made her falter on the third line of the spell, and she began it again.

The magick surged from her, flowing over the wagon and riders.

In the bright moonlight the *gogarin* emerged from the trees to the road ahead. Now they could all see it fully. It was over 20 feet long. Nogusta had earlier described it as having six legs, but Ulmenetha saw that this was not quite so. The hind and middle legs were powerful and treble jointed, but the limbs at the beast's shoulders were more like long arms, equipped with murderous talons, each as long as a cavalry sabre. Rearing up on its hind legs it sniffed the night breeze. One of the spare horses, tied to the rear of the wagon, reared in terror, snapping its reins. Turning, it galloped from the road, and into the forest.

The *gogarin* reacted with sickening speed, dropping to all six limbs and propelling itself forward with incredible power. Ulmenetha stood stock still as it raced towards the wagon. Then it veered after the horse. Its mighty shoulder struck a young tree, uprooting it. Then it was gone behind them.

The horse galloped on, then Ulmenetha heard its death cry.

She could not move, and stood trembling beside the team. Nogusta dismounted and carefully felt his way to her side. 'We must move,' he whispered. Ulmenetha did not reply. Yet even through her terror she maintained the spell. Nogusta led her to the front of the wagon and lifted her to the seat beside the near invisible Bison. Remounting his horse Nogusta rode to the head of the team and reached down for the bridle. At his encouragement the horses moved forward.

Ulmenetha could not stop the trembling in her hands. Her eyes were tight shut, and she almost cried out as Bison's large hand reached out and patted her leg. He leaned in to her and whispered. 'Big whoreson wasn't he.'

His voice was so calm, and the strength of the man seemed to flow with the sound. Ulmenetha felt herself growing calmer. She swung on her seat, gazing fearfully back down the trail. The wagon was moving very slowly, and, with every moment that passed the priestess expected to see the huge, white form of the *gogarin* lumbering out behind them.

They covered another half mile. Slowly the road began to rise, and they climbed to a second ridge road. The wagon filled almost two thirds of it. The horses were tired, and twice Bison was forced to lash them with the reins, forcing them on. The power was almost gone from Ulmenetha now. She tried to draw fresh strength from the mountains, but the old stone would not surrender its magick.

Licking her finger she raised it to the wind. It was blowing from behind them. Their scent could no longer carry back to the forest. With relief she let fall the spell.

'By Heaven, that's better,' whispered Bison.

The ridge road levelled out and Bison paused the team, allowing them to catch their breath. The moon was shining brightly now, and the forest was far below them.

A thin piping cry came from the back of the wagon, as the hungry babe awoke. Bison swore and swung round. Axiana was unbuttoning her dress. The babe's cries echoed in the mountains. The queen tore at the last two buttons, exposing her left breast. The infant calmed down and began to suckle. Bison swore again, and pointed back to the forest.

Far behind them the *gogarin* had emerged from the trees and was moving swiftly along the road.

* * *

Nogusta leapt from the saddle. 'Everyone out of the wagon!' he yelled. 'Kebra, help me unhitch the horses.' The bowman urged his horse forward, then dismounted. He did not even try to release the traces, but drew his dagger and cut them clear. Dagorian edged his horse around the wagon, then jumped down to assist him. Pharis helped the queen down, while Conalin swept up little Sufia and climbed over the side. Bison scrambled into the back of the wagon, picking up food sacks and blankets and hurling them to the roadside.

The giant glanced back down the steep incline. The *gogarin* was running towards them. It seemed small at this distance, a white hound against the moonlit grey of the rock road. The team clattered clear. Nogusta climbed to stand alongside Bison. In his hand was the heavy lance, tipped with a razor sharp throwing knife.

'You know what needs to be done,' said Nogusta. Bison looked into his friend's pale blue eyes.

'I know. Let me take the spear.'

'No! The talisman will protect me from the terror it radiates. Now get down – and set the wagon rolling on my signal.'

Bison jumped to the roadside and summoned Kebra and Dagorian. 'What is he doing?' asked the young officer, as Nogusta settled himself in the back of the wagon.

'He's going to ram it,' said Bison. Stepping back he dropped down behind the front wheels, judging the line which the wagon would follow once they started it down the slope. There was a slight curve to the right some 60 yards ahead. That would be the point where – if they misjudged the speed – the wagon would roll over the edge and plunge hundreds of feet down the mountainside. Sweat beaded Bison's brow and he wiped his sleeve across his face.

'Get ready!' shouted Nogusta. The three men put their shoulders to the vehicle.

On the rear of the wagon Nogusta hefted the lance. He too could see the curve in the road, and was trying to judge the speed of the approaching beast. There was little room for error here. If the wagon rolled too fast it would reach the curve before the *gogarin*, and Nogusta would die uselessly. If too late the wagon might not have picked up enough speed to hurl the creature out over the abyss. Nogusta's mouth was dry, and his heart was beating fast.

'Start her moving,' he called. The three men threw their weight against the wagon. It did not budge.

'The brake is on!' shouted Bison. Nogusta ran to the headboard and vaulted to the driver's seat, pulling the brake clear. The wagon jolted forward. Nogusta almost fell, but then righted himself and ran back to the rear, taking up his lance. Valuable seconds had been lost.

'Push harder!' he commanded. The wagon began to gather speed. The *gogarin* rounded the curve, and saw the rumbling wagon approaching. Rearing up on its hind legs it let out a hideous screech. Nogusta felt the wave of terror strike him like a physical blow. It ripped through his mind and belly, and he screamed and fell to his knees. In all his life he had never known fear such as this. The spear dropped from his trembling fingers and he wanted to fall with it, burying his head in his hands, and squeezing shut his eyes. He could feel the talisman warm upon his skin, but it offered no help. In that moment, when despair threatened to unman him, he saw again the face of his wife, and remembered the Demon Lord's words, of how she had run through the flames. Anger came to his rescue, flaring in his belly and burning into his brain. Grabbing the lance he surged to his feet.

The wagon was almost upon the beast. The *gogarin* reared up high, then dropped to all six limbs, and charged. Nogusta braced himself for the impact. At the last second the *gogarin* reared again, its talons lashing out. The wooden side of the wagon exploded. Then the full weight of the vehicle struck the beast. Lance extended, Nogusta was catapulted forward. The dagger strapped to the lance sliced into the beast, the weapon driving deep into its shoulder. Nogusta's weight powered it on, the wood plunging deeper still. Then it snapped. Nogusta's flying body struck the *gogarin*'s neck, then sailed on to collide with the cliff wall. Searing pain burst through his shoulder as he fell to the road and slid towards the edge. His legs went over the side and he scrabbled for a hand hold. Glancing down he saw pine trees far below. His shoulder was numb, and there was no strength in his left hand. Fear touched him, but he quelled it, and relaxed. Then he slowly hauled himself back up to the ridge.

The *gogarin* had been driven to the lip of the road, and the beast was flailing at its wooden enemy, its sweeping talons ripping at the wagon, smashing it to shards. Nogusta pushed himself to his feet, staggered, then drew his sword and prepared to attack.

Bison came running into sight carrying a lance, followed by Kebra and Dagorian. The bowman sent a shaft slamming into the *gogarin*'s neck. Then Bison scrambled over the remains of the wagon and hurled himself at the beast. As the *gogarin* swung to meet this new attack its right hind foot slipped on the rock. The beast staggered, and tried to right itself. Bison's spear slammed against its chest, barely breaking the skin. But the giant's weight tipped the balance, and the lance propelled the creature back. The *gogarin* fell, tumbling through the air. Twice it crashed against the mountainside, then it soared clear and plunged through the branches of a tall pine, snapping the tree in two.

Bison leapt clear as the ruined wagon slid over the edge. He ran to Nogusta. 'Are you all right?' he asked.

The black man groaned as he tried to move his left shoulder. 'Just bruised, I hope,' he said. 'Is it dead?' Bison peered over the edge.

'I can't see it,' he said. 'But nothing could have survived that fall.'

Antikas Karios was not a man usually given to regrets. Life was life, and a man made the best of it. Yet, strangely, on this misty morning, as he sat on the stone wall of the old bridge, he found himself haunted by the ghosts of lost dreams. He had never before given much thought to the opinions of other men, or their criticisms of him. They had called him cruel, vengeful and merciless. The insults were never said to his face, but Antikas had heard them nonetheless, and had believed himself immune to them. No strong man would be affected by the sneers of lesser beings. As his father used to say, 'A lion is always followed by jackals.'

Antikas Karios had been a man with a mission, single-mindedly following a narrow road. There had been no time for introspection. No time for the casual niceties. No time for friendship. His mind and his time had been fully occupied with thoughts of freeing Ventria from the aggressor.

Not so now, as he gazed into the mist that rolled across the hills. Here in this lonely country there was time for little else but introspection.

He had been waiting by this bridge for two days now, directed here by the spirit of the sorcerer Kalizkan. 'Why do you not lead me directly to them?' he had asked.

'This is where you will be needed most.'

'Wherever they are they will be in peril. My sword could sway the balance.'

'Trust me, Antikas. Wait at the bridge. They will be with you in two days.' The spirit had left him then, and Antikas Karios had waited.

At first the beauty of the mountains had been pleasant to the eyes, and he felt calm, and ready to give his life to the cause of the queen. But as the hours passed on that first day he had found himself reappraising his life. It happened without conscious thought. He was sitting on the bridge, and he suddenly thought of Kara, and the plans they had made to build a home by the sea. Sweet, soft, gentle Kara. He had made her many promises, and had kept none of them. It was not that he had meant to lie. But the war with the Drenai had taken precedence. She should have understood that.

Dreams of love and family had been washed away in a tidal wave of patriotism, and then replaced by the dream of independence. Now both dreams were dust.

During the last five years memories of Kara had come often to him, but, as busy as he was, it had been easy to suppress them. Always there were plans and schemes that required his attention. But here, during these two, lonely, soul searching days, he had found it increasingly difficult to avoid his guilt.

He remembered the last time he had seen her.

'It was not cruelty or vengeance,' he said, aloud. 'She brought humiliation upon me. What then could she expect?' The words hung in the air, and echoed, unconvincingly, in his mind. Kara had written to him, ending their engagement. She had, she wrote, waited three years. She pointed out that Antikas had promised to return home within one year. He had not done so. Nor had he written for more than eight months. It was obvious that he no longer loved her, and she had now fallen in love with a young nobleman from a neighbouring estate. They were to be married within the month.

And married they were. Antikas had arrived late for the ceremony. He had approached them both as they walked hand in hand from the church, garlands of flowers around their necks. He had removed his heavy riding glove and had struck the groom across the face with it. The duel had taken place that evening and Antikas killed him.

That night he had been summoned to Kara's home. He found her sitting in a darkened room, the lanterns unlit, heavy velvet curtains blocking out the moonlight. A single candle burned on a small table, and by its flickering light he saw her, a heavy blanket wrapped around her slender frame. Antikas remembered how hard his heart had felt, and how he had decided to make no apology for her loss. Hers was the blame, not his. He was planning to make her aware of this. But she did not rail at him. She merely looked up in the gloom and stared at his face. There was no hatred in her, he realized, merely a great sadness. In the candlelight she looked exquisitely beautiful, and he had found himself wondering how he could ever have left her for so long. In his arrogance he believed that she had never truly loved the other man, but had accepted his offer knowing that Antikas would come for her. Now he had, and, if she begged him, he would take her back, despite the humiliation. He was prepared to be forgiving. But this scene was not what he had expected. Tears, yes. Anger? Of course. But this eerie silence was intolerable.

'What is it you want of me, lady?' he said.

Her voice when it came was a faint whisper. 'You are . . . an evil man . . . Antikas. But you will hurt us . . . no longer.' Her eyes held to his for a moment more, then they closed and her head sagged back. For a moment only he thought she had swooned. Then he saw the pool of blood around the base of the chair. Stepping forward he wrenched the blanket from her. Both her wrists were cut, and her clothes were drenched in blood. Still wearing her wedding dress and her garland, she had died without another word.

Antikas tried to push away the memory, but it clung to him like a poisoned vine. 'It was not evil,' he said. 'She should have waited for me. Then it would not have happened. I am not to blame.'

Who then do we blame? The thought leapt unbidden from his subconscious.

It had not ended there. Her brother had challenged Antikas. He too had died. Antikas had tried to disarm the boy, to wound him and stop the duel. But his attack had been ferocious and sustained, and, when the moment came, Antikas had responded with instinct rather than intent, his blade sinking into his opponent's heart.

Antikas Karios rose from the wall and turned to gaze down into the rushing water below. He saw the broken branch of an old oak floating there, drifting fast. It stuck for a moment against a jutting rock, then twisted free and continued on its way. Further down the bank a brown bear ambled out of the woods and waded into the water. Antikas watched it. Twice its paw splashed down. On the third time it caught a fish, propelling it out to the bank. The fish flopped against the earth, its tail thrashing wildly. The bear left the river and devoured the fish.

Antikas swung away and walked to where his horse

was cropping grass. From his saddlebag he took the last of his rations.

Thoughts of Kara intruded as he ate, but this time he suppressed them, concentrating instead on the escape from Usa. Kalizkan's spirit had taken him first to an old church by the south wall, and there he had directed him to a secret room behind the altar. By the far wall was an ancient chest. It was not locked. The hinges were almost rusted through. One snapped as Antikas opened the lid. Inside were three scabbarded short swords, each wrapped in linen. Antikas removed them.

'These are the last of the Storm Swords,' said Kalizkan, 'created when the world was younger. They were fashioned by Emsharas the Sorcerer, for use against the demonic Krayakin.'

Antikas had carried them from the city to where the army was camped beyond. There he had obtained a horse and supplies and had ridden out into the mountains.

On his first night he had unwrapped one of the swords. The pommel was inset with a blue jewel, heavy and round, held in place by golden wire. The tang was covered by a wooden grip, wrapped in a pale, greyish white skin, while the upwardly curved quillons were deeply engraved with gold lettering. The scabbard was simple, and without adornment. Slowly Antikas drew the sword forth.

'Do not touch the blade!' warned the voice of Kalizkan. In the moonlight the blade was black, and, at first, Antikas believed it to be of tarnished silver. But, as he turned it, he saw the moon reflected brilliantly on its dark surface.

'What is the metal?' he asked Kalizkan.

'Not metal, child. Enchanted ebony,' replied the

sorcerer. 'I don't know how he did it. It can cut through stone, yet it is made of wood.'

'Why is it called a Storm Sword?'

'Stand up and hold the flat of your hand just above the blade.'

Antikas did so. Colours swept along the ebony, then white blue lightning lanced up into his palm. In surprise he leapt back, dropping the sword. The point vanished into the earth, and only the curved quillons prevented the blade sinking from sight. Antikas drew it clear. Not a mark of mud had stained the sword. Once again he held his hand over it. Lightning danced to his skin. There was no pain. The sensation was curious, and he noticed that the hairs on the back of his hand were tingling.

'What causes the small lightning?' he asked Kalizkan.

'I wish I knew. Emsharas was Windborn. He knew far more than any human sorcerer.'

'A demon? Yet he made swords to fight demons? Why would that be?'

'You have a penchant for asking questions I cannot answer. Whatever his reasons Emsharas allied himself with the Three Kings, and he it was who cast the Great Spell that banished all demons from the earth.'

'Including himself?'

'Indeed so.'

'That makes no sense,' said Antikas. 'He betrayed more than his own people, he betrayed his entire race. What could induce a man to commit such an act?'

'He was not a man, he was – as you rightly say – a demon,' said Kalizkan. 'And who can know the minds of such creatures? Certainly not I, for I was foolish enough to trust one, and paid for it with my life.'

'I loathe mysteries,' said Antikas.

'I have always been rather partial to them,' admitted

Kalizkan. 'But to attempt an answer to your question, perhaps it was simply hatred. He and his brother, Anharat, were mortal enemies. Anharat desired the destruction of the human race. Emsharas set out to thwart him. You know the old adage, the enemy of my enemy must be my friend? Therefore Emsharas became a friend to humans.'

'It is not convincing,' said Antikas. 'There must have been some among his people that he loved – and yet he caused their destruction also.'

'He did not destroy them – merely banished them from the earth. But if we are questioning motivations, did you not cause the destruction of the one you loved?'

Antikas was shocked. 'That was entirely different,' he snapped.

'I stand corrected.'

'Let us talk of more relevant matters,' said the swordsman. 'These warriors I am to fight are Krayakin, yes?'

'They are indeed – the greatest fighters ever to walk the earth.'

'They have not met me yet,' Antikas pointed out.

'Trust me, my boy, they will not be quaking in their boots.'

'They ought to,' said Antikas. 'Now tell me about them.'

Antikas was sitting once more on the bridge wall when the riders emerged from the mist. The black warrior, Nogusta, was leading them. Antikas could see the queen, sitting side saddle, her horse led by a tall, slim, blond-haired woman in a flowing blue robe. Behind them came the man, Bison. Antikas had last seen him tied to the whipping post, on the day that Nogusta slew Cerez. A small, fair-haired child was seated before him. Behind the giant came two more youngsters, riding double, a red-haired boy of around fourteen and a wand-thin girl with long dark hair. Then he saw Dagorian. The officer was holding a small bundle in his arms. Bringing up the rear was the bowman, Kebra.

Nogusta saw him and left the group, cantering his horse down the shallow slope.

'Good morning to you,' said Antikas, rising and offering a bow. 'I am pleased to see you alive.'

Nogusta dismounted and moved closer, his expression unreadable. Antikas spoke again. 'I am not here as an enemy, black man.'

'I know.'

Antikas was surprised. 'Kalizkan told you about me?'

'No. I had a vision.' Slowly the group filed to the bridge. Nogusta waved them on, and they rode past the two swordsmen. Antikas bowed deeply to Axiana, who responded with a smile. She looked wan and terribly weary.

'Is the queen sick?' he asked Nogusta, after she had passed.

'The birth was not easy, and she lost blood. The priestess healed her, but she will need time to recover fully.'

'Is the child strong?'

'He is strong,' said Nogusta. 'It is our hope that he remains that way. You know that we are followed?'

Antikas nodded. 'By the Krayakin. Kalizkan told me. I will remain here and bar their path.'

Nogusta smiled for the first time. 'Not even you can defeat four such warriors. Even with the black swords.'

'It was a good vision you had,' said Antikas. 'Would you care to share it with me?' Nogusta shook his head.

'Ah,' said Antikas, with a wide grin, 'I am to die then. Well, why not? It is something I've not done before. Perhaps I shall enjoy the experience.'

Nogusta remained silent for a moment. Dagorian, Kebra and Bison came running back across the bridge to stand alongside him. 'What is he doing here?' said Dagorian, his face flushed and angry.

'He is here to help us,' said Nogusta.

'That's not likely,' hissed Dagorian. 'He sent assassins after me. He is in league with the enemy.'

'Such indiscipline in your ranks, Nogusta,' said Antikas. 'Perhaps that is why you never gained a commission.'

'Shall I break his neck?' asked Bison.

'How novel,' muttered Antikas, 'an ape that speaks.' Bison surged forward. Nogusta threw out his arm. The effort of blocking the giant made him wince, as his injured shoulder flared with fresh pain.

'Calm down,' he said. 'There is no treachery here. Antikas Karios is one of us. Understand that. The past is of no consequence. He is here to defend the bridge and buy us time. Let there be no more insults.' He turned to Antikas. 'The Krayakin will come tonight. They do not like the sun, and will wait for the clouds to clear and the moon to shine bright. There will be four of them. But riding with them will be a unit of Ventrian cavalry, sent by the demon who inhabits Malikada.'

'You say I cannot defeat them alone? Will you then stand with me?'

'I would like nothing more.'

'No,' said Dagorian, suddenly. 'Your shoulder is injured. I have watched you ride. You are in great pain and your movements are slow and sluggish. I will stay.'

'I too,' said Kebra.

Nogusta shook his head. 'We cannot risk everything

on one encounter. There are only four of the Krayakin directly behind us. Four more are out there, moving to cut us off. We need to put distance between us. Antikas Karios has chosen to defend this bridge. Dagorian has offered to stand beside him. That is how it will be.' He swung to Kebra. 'You and Bison ride on with the others. Keep heading south. About a mile ahead the road branches. Take the route to the left. You will pass over the highest ridge. Move with care, for it will be cold and treacherous. I will join you soon.'

The two men moved away and Nogusta sat down on the bridge wall and rubbed his injured shoulder. Ulmenetha's new-found magick had knitted the broken collar bone, and he could feel himself healing fast. But not fast enough to be of use to the two men who would guard the bridge.

'Bring out the black swords,' he told Antikas. The swordsman moved to his horse and lifted clear the bundle tied to the rear of the saddle. Warning Nogusta and Dagorian to beware of the blades he unwrapped them. They were identical save for the crystal jewels in the pommels. One was blue, the second white as fresh fallen snow, the third crimson. The blue blade Antikas took for himself. Nogusta waited for Dagorian. The young officer chose the sword with the white pommel. Nogusta accepted the last.

'There is little I can say to advise you,' he told Dagorian. 'Stay close to Antikas Karios, guard his back as best you can.'

'You have seen the coming fight, haven't you?'

'Glimpses of it only. Do not ask me about the outcome. You are a good man, Dagorian. Few would have the courage to face the warriors coming against you.'

'This is all very touching, black man,' said Antikas,

'but why don't you ride on? I will take Dagorian under my wing, as it were.'

'I don't need your protection,' snapped Dagorian.

'You Drenai are so touchy. It comes from lacking any sense of true nobility, I expect.' Antikas strode back to his horse, mounted and rode past them down the bridge.

'Are you sure he can be trusted?' asked Dagorian. Nogusta nodded.

'Do not be fooled by his manner. He is a man of great honour, and he carries a burden of shame. He is also frightened. What you are seeing is merely a mask. He is of the old Ventrian nobility, and he is drawing on its values in order to face a terrible enemy.'

Dagorian sat alongside the black swordsman. 'I never wanted to be a soldier,' he said.

'You told me, you wanted to be a priest. Well, think on this, my friend, is it not a priest's duty to keep a lantern lit against the dark? Is it not his purpose to stand against evil in all its forms?'

'That is true,' agreed Dagorian.

'Then today you are a priest, for the demons are coming. They seek the blood of innocence.'

Dagorian smiled. 'I did not need encouragement, but I thank you for it anyway.'

Nogusta rose. 'When your mission here is done, head south, follow the high road. You will see the ghost city of Lem in the distance. We will meet you there.'

Dagorian said nothing, but he gave a knowing smile. Then he held out his hand. Nogusta clasped it firmly. Then he mounted Starfire and rode away.

Nogusta walked his horse to the far end of the bridge. Ulmenetha stepped in front of his horse.

'Did you tell him?' she asked.

'No,' he told her, sadly.

'Why? Does he not have a right to know?'

'Would he fight the better if he did?' he countered.

As the others rode away Dagorian took a deep breath then stared around the bridge. Built of stone it was around 80 feet across and 20 wide. He had seen it on two of Nogusta's maps. Once it must have had a name, for it was a fine structure, carefully constructed. But it was lost to history now, as was the name of the river it spanned. Built when Lem was a thriving city it must have cost a fortune, he thought, picturing the hundreds of men who had laboured here. There had once been statues at both ends of the bridge, but only the plinths remained. It was as Nogusta had said, 'History forgets us all eventually.' Walking to the bridge wall he looked down at the river bank. A stone arm jutted from the mud. Dagorian strolled down to it, pushing the earth away, and exposing a marble shoulder. The head was missing. Casting around he saw a section of a stone leg, covered by weeds. Someone had toppled the statues. He wondered why.

He drank from the river then climbed back to the bridge. 'Time for a little work, Drenai,' said Antikas.

The area around the north of the bridge was heavy with rocks and boulders. Dagorian and Antikas laboured for two hours, rolling large stones onto the bridge to impede enemy horses. The two men spoke little as they worked, for Dagorian remained uneasy in the presence of the hawk-eyed Ventrian. This man had planned to kill him, and had been instrumental in the destruction of the Drenai army, and the murder of the king. Now he was to stand beside him against a terrible foe. The thought was not a pleasant one.

Antikas cut several large sections of brush and used his horse to drag them to the bridge, wedging thick branches

314

into the stone side supports, and angling them to jut out over the rocks. At last satisfied he carefully led his horse through the obstacles, tethering him at the far end of the bridge alongside Dagorian's mount.

'That is all we can do,' he told the young officer. 'Now we wait.' Dagorian nodded and moved away from the man to sit on the bridge wall. The mist was clearing now, and the sun shone clearly in a sky of pale blue.

'We should practise,' said Antikas.

'I need no practice,' snapped Dagorian. Antikas Karios said nothing for a moment, then he stepped in close.

'Your hatred means less than nothing to me, Drenai,' he said, softly. 'But your petulance is irritating.'

'You are a murderer and a traitor,' said Dagorian. 'It should be enough that I am prepared to stand beside you. I don't need to talk to you, and I certainly have no wish to engage in a meaningless training drill. I already know how to fight.'

'Is that so?' Antikas drew his sword. 'Observe!' he ordered. Lifting a thick piece of wood he held the black sword to it. The blade slid through the old wood like a hot knife through butter. 'You and I,' said Antikas, softly, 'will be fighting alongside one another. One clumsy sweep, one careless move and one of us could kill the other. How many times, in close order battle, have comrades accidentally caused injury to one another?'

It was true and Dagorian knew it. Pushing himself from the wall he drew his own blade. 'What do you suggest?' he asked.

'Which side do you wish to defend, the left or the right?'

'The right.'

'Very well, take up your position, and let us rehearse some simple moves.' The two men walked out onto the bridge. 'The enemy will be forced to advance on foot, clambering over the rocks and brush. We will wait for them, and engage them here,' he said. 'No matter what happens you must stay on my right. Do not cross over. Now you are less skilful than I, so at no time try to move to my defence. If I move to yours I will call out, so that you know where I am.'

For a while they practised moves, rehearsed signals and discussed strategies. Then they broke off to eat from Dagorian's ration of dried beef. They sat in silence on the rocks, each lost in his own thoughts.

'I have never fought a demon,' said Dagorian, at last. 'I find the thought unsettling.'

'It is just a name,' said Antikas. 'Nothing more. They walk, they talk, they breathe. And we have the weapons to kill them.'

'You sound very sure.'

'And you are not?'

Dagorian sighed. 'I do not want to die,' he admitted. 'Does that sound cowardly?'

'No man *wants* to die,' responded Antikas. 'But if thoughts of survival enter your mind during the fight, death will be certain. It is vital for a warrior to suspend imagination during a battle. What if I get stabbed, what if I am crippled, what if I die? These thoughts impair a warrior's skills. The enemy will come. We will kill them. That is all you need to focus upon.'

'Easier said than done,' Dagorian told him.

Antikas gave a thin smile. 'Do not be frightened by death, Dagorian, for it comes to all men. For myself I would sooner die young and strong, than become a toothless, senile old man talking of the wonders of my youth.'

'I do not agree. I would like to live to see my children

and grandchildren grow. To know love and the joys of family.'

'Have you ever loved?' asked Antikas.

'No. I thought . . .' he hesitated. 'I thought I loved Axiana, but it was a dream, an ideal. She looked so fragile, lost almost. But no, I have never loved. You?'

'No,' answered Antikas, the lie sticking in his throat, the memory of Kara, burning in his mind.

'Do demons love, do you think?' asked Dagorian, suddenly. 'Do they wed and have children? I suppose they must.'

'I have never given it much thought,' admitted Antikas. 'Kalizkan told me that Emsharas the Great Sorcerer fell in love with a human woman, and she bore him children. He was a demon.'

'All I know of him is that he cast the Great Spell thousands of years ago.'

'Yes, and that I find curious,' said Antikas. 'According to Kalizkan he banished his entire race to a world of nothing, empty and void. Hundreds of thousands of souls ripped from the earth to float for eternity without form. Can there have ever been a crime worse than that?'

'You call it a crime? I don't understand. Humanity was saved by the action.'

'Humanity yes, but Emsharas was not human. Why then did he do it? Why not cast a spell that would banish *humanity* into a void, and leave the earth for his own people? It makes no sense.'

'It must have made sense to him. Perhaps it was that his people were evil.'

'Come now,' snapped Antikas, 'that makes even less sense. If we are to judge his actions as good, then we must accept that he was not evil. Why then should he have been the only good demon in the world? What of the Dryads who lived to protect the forest, or the Krandyl who preserved the fields and meadows? These also are creatures of legend, spirit beings, demons.'

Dagorian suddenly laughed and shook his head. 'What is so amusing?' asked Antikas.

'You do not find it amusing that two men sitting on a bridge and waiting for death can debate the actions of a sorcerer who died thousands of years ago? It is the kind of conversation I would expect to have sitting in the library at Drenan.' His laughter faded away. 'I don't care why he did it. What does it matter now? To us?'

'Are you determined to be morbid all day?' countered Antikas. 'If so you will be a less than merry companion. You do not have to stay here, Dagorian. There are no chains.'

'Why do you stay?' asked the younger man.

'I like to sit on bridges,' Antikas told him. 'It calms my soul.'

'Well I am staying because I'm too frightened not to,' said Dagorian. 'Can you understand that?'

'No,' admitted Antikas Karios.

'A few days ago I attacked five Ventrian lancers. I thought I was going to die. But my blood was up and I charged them. Then Nogusta and Kebra came to my aid and we won.'

'Yes, yes,' interrupted Antikas. 'I saw you had Vellian's horse. But what is the point of this tale?'

'The point?' said Dagorian, his face twisting in anguish. 'The point is that the fear never went away. Every day it grows. There are demons pursuing us. Unbeatable and unholy. And where are we headed? To a ghost city with no hope of rescue. I could not take the fear any more. So here I am. And look at me! Look at my hands!' Dagorian held out his hands, which were trembling uncontrollably.

'So humour me, Antikas Karios. Tell me why you are here on this cursed bridge?'

Antikas leaned forward, his hand snaking out, the palm lashing against Dagorian's cheek. The sound of the slap hung in the air. Dagorian surged to his feet, hand scrabbling for his sword. 'Where is your fear now?' said Antikas, softly. The softly spoken words cut through Dagorian's fury, and he stood, hand on sword hilt, staring into the dark, cruel eyes of Antikas Karios. The Ventrian spoke again. 'It is gone, is it not, your fear? Swamped by rage.'

'Yes, it is gone,' said Dagorian, coldly. 'What was your point?'

'You were right to stay here, Dagorian. A man would have to be a contortionist to both face his fear and flee from it.' Antikas stood and walked to the side of the bridge, leaning upon it and staring down into the water below. 'Come and look,' he said. The Drenai officer joined him.

'What am I looking at?'

'Life,' answered Antikas. 'It starts high in the mountains with the melting of the snow. Small streams bubbling together, merging, flowing down to join larger rivers, then out to the warm sea. There the sun shines upon the water and it rises as vapour and floats back over the mountains, falling as rain or snow. It is a circle, an endless beautiful circle. Long after we are gone, and the children of our grandchildren are gone, this river will still flow all the way to the sea. We are very small creatures, Dagorian, with very small dreams.' He turned to the young officer and smiled. 'Look at your hands. They are no longer shaking.'

'They will – when the Krayakin come.'

'I don't think so,' said Antikas.

His experience within the body form of Kalizkan had given the Demon Lord, Anharat, great insights into the workings of human mechanisms. Unable to halt the cancer spreading through the sorcerer's body Anharat had allowed all the mechanisms to fail, then using magick to maintain the illusion of life. Not so with this body form!

With Malikada slain and departed Anharat repaired the pierced heart, and kept it pumping, the nutrients in the blood feeding the cells and keeping the form alive – after a fashion. The spell needed to be maintained at all times. If the magick ceased to flow the body would decay immediately. This was not, however, a problem, for the spell was a small one. He had more difficulty with the autonomic responses, like breathing and blinking, but, upon experimentation overcame them. Using Kalizkan's corpse had been an effort, especially when corruption and decay accelerated. More and more power had been needed to maintain a cloak spell over the disgusting form. Now, however, he merely needed to keep the blood flowing, and air filling the lung sacs. There were also advantages to this new method. Senses of taste, touch and smell were incredibly heightened.

Anharat sat now in his tent, sipping a goblet of fine wine, swilling it around his mouth and savouring the taste. Although he preferred his own natural form Anharat considered keeping this one for a few years in order to fully appreciate the pleasures of human flesh. They were so much more exquisite than he could have imagined. Perhaps it was because the humans were so short-lived, he thought, a gift of nature to creatures who were in existence for a few, brief heartbeats. Emsharas had discovered these pleasures, and now Anharat understood them. No wonder his brother had spent so much time with the black woman.

Outside the tent he could hear the sounds of the army settling down for night camp, the rattling of pans and dishes as the men lined up for food, the smell of wood smoke from the fires, and the laughter of soldiers listening to tall tales.

He had dispensed with his undead guards. Their blank, uncomprehending stares had unnerved the officers. Equally he had withdrawn the Entukku from the city, allowing the terrified populace to return to a semblance of normality before the army marched. Thousands had died in the riots, and none of the surviving humans had the least notion of what had caused their own murderous rages. Curiously the Entukku, who normally thrived on terror and pain, had gorged themselves equally on the waves of remorse that had billowed forth. These humans were a constant source of all kinds of nourishment.

Anharat could hardly wait to experiment further upon them.

A faint glow shone on the walls of the tent behind him. His skin prickled, and he swung towards the light, his hands opening, the first words of an incantation upon his lips. A pale figure was forming. Anharat saw that it was merely an image, for the legs of the figure were merging with the iron brazier, filled with hot coals. He relaxed, his curiosity aroused. Was Kalizkan returned?

Then the light began to fade and the features of a man appeared. Anharat's rage grew and he began to tremble. His face twisted and he stepped forward, aching to rip his talons through the heart of the figure. The newcomer was dressed in robes of white. His skin was black, his eyes pale blue. Upon his brow he wore a circlet of gold. 'Greetings, my brother,' he said.

Anharat was almost too angry to speak, but he fought for control. If he could hold the image here for a while he could concoct a search spell that would follow it back to its source. 'Where have you been hiding, Emsharas?' he asked.

'Nowhere,' answered the figure.

'You lie, brother. For I was sentenced to exist in the hell of Nowhere, with all the creatures of the Illohir. And you were not there. Nor were you among the humans, for I have searched for you these last four thousand years.'

'I did not hide, Anharat,' said the figure, softly. 'Nor was it – nor is it – my intention for our people to exist in a void for ever.'

'I care nothing for your intentions, traitor. Did you know that I have destroyed your descendants?'

'Not all of them. One remains.'

'I will see him dead, and I will have the babe. Then your evil will be undone. The people of the Illohir will walk free upon the earth.'

'Aye, they will,' said Emsharas. 'But they will not be able to drink the water or the wine, nor will they laze under the sun.'

Anharat's mind was working furiously, and the search spell was almost complete. 'So, brother, will you not tell me where you have been all these centuries? Have you been enjoying life as a human? Have you tasted fine wines and bedded great beauties?'

'I have done none of these things, Anharat. Where do you think I found the power for the Great Spell?'

'I neither know, nor care,' lied Anharat.

'Oh, you care, brother, for you know that you and I were almost equally matched, and yet I discovered a source of power hitherto unknown. You could use it too.

I will willingly tell it to you – if you will help me complete my work.'

'Complete . . . ? What new horror do you have in mind for the Illohir, brother? Perhaps we could create chains of fire to torture our people down the ages?'

'I offer them a world where they can lie in the sun and swim in the rivers and lakes. A world of their own.'

'Really? How kind you are, Emsharas. Perhaps though you would explain why they are not already there. And why we have waited so long for this little discussion.'

'I did not have the power to complete the Spell. I needed you, Anharat.'

Anharat's finger jabbed out, and the completed search spell flowed around Emsharas, bathing him in a blue light. 'Now I will find you,' hissed Anharat. 'I will find you and I will destroy you. I swear it! But first I will kill the third king, and complete the prophecy.'

Emsharas smiled. '*My* prophecy,' he said. 'I left it for you, brother. And it is a true one. Upon the death of the third king the Illohir will rise again. We will speak soon.'

With that the figure vanished.

Anharat closed his eyes and fastened to the search spell. He felt it grow weaker and weaker, as if coming to him across a vast distance. Then it was gone.

The Demon Lord returned to his wine and drank deeply. In all his thousands of years held captive in the void he had used every known spell to locate Emsharas, sending search spells out through the universe. Yet there was nothing. It was as if Emsharas had never been.

And now, with the hour of Anharat's triumph approaching, his brother had returned.

Anharat could have endured threats, but Emsharas had made none. And what did he mean by denying that he had been hiding? A tiny seed of doubt seeped into

Anharat's mind. His brother never lied. Refilling his goblet Anharat drank again, recalling again the words of Emsharas. 'Oh, you care, brother, for you know that you and I were almost equally matched, and yet I discovered a source of power hitherto unknown. You could use it too. I will willingly tell it to you – if you will help me complete my work.' What source of power? Anharat moved to the pallet bed and lay down. *Tell* it to you. That's what Emsharas had said. Not *give* it to you. Not tell you where it *is*. The secret power source was not then an object, like a talisman, but something that could be passed on with words alone. It was impossible.

And yet . . . they *had* been almost equally matched. Where then had his brother found the power to banish an entire race?

There would be time to ponder the question. For now Anharat wished to see his victory draw closer. Allowing his mind to relax, his dark spirit floated free and flew over the mountains towards the stone bridge.

Chapter Ten

Antikas Karios removed his red cloak and neatly folded it, laying it upon the stone work of the bridge. Then he tied his long hair into a tight pony-tail and began moving through a series of routines designed to stretch his back and shoulders and hips. At the beginning the movements were slow, graceful and balletic. Then they grew more swift, becoming a dance, full of leaps and turns. Dagorian watched the man with a growing sense of sadness. Such a dance, he thought, should be to celebrate life and youth, not as a prelude to violence and death.

The sun was falling below the western mountains, and the violet sky was streaked with golden clouds. Antikas strolled across to where Dagorian waited. 'What a beautiful sunset,' he said.

The young officer did not reply. A line of ten riders had appeared from the woods, and were moving towards the bridge. As they cleared the tree line four more riders appeared, tall men, wearing black armour and full-faced helms.

The Ventrian captain rode his horse to the first of the obstacles, then called out to Antikas. 'Give way for the emperor's riders.'

'Which emperor would that be?' Antikas responded.

'Give way, Antikas Karios, you cannot stand against all of us. And I have no orders for your arrest.' The captain shifted nervously on his horse, and continually glanced back towards the black armoured Krayakin.

'I fear I cannot comply, captain,' said Antikas. 'You see I am a servant of the infant king, and I have been ordered to hold this bridge. Might I suggest that you and your men ride away, for you are wrong –' his voice hardened. '– I *can* stand against you. More than that, I can promise you that any man who steps upon this bridge will die.'

The captain licked his dry lips. 'This is madness,' he said. 'What is your purpose here?'

'I have already told you my purpose. Now attack – or be gone!'

The captain dragged back on the reins and wheeled his horse. Dagorian could see that none of the Ventrian soldiers seemed willing to enter the fray. Such was the awesome – and justified – reputation of the man facing them. Still they dismounted and drew their swords, for they were brave men and disciplined.

'Remember,' whispered Antikas, 'stay to the right.'

'I shall.'

'Are your hands trembling?'

'No.'

'Good. That is of some relief to me – for I cannot really take ten men alone.' He grinned at Dagorian then drew both his swords, one of shining steel, one darker than the pit, and stepped up to take his place on the left.

The bridge was wide enough for four warriors to walk abreast and still leave room to swing a sword. The Ventrians advanced slowly, picking their way through the rocks. Antikas stood very still. As they got closer he suddenly leapt at them with an ear-splitting battle cry. His steel sword swept out slashing through a soldier's throat, then the black blade sliced through the chest of a second man, killing him instantly. The Ventrians surged forward. Three made it past the swordsman. Dagorian jumped forward. The black blade licked out and a man died. A sword pierced Dagorian's shoulder. He fell back. The swordsman stumbled over a rock and lost his balance. Dagorian killed him with a straight thrust to the heart. Then Dagorian was struck again, this time by the third soldier. He felt as if he had been kicked by a horse, and could not, at first, locate the wound. Ignoring it he leapt to the attack, blocking a wild cut and sending a riposte that swept through the man's ribs. He fell without a sound.

Dagorian looked up to see Antikas battling furiously, his blades a blur as he cut and parried. There was blood on his face and left arm, but five men were down. Only the captain and one other remained.

Antikas ran at them – and they turned and fled.

They did not get far.

The four warriors of the Krayakin blocked the bridge. Two of them stepped forward and slew the fleeing soldiers.

'Hardly sporting,' called out Antikas Karios. 'Do you often kill your own men?'

'You fight well, human,' came a muffled voice. 'And I see you have found a Storm Sword. It should be an interesting encounter.'

'All at once – or one at a time. I care not,' said Antikas.

The sound of laughter greeted his challenge. Then the tallest of the warriors stepped forward. 'I like you, human,' he said. 'But there is blood running into your eyes. Move back and tie a scarf around your brow. I will await you.'

Antikas grinned then backed away to where Dagorian was sitting with his back to the bridge wall. 'Taking a rest, Drenai?' he asked. Then his smile faded as he saw the blood soaking Dagorian's tunic.

'Do not concern yourself with me,' said Dagorian, with a weak smile. 'Do as he bid.' Antikas had been cut just above his left eyebrow. The gash was around 2 inches long and blood was dripping into his eye. With his dagger he slashed through his shirt sleeve, then ripped it clear. Tearing a strip from it he bound his brow.

'Terrible thing to do to a good shirt,' he said. 'My tailor would be most annoyed.'

Then he rose and glanced down at Dagorian. 'Don't go away,' he said. 'I shall be back soon.'

'I don't think I'm going anywhere,' said Dagorian. 'Take the Storm Sword. I have a feeling you'll need it.'

Armed with the two black blades Antikas strode back to the centre of the bridge. 'What is your name?' he asked the tall warrior.

'I am Golbar,' replied the Krayakin.

'Come then, Golbar, let us dance a jig.'

'Bear with me, human,' said Golbar, removing his gauntlets. Slowly he removed the black armour, unbuckling the breastplate and the shoulder guards, the greaves and the forearm protectors. Lastly he removed his helm. His hair was white, his eyes dark, his skin pale. Drawing his sword he turned to one of his comrades, who threw him a second. He caught it cleanly and advanced across the stones. Antikas watched his movements. They were quick and graceful.

Antikas attacked, and as their swords met lightning crackled from the blades. The attack was parried with ease and Antikas only just managed to avoid a murderous riposte that further sliced the ruined satin shirt. The Krayakin came at him with bewildering speed and Antikas found himself fighting for his life. Never had he faced a more skilful opponent, nor met a man with reflexes as fast as this Krayakin. Antikas parried and blocked with increasing desperation, and slowly he was forced further back along the bridge. Anger touched him then, for the Krayakin was toying with him. Twice he had an opportunity to lance a thrust through the human's guard, and twice he merely sliced small cuts in his opponent's chest.

'You are very good,' said Golbar, conversationally, while still attacking. 'Not the best I ever killed, but close. Do let me know when you are ready to die.'

Antikas did not answer. Despite his increasing weariness and desperate battle for survival he had been reading his opponent's moves, seeking out a weakness. The man was ambidextrous – as indeed was Antikas – but he favoured the right, and sought to kill with thrusts rather than cleaving cuts. Antikas leapt back.

'I am ready now,' he said. The Krayakin attacked. Instead of backing away Antikas moved suddenly forward. As he had expected Golbar sent a lightning thrust with his right hand blade. Antikas swayed to the right, his enemy's sword glancing along his ribs. Ignoring the pain he slammed the black blade through the Krayakin's chest, spearing the heart. Golbar's dark eyes widened in pain and shock, his swords falling from his hands. Without a word he fell back to the stone of the bridge.

Antikas moved forward to face the remaining three.

'Who gets to strip next?' he asked.

'No-one,' came the response. 'Golbar always had a taste for the dramatic.'

Hefting their swords they came at him together. Antikas watched them, determined to take at least one more with him.

The moon was shining now over the mountains, and a cool breeze was whispering over the bridge. It would be so easy to sprint back to his horse and ride from here, ready to fight another day. He cast a quick glance at Dagorian. The young officer was sitting very still, his hands locked over the terrible wound in his belly. He had a sudden desire to tell him why he had chosen to fight on this bridge, to speak of redemption, and the loss of Kara. But there was no time.

The Krayakin were picking their way through the debris. Antikas tensed, ready to attack them.

A colossal, white form burst from the undergrowth, smashing aside trees as it came. It thundered towards the bridge, letting forth a terrifying screech. Antikas stared disbelievingly at the monstrous form, with its huge, wedge-shaped head and gaping jaws. It was moving at great speed. Blood was streaming from a wound high in the beast's shoulder, and Antikas could see a broken lance jutting there.

The three Krayakin swung round as the beast bore down upon them. There was nowhere to run, save to hurl themselves into the river. They stood their ground, dwarfed by the monstrosity looming over them. One Krayakin tried to attack, but a sweep from a taloned arm tore his head from his shoulders. The wedge-head lunged down, fastening to the shoulder of a second warrior, lifting him high. The Krayakin plunged his sword deep into the beast's neck. The beast's head flicked and the warrior sailed out over the river, splashing down into the torrent and disappearing below the waves. The third Krayakin had run in and lanced his sword deep into the fish-white belly of the beast, ripping a great wound, from which gushed a prodigious amount of blood. Talons ripped into the knight, smashing through his armour. He was hurled back against the stone supports of the bridge, his sword wrenched from his hand. The beast's head lunged at him. He tried to avoid it, but the terrible teeth caught him in the midsection, ripping him apart.

The monster reared up and the stone work trembled as it let out a howl of pain. The wound in its belly ripped further open, spilling its entrails to the bridge. Twisting its head it saw Antikas standing alone at the centre of the bridge. It made two faltering steps towards him, then stumbled sideways. The side bridge supports crumbled under its weight and it toppled into the rushing river.

Antikas moved to the edge, staring down. The body was moving slowly out of sight, towards the distant falls.

Remembering Kalizkan's warning about the near miraculous healing powers of the Krayakin Antikas ran to the first body and heaved both sections into the river. He paused at the second, and stared down at the decapitated head. The helm visor was still closed. Antikas flipped it open and found himself staring into glowing eyes, that were alive and full of hatred. The mouth moved, but without vocal chords no sound issued forth. Antikas picked up the head and tossed it into the water, then rolled the body after it. Lastly he moved to the armourless body of Golbar. This too he fed to the river.

Returning to Dagorian he slumped down beside the dying officer. 'How do you feel?' he asked.

'There is no pain, but I can no longer move my legs. I am dying, Antikas.'

'Yes, you are. But we won, Drenai.'

'Perhaps. Then again, perhaps we merely delayed the inevitable. There are four more Krayakin, and the Ventrian army has closed off the road to the sea.'

'Let tomorrow take care of itself, Dagorian. You fought well, and bravely. It was an honour to stand beside you. I do not know much about your religion. Is there a Hall of Heroes contained in it?'

'No.'

'Then you should convert to mine, my friend. In it you will find a palace full of young virgins ready to obey your every whim. There will be wine and song and endless sunshine.'

'It . . . sounds . . . very fine,' whispered Dagorian.

'I will say a prayer for your spirit, Drenai, and that prayer will shine above you like a lantern. Follow it to the palace that awaits me. I will see you there.' Antikas reached across and closed the dead eyes. Then he scabbarded the Storm Swords and walked slowly back to the horses. The cut on his ribs was stinging now as the blood clotted over it. He stepped into the saddle and gazed back along the bridge.

Then he fulfilled his promise and sent a prayer-light to shine for Dagorian.

Swinging the horses he rode after the others.

The cave was deep, and curved like a horn. The biting wind could not reach them here and the group huddled around two fires. Nogusta stood apart from the others, heavy of heart. He had not lied to Dagorian. He had not *seen* him die. Yet he had known that the young man would not survive the encounter on the bridge, for in the vivid flashes of the future which had come to him there had been no sign of the officer.

Kebra moved from the fire and stood beside him. 'How long before we come down from this mountain?' he asked.

'Some time late tomorrow.'

'I have fed the last of the grain to the horses, but they need rest, Nogusta, and good grass and water.'

Nogusta unrolled the parchment map, and held it up so that they could both see it in the firelight. 'Tomorrow we will reach the highest point. It will be bitterly cold and the road will be ice covered and treacherous. After that we begin the long descent to the five valleys and Lem.'

'The fires will not last the night,' said Kebra, 'and it will be below freezing in here without them.' They had gathered wood in the last valley, and Bison had also tied several bundles of dried timber from the smashed wagon. It was these which were burning now.

'Then we will be cold,' said Nogusta. 'Though not as cold as Dagorian.'

'You think we should have stayed?'

Nogusta shook his head. 'The other Krayakin are close by.'

'What have you seen?'

'Too much,' said Nogusta, sadly. 'The Gift is more of a curse than ever. I see, but I cannot change what I see. Dagorian asked me if he was to die. I did not tell him. I think he knew nonetheless. He was a good man, Kebra, a man who should have lived to build, to sire children and teach them the virtues of honesty, courage and honour. He should not be lying dead on a forgotten bridge.'

'We will not forget him,' said the silver-haired bowman.

'No, we will not. And what does that count for? We are old men, you and I. Our time is passing. And when I look back over my life I wonder whether it has been for good or ill. I have fought for most of my life. I defended the Drenai cause, even though most of my comrades either feared me or loathed me for the colour of my skin. Then I took part in the invasion of Ventria, and saw the destruction of an ancient empire. All for the vanity of one arrogant man. What will I say to the Keeper of the

Book when I stand before him? What excuses shall I offer for my life?'

Kebra looked closely at his friend, and he thought carefully before speaking. 'This is probably not the time to consider it,' he said, at last. 'Despair touches you, and there is no comfort to be found in melancholy. You have in your life rescued many, and risked yourself for others. You do so now. Such deeds will also be recorded. I am not a philosopher, Nogusta, but there are things I know. If your Gift sees us fail, and the child is destined to fall into the hands of evil, no matter what we do, will you ride then away and leave him to his fate? No you will not. Even if death and defeat are inevitable. No more will I. No-one can ask more of us than that.'

Nogusta smiled. He would have reached out and embraced the man, save that Kebra was not tactile, and disliked being touched. 'My father once told me that if a man could count true friends on the fingers of one hand then he was blessed beyond riches. I have been blessed, Kebra.'

'I too. Now get a little rest. I will keep watch for a while.'

'Listen for a single horse, for Antikas Karios will be trying to find us.'

'I have to say that I do not like the man,' admitted Kebra. 'His arrogance sticks in my throat.'

Nogusta smiled again. 'Reminds you of us some twenty years ago, doesn't he?'

Kebra nodded and walked to the mouth of the cave. Sitting back from the wind he looked out over the peaks and shivered. They were thousands of feet above the valley floor, and the clouds looked close enough to touch. Drawing his cloak about him he leaned back against the wall. Dagorian's death had saddened him also. He had liked the young man. His fear had been great, his courage greater still. He would have raised fine sons, thought Kebra.

The rocks were cold and he lifted his hood into place. Fine sons. The thought saddened him. What kind of a father would I have been, he wondered? He would never know. And, unlike Bison or Nogusta, there was no chance that he had sired children with any of the whores he had encountered through thirty years of campaigning, for he had never coupled with any of them. He had, of course, visited the brothels with both his comrades, but upon reaching the quiet of the bedroom he had merely paid the girls to sit and talk with him. To make love one had to touch, and Kebra could not even bear the thought of it. Flesh upon flesh? He shuddered.

From out of the past the memory came. It caught him unawares, for he had long ago buried it beyond the reaches of his imagination. The dark walls of the barn, the huge hairy hands of his father, the pain and the terror, and the threats of death if ever he spoke of it. He blinked and focused his gaze on the mountain peaks.

Conalin crept up to sit alongside him, a blanket wrapped tight around his thin shoulders. 'I brought your bow and arrows,' said the boy.

'Thank you – but I don't think we'll need them tonight.' He glanced down at the boy, seeing the fear in his eyes.

'Antikas Karios and Dagorian held the bridge. Antikas will be coming soon.'

'How do you know?'

'Nogusta had a vision. His visions are always true.'

'You said Antikas will be coming. What about Dagorian?'

There was no other way to say it. 'He died for us,' said

Kebra. 'He fought like a man, and he died like a man.'

'I don't want to die,' said Conalin, miserably.

'But you will, one day,' observed Kebra. He chuckled suddenly. 'I had an old uncle, and he used to say, "Only one thing in life is certain, son, you won't get out of it alive." He lived every day to the full. He was a man who loved life. He was a soldier for a while, then a merchant, and lastly a farmer. He never did anything brilliantly, but he always gave it his best. I liked him – and he once did me a great service.'

'What did he do?'

'He killed my father.'

Conalin was shocked. 'And that was a service?'

'Indeed it was. Sadly he killed him too late, but that was not his fault.' He fell silent for a moment. Conalin wanted to ask him other questions, but he saw the sadness in the old man's eyes. Then Kebra spoke again. 'What would you like to be, Conalin?'

'Married to Pharis,' answered the boy, instantly.

'Yes, I know that. But what career do you desire?'

Conalin thought about it. 'Something to do with horses. That's what I'd really like.'

'A good occupation. Nogusta has similar plans. Once his family were renowned for their horses. But his wife and all of his kin were murdered, the great house burned to the ground, the stables destroyed. The herd escaped into the mountains. Nogusta has a dream of returning to the family estate and rebuilding it. He says that deep in the mountains there are many valleys, and that the herd will have grown now. He plans to find them.'

Conalin's eyes were shining now. 'I'd like to do that. Would he let me, do you think?'

'You would have to ask him.'

'Could you not ask him for me?'

'I could,' agreed Kebra, 'but that is not the way it should be. A strong man makes his own way in the world. He does not ask others to do that which he fears himself.'

Conalin moved out of the wind. He was a little too close to Kebra now, and the bowman felt uncomfortable. 'I will ask him,' said the boy. 'Will you be there with us?'

'I might be – if the Source wills it.'

The boy's excited expression suddenly faded. 'What is wrong?' asked Kebra.

'What is the point of talking about horses? We are going to die here.'

'We've made it this far,' Kebra pointed out. 'And I have yet to see the enemy who could defeat Nogusta. And as for Bison . . . well, he is the strongest man I ever knew, and he has more heart than any ten demons. No, Conalin, do not dismiss them so lightly. They may be old, but they are canny.'

'What about you?'

'Me? I am quite simply the finest archer ever to walk the earth. I could hit a fly's testicles from thirty paces.'

'Do flies have testicles?' asked Conalin.

'Not when I'm close by,' answered Kebra, with a smile.

Antikas Karios reached the cave just before midnight. His beard was caked with ice, as was his horse's mane, and both he and his mount were mortally weary. For the last 2 miles he had been swaying in the saddle, and fighting to stay awake.

Kebra stepped out into the biting wind, taking hold of the horse's bridle and leading him into the cave. It took Antikas two attempts before he could summon the energy to dismount. Nogusta approached him.

'Sit by the fire and warm yourself,' he said.

'Horse first,' muttered Antikas. From the back of his saddle he untied a thick bundle of wood and handed it to Nogusta. 'I thought the fuel might be running low,' he said. Dragging off his gauntlets Antikas rubbed life back into his cold fingers, then began to unsaddle the chestnut gelding. His movements were stiff and slow.

'Let me help you,' said Kebra, lifting the saddle clear and laying it over a rock. Antikas did not thank him, but moved to the saddlebags. His cold, swollen fingers fumbled at the buckles, but, at last he opened them, taking out a body brush and a cloth. Returning to the horse he rubbed the animal dry then, with deep circular strokes, brushed him. Conalin watched with interest. He had seen Kebra and Nogusta do the same some hours before, when they had first arrived at the cave. 'Why is it so important for the horse to have a brushed coat?' he whispered to the bowman.

'Grooming is not just about the coat,' answered Kebra. 'That horse is cold and tired. The brush helps to improve the circulation of blood, and tones the muscles.'

Antikas stepped back from the horse, cleaned the brush and returned it to his saddlebag. Then he removed his crimson cloak and laid it over the gelding's back. It was then that the others saw the dried blood on his torn, satin shirt. Ulmenetha rose from the first of the fires and bade Antikas to remove his shirt. He did so with great difficulty. Satin fibres had stuck to his wounds, and as he pulled the shirt clear the small cuts in his chest and the long, jagged slice along his ribs began to bleed once more. Sitting him down by the fire Ulmenetha examined the wounds. The smaller cuts she could heal immediately without stitches, but the wound caused by Golbar's last thrust first needed more traditional treatment. Nogusta handed Antikas a cup of broth, which he accepted gratefully. As Ulmenetha prepared her needle and thread Antikas stared around the firelit cave. The ape, Bison, was asleep by the far wall. Alongside him, huddled close for warmth was a young girl and a child. Beyond them the queen was sitting in the shadows, holding her babe close to her breast. Antikas saw that the child was feeding, and looked away guiltily.

'Stand up,' ordered Ulmenetha. Antikas did so. The priestess came to her knees, and began to stitch the wound, beginning first at the centre, drawing the flaps of skin together. Antikas looked across at Nogusta, and their eyes met.

'He died well,' said Antikas.

'I know.'

'Good, for I am too tired to discuss it further.' He winced as Ulmenetha drew tight the centre stitch. 'You are not knitting a rug, woman,' he snapped.

'I'll wager you did not whine so when the Krayakin faced you,' she responded. Antikas grinned, but said nothing. Three more stitches were inserted, then Ulmenetha laid a slender hand over the wound, and began to chant in a low voice. Antikas glanced down at the priestess, then gave a questioning look to Nogusta. The black man had turned away and was untying the bundle of wood.

Antikas felt a tingling sensation begin in the wound, heat flaring from it. It was mildly uncomfortable, but not at all painful. After some minutes Ulmenetha removed her hand, then, with a small knife, cut the stitches and pulled them clear. Antikas touched the cut. It was almost healed. More than this he felt curiously rejuvenated, as if he had slept for several hours.

'You are very talented, lady,' he said.

'You should see me knitting a rug,' she answered, rising to stand before him. She repeated the Healing Prayer on the smaller chest wounds, then reached up to pull clear the blood-stained satin strip around his brow. 'Bend your head,' she ordered him. Antikas obeyed.

As she healed the cut she spoke again. 'You are a lucky man, Antikas. Had the blow been two inches lower you would have lost an eye.'

'Strangely, the more I practise the luckier I get,' he said.

Ulmenetha stepped back from him, and appraised her work. Satisfied she moved back to the fire and sat down. 'Had you remained at the bridge you might have saved Dagorian,' he said. Ulmenetha shook her head.

'His internal injuries were far beyond my powers.' So saying she turned away from him. Kebra handed him a clean, folded tunic of off-white wool. Antikas thanked him. Lifting it to his nose he smiled. 'Scented rosewood,' he said. 'How civilized. You are a man after my own heart.'

'Probably not,' said Kebra.

Antikas slipped on the shirt. The arms were too long, and he folded back the cuffs. 'Well, Nogusta,' he said, 'what now? What do your visions tell you?'

'We go to the ghost city,' answered Nogusta. 'That is all I can say. I do not yet know the outcome of this quest. But all questions will be answered in Lem.'

The child sleeping beside Bison suddenly cried out and sat up. The girl beside her awoke, and took her in her arms. 'What is wrong, Sufia?' she asked, stroking the child's blond hair.

'I had a dream. Demons in my dream. They were eating me up.' The child began to cry. Then she saw Antikas, and her eyes widened.

'Hello,' said Antikas, giving her his best smile. Sufia let

out a wail and buried her head in Pharis's chest. 'I've always had a way with children,' said Antikas, drily.

The noise awoke Bison, who gave a great yawn, then belched loudly. He too saw Antikas, and looked around for Dagorian. Rising he scratched at his groin then moved to the fire, where he belched again. 'Killed 'em all, did you?' he asked Antikas.

'One of them. A huge beast came from the forest and slaughtered the others.'

Fear showed in Bison's face. 'Is it still alive?'

'No. It fell into the river and drowned.'

'Well, that's a relief,' said Bison. 'Almost makes up for the fact that you survived. Where is the lad, Dagorian?'

'He died.'

Bison absorbed the information without comment, then swung to Kebra. 'Is there any broth left?'

'No, Antikas ate the last of it.'

'What about the biscuits?'

'A few left,' said Kebra. 'But we are saving them for the morning. The children can have them for breakfast.'

Antikas removed his sword belt, and laid it beside him. 'There are four more Krayakin,' he said. 'Believe me, Nogusta, that is four too many. I fought one. He had a sense of honour, and removed his armour to fight me. He was faster than any man I have ever known. I am not sure I could defeat another, and I certainly could not defeat more than one.'

'What then do you suggest?' asked Nogusta.

'I have no suggestions. What I am saying is that I treated them too lightly. I thought of them merely as men, and there is no man more skilled than I. But they are not men. Their reflexes are astonishing, and their strength prodigious.'

'And yet we must face them,' said Nogusta. 'We have no choice.'

'Whatever you say,' said Antikas. He stretched out beside the fire, then glanced up at Bison. 'We could always send him against them,' he said. 'His body odour would fell an ox.'

Bison glared at him. 'I'm beginning to *really* dislike you, little man,' he said.

Breakfast was a sorry affair, with the last of the oatcake biscuits being shared by Sufia, Pharis and Conalin. Pharis offered hers to the queen, but Axiana smiled and shook her head. Bison grumbled about starvation as he saddled the horses.

As she finished her food little Sufia climbed onto Ulmenetha's lap. 'Did you sleep well, in the end, little one?' asked the priestess.

'Yes. I didn't dream no more. It's very cold,' she added, snuggling close. The last of the wood had long burnt away, and the temperature in the cave was dropping fast.

'We are going down into the valleys today,' Ulmenetha told her. 'It will be much warmer there.'

'I'm still hungry.'

'We are all hungry.' Sufia gave a nervous glance across at Antikas. 'He looks like a demon,' she said. Antikas heard her and gave her a grin. She scowled at him from the perceived safety of Ulmenetha's lap.

'I am not a demon,' said Antikas. 'I am earth born, as you are.'

'What does that mean?' Sufia asked the priestess.

'It means that we come from the earth, whereas demons are born of the wind. We are solid. We can touch things. Demons are like the wind. They can blow against us, but they cannot live and breathe as we do.'

Pharis came and sat alongside them. 'If that is true, how can the Krayakin fight us? Are they not solid?'

'There is an old story,' said Antikas, 'that my father used to tell. It is part of Ventrian history and myth. Once there were two Windborn gods, great and powerful. They floated above the earth, and watched the deer and the lion, the eagle and the lamb. They were envious of them, and their ability to walk the land. These gods had many Windborn subjects, and they too looked upon the earth with jealousy. One day the two gods – who did not like one another . . .'

'Why didn't they like one another?' asked Sufia.

'That's not important. Anyway . . .'

'I think it is important,' said Pharis. 'Why would gods not like one another?'

Antikas suppressed his irritation. 'Very well, let us say that one of the gods was evil, the other good. One was a lord of chaos and destruction, while the other loved the light, and delighted to see things grow. They were like night and day.'

'All right,' said Pharis. 'I can understand that. Go on.'

'Thank you. One day these gods decided to use their great power to cast a spell that would allow their people, the Illohir, to take on fleshly forms. These spirit beings floated down to the earth, and wherever they landed they drew matter to themselves, creating bodies that could walk upon the earth.'

'How did they do that?' asked Sufia.

'I don't know how they did it,' snapped Antikas.

'I do,' said Ulmenetha. 'All matter is made up of tiny molecules – so tiny that the human eye cannot see them. They literally drew these molecules to them, like so many bricks and built their bodies.'

'There,' said Antikas to Sufia. 'Does that satisfy you?'

The child looked mystified. Axiana, who had been listening to the tale, walked across to them, the babe asleep in her arms. Antikas rose and bowed to her. She responded with a smile. 'I too heard this story,' she said, softly. 'There is great beauty in it. Some of the Windborn landed in forests, and drew their strength from the trees. They became Dryads, protectors of woodland, their souls entwined with the trees they loved. Others came down in the mountains, building their forms from the rocks and stones. These were the High Trolls. Some groups emerged near living creatures, like wolves. Because they drew particles from everything around them they became Shape-Shifters, manlike during the day, but becoming wolves at night. All over the world the Illohir took on different forms, and rejoiced in their new-found freedom.'

'Did any become birds?' asked Sufia.

'I expect that they did,' said Axiana.

'That means Bison is a demon,' said Sufia, 'because he once had big white wings and flew over mountains.'

'Must have been *really* big wings,' said Antikas.

Conalin joined them. 'If they were all so happy why did they start a war with people?'

Ulmenetha answered him. 'They weren't *all* happy. Some of the Windborn had landed in places that were . . . unclean. Battlefields, graveyards, scenes of violence or terror. What they drew into themselves was dark and fearsome. These became the Hollow Tooths, who suck blood from sleepers. Or the Krayakin, who live for war and slaughter.'

'And these were the ones who started the war?' persisted Conalin.

Antikas took up the story again. 'Yes. The real problem was in the nature of the spell which brought the

Windborn to the earth. They were . . . are . . . creatures of spirit, and though they could build their bodies with magick, they could not hold them together for long. They could not feed as we do, and, as the years passed, some of the Illohir began to wither away, and return to the air. Those that remained needed to find a new source of nourishment. *We* were that nourishment. The Illohir began to feed on human emotions. The Dryads, the fauns, and other creatures of the forest found they could draw energy from human happiness and joy. That is why there are so many stories of wild celebration involving fauns and humans. Fauns were said to have invented wine, to further enhance human joy. But the darker demons fed on terror and dismay – as you saw back in Usa. It was said that the fear and pain inspired in a human tortured to death could feed a demon for years. And because they had magick – which gave them domination over us – they treated us like cattle, as a food source. Mankind suffered through many centuries under their rule, until at last three human kings rebelled against them. The war was long and terrible, the battles many.'

'How did we win?' asked Conalin.

'No-one really knows,' Antikas told him, 'for it was so long ago, and there are so many legends. However, Kalizkan told me that Emsharas the Sorcerer – himself a demon – betrayed his own people and cast a great spell that banished all his brethren from the earth. He made them Windborn again, and locked them away in a great void.'

'And now they are coming back,' said Conalin.

Nogusta stepped forward. 'It is time to ride,' he said.

For the first hour they rode in single file along the

narrowing ridge road, Nogusta leading, followed by Kebra and Conalin. Ulmenetha was walking, and holding to the bridle of the queen's mount. Behind her came Bison, also walking, and leading the horse ridden by Pharis and Sufia. Antikas Karios rode at the rear, leading the two spare horses. The wind was cold, hissing over jagged rocks, whipping snow into their faces.

By noon they had reached the highest point and Nogusta drew rein, scanning the road ahead. It dipped gently, curving round a mountain towards an area of high timber several hundred feet below them. From here Nogusta could see a waterfall and a river emptying into a wide lake. Ducking his head against the wind he urged Starfire on. The road widened, and Antikas Karios rode past the others, drawing rein alongside the black warrior.

'We need to rest the horses,' shouted Antikas. Nogusta nodded and pointed to the distant falls.

'I'll scout the area,' said Antikas, and rode on ahead.

There were patches of ice on the road, and the queen's horse slipped. Axiana lurched in the saddle, and found herself staring down into a deep abyss. Grabbing the saddle pommel with her free hand she righted herself in the saddle. The sudden jerk woke the babe. But, safe and warm in his blanket, he went straight back to sleep.

Kebra spotted movement in the trees below. Several small deer moved out of the trees. Taking his bow he also rode alongside Nogusta. 'I'll see you at the falls,' he said, and followed Antikas Karios down the mountain.

They journeyed on for another hour before reaching the falls. It was still cold here, for they were several thousand feet above the valley floor, but the thick stand of trees dispersed the wind, and there was enough dead wood to light a good fire. Kebra returned with a deer, which he had already skinned and quartered, and soon the smell of roasting meat filled the air.

Nogusta ate swiftly, then walked away from the group to stand at the edge of the falls. Antikas Karios joined him there. 'I see you ride the king's horse,' he said. 'I thought it was dying.'

'It had a lung infection caused by poor stabling.'

'It was a fine beast once,' said Antikas. 'But it is old now.'

'Old it may be, Antikas, but it will outrun any horse among the Ventrian cavalry, and it would ride through the fires of Hell for a rider it trusted.'

'Trusted? It is just a horse, black man. No more, no less. A beast of burden.'

Nogusta did not reply. 'I think it is time to tell me what you have seen,' said the Ventrian.

Nogusta swung back towards him. 'You want to know if you live or die?'

'No. Time will tell about that. But you are carrying a great weight. I can tell. It might be better if you shared it.'

Nogusta thought about it for a moment. 'My Gift,' he said, at last, 'is not precise. If it were I would have saved my family from massacre. What I see are sudden, vivid scenes. You remember the king's birthday celebrations? I was talking to Dagorian. I saw him fighting you in the final of the sabres. I could not see if he was winning or losing. The vision lasted a heartbeat only. But then I saw him beside you again, on a bridge. He was sitting against the wall, badly wounded. I had no way of knowing where that bridge was, or when in the future the event would take place. All I knew was that Dagorian would probably die alongside you. Indeed, you may have been the one to cause the wound.'

'I understand,' said Antikas. 'So now tell me what else you have seen.'

For a moment Nogusta did not speak, and stood staring out over the lake. 'I have seen the death of a friend,' he said, at last, dropping his voice. 'And the question that haunts me is this, can I change his destiny? Could I have prevented Dagorian from standing on that bridge with you? And if I had would you have won alone?'

'Probably not. Dagorian took out three soldiers. Ten would have been too many – even for me.'

'That is what I thought,' said Nogusta. 'Which could mean that, although I could change the future and save my friend, by doing so I might bring about the return of the demons.'

'Alternatively, by changing the future you might bring about the opposite,' Antikas pointed out. 'Have you ever tried to alter events, based on your visions?'

Nogusta nodded. 'I saw a wagon crushing a child to death outside an inn. I knew the inn, and I could tell the event was to happen just before dusk. I went to the area, seeking out the child. I waited at the inn. She came on the second day, and I spoke with her. I told her to beware of running out in front of wagons. I went every day for a week, and we talked often. Then, one afternoon, she was running towards me when I saw a wagon turn the corner. I shouted to her, and she stopped running. The wagon missed her.'

'Then you can alter the future for the good,' said Antikas.

Nogusta shook his head. 'No. I thought I had accomplished the task. The following day she was struck by another wagon and killed. But that was not the worst of it. She was running to meet *me*, because she enjoyed our conversations. Had I not sought her out she might never have been outside the inn at all.'

'It is all very complicated,' said Antikas. 'I am glad that I do not have visions. I do have one observation, however. The Demon Lord needs to sacrifice the babe in order to bring about the end of the Spell. If the child were to die before the sacrifice the Spell would be thwarted.'

'That has occurred to me,' admitted Nogusta.

'And what conclusion did you reach?'

'Whatever destiny holds in store for me it will not be as a killer of children. What the Demon Lord plans is evil. I do not believe that the way to fight great evil is to commit a lesser one. My role now is to protect the child. That I will do.'

'You are very rigid in your thinking,' Antikas pointed out. 'Kill one babe to save the world? It seems a small price to pay.'

'It is not a question of scale,' said Nogusta. 'If it were then ten thousand babes would be a small price for such a great reward. It is a question of right and wrong. That child may prove to be one of the greatest men ever born, a peacemaker and a builder, a prophet or a philosopher. Who can say what wonders he may bring about?'

Antikas chuckled. 'More likely he will be another Skanda, full of vanity and arrogance.'

'Is that your advice then, Antikas Karios, to kill the child?'

'Answer me this first,' responded the Ventrian. 'If your vision told you that the babe was certain to fall into the clutches of the Demon Lord, would you reconsider?'

'No. I will defend it to the last drop of my blood. Now answer my question.'

'I am no longer a general, Nogusta. I am merely a man. You are in command here. As long as you live I will follow your orders, and I too will defend the child to the last.'

'And if I do not live, and you survive me?'

'I will do whatever I think is right by my own principles. Does that satisfy you?'

'Of course.'

Antikas smiled and began to turn away. Then he stopped. 'You are a romantic, Nogusta, and an idealist. I have often wondered how men like you find happiness in such a corrupt and selfish world.'

'Perhaps one day you will find out,' Nogusta told him.

Antikas returned to the camp. Conalin was rubbing down the horses, while Bison sat by the fire eating roast meat, the juices running down his chin and staining his already filthy tunic. Antikas moved to where Axiana was sitting with Ulmenetha and the young girl, Pharis. The priestess was holding the sleeping babe, and the queen was daintily picking at her food.

'A far cry from palace banquets,' observed Antikas, making a deep bow.

'And yet very welcome, sir,' she told him. Axiana's dark eyes met his gaze. 'We thank you for coming to our assistance.'

'My pleasure, highness.'

As Antikas moved away Ulmenetha leaned in to the queen. 'Do you trust him, child?' she asked.

'He is a Ventrian noble,' she replied, as if that answered the question. Reaching out she took back her son, and held him close to her, carefully supporting his head. His tiny hand flapped out from the blanket. 'Look at his finger nails,' she said, 'how small and perfect they are. So tiny. So beautiful.' She gazed down into his face. 'How could anyone wish to hurt him?'

Ulmenetha gave no answer. Stretching out upon the cold ground she released her spirit and flew high above the trees. The fierce winds were merely a sound here, and they shrieked around her, as if angry that they could not buffet her spirit. Like a shaft of light she sped south, searching the land for sign of the Krayakin.

Her spirit soared over woodland and valleys, over tiny settlements and farms. Nowhere could she find evidence of the black-armoured riders. She moved north, back over the canyon and along the Great River. The army of Ventria was marching here, in columns of threes, cavalry riding on the flanks. Ulmenetha drew away from them, afraid that the Demon Lord would sense her spirit.

Back over the canyon she flew, until, far below, she saw the camp-site.

Pain struck her like an arrow, claws digging into her spirit flesh. Instantly she produced the fire of *halignat*, which blazed around her. The claws withdrew, but she could sense a presence close by. Hovering in the air she gazed around her, but could see nothing.

'Show yourself,' she commanded.

Just outside the white fire, so close that it shocked her, a figure materialized. It was that of a man, with ghost-white hair, and a pale face. His eyes were blue and large, his mouth thin lipped and cruel. 'What do you want of me?' she asked him.

'Nothing,' he told her. 'I want only the child.'

'You cannot have him.'

He smiled then. 'Six of my brothers have returned to the great void. You and your companions have done well, and have acted with great courage. I admire that. I always have. But you cannot survive, woman.'

'We have survived so far,' she pointed out.

'By flight. By running into the wilderness. Think about where you are heading. To a ghost city, whose walls have long since crumbled. A stone shell offering no sanctuary. And what is behind you? An army who will reach the city by dusk tomorrow. Where then will you run?'

Ulmenetha could think of no answer. 'You seek to protect a flower in a blizzard,' he said. 'And you are ready to die to do so. But the flower will perish. That is its destiny.'

'That is *not* its destiny,' she told him. 'You and your kind have great powers. But they have not prevailed so far. As you say six of your brothers have gone. The rest of you will follow. Nogusta is a great warrior. He will kill you.'

'Ah, yes, the descendant of Emsharas. The last descendant. An old man, tired and spent. He will defeat the Krayakin and the army of Anharat? I think not.'

Ulmenetha remembered the Demon Lord's words as he floated above the wagon. He had looked at Nogusta and said, 'Yes, you look like him, the last of his mongrel line.' Ulmenetha smiled and looked into the eyes of the Krayakin. 'Do you not find it strange that the descendant of Emsharas should be here now, defying you as his ancestor defied you? Does it not cause you concern? Does it not have a feeling of destiny at work?'

'Yes, it does,' he admitted. 'But it will not alter the outcome. He has no magick. He is not a sorcerer. All his gifts stem from the talisman he wears. It can turn aside spells, but cannot deflect a sword blade.'

'Your evil will not conquer,' she said.

He seemed genuinely surprised. 'Evil? Why is it you humans always speak of evil as something that exists outside of yourselves? Do your cattle think of you as evil because you devour them? Do the fish of the ocean see you as evil? Such arrogance. You are no different to the cattle, and we are not evil for feeding upon you. You wish to hear my view of evil? The actions of Emsharas, banishing his people to a soulless hell, void of sound and smell, of taste and joy. I see our return as no more than simple justice.'

'I will not debate with you, demon,' she told him, and yet she did not move away.

'Not *will not*, woman. *Cannot!* By what right do you deny us a chance at life under the moon and stars?'

'I do not deny you,' she said. 'But by what right do you seek to kill a child?'

'Kill? Another interesting concept. Do you believe in the soul?'

'I do.'

'Then we kill nothing. All we do is end the mortal existence of humans. Their souls go on. And since their mortal existence is fragile and short-lived anyway, what have we really taken from them?'

'Your kind are immortal. You can never know the value of what you so casually remove from others. Death is alien to you. Yes, I believe in the soul, but I do not know if it is immortal. All I know is the pain you cause to those who are left behind. The misery and the despair.'

He smiled again. 'These things you speak of are our food source.'

'There is no point in this conversation,' she told him.

'Wait! Do not go yet!'

In that moment, as she looked into his eyes, Ulmenetha saw a moment of panic. Why did he want her to stay? Could it be she was reaching him, in some indefinable way. She relaxed and prepared to talk on. Then, though he tried to hide it, she saw the triumph in his eyes. And she knew! She was the only one among the group who could use magick. His only purpose was to detain her.

353

Spinning away from him she sped for her body.

It was too late. Three Krayakin burst from the bushes and charged into the camp.

Drasko stepped into the clearing, Mandrak to his left, Lekor to his right. Their swords were in their hands, and Drasko felt the long forgotten surging of battle fever in his veins. The bald giant who had killed Nemor ran at him. Drasko spun and plunged his sword through the man's ribs, then backhanded him across the face, hurling the giant to the ground.

On the far side of the fire a hawk-eyed swordsman leapt to his feet. Drasko saw that he carried two Storm Swords. Beyond him a silver-haired man had rolled to his left, coming up with a bow, and notching an arrow to the string. Opening his hand Drasko tossed a small, black crystal globe across the clearing, then closed his eyes.

The explosion was deafening, and Drasko's eyes, even through tightly closed lids, were hurt by the blinding light which followed. Opening his eyes he saw that the swordsman had been hurled across the clearing and was lying, stunned, beside a tall pine. The bowman was sprawled some distance from him. The queen had also been caught by the blast, and was lying unconscious by the bushes, the babe beside her. A red-headed youngster came running from the trees, grabbing the hand of a skinny girl and dragging her away. Drasko had no interest in them.

He turned towards the queen. At that moment the blond-haired woman lying beside her lunged to her feet. The holy fire of *halignat* burst around his helm. He staggered back. The priestess advanced, holy fire blazing from her fingers. Instantly all was confusion. A fireball enveloped Mandrak, who fell back into the undergrowth. Then Lekor hurled a knife, that spun through the air, slamming hilt first into the woman's temple. She dropped to her knees, the fire extinguished. The stunned swordsman was stirring, and Drasko turned once more to where the queen lay unconscious.

Flipping open the visor of his helm he looked for the baby. It was nowhere in sight. The shock was immense. The infant could not have vanished. He knew enough of humans to know that newborn babes could not crawl! He glanced around. The giant human had also gone, and where he had fallen there was now only a bright red stain of blood upon the grass.

'The bald one has the child,' he told the others. 'Find him, kill him, and then return here.'

Lekor and Mandrak turned and ran back through the undergrowth, following a grisly trail of blood.

Drasko moved towards the swordsman. The man was on his knees now, sucking in great gulps of air.

'Gather your swords and face me,' said Drasko. 'It is long since I killed a Storm Swordsman.'

'Then face me, demon,' came a voice from behind.

Drasko spun on his heel and saw the black warrior, Nogusta standing by the camp-fire. He too held a Storm Sword. 'Very well, old one,' said Drasko. 'You shall be – as you humans say – the appetizer before the main course.'

Behind him Antikas Karios fell once more, then rolled to his side, his vision swimming.

Drasko leapt to meet Nogusta. The black man moved in, then swayed away from a wild cut. Their swords met, and lightning flared from the blades. The sound of clashing swords filled the clearing with savagely discordant music. As his vision cleared Antikas Karios watched the warriors circle one another, their blades shimmering in the sunlight, lightning leaping up from every exchange. He knew what Nogusta was going through, and, worse, he knew the end result.

Drasko knew also that the old man was tiring. Always a careful fighter he took no chances. The moment a swordsman went for the kill, was also the most dangerous time. If such an attack was mis-timed a fatal riposte could follow. Therefore Drasko fought on, making no attempt to end the contest, merely waiting for the tiring old man to leave an opening.

Nogusta leapt back, then stumbled, his fatigue obvious. From the ground Antikas watched him. A slow smile began as he recalled the fight with Cerez. Nogusta was trying the same tactic. It worked. Drasko suddenly leapt to the attack. Nogusta swayed away from the thrust. But not fast enough. The blade slammed home in his shoulder, smashing the bone, and emerging at the back. Then his own Storm Sword swept across and down, striking Drasko's sword arm at the elbow. The enchanted blade slid through armour, flesh and bone, severing the limb in one strike. Drasko screamed in pain. The severed arm flopped to the ground, and the black man stood stock still facing his enemy, the sword jutting from his shoulder.

'Time,' said Nogusta, 'to return from whence you came.'

Drawing a dagger with his left hand Drasko lunged. But the Storm Sword flashed in a glittering arc beheading the warrior cleanly. As the body fell Nogusta staggered, then fell to his knees beside it. Flipping his sword he held it dagger fashion, plunging it into Drasko's heart.

Antikas Karios came to his feet and stumbled to where Nogusta knelt. 'Let me help you,' he said.

'No. Follow the trail. Bison has the babe.'

Antikas began to run through the trees. He had seen Bison stabbed. The wound was mortal. And Bison's sword was still lying where it fell.

Unarmed and dying he was the only hope now for the child.

Bison stumbled on, his body wracked by spasms of pain. Sweat dripped into his eyes as he ran. Sufia's arms were around his neck, and she was crying. He couldn't remember picking her up. He did, however, remember picking up the baby and staggering into the wood. It was all so confusing. He glanced down. There was blood on the baby's head. For a moment he was worried. Then he realized that the blood was his, and that the child was unhurt. Relieved he moved on. Why am I running, he thought, suddenly? Why am I hurting? His shoulder struck a tree trunk and he spun and almost fell. Regaining his balance he pushed on.

The Krayakin had come. One of them had stabbed him, then struck him on the temple. He had never felt such a blow in his life.

The ground was sloping upwards now. He struggled to the top of a rise and stood, breathing heavily. Then he began to cough. He could feel warm liquid in his throat, choking him. He spewed it out, then gasped for air. Sufia pulled back in his arms and stared at him, her blue eyes wide and fearful. 'Your mouth is bleeding,' she cried.

He couldn't remember being hit in the mouth. He coughed again. Blood dribbled to his chin. Dizziness swamped him. 'They're coming!' shouted the child. Bison swung round.

Two Krayakin in black armour were walking purposefully towards him, black swords in their hands. Holding firmly to the babe and the child Bison pushed on. He had no idea where he was going. All he knew was that he had to carry the children to safety.

But where was safety?

Emerging from the tree line he saw a towering cliff face, and a narrow ledge winding along the face. Blinking sweat from his eyes he struggled on.

'Where are we going?' asked Sufia. Bison did not answer. He felt weak and disoriented, and his breath was coming now in short, painful gasps. I've been wounded before, he told himself. I always heal. I'll heal again. Glancing back he saw the Krayakin reach the top of the rise some 70 yards behind him. Where is Nogusta, he wondered. And Kebra.

They'll be coming! Then I can rest for a while. Nogusta can stitch my wound. Blood was pooling in his boot, and his leggings were drenched. So much blood. He stumbled on. The ledge was narrow here, no more than 3 feet wide. He looked down over the edge. They were impossibly high. Below him Bison could see wispy clouds clinging to the side of the abyss, and through them he could just make out a tiny river flowing through the base of the canyon. 'We are above the clouds,' he told Sufia. 'Look!' But she clung to his shoulder, her head buried against his neck. 'Above the clouds,' he said again. He swayed and almost fell. The baby began to cry. Bison focused his mind on movement and continued along the ledge.

Another coughing spasm shook him, and this time there was a rush of blood, that exploded from his mouth in a crimson spray. Sufia was crying again. Bison stopped moving. The ledge ended here, in a blank, grey wall of rock. Gently he laid the baby on the ledge, then pulled Sufia's arms from around his neck.

'Old Bison needs a rest,' he said. 'You . . . look after the baby for me.'

He was on his knees, but couldn't remember falling. 'There's lots of blood,' wailed Sufia.

'Look . . . after the baby. There's a good girl.' Bison crawled to the edge and gazed down again. 'Never . . . been this high,' he told her.

'What about when you had wings?' she asked.

'Big . . . white . . . wings,' he said. He looked back along the ledge. The Krayakin must be close now, but he could not see them yet.

I don't want to die! The thought was a terrible one, and far too frightening to contemplate. I'm not going to die, he told himself. I'll be fine. A few stitches. The sun was shining, but it was cold here on this exposed face. The cold wind felt good. The wind had been cold back at Mellicane. It was winter then, a hard, harsh winter. The rivers had frozen solid and no-one had expected an army to march through the raging blizzards. But the Drenai had, crossing mountains and lakes of ice. The Ventrian army had been surprised at Mellicane. That's where I got my medal, he remembered. The medal he had sold for a night with a fat whore.

She was a good whore, though, he recalled.

He sat with his back to the cliff, a great wave of weariness covering him like a warm blanket. Sleep, that was what he needed. Healing sleep. When he woke up the wound would be mending. That priestess, she can heal me. A few days' rest and I'll be good as new. Where is Nogusta? Why has he left me alone here?

The baby wailed. Bison thought it best to pick him up, but he didn't seem to have the strength. Sufia screamed and pointed back along the ledge. The two Krayakin were in sight now, moving in single file along the narrow finger of rock.

Twisting round Bison scrabbled at the rock face, dragging himself to his feet. So this is how it ends, he thought. And this time there was no fear. He glanced at Sufia. The child was terrified. Bison forced a smile. 'Don't you worry . . . little one,' he said. 'No-one's going . . . to hurt you. You just . . . look after . . . the little prince until . . . Nogusta comes.'

'What are you going to do?' she asked him.

The Krayakin were closer now. The ledge had widened, and they were advancing together.

Bison pushed at the rock wall, and stood blocking their way.

'Did you know,' he told them, 'that I have wings? Big white wings? I fly . . . over . . . mountains.'

Suddenly he launched himself at them, spreading his arms wide. The Krayakin had nowhere to run. In desperation they stabbed at him, plunging their blades into his chest. With a last desperate lunge he hurled his weight forward, into the cold metal that clove through his heart. Dying, he clamped his huge arms to their armour and propelled them over the edge.

Sufia looked out, and saw them spiralling away, down and down, Bison with outstretched arms, falling into the white, wispy clouds.

Antikas Karios had arrived just in time to see them fall. He ran to Sufia and knelt beside her.

'He got his wings back,' she said, her eyes bright with wonder. 'Big, white wings.'

Little Sufia put her arms around Antikas Karios's neck. Instinctively his own arm curled around her. Then he looked down at the baby. This was the source of all their problems, this tiny package of flesh, soft bone and tissue. It was crying still, thin piping wails that echoed from the rocks. It would be so easy to choke off that sound. The baby's neck was so slender that Antikas could crush the life from it by merely pinching the flesh between his thumb and index finger.

The world would be safe from the demons. His hand reached down. As his finger touched the baby's cheek its head turned towards it, mouth open, seeking to suckle. 'Got to look after the baby,' Sufia whispered into his ear.

'What?'

'That's what Bison said before he flew away.'

He pondered what to do. If he killed the baby, then he would have to kill Sufia too. He could toss them both from the ledge and say he had arrived too late to help them. His thoughts turned to Bison. The grotesque old man had run for almost half a mile, with a wound that should have killed him instantly. Then he had carried two Krayakin to their deaths. He had shown enormous courage, and in that moment Antikas realized that, were he now to kill the child, it would sully the memory of Bison's deed. Gathering up the baby he walked back along the ledge, and down the slope to the camp-site. Kebra and the queen were still unconscious, and Conalin and Pharis were sitting by the fire, hand in hand. The girl looked up as Antikas walked into the camp. Her thin face broke into a wide smile. Surging to her feet she ran to him, lifting Sufia clear. The little girl immediately began to tell her of Bison's wings.

Ulmenetha was sitting beside Nogusta. Antikas walked over to them. Nogusta was looking twenty years older, a grey sheen covering the ebony of his features. His pale blue eyes were tired beyond description. The black sword still jutted from his shoulder.

'Can you remove the sword?' Ulmenetha asked Antikas. Laying the baby on the grass he took hold of the hilt. Nogusta gritted his teeth.

'Brace yourself,' said Antikas, setting his boot against Nogusta's chest. With one savage wrench he dragged the blade clear. Nogusta cried out, then sagged against Ulmenetha. Holding her hands over the entry and exit wounds she began to chant.

Antikas moved away from them to where Kebra lay. Kneeling beside him he felt for the man's pulse. It was firm and strong. Conalin appeared alongside him. 'He is just sleeping,' said the boy. 'Ulmenetha has already prayed over him.'

'Good,' said Antikas.

'Did you see Bison's wings?' asked Conalin.

'No.' He gazed up at the boy, angry now. 'There were no wings,' he snapped. 'Such stories are for children who cannot deal with the harsh realities of life. A brave man gave his life to save others. He fell thousands of feet and his dead body was smashed upon the rocks below.'

'Why did he do it?'

'Why indeed? Go away and leave me, boy.'

Conalin walked back to the fire, and the waiting Pharis. Antikas pushed himself to his feet and made his way to the water's edge, where he drank deeply.

The death of Bison had moved him in a way he had difficulty understanding. The man was an animal, ill bred and uncultured, uncouth and coarse. Yet when the Krayakin had attacked he had been the first to tackle them, and had, without doubt, saved the children. He had gone willingly to his death. All his life Antikas had been taught that nobility lay in the blood line. Nobles and peasants, thinking beings and near animals. Only the nobility were said to understand the finer points of honour and chivalry.

The manner of Bison's sacrifice was unsettling. Axiana was a Ventrian princess, her child the son of the man who had spurned Bison's services. Bison owed them nothing, but gave them everything.

It was more than unsettling. It was galling.

In Ventrian history heroes had always been noblemen, full of courage and virtue. They were never belching, groin-scratching simpletons. A thought struck him, and he smiled. Maybe they were. Conalin had asked him if Bison had grown wings. If they survived this quest the story would grow. Antikas would tell it. Sufia would tell it. And the story to be believed would be the child's. And why? Because it was more satisfying to believe that heroes never die, that somehow they live on, to return in another age. In a hundred years the real Bison would be remembered not at all. He would become golden haired and handsome, perhaps the bastard son of a Ventrian noble. Antikas glanced at the sleeping queen. Most likely he would also, in future legends, become Axiana's lover and the father of the babe he saved.

Antikas returned to the camp. Nogusta was sleeping now. Axiana was awake and feeding the child. Ulmenetha signalled for Antikas to join her. 'The wound is a bad one,' she said. 'I have done what I can, but he is very weak, and may still die.'

'I would lay large odds against that, lady. The man is a fighter.'

'And an old man devastated not just by a wound, but by grief. Bison was his friend, and he knew his friend was to die.'

Antikas nodded. 'I know this. What would you have me do?'

'You must lead us to Lem.'

'What is so vital about the ghost city? What is it we seek among the ruins?'

'Get us there and you will see,' said Ulmenetha. 'We can wait another hour, then I will wake the sleepers.'

As she turned her head he saw the angry, swollen bruise upon her temple, and remembered the knife hilt laying her low. 'That was a nasty blow,' he said. 'How are you feeling?'

She smiled wearily. 'I feel a little nauseous, but I will live, Antikas Karios. I have the maps here. Perhaps you would like to study them.' He took them from her and unrolled the first. Ulmenetha leaned in. 'The Ventrian army are moving from here,' she said, stabbing her finger at the map, 'and they have swept out in a sickle formation, expecting us to make for the sea. Within the next two days they will have secured all the roads leading to Lem.'

'There is no proper scale to this map,' he said. 'I cannot tell how far we are from the ruins.'

'Less than forty miles,' she told him. 'South and west.'

'I will think on a route,' he said. He glanced at Axiana, who was sitting just out of earshot. 'It would have been better for the world had Bison jumped with the babe,' he said, softly.

'Not so,' she told him. 'The Demon Lord has already begun the Great Spell. The child's death will complete it, with or without a sacrifice.'

Antikas felt suddenly chill. He looked away, and remembered his fingers reaching for the babe's throat.

'Well,' he said, at last, 'that, at least, adds a golden sheen to the old man's death.'

'Such a deed needs no sheen,' she told him.

'Perhaps not,' he agreed. He left her then and moved

to the fire. Little Sufia was sitting quietly with Conalin and Pharis. She scampered over to Antikas. 'Will he fly back to us?' she asked him. 'I keep looking in the sky.'

Antikas took a deep breath, and he looked at Conalin.

'He will fly back one day,' he told the child, 'when he is most needed.'

Chapter Eleven

Nogusta was only vaguely aware that he was riding a horse. Someone was sitting behind him, holding him in the saddle. He opened his eyes and saw that the company was moving slowly across a verdant valley. Up ahead Antikas Karios was riding Starfire. Nogusta felt a stab of irritation, but then remembered he had commanded the Ventrian to take his horse. Starfire was a spirited animal, and Nogusta was in no condition to ride him.

He glanced down at the hands supporting him. They were slender and feminine. Patting the hands he whispered, 'Thank you.'

'Do you need to stop and rest?' Ulmenetha asked him.

'No.' His vision swam and he leaned back into the woman.

Bison was gone, and the pain of loss struck him savagely. He swayed in the saddle and felt Ulmenetha's arms holding him firmly. Then he drifted into dreams of the past. The day passed in a haze. When they stopped to rest the horses Kebra helped him down. Nogusta did not know where he was, only that the sun was warm on his face, the grass cool against his back. It was blissful here, and he wanted to sleep for ever. From somewhere close came the cry of an infant. Then he heard a child singing a song. He seemed to remember the child had been killed by a wagon, but obviously this was not so. He was relieved – as if a burden had been lifted from him.

At some point he was fed a thick soup. He remembered the taste, but could not recall who had fed him, nor why he had not fed himself.

Then he saw his father. They were all sitting in the main room of the house, his brothers and sisters, his mother, and his old aunt. 'I shall show you some magick,' his father said, rising from the old horse hide chair he cherished. He had lifted the talisman from around his neck. The chain was long, the gold glinting in the lantern light. Father walked to the eldest of Nogusta's brothers and tried to loop the chain over his head. But the chain shrank, and would not pass over the boy's skull. Each of the brothers in turn marvelled at the magick. Then he came to Nogusta. The chain slid easily over his head, the talisman settling to his chest.

'What is the trick?' asked his eldest brother.

'There is no trick,' said father. 'The talisman has chosen. That is all.'

'That is not fair,' said the eldest. 'I am the heir. It should be mine.'

'I was not the heir,' father pointed out. 'Yet it chose me.'

'How does it choose?' asked the youngest brother.

'I do not know. But the man who made it was our ancestor. He was greater than any king.'

That night, alone in their room, his eldest brother had struck him in the face. 'It should have been mine,' he said. 'It was a trick because father loves you more.'

Nogusta could still feel the pain of the blow. Only now, for some strange reason that he could not fathom, the pain was emanating from his shoulder.

He was riding again, and he opened his eyes to see the stars shining in the night sky. A new moon hung like a sickle over the mountains, just like on his talisman. He almost expected to see a golden hand reach out to encircle it. High above him an owl glided by on white wings.

White wings . . .

'Poor Bison,' he said, aloud.

'He is at peace,' said a voice. The voice confused Nogusta. Somehow Ulmenetha had transformed into Kebra.

'How did you do that?' he mumbled. Then he slept again, and awoke beside a camp-fire. Kebra had become Ulmenetha again, and her hand was upon his wound. She was chanting softly.

A figure floated before his vision, blurred and indistinct, and Nogusta fell away into a deep dream.

He was sitting in the Long Meadow back at home, and he could hear his mother singing in the kitchen. A tall man was sitting beside him, a black man, but one he did not know.

'This was a peaceful time for you,' said the man.

'It was the best of times,' Nogusta told him.

'If you survive you must come back and rebuild. The descendants of your herds are back in the mountains. There are great stallions there, and the herds are strong.'

'The memories are too painful.'

'Yes they are painful, but there is peace here, if you seek it.'

He looked at the man. 'Who are you?'

'I am Emsharas. And you are the last of my human line.'

'You cast the Great Spell.'

'I began it. It is not complete yet.'

'Will the child die?'

'All of Man's children die, Nogusta. It is their weakness – and their strength. There is great power in death. Rest now, for you have one last test before you.'

Nogusta opened his eyes. The glorious light of a new dawn was edging over the mountains. He groaned as he sat up. Kebra grinned at him.

'Welcome back, my brother,' he said. There were tears in Kebra's eyes as he leaned forward, and, for the first time, embraced Nogusta.

Anharat's anger had cooled now, as he sat in his tent, listening to the reports from his scouts. The renegades had crossed the last bridge before Lem, and were now less than 12 miles from the ruins. A five-man scouting party had attacked them, but Antikas Karios had killed two, a third being shot from the saddle by a bowman. 'Bring in the survivors,' ordered Anharat.

Two burly scouts entered the tent, then threw themselves to the floor, touching their brows to the rug at Anharat's feet.

'Up!' he commanded. The men rose, their expressions fearful. 'Tell me what you saw.' Both men began speaking at once, then glanced at one another. 'You,' said Anharat, pointing to the man on the left. 'Speak.'

'They were coming down a long slope, my lord. Antikas Karios was leading them. He was followed by a white-haired man, then by the queen and her servant. There was a small child, and two youngsters. And a black man with a bandage around his chest. There was blood on it. Captain Badayen thought we could surprise them with a sudden charge. So that's what we did. He was the first to die. Antikas Karios wheeled his horse and charged us! The captain went down, then Malik. Then the bowman shot an arrow through the throat of Valis. So me and Cupta turned our horses and galloped off. We thought it best to report what we'd seen.'

Anharat looked deep into the man's dark eyes. They

369

both expected death. The Demon Lord wished he could oblige them. But morale among the humans was low. Most of them had friends and family back in the tortured city of Usa, and they did not understand why they were pursuing a small group across a wilderness. Added to this Anharat had noticed a great wariness among his officers when they spoke to him. At first it had confused him, for even while inhabiting the decaying body of Kalizkan, the Warmth Spell had maintained the popularity the sorcerer had enjoyed. The same spell had little effect on Malikada's men. This, he reasoned, at last, was because Malikada had never been popular. He was feared. This was not a wholly undesirable state of affairs, but with morale suffering Anharat would gain no added support from these humans by butchering two hapless scouts.

'You acted correctly,' he told the men. 'Captain Badayen should not have charged. He should have ridden ahead, as ordered and held the last bridge. You are blameless. Had the captain survived I would have hanged him. Go and get some food.'

The men stood blinking in disbelief. Then they bowed and swiftly backed from the tent. Anharat gazed at his officers, sensing their relief. What curious creatures these humans are, he thought.

'Leave me now,' he told them.

No-one moved. Not a man stirred. All stood statue still, not a flickering muscle, not the blink of an eyelid. As if from a great distance Anharat heard the gentle tinkling music of wind chimes. He spun around to see Emsharas standing by the tent entrance. His brother was wearing a sky-blue robe, and a gold circlet adorned his brow. It was no vision! Emsharas was here in the flesh.

A cold fury grew within Anharat, and he began to

summon his power. 'Not wise, brother,' said Emsharas. 'You need all your strength for the completion of the Spell.'

It was true. 'What do you want here?' demanded Anharat.

'Peace between us – and the salvation of our people,' said Emsharas.

'There will never be peace between you and I. You betrayed us all. I will hate you until the stars burn out and die, and the universe returns to the dark.'

'I have never hated you, Anharat. Not now, not ever. But I ask you – as I asked you once before – to consider your actions. The Illohir could never have won. We are few, they are many. Their curious minds grow with each passing generation. The secrets of magick will not be held from them for ever. Where then shall we be? What must we become, save dusty legends from their past? We opened the gateways, you and I. We brought the Illohir to this hostile world. We did not kill when we were Windborn, we did not lust after terror and death.'

Anharat gave a derisive laugh. 'And we knew no pleasures, save those of the intellect. We knew no joys, Emsharas.'

'I disagree. We saw the birthing of stars, we raced upon the cosmic storm winds. There was joy there. Can you not see that we are alien to this planet? It conspires against us. The waters burn our skin, the sunlight saps our strength. We cannot feed here, unless it be from the emotions of humans. We are parasites on this world. Nothing more.'

Emsharas stepped further into the tent, and looked closely at the frozen officers. 'Their dreams are different from ours. We will never live among them. And one day they will destroy us all.'

'They are weak and pitiful,' said Anharat, his hand

slowly moving towards the dagger at his belt. It would need no magick to plunge a dagger into his brother's heart. Then he too would be cast into Nowhere.

'I offer a new world for our people,' said Emsharas.

'Tell me the source of your power,' whispered Anharat, his fingers curling around the dagger hilt.

Emsharas swung to face him. 'Why have you not already guessed it?' he countered. 'All the clues are there, in the failure of your search spells, and the nature of the Great Spell itself.'

'You found a place to hide. That is all I know.'

'No, Anharat. I am not hiding.'

'You liar! I see you standing before me, drawing breath.'

'Indeed you can. Tonight I opened a gateway, Anharat, to bring me through to you. But where is *tonight*? It is four thousand years in the past and I am with the army of the Three Kings, and tomorrow you and I will fight above the battlefield. You will lose. Then I will prepare myself for the Great Spell. You can help me complete it. Our people can have a world of their own!'

'This is the world I want!' snarled Anharat, drawing the dagger. Leaping forward he slashed the blade at his brother. Emsharas swayed aside. His form shimmered.

And he was gone.

Bakilas sat quietly in the dark. The Illohir had no need of sleep. There was no necessity to regenerate tissue. All was held in place by magick fuelled by feeding. The Lord of the Krayakin needed no rest. He was waiting in this place only because his horse was weary.

Truth to tell he had not been surprised when his brothers had been defeated. This quest was flawed from the beginning. The priestess was right. It was no coincidence that a descendant of Emsharas should be guarding the baby. There was some grand strategy here, whose significance was lost on Bakilas.

What do I do now, he wondered? Where do I go?

He stood and walked to the brow of the hill and gazed down on the ruins of Lem. He could remember when this city had been like a jewel, shimmering in the night with a hundred thousand lights.

He gazed up at the stars, naming them in his mind, recalling the times when, formless, he had visited them. In that moment he wished he had never been offered the gift of flesh.

Anharat and Emsharas had brought it to the Illohir. The Twins, the gods of glory. Their power combined had created the link between wind and earth. They had been the first. Emsharas had taken human form, while Anharat had chosen wings. The Krayakin had followed.

Who could have guessed then that the gift was also a curse?

True the sunlight had caused great pain, and the water of the rivers had been deadly, but there were so many other pleasures to be enjoyed, and an eternity in which to enjoy them.

Until Emsharas betrayed them all.

Even now, after 4,000 years of contemplation, Bakilas could not begin to understand his reasons. Nor what had become of him. Where could an Illohir hide? Even now Bakilas could sense all his brothers in the void of Nowhere. Emsharas had shone like the largest star. It was impossible not to know his whereabouts. Bakilas could feel the powerful, pulsing presence of Anharat at his camp a few miles away. Equally, had Anharat been Windborn, he could have felt his spirit across the universe. Where then did Emsharas dwell?

One day the answer will become clear, he thought. One day, when the universe ends and the Illohir die with it.

Bakilas shivered. Death. To cease to be. It was a terrifying thought. Humans could not begin to comprehend the true fear of mortality. They lived always with the prospect of death. They understood its inevitability. A few short seasons and they were gone. Worse yet they tasted death throughout their few heartbeats of existence. Every passing year brought them fresh lines and wrinkles, and the slow erosion of their strength. Their skin sagged, their bones dried out, until toothless and senile they flopped into their graves. What could they know of immortal fear?

Not one of the Illohir had ever known death.

Bakilas recalled the Great Birthing in the Coming of Light, when the first chords of the Song of the Universe rang out across the dark. It was a time of discovery and harmony, a time of comradeship. It was life. Sentient and curious. Everything was born at that time, the stars and then the planets, the oceans of lava, and finally the great seas.

There had been joys then of a different kind; the increase of knowledge and awareness. But there had been no pain, no disappointments, no tragedies. Absolute serenity had been enjoyed – endured? – by all the Illohir. Only with the coming of the flesh did the contrasts begin. How could one know true joy until one had tasted true despair? Contrast was everything. Which was why the Illohir lusted after the life of *form*.

Bakilas moved back from the hilltop and drew his sword. Moving silently alongside the sleeping horse he beheaded it with one terrible sweep of his blade. As the beast fell Bakilas tore out its heart and held it up to the night sky, calling upon Anharat.

The heart burst into flame.

'I am glad that you called upon me, brother,' said the voice of Anharat. 'Emsharas has returned.'

'I do not sense him.'

'His powers are great. But he is here. He seeks to prevent our destiny.'

'But why?' asked Bakilas. 'You and he are the Twins. Since time began you were One in all things.'

'We are One no longer,' snapped Anharat. 'I will defeat him. I will hold his spirit in the palm of my hand and I will torment it until the end of time.'

Bakilas said nothing. He sensed a joy in Anharat that had been missing since the betrayal. He was *pleased* that Emsharas had returned! How curious! Bakilas had felt Anharat's pain, and his sense of loss. His hatred of Emsharas had become all consuming. Throughout the centuries he had never given up the hunt for his brother, sending search spell after search spell. His hatred was almost as strong as his love had been. A thought came to Bakilas then. Perhaps hatred and love were, in some ways, the same. Both echoed an intense need in Anharat. His existence without Emsharas had been hollow and empty. Even now the Demon Lord dreamed only of holding his brother's spirit in his hand. Hatred and love. Indistinguishable.

'You must go into Lem,' said Anharat. 'Hide there until the time to strike! When the babe dies, and my power swells, I will find Emsharas and there will be a reckoning.'

Nayim Pallines had always disliked Antikas Karios, though he had wisely kept this information to himself for several years. He had known Kara since childhood, and was one of the guests at her wedding. He had seen her radiant joy, and had envied the look of love she gave her husband as the vows were made, and the ceremonial cord had been looped about their wrists.

Two days later both were dead, the husband slain by the killer Antikas Karios, Kara dead by her own hand. Love, Nayim knew, was far too precious to be so casually destroyed. When the tragedies occurred his dislike of Antikas Karios turned to hatred.

And yet, as a colonel in the Royal Lancers he had been obliged to serve this man, to take his orders, and to bow before him. It had been hard.

But today – with the help of the Source, and the courage of the fifty men riding behind him – he would put an end to both the hatred and the object of it. His scouts had spotted them 3 miles from the ruins of Lem, and Nayim was less than half a mile behind them.

Soon they would see the pursuing riders. Nayim could picture it. The fleeing group would lash at their mounts in a last, desperate attempt to evade capture. But their tired horses would soon be overhauled by the powerful mounts of the lancers. Nayim half hoped that Antikas Karios would beg for his life. Yet even as the thought occurred he knew it would not be so. Antikas, for all his vileness, was a man of courage. He would attack them all.

Nayim was no more than a capable swordsman. He would have to be sure to hang back when the attack began. While not afraid to die he did not wish to miss the capture of Antikas Karios.

His sergeant, Olion, rode alongside him, his white cape fluttering in the breeze. There was a mud stain upon the cape. Olion was a superb horseman, and a fine soldier, but incapable of smartness, no matter what disciplinary measures were taken against him. The high, curved helm of bronze and the ceremonial cape had been designed to add grandeur to the armour of the Lancers. But for Olion, short, stocky, and round shouldered, his face endlessly marked by angry red spots, the end result was comic.

Nayim glanced at the man as he rode alongside. Yet another boil was showing on the nape of Olion's neck. 'The lads are worried, sir,' said the sergeant. 'I don't like the mood.'

'Are you telling me that fifty men are frightened of tackling one swordsman?'

'It's not about them, sir. In fact they'll be relieved to see a little action. No, it's not that, sir.'

'Spit it out, man. You'll not lose your head for it.'

'I could, sir, if you take my meaning?'

Nayim understood perfectly. His face hardened. 'I do indeed. Therefore it will be better to say nothing. Ride up to the top of the slope there and see if you can see them yet.'

'Yes, sir.' Olion galloped off towards the south-east. Nayim glanced back. His men were riding in columns of twos behind him, the butts of their lances resting on their stirrups. Signalling them to continue at their present pace he flicked his heels and rode after Olion.

At the top of the slope he hauled in his mount, and found himself gazing over the distant, ruined city of Lem. Said to be one of the greatest cities ever built it was now a place of ghosts and lost memories. The huge walls had been eroded by time, brought down by earthquakes, many of the stones removed to build houses at the far end of the valley. What remained of the north wall stood before the ghost city like a row of broken teeth.

Then he saw the riders, still around a half mile ahead. At this distance he could not make out individuals, but he could see that their horses were tiring, and they were still some way from the city. Once his men caught up they would ride them down within minutes.

'Be swift and say what you have to say,' he told Olion. 'For then we must do our duty.'

'This is all wrong, sir. The men know it. I know it. I mean, what happened back in the city? There are thousands dead, by all accounts. That's where we ought to be. And why bring the whole army into this wilderness. There's no-one to fight, sir. So why are we here?'

'We are here because we are ordered to be,' said Nayim, anxious to capture the runaways.

'And what about supplies, sir? According to the quarter-master we only have enough food to bring us to Lem. What are we supposed to do then? We've not even been put on half rations. Come the day after tomorrow there'll be no food at all for three thousand men. It's madness!'

'I'll tell you what madness is, Olion, it is a soldier in the army of Malikada who starts spouting mutinous words.' Nayim tried to make the threat sound convincing, but he could not. He shared the man's concern. 'Listen,' he said, in a more conciliatory tone. 'We will do our duty here, then return the prisoners to Malikada. We saw the tracks of elk a few miles back. Once we have the prisoners secured you can lead a unit after them. Then at least we'll eat well tonight.'

'Yes, sir,' said the man, dubiously.

Nayim cast a nervous glance back. The lancers were almost within earshot. 'I take it there is something else? Make it quick!'

'Why is the queen running away? Malikada is her cousin. They have always been close, so it's said. And why would a general like Antikas Karios be helping her?'

'I don't know. Perhaps we shall ask Antikas when we take him.'

As the troops drew reins behind him Nayim raised his arm. 'Follow me!' he shouted.

Picking up the pace he cantered his mount along the old road, swiftly closing the distance between himself and the fleeing riders. A red-headed youngster riding the last horse looked back, then kicked his mount into a run.

Now the chase was on. Nayim drew his sabre. He could see Antikas Karios now, riding a huge black gelding. The man swung his horse, and, for a moment, Nayim thought he would charge them. Instead he galloped back to the rear of his group, urging them on. Nayim gently drew back on his reins, allowing some of his men to overtake him.

The silver-haired bowman swung in the saddle, sending a shaft flashing towards him. Nayim swayed and ducked. He heard a man cry out behind him. Glancing back he saw the arrow jutting from a rider's shoulder.

Nayim was anxious to catch the runaways before they entered the ruins, for once there Antikas and the others could dismount and take cover. They would not last long, but it would cost him men. One of the reasons why Nayim was a popular commander was that he was careful with the lives of his soldiers. No reckless charges, no seeking after glory. He was a professional soldier who always thought out his strategies.

They were closing fast now. Up ahead Antikas Karios was now leading a second horse upon which sat a young woman in a blue dress. It was with some surprise that Nayim recognized the queen. He had always seen her in gowns of silk and satin, looking like a goddess from myth. Now she was merely a woman on a slow horse.

Only around 40 yards separated them now. Antikas

would have no time to seek cover, for they would catch him at the city walls!

Suddenly one of his men shouted a warning. Nayim soon saw why.

Armed men were pouring from the ruins of the city, forming a deep fighting line before the broken gates. They were Drenai soldiers, wearing full-faced helms and sporting long, red cloaks. Hundreds of them, moving smoothly into place with the easy discipline of veterans. Nayim could scarce believe his eyes.

The Drenai army had been destroyed. How then could this be?

Then he realized with shock that he was charging down towards them. Hauling on the reins he held up his arm. All around him his men slowed their mounts.

The fleeing group rode towards the fighting line, which parted smoothly before them, allowing them access to the city.

Ordering his men to wait Nayim rode slowly forward. 'Where is your commander?' he called out. Silence greeted his words. He scanned the line, calculating numbers. There were close to a thousand men in sight. It was inconceivable!

The line parted once more and a tall, thin old man walked out to stand before him.

Nayim felt a sudden chill touch him, as he gazed into the cold eyes of the White Wolf.

As soon as he rode past the old city wall Conalin jumped down from his horse and ran back, scrambling up a jutting stump of stone and squatting down to watch the soldiers. They looked terrifyingly impressive in their bronze breastplates, full-faced bronze helms and crimson cloaks. Their spears were held steady, and their shields presented a strong wall between Conalin and those who had sought to kill him. For the first time in his young life he felt utterly safe. What force on earth could penetrate such a wall of men. He wanted to leap up and dance, to shout his scorn at the waiting Ventrian riders. They looked so puny now. Conalin glanced up at the blue sky, and felt a cool breeze upon his face.

He was safe – and the world was beautiful.

Pharis scrambled up to sit beside him. He took her hand. 'Look at them!' he said. 'Are they not the most wonderful soldiers you ever saw?'

'Yes,' she agreed, 'but where did they come from? Why are they here?'

'Who cares? We get to live, Pharis. We get to have that house in Drenan.' Conalin fell silent, for the old general was talking to the Ventrian lancer. Conalin strained to hear their words, but they were speaking softly.

Nayim dismounted and approached Banelion, offering a respectful bow, which the old man acknowledged with a brief nod. 'We are instructed by the Lord Malikada to return the queen to her palace,' said Nayim. 'We have no quarrel with you, sir.'

'The queen and her son travel with me to Drenan,' said the White Wolf. 'There she will be safe.'

'Safe? You think I mean to do her harm?'

Banelion looked into the young man's eyes. 'What you do or do not do is entirely your own affair. Malikada – or the beast who inhabits Malikada – intends to kill the babe. This I know. This I shall prevent.'

Nayim was taken aback by the words, but, on reflection, was not surprised by them. If Malikada wished to seize the throne then he would certainly see that all rivals were put to the sword. 'Let us assume, sir, for the sake of argument, that you are correct in your assessment. By my judgement you have less than a thousand men here, and no cavalry. A half a day to the north is the Ventrian army. We are three times your number. And we were trained by you, sir. You cannot prevail.'

Banelion gave a mirthless smile that chilled the younger man. 'I have followed your recent career with interest, Nayim Pallines. You are an efficient, courageous and disciplined officer. Had I remained with the army I would have secured promotion for you. But you are wrong, young man. Armies fight best when they have something to fight for, something they believe in. In such instances numerical advantage is lessened considerably. Do you believe in what you are fighting for, Nayim? Do you believe that two armies should fight over whether a child is put to the knife?'

'I believe in doing my duty, sir.'

'Then go back to the Beast, and prepare to die for him. But do not be deceived, Nayim, you are not following Malikada. Malikada is dead. A Demon Lord has possessed his body.'

'With respect, sir, you do not expect me to believe that?'

The White Wolf shrugged. Nayim bowed once more and returned to his horse. 'The army will be here by sunset, sir. It is my hope that you will reconsider your position.' Swinging his horse he rode back to his men, then led them north.

The White Wolf watched them go, then gave the order to stand down. The troops broke formation and laid down their spears and shields, removing their helms. On the broken wall Conalin watched them, a sick sense of dread flowing through him.

Old men! They were all old men, grey haired or bald.

Where moments before had been an invincible force, he now saw them shuffling around on what he perceived to be arthritic limbs, slowly lowering themselves to the ground. Conalin felt betrayed by them. Pharis saw his anger and reached out to him.

'What is it, Con?'

He did not reply, could not reply. Emotions surged within him. He jumped down from the wall and walked to his horse. Taking it by the bridle he led it further into the ruins. There was only one building mostly intact, a huge structure built from white marble, and it was here that the other horses had been tethered. A flight of cracked steps led to a huge, arched doorway. Conalin stepped inside. There was an enormous chamber within, with a high domed roof, part of which had collapsed. Fallen stones littered the remains of the mosaic which had once decorated the entire floor. There was no furniture here, but against the far wall were several broken benches. Light was streaming into the building through high, arched windows. Fragments of coloured glass still clung to some of the frames.

Conalin saw his companions at the far end of the chamber, sitting upon a raised octagonal dais. Kebra saw him and smiled. Conalin strode to where the bowman sat. 'They are all old men,' he said, bitterly.

'They were our comrades,' said Kebra. 'Most of them are younger than Bison.'

'And Bison's dead,' snapped Conalin. Instantly he regretted it, for he saw the pain in Kebra's eyes. 'I'm sorry,' he said, swiftly. 'I didn't mean it like that. It's just . . . they looked so strong when we first saw them.'

'They *are* strong,' said Kebra. 'And they have the White Wolf to lead them. He has never lost a battle.'

'We should ride on,' said the boy. 'Leave the old men to fight.'

Kebra shook his head. 'This will be the final battle, Con. Here, in this ruined place. I will not run any further.'

Conalin sat beside the bowman, his shoulders bowed. 'I wish I had never come with you,' he said.

'I am glad that you did. You have taught me a great deal.'

'I have? What could I teach you?'

Kebra gave a sad smile. 'I have always wondered what it would be like to have a son, a boy I could be proud of; someone I could watch grow into manhood. You have shown me what it could have been like. And you are quite right, there is no reason for you to stay here. There is nothing you can do. Why not take Pharis and Sufia, and some supplies and head off into the hills. If you head west you will eventually reach the sea. I will give you money. I do not have much, but it will help.'

The thought of leaving touched Conalin like the cool breeze that follows a storm, blowing away his anger and his fear. He and Pharis would be safe. And yet, in that moment, it wasn't enough. 'Why can you not come with us? One man won't make a difference.'

'These are my friends,' said Kebra. 'A true man does not desert his friends in time of need.'

'You think I am not a man?' asked Conalin.

'No, no! I am sorry for the way that sounded. You will be a fine man. But you are young yet, and war is not for . . .' He was going to say children, but as he looked into Conalin's young face he saw the man there, waiting to be born. 'I do not want to see you hurt, Con,' he said, lamely.

'Nor I you. I think I will stay.'

Kebra cleared his throat and held out his hand.

Conalin looked embarrassed, but he gripped it firmly. 'I am proud of you,' said Kebra.

They sat in pleasant silence for a while and Conalin gazed around the enormous building. 'What was this place?' he asked.

'I don't know,' admitted Kebra. 'But it has the feel of a temple, don't you think?'

'I have never been in one,' said Conalin. Sufia was sitting on the floor close by, rubbing at the stones with the ragged sleeve of her dress.

'There's pictures on the floor,' she said, happily.

Ulmenetha moved to her side, kneeling down. 'They are called mosaics,' she told the child. 'They are created with lots of coloured stones.'

'Come look!' Sufia called out to Conalin. He did so. There was no way of telling what the original mosaic had depicted, for many of the coloured stones had been shattered by falling masonry from the ceiling, the rest covered by the dust of centuries. There was a tiny patch of blue, and a line of red. It could have been a flower, or a section of sky.

'It's very pretty,' he told her.

'I shall clean it all up,' she said, with the confidence of the very young, and began to scrub at a tiny section.

'It will take you weeks,' he said, staring around the vast temple.

'Weeks,' she repeated. 'That's all right.' She rubbed at the stones for a few more seconds then sat back. 'I'm hungry now.'

Conalin picked her up, and kissed her cheek. 'Then let us find you some food,' he said. Perching her on his shoulders he walked back out into the sunlight. Pharis was sitting on the steps. Off to the left was a line of seven wagons. Cookfires had been lit close by, and the three of them moved off in search of a meal.

As they approached the cookfires an elderly soldier called out to them. The man had a wicked scar upon his face, and a black patch over what had once been his right eye. Beside him was a trestle table, stacked with pewter plates. 'You look in need of something hot and savoury,' he said. Moving to a huge, black cooking pot he ladled thick stew into three deep plates and handed them to the youngsters. 'Take some spoons,' he said, 'but bring them back, with the plates, when you're finished. Then I've some honey cakes for you.'

Conalin thanked the man. The soup was thick and nourishing, though with too much salt for the boy's liking. But he was famished, and consumed it with relish. The old soldier did not wait for them to return the utensils, but came over with a plate of honey cakes. Sufia grabbed two, then looked anxiously up at Conalin, waiting for a rebuke. When none came she happily devoured them.

'Why did you come here?' Conalin asked the soldier.

'White Wolf brought us,' said the man.

'Yes, but why?'

'He didn't say. Just offered us twenty gold pieces a man. Said there might be a battle.'

'There will be,' said Conalin.

'Good. Wouldn't want to come all this way for nothing,' said the soldier. Collecting the plates and spoons he moved away. Moments later other soldiers began to file past the cookfires, and soon the area was crowded. Everyone seemed at ease, and many of the soldiers took time to speak with the youngsters. Conalin was confused.

'They seem to be looking forward to fighting,' he said to Pharis. 'I don't understand it.'

'It is what they do,' replied the girl. 'It is what they are. We should take some food back to the queen.'

'Can I carry it?' asked Sufia.

'Of course you can, little one.'

'I won't spill any,' she promised. 'Not even a drop.'

Axiana watched as four veteran soldiers erected Banelion's tent at the far end of the temple. Simple furniture was carried in, a hinged bed, several canvas-backed chairs and a folding table. Then they swept the floor inside and laid simple rugs upon it. Not once did the men look at her. It was as if she was invisible. While they were working the youngsters returned. The blonde child, Sufia, brought her a bowl of soup. She thanked her with a smile, and turned away from the soldiers while she ate.

Some distance away Antikas Karios and Kebra were sitting beside the sleeping figure of Nogusta. The black man's wounds were healing, but his continuing weakness was a source of concern.

As Axiana finished her meal the tall, slim, armoured figure of Banelion entered the temple, followed by two soldiers carrying a wooden chest. The White Wolf approached the queen and bowed low. 'I am pleased to see you safe, your highness,' he said. 'My tent is yours, and I took the liberty of bringing some spare clothes for you.' Gesturing the men forward he had the chest placed on the dais before her, and opened. The first item she saw was a dress of sky blue satin. 'I do not have an eye for fashion, your highness,' said Banelion, 'but I borrowed these from a noble lady in Marain. It is a small town, and there was little to choose from.'

'It was kind of you, sir, and I thank you.' Ulmenetha appeared alongside her, taking the sleeping baby from the queen's arms. Axiana reached out and stroked the dress. It was wonderfully soft. Then she noticed – against the clean pure satin – how dirty her hands were. For the first time in days she felt embarrassment.

'There is an antechamber just beyond where the tent is placed,' said Banelion. 'There is a spring there. Some of my men have prepared a fire, and warmed some water. When you are ready you and your maidservant can refresh yourselves. I brought a small amount of scented oil with me to perfume the water.'

Before Axiana could reply another soldier entered, carrying a rough made crib, and a small, woven mattress. Setting it beside the queen he placed the mattress within it. 'Best I could do in the time, my lady,' he said, with a bow. Ulmenetha placed the babe within it. The child settled contentedly on the mattress, his sleep undisturbed.

The unexpected kindness left Axiana close to tears. She smiled at the soldier. 'You are most kind.' The man blushed and backed away.

The White Wolf gazed down at the babe, a far-away look in his eye. Then he straightened. 'There are some clothes for an infant at the bottom of the chest,' he said.

'You seem to have thought of everything,' said Axiana. 'I am most grateful. But tell me, how is it that you are here in our hour of need? We are a long way from the sea.'

He glanced at Ulmenetha. 'First Kalizkan appeared to me in a dream, then this lady came. She told me of your peril, and the threat to your son. She asked me to bring my men to this city. I did so willingly. And, if it is humanly possible I shall take you on to Drenan.'

Axiana sat quietly for a moment, gathering her thoughts. For the last few days she had been like a straw in the wind, swept along without the benefit of choice. Her life as a queen had meant less than nothing in the wilderness, and she had given birth to her child while kneeling in the mud like a peasant. But, here and now, was the moment of decision. Was she still a queen? Would her son live to find his destiny. She looked into the pale eyes of the White Wolf and saw the strength there, the iron will that had carried Skanda to a score of victories. 'And if I do not wish to go to Drenan?' she said, at last.

'Drenan would be safest,' he said.

'You swore an oath to Skanda. Do you accept his son as his rightful heir?'

'I do, lady.'

'Then I ask you again, as the mother to the king, what if I do not wish to go to Drenan?'

She knew this was difficult for him. Continued war between the two nations was more than likely. If Axiana remained in Ventria the Drenai would almost certainly declare independence. If she went to Drenan the Ventrians would find another emperor. At least with her and the child in Drenan the Drenai would have legitimate cause to reinvade Ventria. She held to his iron gaze without flinching. He smiled. 'If not Drenan,' he said, 'then I will escort you to wherever you wish to travel. You are not my hostage, your highness, nor my prisoner. I am your servant, and will do whatever you bid.'

Axiana rose. 'I will think on what you have said, general. But first I would like to bathe and lay aside these garments of travel.' He bowed and one of the soldiers stepped forward to lead the queen and Ulmenetha towards the antechamber.

The White Wolf strode to where Nogusta lay. Antikas Karios and Kebra rose. Banelion gave Antikas a cold look, then knelt beside the wounded warrior. Nogusta opened his eyes as Banelion took his hand. 'Am I always to rescue you, my boy?' he said, fondly.

'It would seem so. It is good to see you, general.' Nogusta's smile faded. 'Bison didn't make it.'

'I know. The priestess showed me his death in a dream. It was valiant, and no less than I would have expected from him. He was an obdurate man, and I liked him not at all. But he had heart. I admired that.'

Nogusta relaxed and closed his eyes. 'It is not over, general. There are three thousand Ventrians riding with the Demon Lord. They think he is Malikada.'

'I wish he was,' said Banelion, sourly. 'I'd have dearly loved to slit his treacherous throat.'

'A feeling I am sure he would have reciprocated,' said Antikas Karios. The White Wolf ignored him.

'I am not troubled by the numbers of the enemy,' he told Nogusta. 'I am more concerned that they are being duped. Ulmenetha tells me that if the Demon Lord is successful the soldiers riding with him will – like Malikada – be possessed and destroyed. It is bad enough having to kill men in a good cause. But those Ventrians are going to die for the wrong reasons.'

'Good of you to concern yourself,' said Antikas, his words edged with sarcasm.

Once again Banelion ignored him. 'Rest now,' he told Nogusta. 'Regain your strength. I will do all that needs to be done.' Then he rose and his pale eyes rested, for a moment, on Antikas. 'I watched you fight alongside Dagorian on the bridge,' he said. 'I loved that boy, and it was good of you to say that prayer for him. I am not a religious man, but I would like to think that a light did appear for him, and lead him to your palace.' Without waiting for a response he strode away, calling his soldiers after him.

'He hates me, yet he praises me,' whispered Antikas. 'Truly he is a strange man.'

'Maybe he does, maybe he doesn't,' said Kebra. 'One rarely knows what the White Wolf is thinking. That's what makes him the best. There's never been a general like him.'

'You think he genuinely cares about what happens to the Ventrian troops?'

'Oh yes,' Kebra told him. 'He does not revel in slaughter. There is no battle madness in him.'

Antikas looked down. Nogusta was sleeping again. He knelt beside the black man and looked closely at his face. A thin sheen of sweat lay upon the skin, and snow white bristles were showing on his shaven head. 'It is easy to forget how old he is,' said Antikas, with a sigh. He looked up and smiled at Kebra. 'I watched him fight Cerez, and I marvelled at his skill. I thought him to be around forty years of age. Had I known he was this old I would have bent my knee to him.'

Glancing down once more he saw the talisman on Nogusta's chest begin to glow, the silver moon in the golden hand, shining like a tiny lantern.

'What does that mean?' asked Antikas.

'Evil is near,' said Kebra, lifting his hand and making the sign of the Protective Horn.

The White Wolf stood outside the ruins and once more cast his eyes over the landscape. There was a line of hills to the left and right, thinly covered by trees and brush, but the ground was flat and uncluttered between the hills. The Ventrian army was mainly cavalry, and he pictured all possible lines of attack.

He glanced back at the ruins. They could, of course, decline a pitched battle here, and move around the ruins, coming at him from all sides, but he thought this unlikely. Cavalry could not operate effectively in the ruins themselves, and by spreading themselves thin they would hand the advantage to the Drenai foot soldiers. No, the best chance of victory for the enemy lay in a direct frontal assault, seeking to sunder the line and scatter the defenders.

Banelion summoned his officers to him, and began to give out orders. They listened without comment, then moved back to their men.

The sun was sinking towards the mountain peaks, and there was perhaps an hour before dusk.

Ulmenetha walked out to stand alongside the old man. 'How is Nogusta?' he asked.

'A little better, I think.'

'Good. It is bad enough that Dagorian had to die. I dearly want Nogusta to survive.'

'Did you mean what you said to the queen?' she asked him, her frank blue eyes meeting his iron gaze.

'I always mean what I say,' he told her. 'I think she would be safer in Drenan, but I am her servant, and it is not for me to gainsay her wishes.'

'But you do foresee problems if she decides to remain in Ventria?'

'Of course. The Drenai nobles will either elect a new king, or declare for a new republic. As for the Ventrians – will they accept Skanda's heir, without an army to back his claim? I doubt it.' He raised his arm and gestured to the surrounding land. 'But then the mountains will still be here, and the rivers will run to the sea. It does not matter to Nature who rules or who dies. However, these are problems for another day.'

'Indeed they are,' she agreed. 'I have not thanked you

for coming to our aid. I do so now. My gratitude is more than my words can convey.'

'You needn't thank me, lady. All my life has been occupied by thoughts of duty and responsibility. I am too old to change now.'

'Even so you have pledged most of your fortune to the men who now follow you. Not many would have done that.'

'I think you would be surprised at *how* many would do exactly that. It has become fashionable to believe that all actions have a cynical base. That's what comes of believing the lies of politicians. I have lived long, Ulmenetha, and I have seen much. There is among many people a desire to help others. Perhaps it is this which binds us all together. Dagorian and Bison gave their lives to protect the mother and child. They did it willingly, with no thought of profit.'

'You say that, and yet your men have followed you here for the promise of gold. Is this not at odds with your philosophy?'

'Not at all. I offered them the gold because a soldier is worth his pay. But had I been penniless and asked them to follow me, most would have. Now let us speak of more pressing matters. I have seen your magick, but not your power. Is there any way in which you might help us tonight?'

'I cannot kill,' she explained. 'Land magick is of a healing nature. If I drew fire from the land and used it against the Ventrians the power would vanish from me instantly.'

'I was not thinking about using it against a human foe,' he said.

'There is nothing I can do to hurt Anharat. He is too powerful.'

Banelion fell silent, staring out once more over the battleground. 'There is no doubt that we can withstand their charges,' he said. 'They will impale themselves on our spears, seeking to break through. They will not succeed. But I would like to avoid unnecessary casualties.'

'I do not see how that can be achieved,' she admitted.

'I think I do,' he told her, 'but I do not know whether your power can achieve it.'

Nogusta awoke just before dusk. His mouth was dry and his left shoulder throbbed with pain. He winced as he sat up. The interior of the temple was gloomy now, save for two lanterns which burned in a tent by the far wall. Nogusta pushed himself to his feet, and, for a moment, felt light headed and dizzy. Twenty feet away Conalin was sitting on some rubble, drinking water from a pottery cup. Nogusta called him over.

The black man sat down as the boy moved alongside. 'I want you to take Bison's sword,' he said.

'Why?'

'If the enemy breaks through then we will be the last line of defence.'

Conalin gazed up at the black warrior, noting his weakness. 'I'll get you some water,' he said. The boy ran off to the antechamber and returned with a full cup of cool, clear water. Nogusta drank gratefully. Then he handed Conalin the scabbarded short sword. The boy flipped the belt around his waist, but it was too big. Using his dagger Nogusta made a new hole and shortened the sword belt. Conalin buckled it into place.

'Draw it,' said Nogusta. The boy did so.

'It is heavier than I thought,' said Conalin.

'Remember it is a stabbing blade, not a cleaver. When

your enemy is close thrust towards the heart. Let me see you practise.' Conalin made several clumsy lunges. 'That's good,' said Nogusta. 'We'll make a fine swordsman of you, given time. But thrust off your lead foot. That will put your body weight behind the movement.'

Conalin grinned, and tried again. This time the thrust was smooth and swift. He looked at Nogusta. 'Your talisman is glowing,' he said.

'I know.'

Pharis and Sufia ran in to the doorway of the temple. 'They're here! So many!' shouted Pharis. They ran back outside.

Conalin went to join them, but Nogusta called him back. 'I want you to wait with me,' he said, softly.

'I just wanted to see them.'

'It is important that you stay.' Nogusta turned away from the boy and climbed to the octagonal dais, then sat back upon the stone altar placed there. 'This is one of the oldest buildings anywhere in the world. Most of the city was built after it. Like the palace back in Usa it was said to have been erected in a single night by a giant. I don't believe it, of course, but it is a pretty tale when heard in full.' He took a deep breath. 'This wound is bothersome,' he said.

'Why do you not want to see the battle?' asked Conalin, stepping up to the dais. 'Antikas, Kebra and Ulmenetha are all there. Why should we not go?'

'I have seen battles, Conalin. I had hoped never to see another. Kebra tells me you want to work with horses. Is that right?'

'Yes, I do.'

'It is my plan to return to the northern mountains of Drenan and find the descendants of the herds my father raised. I will rebuild our house. It was set in a beautiful location. My wife loved it there, especially in spring, when the fruit trees were in blossom.'

'Did she die?'

'Yes, she died. All my family died. I am the last of my line.' He could see that the boy was anxious to leave, and decided to distract him. 'Would you like to see some magick?' he asked.

'Yes.'

Carefully Nogusta lifted the talisman from around his neck and looped it over the boy's head. It settled neatly into place around his neck. 'Where is the magick?' said the boy.

Nogusta was surprised, but did not show it. Pharis and the child had returned looking for Conalin. He called them over. 'Try to place it around Sufia's neck,' he said. Conalin lifted the talisman clear, but when he tried to put it on the child he found that the golden chain was too short by several inches.

'I don't understand,' he said.

'Put it back on me,' said Nogusta. The boy stepped forward, and found, to his amazement, that it was still too short. 'It is yours now,' said the warrior. 'It has chosen you.' Softly he spoke the words his father had used. 'A man greater than kings wore this charm and while you wear it make sure that your deeds are always noble.'

'How do I do that?' asked Conalin.

'A good question. Follow your heart. Listen to what it tells you. Do not steal or lie, do not speak or act with malice or hatred.'

'I will try,' promised the boy.

'And you will succeed, for you are chosen. This talisman has been in my family for many generations. Always it chooses its owner. One day, when your sons are near grown you will play the magick game, and you will see it choose again.'

'Why didn't you keep it?' asked Conalin. 'You are still young enough to sire sons. You could take a wife.'

'It is done,' said Nogusta. 'And I am pleased. You are a fine lad, brave and intelligent. If you wish to come back to Drenan with me we will build the house together. Then we can hunt the horses.'

'Will Kebra come too?'

'I hope that he will.'

From outside came the sound of war horns blaring. Axiana emerged from her tent, wearing a shimmering dress of blue satin. Her dark hair was drawn up, and a string of pearls had been braided there. Pharis gasped to see her. The queen approached Nogusta. She was holding the sleeping babe close to her chest.

'If I am to die,' she said, 'I shall die *looking* like a queen.'

Conalin felt heat upon his chest. The talisman was glowing with a bright light now. A sudden vision came to him. A man in black armour moving through the ruins.

'What did you see?' asked Nogusta.

'The last of the Krayakin is coming,' said Conalin.

'He will soon be here,' said the warrior.

'You knew?'

'It was the last of my visions. You now have the gift. Use it wisely.'

'You cannot beat him. You are wounded and weak.'

'A great evil is coming,' said Nogusta. 'You will need all your courage. Never lose heart. You hear me, boy? Never lose heart!'

*   *   *

The Ventrian cavalry appeared on the hills on either side, lancers in their white cloaks and curved bronze helms, light cavalry with wicker shields and wooden spears, mounted archers in garish red shirts, and heavily armoured swordsmen in black cloaks and breastplates of burnished bronze.

The Drenai soldiers waited. Not a man moved. They stood silently their spears pointing towards the sky, their long, rectangular shields held to their sides.

The White Wolf glanced to left and right, and felt a surge of pride in the fighting men who stood ready. The sun was dipping low now, the sky golden, the mountains crowned with fire. At the centre of the Ventrians came Anharat-Malikada, riding a white stallion. He raised his arm, ready to order the attack.

'Prepare!' bellowed the White Wolf. A thousand shields swept up, and a thousand spears dropped down to face the enemy. The movement was perfectly co-ordinated.

The Ventrians rode slowly down from the hills, creating a fighting wedge.

Anharat galloped his horse to the front of the line, then drew rein.

From the highest point of the ruined wall Ulmenetha watched him. Her concentration grew as she summoned the power of the land, feeling it swell inside her. Her body began to shake, and she felt her heart beating faster and faster. Still the power flowed into her. Pain, terrible pain burst in her head and she cried out. But even through the pain she continued to draw on the power of the earth. Tears flowed, and her vision misted. Raising her arms she released the fire of *halignat*.

A huge ball of white flame flew from her hands screeching above the Drenai defenders, and passing through the Ventrian riders. Not one of them was harmed, though their horses reared in panic. The blazing *halignat* swept on, curling around Anharat, swelling into a white globe that hid him from his army. Slowly the *halignat* faded away. Anharat's horse was unharmed, and the Demon Lord laughed aloud.

'I am safe,' he told the officers around him. 'Attack now, and kill them all!'

But no-one moved. Anharat looked at the closest man. His eyes were wide, and he was staring in horror. 'What is it, man?' he said. He looked at the others. They were all staring at him. Several made the sign of the Protective Horn.

Then he saw the White Wolf walking towards him. Antikas Karios was beside him, and the silver-haired bowman, Kebra. 'There is the enemy!' he shouted, lifting his arm to point at the three warriors. Only then did he see what had terrified his men. The flesh of his hand was grey and rotting. The *halignat* had burned away the spell, and the body of Malikada was decaying fast.

'He is not Malikada,' he heard Antikas shout. 'He is a demon. Look at him!'

All around Anharat riders were pulling away.

The sun fell behind the mountains, and the moon shone in the darkening sky.

Anharat suddenly laughed, and spread his dead arms wide. The body of Malikada burst open, the clothes ripping and falling away. The head fell back, then split from the brow to the chin, and black smoke billowed up into the night sky. Slowly it solidified, forming two wide black wings around a powerful body. The wings began to beat, and the grotesque beast flew above the waiting armies.

Kebra reacted first, notching an arrow to his bow, and

sending a shaft flashing into the sky. It pierced Anharat's side, but did not stop his flight.

He flew on over the ruined walls towards the ancient temple.

Antikas Karios ran to the nearest horseman and dragged him to the ground. Then he vaulted into the saddle and kicked the horse into a run. He thundered through the Drenai line and into the ghost city. The winged beast hovered above the temple.

His taloned hand gestured towards the ground. Red fire leapt up, flames 20 feet high encircling the building. Antikas Karios tried to ride through them, but the horse reared and turned away. Antikas leapt to the ground and tried to run through the flames. His shirt caught fire and he fell back, hurling himself to the ground and rolling through the dirt. Two soldiers ran to him, covering him with their cloaks and beating out the flames.

Antikas glanced up and saw the winged demon land upon a high window and disappear into the temple.

Nogusta stood on the dais and gazed around the temple. Some 30 feet to his left was the queen's tent, and beyond that the entrance to the antechamber. Two hundred feet ahead of him were the main doors. He glanced up at the high, arched window above the doors. From here would come the winged terror.

The queen emerged from her tent. Nogusta smiled at her. Carrying the babe she walked to the dais. There was in her movement now a renewed pride and strength, and her bearing was once more regal. Nogusta bowed.

'I thank you for your service to me,' she said. 'And I apologize for any apparent lack of gratitude upon the journey.'

'Stay close to the dais, your highness,' he told her. 'The

last hour is upon us.' Pharis and Sufia were sitting close by. Nogusta ordered them to move to the far wall.

'Where do you want me?' asked Conalin.

'Stand before the queen. The beast will come from that high window.'

Conalin looked up fearfully, but then strode to the dais and took up his position.

Nogusta drew the Storm Sword and stepped from the dais. At that moment a figure in black armour moved from the shadows behind the queen's tent. He too held a sword.

'We meet at last,' said Bakilas, removing his helm. 'I commend your bravery.'

Nogusta swayed, and reached out to steady himself. He took a deep breath, and his vision swam.

'You are sick, human,' said Bakilas. 'Stand aside. I have no wish to kill you.'

Nogusta's vision cleared. He wiped the sweat from his eyes. 'Then leave,' he said.

'I cannot do that. My Lord Anharat requires a sacrifice.'

'And I am here to prevent it,' said Nogusta. 'So, come forward and die.'

Beaten back by the pillars of flame surrounding the building Antikas Karios stood with the White Wolf and his men. Ulmenetha ran to stand alongside them. 'Is there nothing your magick can do?' hissed Antikas.

'Nothing,' she said, her voice echoing her despair. Antikas swore, then ran for the horses. Starfire was still saddled and the warrior heeled him back towards the temple. The White Wolf stepped into his path and grabbed the bridle.

'No horse will run into those flames – and even if it

did, both horse and rider would be burned to a cinder.'

'Get out of my way!'

'Wait!' shouted Ulmenetha. 'Fetch water. There may yet be something we can do.'

Several soldiers ran and collected buckets of water. Under Ulmenetha's direction they doused the gelding. Antikas pulled off his cloak, and this too was drenched. The priestess reached up and took hold of Antikas's hand. 'Listen to me. I shall lower the temperature around you, but I will not be able to hold the spell for long. You must ride through at full gallop. Even then . . .' her words tailed away.

'Do what you can,' he said, drawing his sword.

'The horse will swerve and throw you into the flames!' said Banelion.

Antikas grinned. 'Nogusta told me he would ride through the fires of Hell. Now we will see.' Tugging on the reins he rode the giant gelding back 50 yards, then swung again to face the flames. Swirling his dripping cloak around his shoulders he waited for Ulmenetha's signal.

She gestured towards him, and he felt a terrible chill sweep over him. With a loud battle cry he kicked Starfire into a run. The gelding powered forward, his steel shod hooves striking sparks from the stone.

Soldiers scattered ahead of him. Antikas continued to shout his battle cries as Starfire reached full gallop. As they came closer to the pillars of fire he felt the horse begin to slow. 'On Great Heart!' he shouted. 'On!'

The gelding responded to his call.

And the flames engulfed them.

Bakilas was about to attack when suddenly flames burst around the temple, and a fierce glow shone through the windows bathing the temple in crimson light. Then came the beating of giant wings and Nogusta saw the monstrous form of Anharat glide down from an upper window. The wings beat furiously as his huge form descended, and a great wind blew across the temple sending up a dust storm, and exposing the mosaic at the centre of the floor. It was a surreal sight, for the exposed mosaic depicted a winged creature, with long talons, and blood-red eyes – the mirror image of the creature now hovering above it.

Conalin stood on the dais, the queen and her babe behind him. The boy wanted to run, but in that moment remembered the bravery of Dagorian and the courage of Bison. He drew his sword and stood his ground, tiny against the monstrous creature before him. The beast's talons scrabbled on the mosaic floor and his wings stretched out a full 20 feet in both directions. He gazed at Conalin through blood-red eyes. 'It is fitting that I find you all in my own temple,' he said. He looked beyond the boy, his gaze fixing on Axiana. 'Your work is done, my queen,' he said. 'You have delivered salvation for my people.'

Nogusta was about to attack the beast, but felt a cold blade against his throat. Bakilas spoke. 'You have done all that you can, human. And I respect you for it. Lay down your sword.' Nogusta's blade flashed up, knocking away the Krayakin's sword. He lunged at the black-armoured warrior, but Bakilas sidestepped and parried the Storm Sword, sending a riposte that slammed into Nogusta's ribs. As the blade plunged home, and terrible pain tore through him, Nogusta reached out and grabbed Bakilas's sword arm. Then, with the last of his strength he rammed his own blade into Bakilas's belly. The Krayakin cried out, then fell back, pulling Nogusta with him. They both fell to the ground. Nogusta struggled to rise, but his legs failed him, and he slumped down. Bakilas reared over him, dragging his sword clear of Nogusta's body. Then he rose unsteadily and advanced towards the dais.

Anharat moved towards Conalin, who stood on the dais, holding Bison's sword before him.

'You have only moments to live, child,' said Anharat. 'I shall tear out your heart.'

He started to move, when suddenly there came the sound of distant chimes. Dust motes hung in the air, and the boy stood unblinking before him.

Time stood still and the shining figure of Emsharas appeared on the dais, next to the statue-still queen and the frozen, armoured figure of Bakilas.

'You are in time to see my victory, brother,' said Anharat.

'Indeed I am, brother. And tell me what you will achieve?'

'I will undo your spell, and the Illohir will walk upon the earth.'

'And they will be consigned to the void, one by one. It may take centuries, but in the end you will all be returned to the place that is Nowhere,' said Emsharas.

'And where will you be?' roared Anharat. 'What place of pleasure have you found that you have not shared with your people?'

'You still do not see, Anharat,' said Emsharas, sadly. 'Do you truly not know what became of me? Think, my brother. What could prevent you finding me? We are twin souls. Since the dawn of time we have been together. Where could I go that you could not feel my soul?'

'I have no time for riddles,' said Anharat. 'Tell me, and then be gone!'

'Death,' said Emsharas. 'When I cast the Great Spell in that tomorrow that is already four thousand years past, I shall power it with my life force. I shall die. Indeed, in this time I am already dead. That is why you could not find me. Why you will never find me. From tomorrow I will no longer exist!'

'Dead?' echoed Anharat. 'That is impossible. We cannot die!'

'But we can,' said Emsharas. 'We can surrender our souls to the universe. And when we do so the power we release is colossal. It was that power which dragged the Illohir from the surface of this planet and held them in the limbo that is Nowhere. But it was only the first step, Anharat. Not even my death could propel our people to the world I found, a world where we can take form, and eat and drink, and know the joy of true life.'

'No,' said Anharat, 'you cannot be dead! I will not have it. I . . . I will not believe it!'

'I do not lie, brother. You know that. But it was the only way I could think of to save our people, and give them a chance of life in the pleasure of the flesh. I did not want to leave you, Anharat. You and I were a part of each other. Together we were One.'

'Aye, we were!' shouted Anharat. 'But now I do not need you. Go then and die! And leave me to my victory! I hate you, brother, more than anything under the stars!'

The shining figure of Emsharas seemed to fade under the power of Anharat's rage, and his voice when he spoke again was distant. 'I am sorry that you hate me, for I have always loved you. And I know how much you want to thwart me, but think on this: With all the power you have amassed what have you achieved? The Krayakin are returned to the void, the *gogarin* is dead, and an army awaits you outside the temple. Once you

405

have killed the child you will need all your power to draw back the Illohir. After that you will be merely a sorcerer. The army will kill you, and all across the world mankind will unite against our people. But you will have thwarted me. You will have made my death useless and unnecessary. It will be your final victory.'

'Then that will be enough for me!' roared Anharat.

'Will it?' asked Emsharas. 'Our people have two destinies, and both are in your hands, my brother. They can pass to a world of light, or they can return to the void. The choice is yours. My death alone could not complete the spell. But yours will. If you choose to be the third king to die then our people shall know joy. But whatever your choice I shall not remain to see it. We will never speak again. Goodbye, my twin!'

Emsharas stepped back and vanished. Anharat stood very still, and a great emptiness engulfed him. He realized in that moment what Bakilas had sensed the day before. His hatred of Emsharas was almost identical to his love. Without Emsharas there was nothing. There never had been. Throughout the last four thousand years thoughts of Emsharas, and the revenge he would know, had filled his mind. But he had never desired his brother's death. Not to lose him for all time.

'I love you too, my brother,' he said. He looked around the temple, and saw that the humans were still frozen. Against the wall a young girl had her arms around a child, and upon the dais a teenage boy stood holding a sword. Behind him the queen had turned away, shielding her baby with her body. Bakilas was close by, his sword raised. The black warrior was lying sprawled beside the dais, his blood pooling on the mosaic floor.

Anharat blinked and remembered the journeys upon

the cosmic winds, when he and Emsharas had been as one, twin souls, inseparable.

To die? The thought filled him with terror. To lose eternity? And yet what joy would there be in immortality now?

Then the music of the chimes began to fade, and the humans started to move.

Conalin watched the beast as it landed on the mosaic floor. 'You have only moments to live, child,' said Anharat. 'I shall tear out your heart.' The beast seemed to flicker for a moment, then it moved slowly forward, towering above the boy. Suddenly it dropped down, arms outstretched, its huge dark head lunging forward. Conalin leapt, plunging the sword deep into the thick, black neck. The talons swept down and settled over Conalin's shoulder. But they did not pierce the skin. Gently the beast pushed Conalin aside. Cream-coloured ichor spilled from the wound as the sword was torn free. Anharat dragged himself up onto the dais. Conalin hacked at his back, the blade slashing open the skin. The demon crawled past the queen and hauled himself up onto the altar. Twisting he spread his wings and lay back. Conalin jumped up and holding his sword with both hands drove it down into Anharat's chest. The boy stared down into the demon's eyes. Only then did he realize that the creature had made no move to attack him.

Confused, Conalin released the sword. Anharat's taloned fingers curled round the hilt. But he made no attempt to draw it forth.

'Emsharas!' whispered the demon.

A black shadow moved alongside Conalin. He swung to see the armoured knight moving towards the queen.

'No!' he shouted. With no weapon he sprang at the knight. A mailed fist hit him with a back handed blow that spun him from his feet.

Bakilas struggled on, the Storm Sword still thrust deep in his belly. Clinging to life he raised his blade. Axiana backed away. 'Do not harm my son,' she pleaded. Twenty feet away Nogusta pushed himself to his knees and drew a knife. His arm snapped forward. The blade flashed through the air, plunging deep into Bakilas's left eye. The Krayakin staggered back, then dragged the knife clear, hurling it to the floor. Nogusta tried to draw another. Then he passed out.

The sound of galloping hoofs filled the air. Bakilas turned to see a horseman with a cloak of fire bearing down upon him. Desperately he swung towards the queen and made one last attempt to reach her. Antikas Karios lifted the Storm Sword high and threw it with all his strength. The blade scythed through the air and slammed through Bakilas's neck. The Krayakin crumpled and fell across the body of Anharat.

Casting aside the blazing cloak Antikas leapt from Starfire. The horse's mane was aflame and the warrior smothered the fire with his hands. The gelding was burned across the lower body, and his legs were blistered and bleeding. Antikas himself had injuries to his arms and hands, and the skin over his cheek bone showed a vivid red burn.

Upon the dais Anharat's body began to glow with a brilliant, blinding light which filled the temple. Temporarily blinded Antikas fell to his knees, his hands over his face.

Behind him he could hear the pounding of feet, and guessed the pillars of fire had vanished.

Hands grabbed him, hauling him upright. He opened

his eyes. At first he could see only vague shapes. But then he saw the face of the White Wolf swim into focus.

'That was a fine ride,' said Banelion. Antikas gazed upon the altar. There was no sign now of the Demon Lord, nor of the dead Krayakin. Both had vanished.

Conalin ran to where Nogusta lay, and knelt down beside him. 'I killed it,' he said. 'I killed the beast!'

Nogusta gave a weak smile. 'You did well, my friend. I . . . am proud of you.' He took the boy's hand and lifted it to the talisman. 'What . . . do . . . you see?' he asked, his voice weak and fading.

Conalin closed his eyes. 'I see a strange land, with purple mountains. The Krayakin are there. They are bewildered.'

'What . . . else?'

'I see a woman. She is tall and black and beautiful.'

Nogusta leaned against the boy. 'I . . . see her too,' he said. Kebra ran forward and threw himself down by Nogusta's side.

'Don't you dare die on me!' he said.

Nogusta released Conalin's hand and gripped Kebra's arm. 'No . . . choice,' he whispered. 'Take Starfire . . . back to the mountains.'

'Ulmenetha!' shouted Kebra.

'I am here,' she said. Conalin moved back and allowed the priestess to kneel beside the dying man.

'You can heal him,' said Kebra. 'Lay your hands on him.'

'I cannot heal him,' she said. 'Not now.'

Kebra looked down into Nogusta's dead eyes. 'Oh no,' he said. 'You can't leave me like this! Nogusta!' Tears fell to his cheeks. 'Nogusta!' Ulmenetha leaned over and closed the bright blue eyes. Kebra hugged the body to him, cradling the head. Ulmenetha moved back, and, as

Conalin tried to reach Kebra she took hold of his arm and drew him away.

'Leave them together for a little while,' she said.

'I just wanted to tell him what I saw. He found his wife. On a world with two moons.'

'I know.' Ulmenetha walked to where Starfire was standing. The horse was shivering, and in great pain. She stroked his neck, then went to work on his wounds, healing the blisters and the burns. The worst of the wounds was in his right eye, which was almost blinded. But this too she healed.

Antikas approached her. 'He is a great horse,' he said. 'Nogusta was right.'

'Let me heal your burns,' she said, reaching up towards his blistered face. He shook his head.

'I will carry the pain. It will remind me of what we lost here today.'

She smiled up at him. 'That sounds dangerously like humility, Antikas Karios.'

He nodded. 'Yes it does. How depressing. Do you think it will wear off?'

'I hope not,' she told him.

'I will see that it does not,' he said. Offering her a bow he turned and walked back to the queen.

The White Wolf stood silently gazing down at Kebra and Nogusta, his expression unreadable. Then he moved to the queen's side. 'Where would you like to go, highness?' he asked, his voice weary.

'Back to Usa,' she said. 'And I would like you and your men to help me restore order in the city, and bring peace to the land. Will you do this for me, Banelion?'

'I will, highness.'

Stepping forward she summoned Antikas Karios. He

bowed deeply. 'Will you swear allegiance to me, and promise to defend the rights of my son?'

'With my life,' he told her.

'Then you will take command of the Ventrian army.'

Lastly she called Conalin to her. 'What is it I can do for you?' she asked. 'Name it and it is yours.'

'Kebra and I are going to Drenan,' he said. 'We are going to find Nogusta's horses and rebuild his house.'

'I shall see you have gold for the journey,' she said. Conalin bowed then walked to where Pharis was sitting with Sufia.

'Will you come with me to Drenan?' he asked them. Pharis took his hand.

'Where you are I will be,' she said. 'Always.'

'And me! And me!' said Sufia.

Kebra walked out into the night, grief overwhelming him. Ulmenetha stepped out of the shadows and took his arm. 'He knew he was to die,' she said. 'He saw it. But he saw something else, something incredible. He wanted me to tell you. He was descended from Emsharas, and that meant he was part Illohir. As was Ushuru, for they were cousins. He saw himself walking with her in a strange land, under a violet sky. The Krayakin were there, and Dryads and Fauns and many other Illohir. I think he saw it as some kind of paradise.'

Kebra said nothing, and gazed up at the bright stars. 'I know the pain you are feeling,' said Ulmenetha. 'I too have lost loved ones. But the three of you saved us all. None of you will ever be forgotten.'

Kebra turned on her. 'Do you think I care about fame? They were my family. I loved them. I feel their loss as if someone has cut them from me. I wish I had died with them.'

Ulmenetha was silent for a moment. Conalin came out

of the temple, holding hands with Pharis and little Sufia. The child broke away and ran to Kebra, who was weeping once more. She reached up and took his hand.

'Don't be sad,' she said. 'Please don't be sad.' Then she too began to cry. Kebra dropped down beside her.

'Sometimes,' he said, 'it is good to be sad.' He brushed her blond hair back from her eyes. Conalin came alongside him and laid a hand on his shoulder.

'You are not alone, Kebra,' said Ulmenetha. 'You have a family to raise. Conalin and Pharis and Sufia. And I shall come with you for a while, for I have an urge to run over mountain trails and see the wild flowers grow.'

'We will find Nogusta's horses,' said Conalin. 'And we will rebuild his house.'

Kebra smiled. 'He would like that.'

THE END

THE LEGEND OF DEATHWALKER
by David Gemmell

Under the brutal oppression of the Gothir, the Nadir tribes dream of the Uniter, the Great One, who will bring the tribes together, and end their centuries of torment.

But for one man it is more than a dream. Tailisman, a mysterious and enigmatic Nadir warrior, rides out to the Shrine of Oshikai Demon-bane, seeking the legendary eyes of Alchazzar, twin jewels of enormous power that will light the path to the Uniter. With him rides the beautiful Zhusai, a mystic tormented by the ghost of a long-dead Nadir queen.

But others desire the secret of the jewels.

Garen-Tsen, the sadistic power behind the Gothir throne, believes the magical gems will lead him to glory, and send the elite soldiers of the Gothir army to sack the Shrine, and butcher the few defenders. They cannot lose: five thousand men against a handful of savages and a renegade Drenai warrior.

But the savages are led by one of the most brilliant strategists of the day. And the renegade is Druss the Legend.

The Legend of Deathwalker is the latest battle-charged story of love, romance and heroism from the author of *Ironhand's Daughter*, and continues the cycle of Druss stories begun in *Legend* and *Druss the Legend*.

'Gemmell is several rungs above the good – right into the fabulous'
Anne McCaffrey

0 552 14252 2

DARK MOON
by David Gemmell

The peaceful Eldarin were the last of three ancient races. The mystical Oltor, healers and poets, had fallen before the dread power of the cruel and sadistic Daroth. Yet in one awesome night the invincible Daroth had vanished from the face of the earth. Gone were their cities, their armies, their terror. The Great Northern Desert was their only legacy. Not a trace remained for a thousand years . . .

The War of the Pearl had raged for seven years and the armies of the four Duchies were exhausted and weary of bloodshed. But the foremost of the Dukes, Sirano of Romark, possessed the Eldarin Pearl and was determined to unravel its secrets.

Then, on one unforgettable day, a dark moon rose above the Great Northern Desert, and a black tidal wave swept across the land. In moments the desert had vanished beneath lush fields and forests and a great city could be seen glittering in the morning sunlight.

From this city re-emerged the blood-hungry Daroth, powerful and immortal, immune to spear and sword. They had only one desire: to rid the world of humankind for ever.

Now the fate of the human race rests on the talents of three heroes: Karis, warrior-woman and strategist; Tarantio, the deadliest swordsman of the age; and Duvodas the Healer, who will learn a terrible truth . . .

'As a weaver of genuinely stirring heroic tales, it's hard to see anyone in the field to touch him'
The Dark Side

0 552 14253 0

ECHOES OF THE GREAT SONG
by David Gemmell

The Great Bear will descend from the skies, and with his paw, lash at the ocean. He will devour all the works of Man. Then he will sleep for ten thousand years, and the breath of his sleep will be death.

The prophecy had come true. The world spun. Tidal waves lashed the planet, and a new ice age dawned. The few survivors of a once great empire stuggled to rebuild, to hold their ground against the rising barbarian tide. Then two moons appeared in the skies, unleashing a terrible evil that threatened not only the new empire, but the survival of the world itself.

'When it comes to heroic fantasy, nobody does it better than David Gemmell'
The Dark Side

'Gemmell is several rungs above the good – right into the fabulous'
Anne McCaffrey

'The best fantasy inspires genuine involvement. David Gemmell's novels do just that'
Interzone

0 593 03715 4

NOW AVAILABLE AS A BANTAM PRESS HARDBACK

A SELECTED LIST OF FANTASY TITLES
AVAILABLE FROM CORGI BOOKS